OUTSIDE WOMEN

OUTSIDE WOMEN

A NOVEL

ROOHI CHOUDHRY

UNIVERSITY PRESS OF KENTUCKY

Published by The University Press of Kentucky, scholarly publisher for the
Commonwealth, serving Bellarmine University, Berea College, Centre College of
Kentucky, Eastern Kentucky University, The Filson Historical Society, Georgetown
College, Kentucky Historical Society, Kentucky State University, Morehead State
University, Murray State University, Northern Kentucky University, Spalding
University, Transylvania University, University of Kentucky, University of
Louisville, University of Pikeville, and Western Kentucky University.
All rights reserved.

Editorial and Sales Offices: The University Press of Kentucky
663 South Limestone Street, Lexington, Kentucky 40508-4008
www.kentuckypress.com

Book and Acknowledgments epigraphs are from "You Are Who I Love," copyright
© 2017 by Aracelis Girmay. Reprinted from Split This Rock's The Quarry: A Social
Justice Poetry Database, https://www.splitthisrock.org/poetry-database.

Cataloging-in-Publication data is available from the Library of Congress.

ISBN 978-1-9859-0196-4 (hardcover)
ISBN 978-1-9859-0199-5 (pdf)
ISBN 978-1-9859-0198-8 (epub)

This book is printed on acid-free paper meeting the requirements of the American
National Standard for Permanence in Paper for Printed Library Materials.

Manufactured in the United States of America.

Member of the Association
of University Presses

For the women I love

For the women I love

You who did and did not survive . . .
You whose blood was taken, whose hands and lives were
taken, with or without your saying
Yes, I mean to give. *You are who I love.*

. . . and each of us looking out from the gorgeous
unlikelihood of our lives at all, finding ourselves here,
witnesses to each other's tenderness, which, this moment,
is fury, is rage, which, this moment, is another way of
saying: You are who I love You are who I love You and
you and you are who

—ARACELIS GIRMAY, "YOU ARE WHO I LOVE"

ONE

I should board the train home. But it runs above ground, so the city will dance far below me as I ride past. When I tap my head against the window, I'll watch blurred movement through glass. I prefer to wait until dark when my own reflection is all that stares back.

For now, I'll walk along the East River and imagine I'm part of the city, like a grain of sand seen from above. Here's a couple on their first date. Carefully unsaid words rest between them on the bench. A woman pulls up the zipper to her daughter's bright pink jacket and pats her chest safe. An old man feeds gulls from a plastic bag pocked with reuse. His stale bread spins like a cricket ball across the water.

A taxi driver pulls up to the curb. As he idles for his next ride, he nudges his door open. He spits onto the sidewalk and glances up as he pulls the door shut. He licks the spittle off his lips and sucks in his mustache a little. His eyes are bloodshot and circled dark. His beard is more stubble than purpose.

Can it be? He is older than I remember—but, then, so am I.

In an unexpected blink, my secrets are on display. My body frozen breath tight. Surely he is not permitted here. This city is my sanctuary.

We exchange glances for a single instant. In that pause, his eyes widen. I think his expression changes. Boredom to recognition. A siren breaks through, and he shifts his gaze. He leans back in his seat and stretches his arms in a yawn. I am no one to him.

Almost five years have passed since I arrived in this city from Pakistan. I've made it mine. At the university, I've struck up friendships with other graduate students and adopted their jeans and T-shirt uniform, though it fits uneasily over my curves. I've softened the edges of my name to suit their tongues—the hard jeem in the middle of my *Hajra* has become a languorous *zhhh*. I even met and lost a man who loved me. An American who thought he knew me.

But now, the New York cyclists and playground and seagulls fade. Instead, ghoulish images from my old world rear up.

A woman who twitched and breathed shallow at my feet. My outstretched fingers were afraid to touch her.

I saw the beat-up blue sedan screech away that day but not before I exchanged a look with the man in the passenger seat. His eyes were sharp with righteous scorn. I could recognize them anywhere. Even here, half a world away.

I must not think. I must not lose my nerve. One foot in front of the other, pull open the door and slide into the cab. First address to mind is a classmate's old place on the Upper West Side. I dare not give him my own.

Inside, the taxi company ID card confirms: Mohsin Khan. His picture sports the unkempt beard I remember.

The cab peels up a few streets to First Avenue. Look up. Look up! He is focused on the road but glances at the rearview. Our eyes meet. I duck my head. Quick tug at my ponytail so knotted curls obscure my face.

What have I done. I'm trapped in his back seat. Once again, I'm just a girl in his domain.

His eyes are still on me, brows pulled into a question. My jaw is tight. I want to bare my teeth and growl.

Don't you remember me? Or am I only another voiceless animal from your crosshairs?

Here in my bag is a pen. A trembling scribble, and I've got his medallion number on my hand. My hand is a fist. He brakes, and I am ready. My door swings open. Every door is wide open. I'm running without sight through the sirens and descending darkness and steam rising up from grates and a burst of sparrows fluttering over crumbs.

A second time—on a second continent—I've escaped him.

* * *

There are days when escape is a relief. On those days, I'm convinced of my victimhood. It's what my New York neighbors and professors want: a Muslim woman who doesn't challenge their assumptions.

So I read books censored by the brown men they hate. I study the history of forced Islamic conversions in northern Pakistan and prepare to present at a prestigious conference. I hold my breath in between visa renewals and grant applications. Memories of home turn to ice.

On frostbitten days alone in my room, I recite out loud every piece of Urdu verse I ever learned by heart. Iqbal dangling spider and fly aao jo mere ghar mein tho izzat hai ye meri; Ghalib's melodramatic dil hi jab dard ho to kya kijiye; Bahadur Shah Zafar laments his fate dum lubbon per hai nikal jata nahin.

I ride the train to Jackson Heights and buy Shaan Easy Haleem Mix from Patel Brothers and goat stew meat and bones from the Bangladeshi butcher shop. I spend Sunday stirring the largest stockpot Canal Street sold. Barley and lentil and broth collide against the ladle I scrape to the bottom. Steam condenses against the window and obscures the frozen port city I have chosen for my foreigner's life.

Inside, Pashto lyrics twist around the twang of rubab from an old tape deck. My kitchen is dense with familiar words. I shut my eyes, and my mother's palm rests on my back. "Hajra?" she calls as if looking up to find me. My father coughs from the next room. The world swirls off its inexorable axis for one moment.

Before it pivots back to concrete sidewalk and the drawl of my roommate though thin walls.

Still, I have a bowl of haleem for my dinner, and all is not lost.

Since seeing Mohsin in his cab, I've been preoccupied and jumpy. I try to concentrate on my presentation for the conference I'm attending soon—a coup for my résumé. It's likely I was added to the panel as a token Muslim representative, but I am accustomed to my role and make the best of it.

Soon, I'm startled to find I'm standing in line at LaGuardia Airport. The days stop and start this way now. My mind so firmly in Peshawar, my body believed it too. My throat is hoarse from words I should have screamed out loud when I had the chance years and miles ago.

Pulling up to the midwestern campus, I finally notice that the conference is hosted by a Catholic university housing an order of Benedictine monks. At the curb, suitcase in hand, I pause as church bells sing above rustling leaves and the faraway cawing of ravens. I inhale the gentle evening and wait for its calm to settle me.

None comes. Instead, my chest tightens. The break in routine creates space for fresh panic. What is Mohsin doing in this country? Maybe he came here to pursue me.

Blond students wearing identical sweatshirts glance over and appraise my dark skin. Perhaps they notice my ghosts and take them for foreignness. I try to shake off the strain in my shoulders and introduce purpose into my gait. I find my lodgings and, as usual, lose myself in work.

The next morning, I rise flush with anxiety. Stumbling through my rehearsed presentation, I'm distracted during the ensuing discussion. One of my senior professors in the audience frowns and makes a note. Afterward, I scoop up my papers and dash from the building.

I wander across campus through sheets of icy rain as if making a kind of penance. All the blond students are in class or at the conference, and I am alone in a bleak landscape. Pine needles crunch underfoot. A car swerves to avoid me as I wander mindless into the street. On the other side, I find a board marking a trail into the woods. It's a treacherous path today, and I slip in the mud a few times. But once the buildings and paved roads are behind me, the quiet is a comfort. Most of the trees are still bare this early in the spring, but the alternating grays of bark and shadow make a kind of canopy that shields me from the world. My path widens out into a marsh, and the miasma of decay becomes more pungent here. Bright orange mushrooms peek up through the mulch underfoot. Ahead, an egret tiptoes at the lakeshore before it is startled by my step and flutters into mist.

Across a rickety bridge, I take a path that leads back up toward campus just beyond. Shivering against the rain dripping into my upturned collar, I find shelter under the eaves of a brick building covered with ivy. It turns out to be the Abbey pottery studio, which sounds like a warm refuge. Wiping my fogged glasses, I edge inside. Three young men are busy at their potter's wheels and pause without surprise, as if expecting my visit.

One steps forward and offers me a tour of the studio. He wears a newsboy cap and tortoiseshell glasses and would have fit right into my New York neighborhood. He has no halo of fair hair, no potbelly encircled by a drawstring belt. Though I try to hide it, he seems to notice my surprise when he reveals he is a monk.

"There aren't many of us joining now," he says cheerfully. "I was the only one in my year." The monastery on campus once housed 400 monks, he adds, but now only 120 remain as the elderly pass away.

I want to ask why men no longer choose this life—the certainty of service and purpose. A readymade tribe. After all, religiosity does not seem to be ebbing anywhere. Its insistent demands have shaped the course of my life. But instead, I ask, "Is that sad?"

He assumes a carefully solemn expression. "Yes, I think so."

As I retrace my steps back to the conference center, chin tucked against the wind, I think about Ali. I'm unable to shut him out of my mind lately. Even though I've spun a careful web over the years to muffle his memory. I've almost managed to forget I have a brother.

Ali was around the same age as this young monk when I left Peshawar. If presented with the option, maybe my brother could have pursued a monastic life. He could've risen and slept by devotional rhythms. That might have satisfied his yearning for community.

If he had not met Mohsin, whose offer of belonging was only a ruse. Instead, Ali could have worked clay and planted trees, given the chance. But maybe there was something else wrong inside him, too hard and jagged to be shaped at the potter's wheel. More questions to accompany the others that haunt me.

It is as far as I can go today. So I push away my musings. It's no use thinking about what Ali could have been or what he could have let me be. It's no use thinking about him at all.

Back at the conference center, I drift through hallways. There are talks I've been advised to attend and contacts I should track down at the book fair in the basement. Instead, I wander until I reach the farthest nook of the building—a windowless room that seats only a handful of attendees. Without bothering to note the topic on the board, I slip inside and find a seat toward the back. The speaker's academic drone washes up against my own thoughts.

The panelist wraps up his subject to a smattering of reluctant applause. Startled from reverie by the familiar clink of bangles, I glance up to find a brown woman taking the podium next. She is clad in an elaborate sari, and her gray hair is cropped close to her head. Silver jewelry drapes her neck and jangles from her earlobes. Her lips are purple and stretch into a gap-toothed smile as she loads up her presentation.

On the screen behind her, a single black-and-white photograph looms over the room. A young Indian girl, no older than fifteen, squats back on her heels. Her sari's edge is pulled over her dark curls, and she rests her chin on her knees. One arm is outstretched over a small pot on a campfire. Her eyes are narrowed, but a smirk plays across her lips.

"Who is she?" asks the presenter.

"Indentured Labor: A New System of Slavery," the next slide proclaims as she takes us through a collection of images. Women hunched over seedlings, others hidden among towering crops, a group hacks at piles of sugarcane with machetes. Another holds up a white baby swaddled in frothy lace. And three of them dressed in saris, side by side, hold a cloth banner with dark fingertips. The words on the banner are blurred by the years. One of the three women is caught in the middle of an unlikely laugh.

"Female laborers taken to the colonies were uniquely placed," the presenter says. The silver ropes around her neck shift and glint. "They occupied a space outside of the colonial struggles of men and also outside of traditional custom and ritual in India. Journeying across the sea to work, they became—outside women."

Warmth fills my throat. My seat is hard. The air I breathe is dry from artificial heating, and the false walls of the conference room are too close. In English, the phrase is newborn, but it still stings. Because I, too, have been called an outside woman.

TWO

Madras Presidency, British India, 1891

"Tomorrow, we'll go to the river," said Sita's father as he shook off the day's cares. He lifted a little cup high above his face, and a stream gurgled down his throat. He wiped his mouth. "It will be a good day to bathe."

In the morning, her grandmother woke her well before dawn. Sita tiptoed to the urn in a corner of their courtyard, and the flame from her oil lamp danced inside its reflection. The image shattered when she scooped cool water to splash against her face.

Her bleary thoughts skipped ahead to the coming excitement. Baskets and vessels of food were already packed up for their river picnic. Strong men like her father would heave them onto ox carts and make the packages fast with rope.

Her grandmother's soft palm at her shoulder. "Come now, kutti."

Everyone revered Lord Shiva, but Ayamma taught her to honor the old gods. The guardians who stood vigil at their doorstep must be appeased before any journey from home.

They edged around sleeping mats to avoid splayed fingertips and toes peeking from covers and slipped from the compound's back gate. Outside the walls, night swarmed around their circle of lamplight. A scrap of Ayamma's mundhanai in hand, Sita stumbled in her sure-footed wake and watched for snakes in the undergrowth.

A few steps away, the guardian deity sat squat and dull. Moss bloomed across his rocky brow. Insects burrowed their homes inside his crevices. Ayamma muttered a prayer under her breath while Sita knelt and arranged marigolds in a garland around him. Before she could rise to her feet, her grandmother grasped her hand and guided it to rest against the god's scarred countenance.

A cold shock transferred from stone through her blood. The roots beneath the god seemed to twist around her wrist like vines. She wriggled her grip free.

They rode in three carts, one borrowed from a friend's family. The bullocks flipped their ears and swished their tails at flies as they clambered and kicked up dust clouds. Sita's older brother, Maalan, drove one, her father a second, and a cousin manned the third.

"Brrr-u-ah!" Maalan urged the oxen up the hillside with his switch.

Already, their village wasn't even a dot in the distance. They were surrounded by rustling thorn bushes and the thrum of crickets and a path ahead flattened by other hooves.

Green by green, forest raged forth until the path was overgrown. They'd arrived as far as carts could go. The men strapped packages onto the bullocks' backs and coaxed them into the woods abundant with karamani trees. Red and black seeds glittered across the crunchy layers underfoot. Sita collected them in a small sack Ayamma had stitched and tied it to one corner of her davani for safekeeping. These humble seeds would become Lord Pillaiyar's gleaming eyes for the coming festival season.

"Look, Ayamma, I found so many." The task was an important one, and she assumed a suitably grown-up expression as she held up her treasure.

Meanwhile, her cousins scurried up trees and had to be shouted down. Sita gazed after them, uncertain of her feelings. She could climb higher and faster than any of them. But she was almost a woman and must tread the forest path with appropriate gravity. Even though the banyan vines hung low and beckoned as she brushed them aside. Moist loam in among the roots promised discovery. A millipede that she longed to tease into ancient spiral.

Soon enough, branches parted, and the river was already a roar in her ears. Unable to contain herself any longer, Sita raced forward past the oxen, not caring about the burrs from the adai-otti that scratched her shins and arms. They were no more nuisance than the boys' jeers or her grandmother's call behind her. At the riverbank, she squelched past reeds and jumped over toads and slipped on mossy pebbles.

Practiced, she gripped each stone in the riverbed with her toes and found the midstream spot that was her favorite. By degrees, she lowered into the cool until she was soaked through. If she lay back and closed her eyes, she could drift far away from instruction and caution.

"Sita! Stop being childish. Come quick out of there and help us." It was Anjali, of course. Her sister-in-law's voice was as bitter as lime peel.

Sita made herself heavier. Under the water's surface, she blew bubbles and became a creature with an oily coat slithering along the currents. But her lungs betrayed her, and she sat up gasping for breath. Dripping, she wrung out her pavadai and trudged over to the women busy with their usual sorting and cleaning and making.

Her grandmother pushed her away. "Go and play, ma. We can manage here."

Anjali scowled, but she dared not contradict Ayamma. She could only sigh and stamp through her work. Stifling a smirk, Sita skipped away.

Later, after she'd swum her fill and shafts of sunlight lengthened through the boughs overhead, she waded over to the rock she'd chosen. It was flat and half-submerged, so she could sit with her toes wriggling in water. A smaller rock next to her held a convenient divot for the handful of coconut sauce Ayamma ladled out. Here, she sat and squeezed water from the tip of her braid and waited.

Ayamma was seated on a large rock farther upstream, as befitted her station. Beside her was Anjali, not much older than Sita, but her duties were lent the weight of her new marriage. Sita's father tied up his drenched veshti around his knees. His soft belly slumped over the knot. He sat on a rock near the women and teased his mother and shook water from his long eyelashes.

Maalan perched nearby. Unloading the packages earlier, he'd ordered his cousins around with an authority they readily mocked. Last season, he'd been one of them—the boys who competed over push-ups in the shallows and hid a snake under the women's baskets. Now, his married status lay heavy on his shoulders. He glanced over at Anjali often—too often—but his bride was irritated and averted her eyes.

"Ayamma! Please, we're so hungry." One of the boys held out his banana leaf like a prayer.

Ayamma wagged her head. "You are always hungry. You are made only of stomach."

But she tucked her mundhanai to her waist and began. From the woven basket as tall as her knee, she picked out a single idli between finger and thumb. A few crumbs shed like white blossoms from her hands.

She placed the pillow gently into water, and it rocked away. Curious fish nibbled at its rounded edges, but it floated mostly intact to Sita's father. By rights, he would eat first.

As the idli reached him, he glanced up and met Sita's eyes. His hair was marked by early gray at the temples but was still a lush thicket. The lines forking from his eyes deepened as he broke into a wide grin. Lazy sunshine caught his brilliant teeth and the dip of his throat as he spoke: "My kutti will eat first." And he splashed the idli expertly across the rushing river between him and his only daughter.

Basking in the jealous hunger cast her way by her cousins and Anjali, Sita rescued the waterlogged cake. She hooked two fingers and scooped a morsel of coconut to smear over the top and sank her teeth in.

First, mustard seed tugged at her tongue, and, too, pepper eager within. Slower, coconut nestled its trove of memories. Full bellies, glistening skin, black hair.

Last, but more persistent than flavor: the river. Soaked tight into each grain and dissolved in her mouth. The river sang of its birth in long-ago mountains and the sea for which it yearned. A body of water, one with Sita's own.

* * *

Awake on her sleeping mat in the courtyard at home, Sita sifted through daydreams. Smoke from stoves snuffed out for the night still hung in the air. Everyone else slept soundly on their mats under moonless night.

She knew each person who slumbered in the streets around their compound. The barber's street on the left. Chickens roosted in the coop behind the tea shop a few streets away. At the pond near the temple, delicate lotus would soon blossom over floating pads, and she'd collect the blooms with her grandmother for puja.

She was powerful in this village, where her father was a rich man. He'd inherited an expanse of paddy fields, and abundant harvests filled their granary to capacity. Ayamma told her stories of parched earth and cattle felled by thirst. An epidemic took her own mother when Sita was only a baby. She was still a young woman, and it was a tragedy. But these were stories of adversity from another era.

Closing her eyes, Sita imagined lying on her mat in a different place—one that was far away from her compound's ancient stone wall. Where she did not know the precise distance in steps to the school run by Anglo-Indian nuns.

Once, the nuns showed them a map held in place by pebbles at each corner. An India so vast, Sita could not even carry the image in her head. Networks to the left and right reached fingers to the blue edges of the ocean. She tried to imagine such faraway places—like Madras, which she knew from her father's college reminiscences. That was where he'd developed what her grandmother called his "big ideas." She did not approve of school for a girl.

A droplet splashed against Sita's wrist as she was finally drifting to sleep. She got to her feet and extended her palms to catch the first rain of the season. But that first drop seemed to rip through and tear a celestial water sack. Torrents of water roused Sita's family, and they ran through the courtyard collecting bedding and clothes from the line. Drenched, they huddled inside one of the two large rooms that made their home. They watched as rain dug craters in the mud courtyard.

Sita was thirsty. She wanted rain pummeling her scalp and flowing down her back. But she was too old now to run shrieking through the storm. She'd started bleeding a few months ago. In a year or so, she would be married to her betrothed from a nearby village. And she was an aunt now, too, and was responsible for setting an example.

She tickled the soles of baby Kavita's feet, and her niece kicked her away with delight. Nearby, Maalan watched as his daughter tried to wind her fist around the tip of Sita's long plait. It was still hard to believe that Maalan was Kavita's father. Yes, he'd changed soon after his wedding to Anjali, becoming kinder, less foolish. He'd even escorted Sita to borrow books from the nuns because she couldn't go to school anymore now that he'd left.

Anjali seemed to befriend her at first. She lent Sita bangles and plaited her hair into coronets that Ayamma could not manage. But she was short-tempered. She would turn without warning and snap at

Sita's little mistakes. Still, they were sisters now, Ayamma explained, and bickering was only a form of love.

Sita was glad for the cool evenings of the rainy season. But in the days that followed, neighboring farmers came to consult with her father on his veranda. She caught snatches of their conversations when she carried out tea and steaming vada. The monsoon was too much and too early, they worried together.

The rains didn't cease for a week, then two. Water rose up river-banks and rushed down pathways cut into the reeds. Fields became lakes. They worked to make crude dams and divert the river or else bucket the excess water from paddy fields. Children as young as five were drafted to help. Sita worked alongside their hired laborers, carrying and stacking sacks of soil.

She was eating her evening meal in the room where they were now confined when a trickle of water reached her bare foot. She jumped up. A sheet of water slithered under their back gate into the courtyard. Quickly, they grabbed more sacks of mud and piled them against the leak. But their backs were turned to the real deluge. A mass of water broke through their neighbor's dam half a mile away. The flood roared down the village main street. It flattened every obstacle they'd set up.

Before they even knew to escape, the wave battered down their compound's defenses. Knocked to the ground, Sita choked on water carrying grain from destroyed rice fields. Silt from deep in the river-bed. Coughing, she fought to steady herself upright. The wave swelled to her hip. They had no time to take anything. Rain lashed against her scalp. Broken bits of an urn tossed up against her bracing arms. They half waded, half swam toward the stairs to the rooftop. Each step loomed as water snapped at her ankles. Anjali's sobs rang in her ears.

On the roof, they shivered under the shelter of a woven lean-to and watched the tide climb step after step like a predator stalking their hiding place. The water finally stopped rising only two steps away. At sunrise, Sita crept against the rain to the edge of the flat roof. Their fields were covered by water black with dirt dredged from the river's journey. Not a single blade of rice was left standing.

Stranded on the rooftop for two days, they collected rainwater to drink. Closer to the center of the village, the barber's family waved from their roof. And farther away, the topmost dome of the Shiva temple was a red and white island. But no other houses were tall enough. Every other building in the village was submerged. Corpses of livestock floated past. A dog paddled feebly, whimpering before it disappeared around the corner. Little Kavita cried without pause in Anjali's arms.

By the third day, after their rescue by neighboring villagers in a fishing boat, a raging fever took hold of the baby. She survived that roof with the rest of them once the flood receded to join the river drifting south. But Kavita only lived another week after that.

* * *

When had Sita become a stranger to the places she once loved? Perhaps it happened when the same river she played in—cherished pet turned villain—broke through the walls of her home. Or maybe it was when drought and disease followed the flood. After she lost the soft crook of her grandmother's body and the shelter of her father's protection. Year after year, shadows burned across the village where lush green had once reigned.

Or earlier. Maybe she'd become a stranger when she first argued her headstrong way into attending school with her brother. When she lay awake on her sleeping mat and plotted adventures not meant for girls. But she understood without a doubt that she was an outsider on the day a child escaped from her family's compound.

As usual, Sita was minding the young ones. The sun beat down on the courtyard, and she edged back into the meager shade cast by the eaves. The children seemed unperturbed by the heat as they played. The neighbors' bossy little girl was supervising. "Here, this is the kitchen. These dried leaves are rice when you crumble them. With this stick, I am cooking them. Isn't it delicious?"

Three toddlers crouched close and followed her instructions. A pair of boys refused the game and ran in circles as they flew an imaginary kite.

In her dusty corner, Sita bent over a pile of mending. Anjali's blouse needed a new patch. This had been another woman's garb once. She could see the line where it was altered for Anjali's smaller bust. She ran her fingers over the row of tiny stitches. The children shrieked and pretended in the background.

One little boy slipped out unnoticed. Naked, the child ran through paddy fields fallow from flooding and drought and across the inauspicious cremation ground. He crept around the village streets until the watchman found him and carried him home before anyone even knew he was gone.

Her father would have attempted sternness in response, but he wouldn't have been able to suppress his laughter at the plucky boy. Her grandmother would have pursed her lips and sent coins to a Brahmin for the cleansing ritual required.

But they were both dead. And the money was gone too. The flood and years of drought had stolen every warm embrace. Anjali was matriarch now.

When the child was returned, Sita was still mending in her corner. Some of the children continued their play; others had tired of the heat and fallen asleep. Anjali stormed into the courtyard, the little boy slumped over one hip. Her cousin's son. His parents had left him when they went to the city in search of work.

"Sita! Are your eyes open, or are you sleeping?"

"Akka?" Sita scrambled to her feet, Anjali's tone a warning.

"This child. You were supposed to look after him. This one job you were given. Even servants can follow simple instructions. Can you do this much in exchange for the roof your brother provides?"

"I was watching them, Akka. I—"

"Watching them with your eyes closed?" Anjali rubbed her pinched face with her free hand. "What sin am I atoning for? To be burdened with this snake bringing disaster after disaster upon our heads."

Sita's face burned as she backed against the wall. Perhaps if she remained silent, her sister-in-law would stop at words.

"Anjali, enough, da. The neighbors will hear." Maalan stood at the back gate. His voice was tentative, almost pleading. He wiped his brow with the crook of his elbow and let out a sigh.

"Don't you get involved. You're a bigger fool than anyone here."

In response, Maalan licked his lips and seemed to consider. But he didn't speak. Instead, he fixed his gaze at a point just beyond the far wall.

Anjali barreled on. "Oh yes, she acts like a harmless thing. Your sister who thinks she's better than us because—she can read? Hnnh.

She thinks I don't see her evil. How she plots and schemes. She fills her stomach so my children starve. She prays for us to die so this house may be hers."

As her voice grew louder, the child on her hip roused and let out a low wail. Anjali seemed not to hear him. With each word, she took a step closer to the corner where Sita had retreated. She pushed at Sita's arm with the heel of her palm. "Well? Say something. Cursed girl. Put on this earth to test me."

She continued to slap at Sita's arm with a flat hand. But then she seemed to gather steam, and her palm became a fist, finding Sita's sternum and collar. The child squirmed and escaped to the safety of his playmates. Cowering to protect herself, Sita raised her arms around her head and glanced toward the gate. Maalan had never seen one of these episodes for himself, though he must have known. Surely, he couldn't ignore it this time. But the threshold was empty. Her brother was gone.

Anjali was small and narrow-framed. Sita was a full head taller, her shoulders and hips broad. Under her frayed davani, her ribs stood out stark from her torso without enough sustenance. But though Sita's stomach buckled into its cavity, her muscles were still resilient from years of climbing trees and long days of work. She'd always been as strong as the boys. So, worse than Anjali's feeble blows were the children's stares and the neighbors eager for gossip. The absence of her brother. He, too, had abandoned her.

Sita could take no more. She grabbed Anjali's fists and held them together in both hands. In that paused beat, their gazes locked. Anjali's eyes widened in disbelief mingled with rage. Never before had the younger girl resisted. Sita didn't wait for the eruption sure to follow. She cast her sister-in-law's fists from her and ran through the courtyard out through the back gate. Anjali's taunts echoed behind her. *Unlucky, useless, burden.*

Sita stumbled into the gully behind their compound. She did not belong inside anymore. An unmarried girl of eighteen, her dowry sold piece by piece for food. No prospects, no father. Nursemaid to her brother's children, no better.

She wandered through withered brush. Ketaki flowers once flourished here by the ruins of the village guardian's shrine. As a child, she'd filled her skirt with blooms and strung them into fragrant ropes for her grandmother's hair. Only wisps of yellow leaves now remained to crackle underfoot.

A little farther, she ran her fingers over the stump of the banana tree that used to bear the variety her father loved best. Fruit no larger than two thumbs and tart thread to brighten the sweetness within. He loved sweetness. He'd been a soft man fond of indulgences, with a full head of black hair. But worry had turned him gray. Worry had stopped his heart. As the famine raged and his children grew more gaunt and his mother wasted and still the British taxman took what was left in their granary and he was powerless.

Once, the gravity of his voice had been an anchor. Her father's timbre, "Sita—" He'd called to her at dusk from his veranda. The one-two music of the name he'd chosen for her. Different from all the other girls in the village.

Once, she'd collected leaves from this same banana tree and woven their strips into rafts for baby frogs she'd raised from tadpoles. She sailed them on her uncle's lily pond, where turquoise fish darted beneath the surface. That pond was now dry with zigzag cracks that yawned from one end to the other. A padlock grew rusty at her uncle's front door since he'd left for the city.

Here was the corner where a palm vendor used to set up his summer treat of padhini with chewy nongu pooled inside palm fronds. He'd twist the fronds into cups with a flourish while the children begged for a few tasty gulps. Near the old barber's, grass still crept through the gaps in a pile of driftwood where an urn, tall as her thigh, was dry without the drinking water he'd offered customers.

She rested for a while on the steps of the deserted Shiva temple, reluctant to return to the compound that was no longer her home. But she was careful to avoid other villagers too. She was marked here as the unmarried girl, conspicuous in the childish pavadai davani Anjali still made her wear instead of a sari. She was the unlucky one who was once betrothed, but no more. Her brother was only a weak man unwilling to stand up to his wife.

As the afternoon lengthened, Sita finally trudged back down the main road past the old tea shop where her father had spent so many afternoons. The shop owner had long since packed and left. But three of the men her father had loved to debate with still lingered on the broken benches.

"Daughter!" one of them called to Sita. Like the old days when the respect commanded by her father had extended to her too. Today, the men hunched over a meal one had brought and savored the pleasure of idlis and watery sambhar. They insisted she sit with them awhile.

"So tall," one exclaimed as she bent to touch their feet in greeting. "I remember when you would ride around the village on your father's shoulders. Like a queen on an elephant!"

They chuckled. She tried to join them, but no laughter would come. And they, too, sobered soon. They chewed their meager meal slowly, as if considering.

"Daughter," another finally said, his voice tentative. "Life has been unkind. But it is long."

"Yes." His friend nodded. "You are shivering in the cold now, but the season will change. Prosperity will return to our village."

Sita bowed her head. The old men meant well, but their advice belonged to another time. "Thatha, there is nothing here. Everyone who could has left. There are cities out there full of machines and new ideas—" Here, Sita's imagination faltered. But gathering momentum, she plowed on. "Anyway, prosperity is there, away from this place. Not here."

The old men smiled, benevolent. "Still the same kutti. Full of dreams."

"It's good, good." Another patted her head. "You have hope. Like the child we remember."

She frowned at his indulgent tone. To these old men, she was still her father's little girl. What did they understand of her life, waking or sleeping? She dreamed not of prosperity but of refuge. In her dreams, beasts thundered and chased her down the streets of the village. Sometimes she was pulled from the streets to the safety of a home. More often, when she woke, she was still running.

THREE

Peshawar, Pakistan, 1989

Uncle Mukhtar—my father's friend—had a new Jeep painted all black with gleaming hubcaps. The tires purred over potholes and garbage and pebbles from the river as he drove up to our house. We didn't have a car; back in the eighties, no one in our part of Peshawar did. Especially not mohajirs—refugees from India, like us. Our father had a Vespa, and that was a marker of accomplishment.

Ali and I skipped as pilgrims around the Jeep, inspecting headlights and spare tire and exhaust pipe. Our eager faces distorted in the veneer. No touching. We were promised a ride around the block later, and the wait was excruciating. Uncle Mukhtar and our father told their tales and smoked their cigarettes for hours. Ali and I paced outside and peeped into the living room every minute. Finally, the men shuffled to their feet, and we thought our torture might be over. But they announced they were strolling down the street to visit a neighbor. I jumped up and down in place. Ali banged his forehead against the wall. We might have to wait hours more, but this was impossible.

"Hajra! Look what I found," Ali said, his voice low though we were alone. The keys. Uncle Mukhtar had left them on the table with his scarf. I stared at Ali, thrilled and terrified. I was ten then, maybe eleven, and he two years older. We'd been in cars a few times but never behind the wheel. And never a Jeep. We couldn't do this.

But Ali was the adventurous one. He'd jumped off the rooftop water tank in his makeshift superhero cloak when I clung, paralyzed, to the edge until my father climbed up and rescued me.

"Come on, just until the end of the street," Ali said now. "Don't be such a darpok."

So we ran out to the Jeep, Ali to the driver's side. I sank into delicious leather as Ali danced up and down the wood-beaded cover Uncle Mukhtar had installed on his seat. We couldn't stop laughing as we breathed in the smooth, expensive machinery. Ali slid the key into the ignition and turned it once. The Jeep hummed, alive. He turned the key once more, and it seemed to beg to spring forward.

Ali had some idea what to do. He talked about cars with his friends all the time. He depressed the hand brake, one hand on the gearshift. We darted forward, and immediately, the Jeep sighed to a standstill. Again. We moved forward a few feet before another abrupt stop, and we were thrown back in our seats. By now, we only had to look at each other to burst out laughing. Ali wheezed as he rested his forehead on the wheel, and tears ran down his cheeks.

We had to get going before our mother found out. Ali started the Jeep again, and we inched forward, jerk by jerk. We crawled along the alley and then the next.

"You said just up the street!" I squealed. But I didn't want to go home either. We made our way down the street near the tandoor, where one of our neighbors saw us and called out. Quick, Ali turned into a crooked alley with gutters running down the edges. Would the Jeep fit?

"Of course," Ali scoffed but with a note of uncertainty.

The screech, metal on metal, was the worst. Ali misjudged one of the alley's curves, and the Jeep plowed into a rusty gate. We watched its progress, frozen. By the time I remembered to pull up the hand brake, the gate had bowed into us. The Jeep was several inches inside the house's porch. Ali and I turned slowly to look at each other. At the very same moment, he began to laugh, and I began to cry.

* * *

"Ammi, we should really talk to the laundry. Look, they've shrunk Ali's shalwars."

My mother frowned a warning at me, though its effect was spoiled by her stifled laughter.

Ali shook his head as he skipped downstairs, chappals clattering. "You're getting too old for such childish jokes," he called behind him. His voice echoed up the stairwell. I ran to the railing to return his barb, but the front gate was already slamming shut below.

So much was changing in Peshawar when I was a teenager, though I was too busy with my friends to notice most of the time. We spent whole summers flicking through romance novels to the good parts, or rewatching pirated Keanu Reeves movies, or making grunge mixtapes on a friend's boom box. Of course, no one could miss the change in Ali once he began college, but usually, it was beneath my notice.

"Why must you tease your brother? He's your elder." My mother returned to the bowl of peas she was shelling in her lap and turned up the latest episode of *Uroosa*. I plopped down on the divan next to her and hugged my knees as the green-eyed star of the PTV serial adjusted her headscarf.

"Oof, but she's just woken up! What, she goes to sleep with her perfectly pinned dupatta?"

"Why do you care?" My mother sighed and pushed the peas at me.

I rolled my eyes and began popping peapods with teenage vehemence. "I *care* because it's all so stupid. And it's everywhere. I mean, Uroosa can't even get out of bed without her dupatta thanks to these new modesty rules. And Ali—have you seen him? He's starting to look like one of those Taliban nutjob friends of his with their too-short pants and topi and everything. Like that Mohsin he's so in love with."

Ali had recently begun hanging around a group of young men he met at college. Most were engineering students like him. Mohsin Khan, their natural leader, was a cipher. He was polite to a fault but remote in a way that inspired worship. Ali gushed about him at every mealtime—*so humble, Mohsin only wears khaddar cotton and Peshawari chappals, not joggers like those Western copycats. You'd never know how rich his family is.*

"Shhhh." My mother turned up the volume. For a while, I was content to sulk, coax peas from their shells, and glare at the simpering ingenue.

Finally, a blue and white foam mattress danced across the screen, and my mother turned it down. "Look, beta, your brother is . . . trying something new. So what if he's wearing different clothes for a while? It's not hurting anyone. And Mohsin is such a good boy. Prays five times a day."

I opened my mouth to protest that his religious guise was part of the problem. But then, Uroosa and Sheheryar returned from the commercial break and mooned at each other across a tea trolley. Our conversation was over.

I didn't bother trying to continue the topic that day or in the weeks that followed. I was busy with my own preoccupations balancing my chores at home with an ever-increasing workload at school. Also, around this time, I'd discovered Ruth Rendell at the British Council library and stayed up late devouring murder mysteries under the covers while Ali snored in the room we shared.

"Sleeping with your eyes open. You'll be late again!"

How long had I been sitting in front of the tiny gas heater with one sock in hand? I shook my head to expel the tenacious dregs of sleep and stumbled from my room. A screech from my mother. I lurched into the kitchen, sure I'd find her scalded. But instead, she reached up and squashed Ali's face in her hands.

"Look! Look at my boy," she exclaimed, turning his face to me as if showing off a newborn.

"Uff, Ammi, it's too early for your hysterics." I sighed. "Did you make chai yet?"

"The pot's under the cozy, but I didn't make it! Look, your brother has made tea for all of us. And—what? Last night's clean dishes put away? Oh, Ali, mere laal."

She kissed his cheek noisily; he had the grace to blush and squirm from her grip. "It's nothing much in exchange for your motherly prayers . . . it's all right, Ammi, really," he protested as she lapsed into more proud exclamations.

How many cups of tea have I made in my life? How many glasses of water I've carried to friends of my parents, how many samosas I've fried and kababs patted into rounds, how many lunches I've cooked for us when my mother was late from work. Even though he's the older one. I poured out a cup of chai and took a sip. Steeped too long. Bitter.

"Who won the lottery?" My father stood at the doorway, tie loose around his neck and one eyebrow raised.

"We all did, it seems," I retorted. "The prize was a chaiwallah."

He took in the scene with a shrug and retreated before my mother could rope him in. I grabbed a stale piece of chapati left over from last night and rolled it around a sprinkle of coarse sugar.

I expected my mother to yell after me—that's not breakfast—but she was too busy with Ali to notice. I left my tea to turn cold in the sink. Occasionally, I emerged from my resentment of Ali long enough to appreciate some of his changes myself. Like the day we saw him in the city center, when I'd accompanied my friend Zohra to the tailor for a fitting. Her new outfit for the senior farewell party was almost ready, and she'd begged me to come along for a second opinion.

"Isn't that your brother?"

I snapped around, scanning the square. "Where?"

Both Zohra and I were under strict instructions to come home straight after school and study for our all-important board exams coming up. I wasn't eager to run into Ali, who would definitely rat us out.

I spotted him at the opposite end of the dusty lot in between shopping arcades. He was helping hoist a large vat—secured shut with rope—from the back of a dabba van. A few ragged street children gathered around him, and I recognized a couple of other men from his university crowd. Mohsin was supervising the heavy lifting but standing back at a safe distance. His rough-spun kurta was pristine, hair slicked back with gel and beard shaped just so.

Zohra and I slipped into a bangles stall, where we were anonymous among all the chaadar-clad schoolgirls but still had a clear view of the operation. Ali squatted beside one of the vats while Mohsin tried without success to organize the clamoring children into a queue. Instead, they grabbed plates faster than Ali could ladle rice into them and jostled Mohsin aside.

"Hutt! Chal hutt!" Mohsin shrieked, his voice high-pitched as the kids swarmed him. He brushed their handprints from his clothes frantically, as if he'd been contaminated.

We broke into laughter as he stumbled back to the van and hid while Ali and the others tried to keep up with demand. I caught Ali's expression in between the children pushing around him. He seemed flustered but not as much as I might have expected. Handing a plate to a little boy with matted hair, he flashed him a grin. Playful in the benevolent manner of an elder, not the smirk of one child to another.

I could hardly recognize him. He wasn't my teenage brother anymore as he laughed at a quip from another volunteer. His face was bright and flushed from effort. I was glad he was happy. At least he no longer frequented the downtown snooker club where he used to go and smoke hookah all the time. Most of the young men I'd seen disappearing into the club were the idle sons of Pashtun landowners. We were none of those things. If he's here doing good, he no longer wants to be someone else, I reasoned. I wish I'd been right.

I managed to sneak home undetected that day. And despite the tailor fittings and murder mysteries hidden in between my study notes, I managed to make it through the dreaded exams all right too. Some of my wealthier friends like Zohra left that summer for vacations in Murree or Dubai while I sweltered at home. I'd moved on to ancient used paperbacks scoured from the old city bookstalls—Danielle Steele and Sidney Sheldon were particular favorites. My mother dragged me from my books when she could and dispensed cooking lessons because making perfect bhagare baingan was going to get me far in life, she promised.

For Chhotu Chacha's birthday, we cooked paaye. I never understood the appeal of the gluey vat of trotters, my fingers webbed and sticky when I tried to mop up the gravy with naan. But paaye was the absolute favorite dish of my favorite uncle, so I helped my mother with the elaborate preparation. A fog of garam masala and goat fat permeated the house all morning.

To make room for everyone, we pushed the furniture aside and sat cross-legged on an old bedsheet spread out in the living room. A stockpot steamed on the dining table out of reach of the many kids dashing through their obstacle courses. We were halfway through the raucous meal when Ali walked in and slipped off his chappals at the doorway.

"Ali mian! Where has Allah hidden you?" our uncle called out. "Come, I assure you the meat is halal. That goat never missed a day of prayers, bless him."

A titter rippled through the room as my mother hissed, "Chhotu! Astaghfirullah, have some shame."

Ali's expression remained tranquil as he doled out a generous helping of paaye for himself and came to perch at the outer edge of our circle.

"What?" Chhotu Chacha protested. "I merely wanted to ensure that our imam sahib here would sanction our humble gathering.

What do you say, Ali mian? Will you tolerate us sinners in your home?"

"Chhotu, you're too much," my mother muttered as we glanced at Ali. For a beat, only the children continued their racing and shrieking as the rest of us waited for the shouting match. Ali had never been very good at taking a joke.

He swallowed his morsel before reciting, as if rehearsed, "All are welcome in a true Muslim's home. The lowest servant, the greatest king. All are equal before Allah."

Chhotu Chacha bowed as low as his ample belly would allow. "And we are so grateful, my lord," he began before my mother smacked the back of his head with a dish towel.

Eventually, even Chhotu Chacha wearied of his jokes when Ali wouldn't take the bait. We all settled into our roles around my brother's no-longer-new persona. That autumn, I began attending the same university but kept a wary distance from his crowd. At home, though, Ali and I still climbed up to the roof at night sometimes to share an illicit cigarette. Huddled in the dark under the web of clotheslines, pretending we knew how to blow smoke rings, we were still teenagers. We hadn't become anything yet.

"What does Mohsin huzoor think of your bad habits?" I teased as I passed the cigarette back.

"He's not a saint!" Ali coughed, indignant. "I don't smoke in front of him," he admitted. "But he's patient with our vices. Last week, he told us a story about how the Prophet took a known robber into his home because he repented. You see? He really believes. It's not easy for the son of such a prominent family to relinquish his expensive tastes and serve others."

"Well." I searched for a diplomatic way to phrase my skepticism. "Is that all he wants? He doesn't have—political aspirations? Like that uncle of his who leads the Islamic party?"

Ali shrugged and pushed his glasses up his nose, clearly uncomfortable. "Who can know what's in a man's heart? I see his good deeds. I believe what I see."

Most of the time, Ali was gentler than before. The hardness inside him—his resentment of our refugee family's circumstances—had always driven him to extreme experiences. But he was calmer now. My father and I talked one evening and decided he'd "found himself." I had my doubts about Mohsin, who would not speak to the women of the house nor meet our eyes when he visited. Still, he seemed harmless enough. Even though his dogma that Ali regurgitated at home was worse than tiresome. It felt connected to a religious conservatism that was sweeping the city, making it ever more inhospitable to me.

Peshawar had been a conservative city all my life. As the precocious child of refugee intellectuals, I was used to being the only girl speaking up in rooms full of men. Still, coming from a sheltered convent girls' school, I was unprepared for the current atmosphere at university. Much like Mohsin, many male professors did not meet female students' eyes when speaking to them. Most of my lecture halls included only a handful of women to scores of men. And when I dared ask a classmate if I could share his table during a science lab, he spat out *whore* just loud enough for the surrounding tables to hear him.

Eventually, I found my people and spaces. The "ladies only" section of the ramshackle but beautiful old library. A few friends, a few progressive teachers.

Around the beginning of my second year at college, I wanted to attend an evening talk by a visiting scholar, and my mother insisted that Ali accompany me for safety. The lecture was organized by one of those progressive professors: an earnest man trying to make the best of the college's limited resources. He'd invited an expert on the history of Islamic conversions in Waziristan and other northern areas, which would later become the subject of my thesis. The evening marked the beginning of an academic obsession.

I arrived early with a friend and sat at the front, eager for the rare event of interest. I didn't bother looking around for Ali. He was only my chaperone home and probably wouldn't even attend the talk. So I was startled when the "young man in the back with a question" during the post-lecture discussion turned out to be my brother. He stuttered over his words spoken too low for anyone to understand and had to repeat himself over jeers from other "young men in the back"—including Mohsin.

"How can any acceptance of Allah t'ala and his messenger be questioned?" he asked. "We should welcome these people's entry into Allah's fold."

I squirmed in my seat. I should have expected Ali's objection to the topic. But the speaker was unfazed. "Naturally, newcomers to our deen are to be celebrated," he observed. "But only when they have accepted faith of their free will can it be true iman." Well-prepared, he went on to cite the words of a religious figure in vogue in Peshawar as evidence. Our teacher hastily wrapped up the session.

Afterward, Mohsin melted away without a word. Ali and I emerged from campus into the chaos of early evening traffic. Vendors called out roasted peanuts, and urchins ran beside us with plastic roses. At the bus stop, Ali capitulated to the marketing tactics of a girl dressed in an oversized shalwar kameez. She sold him a miniature copy of the Quran the size of her own tiny fist and wished him many healthy children as she scampered off.

"We'd better get going, or we'll be inundated by any rascals who saw you," I told him, feeling, even as I spoke, that it was a cold thing to say.

Ali only laughed as we fought our way onto the next bus. He pushed aside the milling crowds of men to make sure I got a seat.

It was twilight when we reached our neighborhood and walked toward home. The gathering darkness seemed to invite confidences daytime forbade. "What did you think of the talk?" I asked.

He was quiet for a moment. "You know what I think. Those people in the north are . . . fortunate. They were doomed to die as heathens. Now they have a chance at jannat. What more is there to say? All these books, and for what?"

"But you heard what he said. If it was not of their own will? If they just converted without meaning it, what's the point?"

"Yes, that was true." He nodded. Quiet awhile, he seemed deep in thought.

Maybe there was hope still. "There are so many ways of thinking," I ventured. "If you'd just consider. Mohsin's fixed attitudes aren't everything. God doesn't have to be so harsh."

He clicked his tongue in irritation. "Why bring it back to Mohsin? I can decide for myself. Think about us, Hajra. If Islam hadn't come to India, we would be worshiping idols. Our ancestors, maybe they said the kalima out of convenience or because they had to, I don't know. But thanks to them, we have our faith."

Our ancestors. It was an easy phrase for Ali, eldest male, to throw around. What connection did I have to those shadowy figures from the past? I could well imagine how they'd receive a girl who loved books and spirited debate. What little they'd permit me.

"So you're saying the end justifies the means." The tone of my voice was more combative than I'd intended.

He responded with a challenge as well. "Yes. Sometimes, it does. Do you believe different?"

"I do. Faith resides in one's heart and can't be forced. Allah wouldn't want that."

He shrugged. "We can only guess what Allah wants. Read the Quran and practice ibaadah. Let that guide our actions. It's not simple."

I unlocked our creaky front gate and stepped onto the tiny porch, where our father's scooter was parked alongside the downstairs neighbor's. Insects fluttered around the tube light overhead, and we picked our way gingerly over rows of red chilis laid out to dry over newspaper. My mind tumbled in between the mundane and the ancient. I wondered whether I even believed my own words or if I just relished arguing with men. I'd grasp any opportunity to raise my voice in this city that allowed me precious few.

"We can agree on that," I replied. "None of this is simple."

FOUR

I wake shivering. My window is open, and the night still remembers the winter. It's barely 4 a.m., but I give up on slumber. I throw on clothes and pull my hair into a knot before running down the many stairs of my Brooklyn walk-up. A candy wrapper sashays down the street just ahead. A garbage truck beeps from the next block. I turn up my collar, tuck my chin under, and push through the wind to the diner nearby.

At my usual booth, the waitress approaches me with a tired eyebrow: "Hot tea again?"

By now, I take the book on indentured labor everywhere. It opens to the page I've saved with a pencil. I've found the picture from that conference presentation—three women in saris standing together in Durban, in what is now South Africa. "Kasturba Gandhi's Satyagrahis," says the caption. They're indentured laborers who followed Gandhi's wife in nonviolent protest.

I've been reading about them for weeks: Indians taken across the sea in the nineteenth century by British colonists to work on sugar plantations. The British called them "coolies"—originally from Tamil—and continued to use the word both casually and officially though it was already a slur. Indenture became a substitute for the abolished slave trade. Scholars in my books debate the line between the two evils. And I already knew about Gandhi's time in South Africa—that he started his activism fighting for the rights of laborers in the Natal province.

But I don't understand these three women or why they would make the effort to protest. A few more years of their indenture contract or agreement—which came to be called girmit—and they could have returned to India. Why would they risk arrest for a land that took so much from them?

I crush my tea bag against the cup with a spoon. The tea is weak amber, never black enough. But the chipped cup is warm between my palms. A grizzled man is perched on a stool at the counter. He drags a piece of toast through the pool of yolk on his plate and catches my eye midchew. I avert my gaze.

As always, my attention focuses on the woman in the middle of the photograph who laughs in the face of captivity. I don't know why I'm drawn to her. We are nothing to each other. No relation, no religion joins us. If we met, the only language we might exchange belongs to our colonizers. I wonder if her laughter is brave or foolish. Or maybe I'm the fool because she's come and gone but her laugh survives her. Preserved between the book's covers, she'll taste the salt of the Indian Ocean long after I've stayed up a thousand nights beside the cold Atlantic.

What will survive me: Unfinished academic research I no longer care about. A brother lost; our shared childhood corroded. Parents who only remember the contours of my younger face. Memories of who I used to be: the loud one holding up banners with words I once believed. And, too, the women who placed their faith in that past me—abandoned five years now.

A white man who said he loved me but knew nothing about me. He tucked two years of my life under his arm and left me ever more foreign and alone. "No one could make it past the walls you've got up, Hajra." I've turned over those words in the year since he left, though I scoffed when he said them. Walls. American pop psychology over-sharing intimacy. Why should I cough up data for his analysis?

In the diner, my tea swirls around stirred-up dregs. The classmates I call friends are familiar only with a stick-figure past I've sketched. The man who wanted to share my life subsisted on scraps: hints of a family estranged, a culture he couldn't understand. For a time, mystery sustained him. It was enough until it wasn't.

The waitress pours hot water into my cup, and the tea diffuses to dirty beige. Scanning the photograph, I search the women's expressions. In the weeks since I saw their picture at the conference, I'm tempted by the thought that we belong together. Bereft of any country or man that wants us, we could be a kind of countrywomen, as these three must have become to one another. I've known that sort of kinship. Like them, once, I stood taller with women at my side, when we raised our voices together.

But no longer. A familiar guilt obscures my warmth for the picture. I shut the book and count out change. We are not the same. Protest was no kind of choice for them. Many of the women laborers were likely kidnapped, as scholars now guess. Those women must have known they'd be shunned in India after the taboo ocean crossing. At the end of their five-year labor terms, they were told they could stay or return. They were offered their own patch of the hostile new land or a ticket back to one that didn't want them. My choices are infinite compared to theirs.

The neighborhood is still dark when I leave the diner. Layers of old cardboard shield someone asleep at a church doorstep. Dim movement skitters against cracks of light.

"Too late at night for a nice girl." The bodega cashier wags his finger when I stop for milk. "Not safe, this city."

But the city doesn't scare me. It demands only ordinary sacrifices. Tutoring wealthy children under the table, staying up to keep up. In return, indifference—the glorious flip side of loneliness. Men admonish me here, but no one has cared enough to enforce his disapproval.

Outside the bodega, dawn is beginning to lift the edges of the sky. Magnolia blossoms litter the roofs of parked cars. Two men in hoodies hoist crates of fruit from a truck and carry them into a grocery store. The owner arranges buckets of fresh tulips in staggered rows.

My New York life has been a stasis. But ever since that day in Mohsin's taxi, I'm unable to sleep. I'm woken by long-buried images and dreams. I read book after book to understand why I'm channeling this insomniac energy into women who lived a hundred years ago. But none of the books can answer me this: why did the woman in the photograph laugh?

Her fingers must have been calloused and raw from the punishing sugar fields. She might have been thrown in a jail cell, or worse, after her protest. But her laughter tells me she was glad for that moment. I imagine the sun warm on her arms and a cotton sari soft against her skin. For a moment, away from the plantations, her spirit was light.

Who are we to each other? Is this enough: we are women outside of home. We found our kin standing shoulder to shoulder with strangers.

In New York, politically correct America clashes with the brash city. At the university, they don't quite say, "Your country's tragedy is your meal ticket." Instead, they say, "This diaspora idea is interesting, but Pakistan is so *timely*."

Luckily, I've learned the language of Western academia too. Transnational feminism. The historiography of displacement. Circuits of power. Forced movement. I know how to make connections between my area of expertise and this new obsession with indentured labor.

Area of expertise. That phrase from networking events and funding proposals. To them, it means a few hundred square miles of car bombs and chanting men. To me, a room I once shared with my brother. Yards of white cloth embroidered with flowers blooming and withering.

They say this is timely, but no measure could account for the lifetimes between then and now. I've fallen out of time.

After a tense meeting with my dissertation committee, I succeed in persuading them. Though I'll receive no funding from the department, I can conduct archival research on indenture in Durban, South Africa, during the summer and revise my proposal. The timeline required is impossible enough to ensure I'll abandon my foolishness and stick to the "Islam stuff" everyone likes so much.

I continue to read about indentured labor on the subway, between classes, with my meals. In the moments when my mind is blank—when I lie awake at night or step into the shower—old questions pounce on me afresh. Why I made any of the decisions that brought me here or will take me elsewhere.

I'm startled from my brooding once by a harsh cry and spy a flock of wild geese in formation overhead. They make an effortless arrow toward the north following a homing instinct that has guided generations. No one needed to teach them this path. But I don't have such confidence in the instincts passed to me by my foremothers. Their concerns never resembled mine. Surely, they never left their husbands and tribes and hearths and survived.

I decide I've been charged with a quest. The women in my books are not my ancestors. This charge was not passed to me by blood. But that knowledge only strengthens my conviction. Because what can a child of refugees understand about ancestry anyway. I've never been able to visit the places in India where my parents were born, and I likely never will. Most of our family lore survives in a few photographs and fragments of stories rarely told.

But maybe I was never meant to find my lineage in bloodlines and gravestones.

My quest is composed of many smaller tasks. Apply for a visa. Buy a plane ticket. Arrange housing. Correspond with universities. On my way home every night, my steps are powered with the exhilarated urgency of purpose. On an evening like that, I receive the letter.

My elderly landlord is flipping through the mail in our shared entryway. "Miss Hajra! You went out with your friends, boyfriend? No? You work too hard."

I smile over my grimace and take the letter he hands me. A small white envelope. The handwriting addressing me is neatly sloped. Jinnah's profile is on the stamp and the lawyer's return address on the back. I run upstairs without another word. Inside my room, without taking off my shoes or coat, I crouch at my desk and open the bottom drawer containing a pile of identical white envelopes.

It's been a year or longer since I received one of these letters. For a moment, I pause over the stack that measures out my years in this country. The expectations of a person I used to be from someone I used to know.

I throw the new envelope inside, unopened, as if it is contagious. I shut the drawer.

After the letter arrives, old wounds knitted tight begin to unbind. My mind strays along paths I didn't take and words I didn't say when I still had the chance. Instead, I came here, to a bland and safe life in a city where no one could challenge me. Some part of me longs to find parallels between my choices and those of the women in the photograph. Maybe, before raising their voices in protest, they were tempted by the safety they were giving up too.

Nothing is that simple. Still, I would be a hypocrite to travel oceans searching for the truth about their protest while remaining mute in my own life. I need not even go far to interrupt my silence. Now, there's a man here in this country I can confront. But weeks pass before I can work up the nerve to find him.

I pretend I've lost my earring in his taxi. A few calls and, remarkably easy, I have shift change timings and an address for the depot that owns Mohsin's taxi medallion. Coney Island Avenue in Brooklyn, also known as Little Pakistan.

I've avoided this neighborhood since I arrived in New York. My classmates once arranged an expedition to its restaurants, but I made excuses. Of course Mohsin would be the one to drag me to this place I've dreaded.

At the corner near the subway station, a fenced playground is full of screaming children in neon parkas. Their hijab-clad mothers chatter over strollers and glance at me as I wait for the light. I wonder what they think of me in my corduroy jacket and jeans.

On Coney Island Avenue, I pass old men in prayer caps and yeshiva schoolgirls in pleated skirts that flap around their ankles when they run. A row of mechanics and lube shops thrum with low bass. Panjabi MC raps atop the *Knight Rider* theme from my childhood. For a second, I'm transported to the weekly thrill of Kitt and the swaggering American at the wheel. Screeches and horns at the intersection, and I'm back among the broken-down engines and stink of motor oil.

My feet are reluctant, but I push forth. Here is the taxi depot with yellow cabs parked along the sidewalk. A man dozes at the entrance on a folding chair. He startles awake to my footsteps and stares at my body, up and down. His gaze follows me as I approach the booth and its bulletproof window.

The dispatcher tells me to wait while he disappears into the garage, yelling, "Mo! Some lady say she lose something."

Mo? Laughter bubbles up and threatens to rattle me like a leaf in the wind. But then, as sudden as the impulse came, it dies away. The shape of a man emerges from the back, someone only a couple inches taller than me. He's all sinew and bone. I could take him, I assure myself, though I'm unsure about the source of this false bravado.

My pulse quickens as he draws closer. But his brawn has never been his threat. Instead, I remember the glimmer of his mocking gaze as he sped away all those years ago, secure in the immunity granted by power. That was his danger.

Mohsin scratches the stubble on his chin. His hair is unwashed, and his stained T-shirt is half tucked into wrinkled khakis. He was once accustomed to women washing and cooking for him. His apparent lack of home comforts almost feels like a victory.

He comes to an abrupt halt a few feet from me. Outlined by the afternoon sun, perhaps my identity is more obvious today. He purses his lips and tilts his head back. "So it *was* you." His voice echoes lightly in the garage. "I had a feeling . . . saala." He spits to one side. "I didn't know you were here. Abroad, I heard . . . Ali could have told me. Khussy."

I'm startled by his language. I know he's capable of violence, but I suppose I still thought him a religious man. But he was never pious, just opportunistic.

"I thought you knew everything—a big man with friends all over town."

He sniggers, but it's a sound made bitter by our surroundings. Driving a taxi can't have been part of the big man's plans. "Ali is not a friend." He straightens into some of that old swagger before he adds, "I don't spare time for small people."

Chhote log—small people. Does Ali know that's all he is to his idol? "Trouble between comrades?" I ask.

He shrugs. "People change. They abandon you like rats. You should know about that, running all the way here." He assesses my reaction. It's not a casual accusation. He wants to know whether I could still prove troublesome to him.

"I'm not interested in reminiscing." I pause to register his arms folded in defense. It helps propel me across the tremor in my voice. "I want to know why you did it."

"Did what?" he asks, spreading his palms out in mock innocence. He looks around as if to ask an audience amid cheers.

His manner incenses me. "'Did what?' How dare you pretend? I saw you, it was even your car, did it even occur to you to use someone else's car? Or are you just that stupid."

"Why should I hide? We—" He pauses and emphasizes his plurality. "*We* don't have to be afraid of people like you."

Indignation fires through me. "Oh? I'm sure Immigration would be very interested in what people like me have to say about dangerous criminals entering the country."

His expression sours. I'm sure no woman in his sorry life has dared address him like this. "You think your American baap will protect you?" he growls. "White people won't dirty their shoes for you. Me, I have brothers here. We look out for each other. You're not as far from home as you think."

Smell of petrol through my inhale. Metal tools clank inside the cavernous darkness that shades half of his body. He's right. I have nothing and no one here. And cockroaches like him do stick together.

The fight I'd gathered up in the past few weeks begins to drain from me. But it's not all gone yet. "If you're so fearless, why are you hiding here? Why aren't you leading some party of mullahs like your daddy planned for you?"

He scowls and begins to turn away. "I'm done with this."

"Wait." This whole meeting has spooled away from me. I must reel it back to my purpose. "Tell me one thing, and I'll go."

He glances back, curious.

The question almost dies in my throat, but I manage to croak it out. "Who was with you in the car that day?"

A slow smile spreads across his wolfish face. "Well, well. If only you had asked nicely. But why ask me? Ask him yourself. He's your brother, after all. Run along now. I'll find you when I need to."

With that, he melts into the shadows of the garage.

FIVE

The foreigner arrived toward the end of another monsoon season that ran dry. He called at Sita's home before any other, as custom required, and spoke with Maalan. Sita listened from the shadows beyond the veranda.

The man was fair-skinned like the nuns, but his hair and eyes were dark. His Tamil words were mismatched and sentences broken. Many times, Sita suppressed a giggle at his phrasing. She couldn't decipher all of his odd speech, but she understood that he brought hope.

He needed hardy people unafraid of work in faraway places. This famine was a tragedy in their region. But in other places, fields flourished, and workers were overburdened. He'd been sent to look for people willing to travel to make their fortune. They would be compensated handsomely for the inconvenience. And when they returned to their own lands with money to buy new seeds, their earth would be pliant to crops again. Would Maalan consider the offer seriously and talk to his family?

"I will speak to my cousins," Maalan agreed. "But it will be each man's own choice."

"Of course, you are progressive, I can see," said the man. "And in that spirit, please to speak with your sisters also. Women are just as hardworking as men in these parts, I have heard."

Sita could hear the shock in Maalan's voice. "Send my sister away? Who would marry her if she were to travel alone?" She heard Maalan rise to his feet, and the man understood it was time for him to go.

The foreigner apologized before he left. "I did not mean offense. But these are not times for the old ways. Proud and blessed how much your sisters would be to save their family from starvation?"

Before Maalan could respond, he added: "Just think about it, aenga. You say yourself, it is their own choice."

Afterward, Anjali—who had also eavesdropped—emerged to plot urgently with her husband: "You heard him. They need strong girls. Let Sita go. Lighten our burden."

"What are you saying?"

"There's nothing left for that girl's dowry. She'll stay unmarried like a stone around our necks. Let her work."

"My father would never forgive me if I sent her away."

"Your father is dead. We have to live."

Maalan did not mention the foreigner's visit to Sita, though the village was abuzz as he visited every home and made offers. A friend's brother agreed to leave, and another's as well. But none of Sita's friends signed up. They were busy with their own husbands and infants. They shook their heads, tongues between teeth in disapproval, when Sita repeated what she'd overheard. A girl traveling alone from home was unthinkable. And to earn money by working for strangers. Their families would rather starve than suffer such shame.

But Sita ran through the man's offer every day until she could think of little else. Anjali's feelings might change if Sita were not simply a burden on Maalan. She might even welcome Sita again into her home.

Or, dowry secured, would Sita be able to make a new home with a man? She could leave this village fading into sorrow and strife. She could see cities, machines, tall buildings. Her family could regain their wealth and standing in the village—all for a year's work.

She slipped away one afternoon and ran to the old barber's, where the foreign man was paying for room and board. She hid until he emerged, then sprang out.

"I want to speak with you," she said. "About the work. But I can't be seen. I will meet you at first light. Near the large gulmohar tree. Behind the temple."

He nodded. "I will be pleased to meet you."

The following morning, Sita found the man perched uncomfortably on a rock. She greeted him and sat on another rock, once moss-covered but now bare. Only then did Sita realize she was alone with a man—a stranger. Shyness overtook her quick tongue, and she stared at the ground as she tugged her davani across her shoulders and over her mouth. Unconcerned, the man ran through his script: just a year on the farm of a British person with lots of other girls her age. He'd been waiting to sign up a strong girl, and so, they could be on their way immediately.

He took a sheet of paper from his satchel. "This is the paper the British use to make laws and write letters. It talks about this work, see? They take this all very seriously."

Sita craned her neck forward and tried to read the paper. The jiggly typeface was not so different from the books she'd read at school. She could only make out a few words with the paper upside down. At the top: "Notice to Coolies."

It had been years since she'd read a book. The nuns had long since abandoned this drought-stricken region and taken their texts with them. She would need time to remember and decipher these words. Besides, the man already told her what the paper said. She should begin the journey before Maalan found out and stopped her.

But then she looked up at the foreigner's narrow face. He was a cat eager to pounce on his prey. The expression gave her pause. "Can I touch this . . . paper?" she asked with what she hoped was convincing awe. "I have never seen its like."

The man hesitated but handed it to her gingerly. Sita straightened the notice and struggled to read it while appearing to admire the paper on which it was printed. But only a few of the words made sense: *sugar, ship.* Others were unknown: *emigration, Natal.* She let the words swim into place and strung them end to end in her mind, the way she'd read difficult pages in school. In this way, she understood enough. It was a notice to workers calling them to work for the British queen and her people and leave on a ship to a place called Natal, where she would earn money and live in her own comfortable house.

Sita scanned the paper again. She knew what a ship was; she'd seen pictures. The nuns said it was a vessel to travel the sea. The foreigner had mentioned none of this. Traversing the black water of the ocean was something only strange beings like the whites attempted. It meant abandoning one's name and personhood, as Ayamma had warned the children. Emerging from the black water's deeps, an evil would seize people who attempted to reach beyond their land.

The nuns said this was nonsense—a heathen superstition rooted in caste evil. After all, their own ancestors had traveled to India by sea and suffered no curse. Running the nuns' words over in her mind until she could almost believe them, Sita returned the paper to the foreigner and said nothing.

Ayamma had small hands whose joints could bend almost all the way back. When she'd pulled her fingers taut, they'd made such an improbable shape that Sita's stomach flipped, and she'd begged her to stop the game.

After Ayamma was gone, Sita longed most of all for those hands. "Your people are alive as long as you remember them," Ayamma had said, perhaps to prepare her for the long season of absence to come. But without her grandmother's calloused fingers to scratch Sita's scalp or pat her cheek. Without her father's hand over her head. Without touch, Sita was cut off from her people. She was allowed a sleeping mat in the compound, but she'd become an outsider already.

So why not embrace the outside. Perhaps, in that wilderness beyond people, she'd find a new home to store her loneliness.

That night, she hid in the back of the foreigner's cart as instructed. As she lay there muffled by blankets, one of Ayamma's strange stories about the curse of black water returned to her.

When she'd first told the story, it was an afternoon during the full force of the monsoons. Sheets of rain swept through the courtyard, and Sita was crowded inside with the other children. The younger ones fretted and wept from boredom, and the older ones fought over beloved toys. But when Ayamma began her story, they all quieted. Tears hung suspended from lashes, thumbs stuck in mouths. Their grandmother's voice had a sense of command that wound through her words and lent them the weight of fact.

A young, betrothed girl ventured deep into the jungle to play, Ayamma told the gathered children. There were plenty of trees near the village, but she'd climbed all of them. Even though girls were expressly forbidden from venturing beyond the village boundary, she decided to hack through the overgrown forest and seek out its tallest tree, the naaval maram. Strong and nimble, she climbed it easily and nestled far up in the boughs, where she picked tart fruit to eat and forgot the setting of the sun. When she shimmied down, it was night already, and her sari was stained dark purple by the tree's fruit. She crept back into her sleeping village and scrubbed her sari at the well but to no avail. So she buried the sari there at the base of the well to escape discovery.

When the villagers gathered at the well the next morning, bucket after bucket of their drinking water came up black as ink. Men lowered inside on ropes to investigate the contamination and dug the earth all around. They found the stained sari. The girl's brother wept for her fate, but he had no choice. Fruit from the depths of the jungle was cursed, so the elders told, and they had to get rid of the poison she'd brought back. A group of village men carried and tied her to that same naaval tree as a sacrifice. They prayed the spirit beasts that raged beyond the village bounds at night would devour her. Once they were appeased, the curse would be lifted.

But their well water still ran black. Her banishment was not enough to lift the ancient curse that would infect everyone in the village and even their descendants to come. Undone by thirst, the people abandoned their village and scattered. Though they told no one about their black water curse, it tainted them forever.

In some weeks, the girl's groom-to-be and his wedding party traveled through the jungle on their way to her house. They did not know what had befallen the village. As they traveled, a laughing voice began to pursue them along their path. A melody sung by the naaval tree and the girl become a forest witch:

> *Beloved,*
> *Hear my song.*
> *My blood runs as rain.*
> *My skin is brittle as bark,*
> *Leaves rustle along my empty wrists,*
> *My lips are the darkest fruit in the forest.*
> *They threw me away, beloved.*
> *Take me away.*

The groom panicked when he could find no singer for the words drifting through the trees and vines. He turned and fled the way he'd come. The naaval tree's witch sang alone in the jungle, unavenged.

SIX

The bomb separated us.

India had an atomic bomb, and everyone in Pakistan celebrated when we learned that we had one too. The day after the nuclear tests, shadows crisscrossed the arched courtyard of our Peshawar college. They fell in geometric patterns across the faces and fists of men who gathered to cheer the news. My friends and I watched from a third-floor corridor above them, as if banished to watch from the wings. From our vantage point, the men were a pack of black heads and white prayer caps. The white and black circles jumped and dipped. Courtyard acoustics made their voices into cacophony. One burst into a kind of dance, and soon, others followed suit with arms outstretched.

Mohsin faced the crowd and led them in slogans cobbled together from old truisms. His expression was triumphant and satisfied—he was clearly so ready to gather up the energy of this moment toward his own purpose. I scanned the faces around him and dared hope I'd be wrong. But there, steps from Mohsin. Ali's lips were set in a line. His hands clasped before him were not empty. At a shout from Mohsin, Ali hoisted a large poster high up above his head. A drawing of Dr. A. Q. Khan—the physicist an unlikely hero for their cause. The cheap cardboard seemed to vibrate as it loomed. Mohsin riled the crowd in a repeated chant. Bhaarat? Murdabad. Pakistan? Zindabad.

As if the fiery destruction of one could spell anything but the end of us all. Our fragile bodies could not be safeguarded by a border. Each chanted call cracked deeper at the fissure separating me from my brother. We'd never find our way back to each other.

"All You Need Is Pyaar" came to me in a pamphlet during those churned-up weeks after the nuclear tests. The yellow paper photocopy bore a clumsily sketched origami crane on its cover along with Pakistan and India flags crossed back to back. At the meeting I attended, a handful of would-be peace activists showed up in search of a home amid the bloodthirsty celebrations.

Marjan—a gray-eyed girl with a golden fringe peeking out from her chaadar—spoke Urdu with Afghan cadence. She stood on a chair to project her soft, assured voice: "We need a show of peace. Let's show the world we're more than a nation of warmongers."

I glanced around at the solemn nods and murmurs. Twenty or twenty-five students had gathered for what was likely their most successful meeting ever. Hundreds assembled in the courtyard for Mohsin's impromptu demonstration. What chance did the meek have?

I was skeptical, but I didn't know where else to go. The courtyard chants had stirred a deep anger in me. I didn't understand it then, but I was already a student of history. I didn't have to look far to know this gathering nationalism was false and dangerous. But more than anything, I seethed at the idea of men in power directing my allegiance. They would not manipulate me into offering up my life for their greed.

Without anywhere else to channel this indignation, I copied down the details of the organizing committee meeting. A few days later, I found Marjan at the back of Zaheer Books, moving piles of dusty hardcovers aside to make room for a few folding chairs.

"The owner's a friend of the family," she explained with a smile and thrust a stack of economics textbooks at me. He'd allowed the group to meet at the back of his conveniently located bookstore.

Saeed—a lanky student in oversized glasses and a patchy mustache—arrived soon and helped snap open five chairs. A quiet, wide-eyed woman I remembered from my sociology lecture hall also showed up. The bookstore assistant brought us an enamel teapot of hot doodh patti and four chipped cups. Over chai and a box of zeera biscuits, we commiserated about our patriotic family members and jingoism on the news. Marjan eased the conversation from complaint to action, and we batted around ideas for a peaceful counterpoint: An opinion column for *The News*, where Saeed had a journalist uncle. Pamphlet distribution at the Sunday bazaar.

None of us were particularly excited by the proposals. But we emerged blinking into sunlight with another meeting date planned and tasks assigned for the meantime. On the bus ride home, I noticed my chest lighter and my hands steadier. I leaped off at my stop, took quick steps down the street, and ran up the stairs to our home— because I could, because my feet wanted to.

A car was on fire. My friend Samina and I came upon the blaze in front of the old canteen at the edge of campus. The silence unnerved me. No one to cheer on the flames or put them out. The air shimmered as a halo, foul stench trapped in my hair. Though the torched car was only one symptom of rising unrest at our college, I would remember it as the beginning. A flare signaling danger to come.

"Hartal," Samina said breathlessly some days later, arms crossed over her chest. A few of us were waiting for our professor in a mostly empty lecture hall. Samina slipped out to investigate the delay and spotted signs of riots in the distance.

We hastily packed up our belongings. Hartal had been declared at our college in the past and could mean stampedes, crowded buses, shuttered shops in the surrounding neighborhood. We hurried toward the college gates like beleaguered itinerants, weighed down with bags, papers, library books. Who knew when we would be allowed back inside.

Clouds had begun to gather that morning, and at midday, thunder murmured ominously. A susurration of chants rose and fell. The sound took shape and grew closer, but we couldn't identify the words. Samina wrapped a corner of her chaadar across her nose and mouth as if to shield herself.

Beyond the gates, we dispersed and hailed auto-rickshaws, not caring to trust our safety to buses or dabba vans if we could help it. Samina raced ahead, pushed others aside, and grabbed hold of an auto-rickshaw with both hands. She yelled at me to catch up, and I swung in beside her as the auto zigzagged past me. We were off in a roar of fumes, scattering pigeons in our wake.

Samina leaned back and hugged her book bag. Her family was strict, and Samina's permission to attend classes already hung by a frail thread. If she were stuck without transport during a riot, that could spell the end of her college career. I reached out and squeezed her arm.

She glanced up, and our eyes met in a brief moment of sympathy—too brief. We were jolted forward as the auto-rickshaw screeched to a halt. I stuck my head out and was almost thrown clear as the driver swerved in a wild reverse U-turn. He swore at us, our forefathers, and his own fate as he struggled to keep the vehicle upright through his maneuvers.

Samina's shrieks in my ear, I spotted the overturned car. The man curled into a ball on the ground clutched his head as another kicked him until his chappal flew off into the dust. Other men rammed cricket bats and hurled rocks at the car. One of them dragged the tape deck through a window. Wires trailed through broken glass.

The auto-rickshaw sped a few blocks in the opposite direction, then another. The driver continued muttering oaths. We were too stunned to ask where he was taking us. Eventually, he raced down a wide avenue toward the safe Cantonment district. Neither of us tried to stop him, though it was far from our own neighborhood. Letting us out at a busy market, he entreated us to call our families before he slumped forward and retrieved his snuffbox with shaking hands.

It was hours until Samina's family could cross town and rescue us from the video store where we camped out and waited. She wept all the way home in the back seat of her uncle's car. She knew she'd never be allowed out on her own again.

In the weeks that followed, I had to stay home too. It turned out the Islamic groups on campus were protesting pro-India comments a professor had made. But that was just the spark that lit a fire. Hostilities between India and Pakistan had worsened since the nuclear tests. The many factions across our university were eager to manipulate emotions riding high. Mohsin had recently formed one such student group, attached to the political party his uncle commanded as a member of parliament. Islam was their fashionable excuse.

I suppose it's easy to understand why Ali threw himself into the riots. Son of Indian refugees, he'd always been desperate to prove he belonged in Peshawar. What better way to shout his allegiance than by denouncing a traitor.

I was cleaning when Mohsin brought him home. Cooped up while college was closed, I'd pulled out stacks of old notes and was attempting to organize them when I heard labored steps on the stairwell.

"Y'Allah!"

I ran out to find my mother frozen, an end of her dupatta clutched at her mouth. I skidded to a stop at the railings as Mohsin heaved Ali up the last few stairs. Ali leaned against him and seemed to favor one leg over the other. One side of his face was covered with blood.

"It's not so bad," Mohsin panted as he gave up his burden to my mother's trembling hands and a chair I had pulled in from the dining room. "It looks worse than it is. Things got a little . . . messy at the rally today."

"What, what is this?" my mother whispered as she ran her fingers over her eldest's face.

"It's just—" Ali tried to speak but grimaced midsentence and ran his tongue over his split lip.

"Hajra! What are you staring at?" My mother gave me a push without turning to look at me. "Go, boil a kettle of water, get Dettol, a towel, go, go!"

A flare of anger shot up in my chest. She could look after her fool-hardy son herself. If he wanted to risk his life on his war cries, why should we care?

But I'd been well taught to swallow my bitterness, so I did as I was told. I wrung bloody towels into a bucket of hot water while my mother bound Ali's foot and raised it onto a stool. Her lips were pressed firm, her silence deadly. Mohsin was long gone.

"Ammi, leave it, really, this is too much," Ali tried to protest as she fussed with the binding. A mistake. She dropped the bandages and rose to her full five-feet-zero. He cowered in his dining chair.

"It's too much. Too much," she repeated. "Are we too much for you? Are we giving you too much trouble? Inconveniencing his high-ness, who has many important tasks out there in the world? Who—"

I tried my best to be unobtrusive as I gathered up the bloody rags and bucket and tiptoed to the bathroom. She was just getting started.

Ali didn't spend much time at home anymore. On those nights when he returned from the demonstrations, his clothes were filthy. My mother begged him to stay, especially after that bloody episode. But he'd just bathe, change, and leave again. Occasionally, he'd fall asleep on the sofa for a couple of hours. I found him like this one night when I woke to get a glass of water. I was seized by reflexive terror at the stranger prone in our living room. In the next instant, I saw that it was my brother. But my fear did not abate with the knowledge. That was how I learned I was afraid of him.

I tried to focus on my work with Pyaar instead. We met a few more times while college remained shut; the meetings provided an outlet for our frustrations. Materials began to spill over my desk and accumulate around the house. A pile of photocopied pamphlets in a shoebox by the front door was ready for Sunday. Newspapers were spread out on the dining table, where I analyzed opinion columns and underlined inspiring phrases.

One evening, I found Ali leaning against the kitchen counter. A Pyaar pamphlet was propped open in one hand; his other held a stale chapati rolled around a shami kabab. We exchanged a glance heavy with implication before I turned to the sink to wash my teacup and bowl and place them on the rack. I was drying my hands on a towel when he spoke.

"You're better off spending your free time on ibaadah and Quran study. Don't waste it on this silly nonsense, Jerru." His rubber slippers squeaked as he left.

I spun around—my mouth open to respond—but he was already gone. I was confused by the kindness in his voice and the childhood pet name. Layered through with condescension, the medicine was sweetened but still bitter. I gritted my teeth and flung the towel hard against his dirty plate. The greasy frying pan he'd left to crust on the counter.

"Pamphlets and articles are not enough."

College had been closed for weeks. Our core Pyaar group met and papered the old city walls with posters and handed out fliers at bazaars. We even managed to get a letter to the editor published in *The News*, in which we pled our case for peace with India.

So when I made my pronouncement that day, the others looked at me with surprise. Things were going well, they countered.

"Who's going to take us seriously with all this pen and paper nonsense?" I stared each of them down in turn.

"Serious people, those who *think*. They will take us seriously." Marjan returned my stare coolly. "The others are not our concern."

"But 'the others' are the ones who've shut down our college! They're the ones holding us hostage."

We argued back and forth as the other members watched our tennis match in silence.

"Look who we're dealing with." Marjan threw up her hands in frustration. "You want to reason with these people? Like the Taliban, who would chop off my head in a football stadium? They're all ready to die for their madness. Is that what you want?"

I bowed my head, momentarily silenced, but my indignation fumed. I knew Marjan wasn't the right target for my anger. Those men were—the stadium murderers, the nuclear bullies. The men who had shut down my campus, scattered my freedoms, and left me trapped indoors. My only brother, who might one day become one of those martyrs ready to die for someone else's profit.

I glanced up, mind racing. Maybe death was what I wanted after all.

"I have an idea."

We chose the day of their rally in the old city. Mohsin's uncle and his party had teamed up with the student association to bring attention to the young people's cause. Cloth banners called the faithful to gather after Friday prayers at Chowk Yadgar, the domed monument in the heart of the old city, where stray cats and heroin addicts spent their nights.

We moved through the ancient alleys covered in shuttlecock burqas. Ten of us were split up in twos and threes. Shops were shuttered for afternoon prayers, but women and children loitered in the streets, where they picked through rubbish and gathered crumbs. We were not out of place among them.

When the men streamed out of mosques and spilled through the arteries toward the central Chowk, we slipped into the current. We were not invisible in our burqas but close enough. As planned, we tried to follow older men so we'd be mistaken for their women and left alone. It seemed to work.

In the grounds around the Chowk, some 100 or 150 men assembled and called out slogans as party leaders climbed inside the dome and took up loudspeakers. Dispersed among the crowd, we waited for our moment. Under the burqa's anonymity, we could check our wristwatches as often as we liked.

It was time. Heat flushed through my body up to my temples. I shut my eyes to the dust of old places, stink of refuse, buzzing flies, crackle and hiss of men listening to their leaders. I unpinned the white sheet splattered in red paint from around my torso and let it drop under the burqa. As practiced, I pulled one corner over my shoulders and head. For an instant, I panicked as cotton layers stifled me. But I found the holes I'd cut for my nose and mouth and inhaled deeply.

One hand free, one pushed against the bodies around me, I flung the burqa from me onto the ground, buckled my knees, and let my body collapse. Abandoned burqa beneath me, I lay on the ground clad in a white shroud and trembled as I attempted deathly stillness.

Later, our friend from *The News* told us the crowd quieted when we all fell. In that instant, confronted by our scattered and shrouded bodies, the men were somber. The party leader's voice up front faded into confusion. A photographer captured Mohsin's stricken face caught between fury and bewilderment at our theft of his limelight.

On the ground, I knew only chaos. I lay still for moments of terror before I was pushed from the space I'd claimed. We were lucky. Most of our bodies were only bruised by the stampede. One protester twisted her ankle when she scrambled to her feet. Marjan chipped a tooth in the tussle with an enraged man who pulled her up by her hair and tore off her shroud. He shook her hard and slapped her across the face before she got away. I was kicked once. The shape of a chappal bloomed across my hip later. But I suffered no lasting damage.

"Police." An urgent voice to my left. Sirens. I pulled the shroud over my head, and inside out, it became an ordinary chaadar. I became another small woman scurrying through empty streets, escaping the sudden violence of men.

Chhotu Chacha lifted his copy of *The News* above his head as he walked in. "Did you know? We're famous. Look, black and white." He slapped the paper for added emphasis. "Famous, our own bitya."

My mother sighed over her prayer beads. She didn't bother to emerge from her sulk for the visitor. The previous day's paper had printed a small article with a black-and-white photo to cover Pyaar's die-in at Chowk Yadgar. Since then, we'd alternated between shouting matches and icy silence at home. How-could-you and think-of-your-parents and this-is-the-real-world and danger and forbidding and tears. I was grateful for Chhotu Chacha's interruption of the cycle.

Since it was Sunday and no one seemed to have anything better to do, the elderly sisters from across the street dropped by soon too. Our flat buzzed with their gleeful horror at my daring as everyone sat around in clumps of conversation.

My mother sniffed loudly and got to her feet—she wanted no part of this gossip. "I'm going to pray," she said with a regal flourish of her dupatta and left the room.

"But weren't you afraid?" whispered Chhotu Chacha's young wife, Nusrat. Wide-eyed, kohl-rimmed, frost-lipped. Only a year older than me. Her little son slept in her lap, toy car sticky in his grip.

"Afraid of what?" I tried for nonchalance, and perhaps I managed to fool her.

"Wah, Hajra." She grimaced as she shifted the slumbering child from one knee to the other and shook out her numb foot. "No fear? Of those men looking at you and Allah knows what they want and no one to protect you. Astaghfirullah, all alone out there." She indicated the window with her chin and let a stage shiver run through her. Then, she paused. "What is that sound?" Strains of guitar drifted in from the next room. "It almost sounds like a . . . helicopter," she mused.

Any words I might have chosen in response were drowned out. "WE DON'T NEED NO EDUCATION." Chhotu Chacha burst in, shouting along to the blaring boom box on his shoulder: "LEAVE US KIDS ALONE." He got through another few bars before my father managed to grab the boom box from him and turn it off.

"What are you *doing*?" Nusrat bounced the wailing child woken by his father's music. The neighbor sisters shook their heads and whispered among themselves.

"Just thought Hajra would appreciate some Floyd. Our fighter bitya."

He grinned at me from the doorway, irrepressible. I couldn't help but grin back. Because behind his usual silliness was also pride in his own. No one else in my family had expressed any so far. Instead, they looked at me with disbelief, as if they couldn't recognize this stranger among them. Aside from my mother's warnings and my father's disappointment, Ali was conspicuous by his absence. He came home late at night and slept on the sofa, then rose early for Fajr prayer and left before any of us woke. He said nothing about the protest.

As Chhotu Chacha flashed me an exaggerated thumbs-up, gratitude welled in me. Maybe there was room in my family for me to become the kind of woman I longed to be. This fighter bitya.

My mother shuffled back into the room, her pale face stained by tears. Her eyes were rimmed with dark circles, and blotches of red streaked her skin. Muttering prayers under her breath, she made a beeline for me on the divan. As I looked up and met her gaze, she took my cheeks in her hands. My lids fluttered shut as she breathed her prayers cool around the dips and crevices of my face. She kissed my forehead once with trembling lips before she withdrew. Her blessing lingered on my body.

SEVEN

Sita lay in the back of a cart jolting along an uneven road. She inhaled mildew and dust motes in quick breaths. Blankets covered her so no one would know she was stealing away.

In that shadowy hour before dawn, she and the foreigner alighted in a silent place. He opened a large door and pushed her in with one hand at her back. She stumbled into darkness as the door shut. A bolt slid into its groove. Released breath, and the noise began: weeping, whispered fates, prayers to mothers and gods. So many voices. Every one belonged to a woman.

A single window was set too high for anyone to reach. Sita sat on the ground exactly where she'd been pushed, afraid to move farther into the noise. Soon, sunlight began to tinge the high window and revealed the contours of her surroundings. A cavernous cowshed but no cattle. Packed mud floor in between a tangle of hair and arms and toenails. Thirty or forty women, more than she'd guessed.

At midmorning, the foreigner and two other men carried in a cloth bundle of food and rusty buckets sloshing water. Women rushed forward and pushed others aside to grab what they could. Sita turned queasily into the corner she'd claimed. These women stank of urine and tore into grain like animals. They picked at crumbs that fell to the ground or gathered in their bosoms. She couldn't share sustenance with such filthy strangers.

She'd anticipated sacrifice and labor on this journey, but her imaginings had been abstract. The possibility of this kind of hardship had never occurred to her. These women were no better than the lowest sharecroppers or the bonded laborers once in her father's employ.

Ayamma had a cup and plate, separate from their own, set aside for such people.

Tap at her shoulder. A woman bent over her, a cholam cake wrapped in a corner of her green sari. She was at least a decade older than Sita and perhaps many years more by experience. A silver pin was threaded through one of her nostrils. Lines forked away from her eyes and dug deep around her mouth. Her skin was stretched tight and leather-dry. But softness, too, seemed native to her jaw and brown eyes.

"None of that matters here, girl," she said, guessing the reasons behind Sita's unease. "You've left everything behind. You have to survive like all of us now. Eat."

Sita took the coarse cholam cake and held it for minutes before she could calm her gagging throat and eat a morsel. Her body couldn't possibly accept this meager nourishment. But she had to survive, after all. The woman nodded as Sita ate, then supervised as she gulped down a handful of water at the bucket.

"You'll learn to keep it down," she said, thumping her back.

Afterward, she chatted animatedly with Sita, seemingly unperturbed by the younger woman's silence and their grim surroundings. Her name was Tulsi. Unafraid of the pale foreigners she mocked, she was the kind of woman Sita imagined her own mother to have been in that picture memory she'd made in her mind.

"Why?"

Night had fallen, but Sita lay awake. She searched for the woman who'd spoken the question aloud. The moon was almost full and hung near the window in a cloudless sky. In the half-light, the woman's face was silver. "Why have they brought us here? They said we would work at a white man's home in Cochin. But it should have taken us a long time to get there. Why am I here?"

Other women offered their own theories knitting the arkati's promises with rumors of old disappearances. Most expected work at white people's estates, where they would be well paid. Some had traveled with their husbands or brothers for this work but were forcibly separated from them. They suggested the supernatural was to blame for their situation. Demons, tests of strength. One spun impressive tales of emperors' harems gilded with silks and depravity.

Sita wished she could shut out their imaginings. Not one mentioned the black water. Maybe none of them knew. They didn't ask her what she thought. Her haughtiness erected a wall none except Tulsi tried to cross. So perhaps Sita alone knew what truly awaited them. And yet, she'd thrown herself before this fate willingly. She was the only one arrogant enough to wade into black water as if it were nothing.

"And you, how did you come to be here?" The women looked expectantly at Tulsi, whose head was bent low. So far, she'd been silent.

"I met a foreign man," she began. "Years ago. He told me about riches in other lands—I only had to sign a girmit to work there. I was afraid. I didn't want to leave. But my sister-in-law—she didn't want me. My brothers didn't want me. They didn't touch me. My nieces were forbidden to come near me."

Sita glanced at her slumped figure and began to understand. A widow who was an impostor. Long hair in a plait down her back. Color for her clothes a deception. And she, Sita, had eaten food this woman touched. She'd drunk water from the same bucket.

"My father was so sad because of me," Tulsi continued. "I didn't want to stay. I know it was wrong. But I wanted something. I wanted better—"

She fell silent abruptly, and the women did not ask for more. Another began telling her own story. Tulsi glanced up and met Sita's eyes. Her irises were black, not brown, now. Night sky against the whites. Something seemed to pass between them in that moment.

Sita wondered what it meant—she'd met a man years ago? She was sure of one thing: Tulsi knew more about the journey ahead than she had revealed.

The foreigner cradled a heavy ledger in the crook of one arm. Neither he nor his helpers spoke as they dragged a small table out to the middle of the cowshed.

The women were corralled into a line. Each was asked her name in turn, and Sita could hear the scratch of a nib and rustle of paper as she waited. This must be what Tulsi had called the girmit—the paper she said she'd signed.

Sita glanced out the doors left open behind her. At least three men loitered there and chewed on raw sugarcane. Beyond them were fallow orchards littered with twigs and ugly words. *Burden, useless.*

Her turn. The foreigner asked her name. She could read his English letters upside down. He gave her the pen and showed her where to mark an *X*. She could sweep words across the page if she wanted. But her fate now was labor under the sun. It was best her body forget how to form letters. She dipped the pen in ink and crossed two lines.

Afterward, the arkati and his men led them outside. They squeezed onto three carts. Wood slats sagged as each climbed on. Mules brayed and stamped their feet, then clopped along a country path. Dried peepul trees brushed their skin along the way and provided little shade from the sun. The road ahead was marked by cracked lines. Dust clouds rose as hooves struck earth. Women coughed and held saris to their mouths as they traveled.

They spent a day this way and most of another on a train and then a second set of carts. At dusk on the second day, they reached a sprawling set of enclosures no better than the fenced pens where Sita's family once corralled cattle. The sheds were open at the front with slatted roofs above. Wood posts separated sections of mud and insects and yellowed shrubs. A row of them stretched until the divider from the men's section, which extended much farther. Excited, some of the women pointed to monstrous shapes that loomed far away in the gathering darkness. That was Madras port, they said.

That night, Sita lay awake in her corner of the shed and listened to scrabbling rats and the drip-drop from roof to ground. Farther away, she could make out the drunken calls of men who worked at the harbor. All around was a symphony of grumbling stomachs and guts. In between, a whisper—her name. Tulsi beckoned her. Clambering over their neighbors, they emerged from the shed into open night.

Sea breeze whipped ringlets from Tulsi's plait. "Let's explore," she said.

Before Sita could object, Tulsi slipped into the narrow space between sheds. Sita paused only an instant before squeezing behind her.

The harbor was another world. They skirted around mysterious shapes that dotted the landscape. At night, they were living beings in bodies of metal and rope that spilled salty blood in puddles. The two women watched for broken glass and splintered wood as they crept around moonlit shadows and hid behind iron beams.

Around one corner, they leaped back to hide—a trio of crewmen leaned against crates and smoked beedis around a circle of lamplight. Their words drifted into indistinct murmur punctuated by grunts and laughter. Sita and Tulsi could advance no farther unseen, but neither suggested returning to the sheds. They settled behind a long shape covered in tarp and told each other secrets in voices so low, they melted into the wind.

Tulsi had been here before. She'd left her village years ago for this journey and crossed the black water. She'd worked in a land where the people were darker than Sita—about the same hue as Tulsi. Birds and insects were different there. Tulsi eased a small bundle from her waist as she spoke and untied the knot carefully. "See?" A pile of pits and seeds lay in her palm. "I collected them before leaving—nellikai, naaval pazham, palappalam. I'll plant them there and make my own orchard, and I'll be rich."

"Is there no fruit in this place, then?" Sita asked.

Tulsi smirked. "Silly girl. It's all different. The fruit, the people—the sky, even, turns such strange colors." She paused, and her smile faded. "But the white people, they are just the same." The plantation where she'd worked had been a misery, she hinted, though she did not volunteer details. So when her contract was over, she took a ship back here. "You can imagine how my family greeted me." Her voice was a bitter grate.

"I can't imagine. Tell me," Sita whispered, her stomach in a knot. Though she hadn't spoken it aloud, she still nursed her fantasy of returning to the village, rich and triumphant, one day. Tulsi simply shook her head.

"I'm back here." She closed her calloused palm tight around the seeds. "I'm signing another girmit, aren't I? That should tell you enough."

In the weeks of waiting, everything that had once only existed in books became familiar to Sita. The rotten smell of the ocean, the loading and unloading of ships. Jungle of masts towering as far as she could see. Ropes as if vines, and men scampering far above, acrobatic as monkeys. Wood crates—each so huge she could have stood inside touching neither head nor shoulder to its corner—hoisted on pulleys and stowed aboard by straining men.

To keep busy, they were instructed to plant a new vegetable garden at the back of the depot. The rest of the time, she remained aloof
from most of the women in the enclosures and declined to join their
card games. Still, their chatter filtered through. Some had lived in cities and traveled many times. Others spoke coarsely about their own
bodies and the bodies of men they'd embraced, as if this were nothing. She'd never known such women or seen her life stretch ahead as
mysterious as the ocean they would cross. For a while, the anticipation of the unknown was enough to distract from her fears.

But her thoughts drifted to the black water and Ayamma's warnings eventually. The curse the girl-turned-witch brought back from
the jungle had spared no one—it had stained even generations to
come. Sita reminded herself that she'd never really believed those
tales. Old women spun stories out of the bits and pieces permitted
them. She was the girl who went to school. Myths and rituals were
backward foolishness she had long ago rejected.

Sita licked her lips. They tasted of salt. She was another of a string of
women preparing to board a ship. The salt wind filled her lungs and
chapped her lips raw. She tugged at the unfamiliar pleats at her waist
and straightened her shoulders in an ill-fitting blouse. They'd been
given new clothing yesterday, and finally, Sita was able to cast aside
the girlish pavadai davani for a real sari. Now, she was just the same
as the women in line with her.

They were alike in other ways too: none of these women with her
wore any marriage markers—no vermilion, no tali. Earlier, though,
Sita had spotted two of them shuffled in among the married women.
Tulsi explained about their dockside weddings with men who were
also destined for the new land. She turned her nose at the women and
said they were weak to partner with unknown men. Sita said nothing.
Because the men were strangers but less strange than a new world
without the warmth of a body by one's side.

Stepping onto a swaying jetty bridge, Sita closed her eyes to the
nauseating sway of her body over water. She tried to remember
something stable. She used to sit in the courtyard with her grandmother. Rays of early morning sun would filter through the boughs of
a neem tree to their bare arms. A rattan tray lay at their feet. Ayamma
had taught her to clean rice of stray dirt. She'd held the floppy tray

with hands steady as only practice could make them. One twist of her wrist, and rice flew high in the air, so high that Sita thought the lot would scatter far across the courtyard. But Ayamma caught the grains back in her tray. She laid the rattan back on the ground, and they both looked for offending bits of grit. Ayamma's sari was gray-edged cotton. Her fleshy arms were firm against Sita's side.

A ladder led them down from the ship's upper deck into humid darkness. Below was a space crowded with more bodies than she could count. Men, women, babies crying. All clutching the bundles they were given at the dock: lota, sleeping mat, blanket and spare outfit, and the precious certificate bearing their name and destination. Stamped metal disc hung from a piece of string around each neck.

In those first moments, the ship's lower decks took on the air of a bazaar. A cacophony of voices—men calling across the crowd or pushing against neighbors. Scuffles broke out but also simple kindnesses. A weeping infant was reunited with his mother, passed hand to hand above the herd. A man who tripped was raised to his feet by unknown arms. Women were corralled at the far end behind a barrier of sacks heavy with supplies. One lantern hung atop cast weak light into this area.

Jostled, Sita dropped to her knees and crawled as far as she could go. She came to a stop at the very back and crouched next to a stack of crates. All she could see were the spindly ankles and shifting drapes of women claiming their tiny allotments. Some splayed their knees or extended arms to gather more space than they were due.

Sita remembered most of their faces from the days of waiting at the harbor. But today, they all kept to themselves. The strangeness of this cramped dungeon seemed to silence gossip. And the stench of so many unwashed bodies. A nuisance at the harbor, the smell was now unbearable mingled with the sour odor of the ship. She curled against a wood crate, hay from between its slats poking her side, and closed her eyes.

A shadow fell over her. The woman to whom it belonged crouched down. Tulsi. She took Sita's hand and squeezed. With her other hand, she reached up and pushed strands of loose hair from Sita's face and tucked them behind her ears.

Sita reached out and clutched her arm. "Stay with me, Tulsi akka," she whispered.

Release. Ropes sliced and latches broken. The two women hunched together as the ship detached from shore. Tulsi's eyelashes trembled. Her shoulder rose and settled. Sita pulled an edge of the blanket from her bundle between her teeth and bit hard. The ocean roiled beneath her as the ship moaned its departure.

A lurch as if the ship tugged at their navels, as if mothers struggled to keep them. But it was too late. Sita's breath caught because something broke. Veined leaves that once fluttered in her palm. A snail had coursed its sticky trail across her foot. Grains of red earth that clung to a new stalk. The solid threshold of her home connected to her by the ages—stretched taut until the thread snapped.

* * *

That first morning after they set sail, a crewman named Raju led them to the upper deck. Light-skinned, he dressed like the English but still wore a turban wrapped around his head. He spoke Tamil and sometimes interpreted the foreigners' orders with a clipped accent. And though she first expected sympathy from him, soon Sita saw that Raju was more unforgiving than the English themselves.

Sita had already climbed the ladder at dawn to wash and stretch when they were allowed to do so in small groups. Then, she'd averted her eyes from the railings and water beyond. Now, huddled on the upper deck midmorning, she could no longer ignore the roil underfoot or the salt breeze whipping curls from the nape of her neck. A crewman hung precariously from one of the masts with a tool in hand and called to his mates below.

All of them were working, she could tell that much, but their actions were as opaque to her as the strangeness of iron floating on water. The forward momentum of their vessel filled her chest with a thrill—but only for a moment. In the far distance, across the sails and foredeck, she glimpsed endless darkness. Waves salivated foam and licked hungrily toward them. Sunlight skimmed the surface. In that instant, her chest deflated, and fear rose up as a viscous tide.

Blinking hard, she looked away. Averting her gaze from the wild ocean would be the only way she could survive this journey. So she turned her attention to Raju. He'd pulled two jute sacks as tall as his thigh up from the hold. Now, he took a knife from his belt and slit one open. Pale grains of cumbu slipped from the sack onto the cloth he'd spread out. "Clean," he said. He slit another sack, almost as large as the first, and dipped his hand in, drawing a palm of green moong. "Clean," he said.

Days or lifetimes elapsed this way. Sita followed the daily tasks set for them. At dawn, she rolled her bedding and helped prepare breakfast. Midafternoon, she joined a smaller group of women for their mandatory exercise: walking the length of the upper deck and back five times. This was when averting her eyes from the hungry waves became hardest.

While other women worried aloud about what awaited them on the other side of the crossing, she remained silent. She could not bring herself to form friendships with these women, though she had abandoned so many of the rites that demanded separation from them. After all, she had cleaned their shit during her turn scrubbing between decks. She'd eaten from the tin plates they all shared and perfunctorily washed with salt water. She'd slept and risen alongside them in quarters where every bodily function, noise, and odor were laid bare. Still, Sita kept herself at a remove in her mind. It was the only part of her body over which she still had dominion.

She made an exception for Tulsi. Sita felt a kinship with her she could not readily understand. Perhaps it was because Tulsi grew up a fisherman's daughter in a village not far from Madras, where she experienced things the other women had not. Or perhaps it was because she, too, had been driven from home by the cruelty of her brothers and sisters-in-law. In turn, the older woman adopted Sita as a little sister. Much later, looking back, Sita understood that this was the only reason the other women tolerated her superior attitude toward them—because Tulsi, beloved by all, had commanded them to do so.

The ship surgeon resembled a lumbering ox, his skin like leather. He was the most important man on the ship, so Raju said, and also a medical man like those who'd inspected them at the docks. The women squatted on the deck and were taken to see the surgeon one at a time. Inside his cabin, Sita was alone with him. He ran his tongue over his lips as he held a strange contraption to his ear. It resembled a trumpet whose horned end he held at her chest. His cold hand pressed the instrument to her skin, front and back.

He held Sita's wrist and pressed her vein. His thumb was flaky as dough, and a nest of gray hair sprouted from his knuckles. Wet patches spread across his shirt from his armpits to his chest. A trickle of sweat coursed from behind his bright-red ear and disappeared into his collar.

As he waved her to the cabin door, the surgeon spoke—English but different entirely from the nuns' melodic, round words. She understood nothing. Still, she didn't need to catch the words to interpret his leer. She'd been taught by her grandmother to cover and shield her body from that look. She understood that the surgeon would make sure she returned to his cabin.

* * *

Again, the same dream of running. She was racing down dusty streets, her heart in her throat. Something pursued her. This part changed sometimes. A tiger, a bull, a monster twenty feet high. Faster, she ran faster; her breath was beginning to catch. Any moment now, the beast would set upon her.

But then, as always, an open door. A girl stood at the threshold. She reached out and pulled Sita to safety. In that moment, Sita turned around. On the street behind her was someone else—a woman who paused and stared. But it was too late for her. The woman would be devoured. And Sita woke, her cheeks wet because she was certain it was her mother. She'd left her own mother out there to die.

Crickets sang out and mingled with snores from around the courtyard. The night was still, and Sita kicked away the sweaty tangle she'd made of her coverlet. Ayamma lay on the mat to her left, flat on her back with both hands clasped against forehead. Sita slid over and nestled against her grandmother's body, breathing deep the smell of withered jasmine crushed against cotton and stale sweat. Some calm returned to her chest.

"Hmph." Ayamma shifted irritably. "It's too hot for your nightmares, ma."

Sita considered returning to her mat, but even the thought reduced her to tears again. She whimpered not because of the monster, not even the breathy pursuit, but that moment at the end. The abandoned woman who met her gaze for an instant.

"Aa ra ro, aa ra ro." Ayamma cradled her. "Let's dream of sweets and bangles, hmm?"

"But I left her there." Sita wept into the crook of her side.

"Who? Who's worrying my little one?"

"It's my mother!"

Ayamma stiffened. "How do you know who it is, kanna? Don't distress yourself."

"I know . . . I know it's her. And that stranger who pulled me to safety. Why didn't she save us both?"

Ayamma sighed. Sita had related some version of this dream for years. And each time, her grandmother had comforted her back to sleep with crooning platitudes. Tonight, she seemed to have decided different.

"That girl at the door, she is no stranger, ma. She is your daughter."

Sita started up. "My daughter?"

"Shhhh. You'll wake the others. Kanna, one day, your daughter will save you. It's the way of the world. I am old now, but your father's good deeds will rescue me. Just the same, your daughter will rescue you. That is what your dream means."

"But how can you be sure?"

Ayamma took her little hand and kissed it. "I just know. Dreams are old—as old as old women."

Sita was quiet awhile before venturing the thought that still plagued her. "And the woman left outside. She is not my mother?"

But Ayamma seemed to have run out of wakeful patience. She let out a shuddering yawn that jiggled the rolls of fat at her waist. "Let's make our own sweet dreams, shall we?" She kissed Sita's forehead. They drifted away together.

EIGHT

Most of the time, I conserved space. I tidied my belongings around the house, folded my legs under on the divan, and hugged my shoulders close on the bus. But now, after the die-in at Chowk Yadgar, I began to push outward. I wanted to kick cracks against the facade men like Mohsin and my brother were building around our daily lives.

After the newspaper story about our protest, Marjan—whose number was printed on the Pyaar pamphlet—received calls at all hours. Some were congratulatory, some threatening, most were deep-breathing lechery. Her father looked into changing their number, but the calls petered out once we became last week's news. None of the groups behind the campus riots deigned to respond to us. Nothing, it seemed, had changed.

On the day college reopened after the riots, Marjan and I met up and rode the bus to campus together. At the gates, people stood around clumped in animated groups or perched on the front steps. We slipped in among the crowd, anonymous. Or so we thought.

"Wait, excuse me, please." A man ran up to us, satchel flapping against his hip. "I saw, I read, in *The News*," he stuttered and pushed a lock of hair out of the way of his glasses. "That is to say, I want to join. Please, how can I help?"

Marjan and I exchanged a brief smile—he was so earnest—as I jotted down information about our next meeting. In that moment, two more students rushed up—a red-cheeked woman with a friend in tow.

"That was so cool, yaar." She glanced up and down at us with frank curiosity while her more skeptical friend only glared. But the friend, too, asked for information before she left.

It took us forty minutes to get into the building; we were stopped so many times on the way. Finally, we ran the rest of the way to class.

"Posters," I panted at the lecture hall door as Marjan opened her mouth to speak.

She laughed. "You read my mind. Let's sit at the back and draw a quick one with the information. We can photocopy at lunch."

Our next meeting was standing-room-only. Afterward, we pressed forward, energized by all the new ideas. Candlelit vigils for soldiers killed on both sides of the border. Letter-writing campaigns to all the newspapers and talk shows—in English, Urdu, and Pashto—arguing for disarmament. Paper cranes folded by hand for weeks and strung across every arched doorway on campus. The relatives of some of our wealthier new members even gave us money.

Salma, one of the new members and an art student, took charge of design. With donated funds, we could print full-color posters. She pulled in protest imagery placing us within the context of the wider world. Photographs of Asma Jahangir and Medha Patkar collaged with Beatles album covers—a nod to our name. American civil rights spliced with Partition-era nonviolence. Newspaper headlines from *Jang* broken up and subverted. They were smart and eye-catching and empowering. They didn't last.

We came in one morning to find each poster carefully vandalized. The ones plastered around the main entrance were shredded as if by long fingernails. A few on the bulletin board were painted over—eyes of each male protester blacked out, the women's faces scored with ballpoint until invisible. Other posters were simply covered by edicts from local mullahs or the jeweled dagger symbol of the political party led by Mohsin's uncle.

I found Salma in front of a particularly vicious defacement on a wall near the cafeteria.

"Are you all right?"

She turned and blinked slowly as if returning from afar. "What?"

"I'm sorry. I know you put so much effort into these." I ran a finger across the scratched circle over what used to be Fatima Meer's face. Next to her, Ahmed Kathrada's visage was whole, but his eyes were swiped with black marker.

"Oh! You think I'm upset? No, this is amazing."

"It is?"

"Yes! I've been scribbling in my sketchbook since I got in today." She leaned toward me conspiratorially. The end of her brown plait peeked from the side of her chaadar. She pulled the chaadar back over her head, impatient, her fingers smudged with ink. "Don't you see?" She pointed to another poster. "The possibilities? I mean, these are inspired! Censorship, erasure, blindness. So many new poster ideas. The possibilities . . ." She trailed off as words escaped her.

I laughed, and the morning's disappointment slid from me as easy as fabric from silky tresses. "I'll leave you to it, then."

Outraged by the vandalism, many of our newer members wanted a loud demonstration. Marjan and I insisted on preparation, though, having learned from the die-in. We brainstormed communication and safety strategies and wrote letters to organizations around the country for advice. One of the groups we contacted in Islamabad shared our letter with an American colleague based there—Meghan Jennings—who reached out to us.

"I'll be visiting Pesh-a-WAAR next week. I'd love to meet you girls while I'm in town," she gushed on the phone. Flattered a foreigner wanted to speak with us about anything, we agreed readily.

We met at her guesthouse in a wealthy neighborhood it took us many bus changes to reach. The historic lobby had been remodeled to appeal to foreigners in Peshawar on their way to the mountains. The few Pakistanis around were men in suits. I felt distinctly out of place in my chaadar and shalwar kameez, ratty book bag slung over one shoulder.

The manager led us to a café on the second floor, where a middle-aged woman with a blond topknot and long skirt rose from her table to greet us.

"How lovely," she said as she clasped our hands in turn with both of hers. She turned to the obsequious manager: "Bring these girls a cold drink, would you?"

"Thank you, Miss Jennings, we—" Marjan began, but the woman waved her silent.

"Please! You must call me Meghan. I insist."

We exchanged a glance. Addressing someone of her age by their first name was unthinkably rude. But, of course, we knew from the movies that this was commonplace in America.

"All right, uh—Meghan—tell us, please, how may we help you?" Marjan tried again.

"What's important is how I can help *you*, of course! You're doing *such* important work here, and I'm beyond impressed. Beyond."

"Actually, we have just recently started simple peace activities—" Marjan began.

But I had the notion that Americans disliked humility. And I didn't want to lose whatever funds or resources Ms. Jennings might be able to procure for us. I hastily cut in. "She means that we have just started a new *stage* of our long-standing activism. So we asked others to guide us at the beginning of this stage. But we have been planning for a long time. We want to provide a counterpoint to the hardliners and warmongers at our college."

Meghan Jennings stared at me as if I were a barnyard animal abruptly gifted with speech. "Where did you learn such beautiful English?" she burst out in astonished delight. Then, understanding seemed to strike her, and she added, "Was it at one of our mission schools?"

Stunned for a moment, I finally said, "I studied at a convent school."

Meghan nodded as if this confirmed all her suspicions. "Yes, that's the foundation of everything, isn't it? Learning about God's grace from women who serve Him." She leaned forward. "Girls, I really see something special here. Such passion! But you must have access to more opportunities than you can find here." She waved dismissively to indicate our bottles of Pepsi with straws, the window with a view of the lush suburb around the guesthouse. "You can't stay in this backwater."

"Back-water?" Marjan repeated. "But Miss . . . Meghan, we want to make a difference here. And where else can we go?"

"Indeed, well said. Pakistan needs girls like you! Especially here on the Frontier." She jabbed at her place mat. "You have the raw materials. The *verve*. But you need resources. Exposure. Our church has a fund for just this kind of thing, you know. Seminars, training in the States, fully paid. And we've set money aside for Moslem girls dreaming big, just like you!" She finished with a flourish, her jabbing finger now pointing to each of us.

My cheeks began to hurt from all the polite smiling. I decided it was time to wrap up this tiring encounter. "That is—so generous.

We will think about this seriously. But now, we must go home. Our families may be worried," I added with a flash of inspiration. "They don't allow us to be out." I arranged my features into an appropriately forlorn expression and hoped Marjan had done the same next to me.

"Oh dear, of course." Meghan Jennings stood and handed us a Dubai Duty Free plastic bag bulging with books and pamphlets. "Here, some materials I brought for your movement. I hope they'll be helpful. And please, you know how to reach me, yes? Any time. God bless you, girls."

Safely outside, we fell over each other, laughing. "What a character!" Marjan exclaimed. "Are they all like that? Americans?"

I shrugged. "Must be. But training in America—why not? Let's stay in touch with her."

Marjan nodded enthusiastically as we found our way to the bus.

When Mohsin called a rally in support of soldiers at the Kashmir line of control, we were ready. Marjan had developed a communication chain based on an organizing handbook Meghan Jennings had given us. Each member was assigned two others to alert about a new action. Now, she tipped the first domino with details—rally at the gates tomorrow afternoon after classes. Whispers eddied around Peshawar's nooks and crevices like the breath of a wind god.

At four o'clock the next day, more than fifty of us picked up our signs. Ready with comfortable shoes and warm clothing, we streamed to the gates from all directions like a swarm of ants.

Mohsin's ragtag group was already assembled there, having pushed aside the samosa and fruit vendors. Twenty or so men gathered around Mohsin, who held up a blood-and-guts photograph of a soldier killed at the Siachin glacier by Indian forces. From a distance, their cries were too muddled to decipher. As I drew closer, some words emerged: the usual *Bharat Murdabad* and *Ya Nabi*.

Marjan chose a spot at the opposite end of the gates and raised a fist—our signal. She met my eyes through the bodies and colors between us. Her fierce expression matched my swooping heart. As planned, we raised our signs together, and I began the first of our chants: *What is our right? Justice. What is our demand? Peace.* Above my head, *We are warriors for peace.*

Louder and louder, our chant rose in ferocity like a vibration. Sound thrummed through my skin and out my mouth as if each of us strung a single instrument.

I glanced over at Mohsin's group on the other side—a mass of bewilderment. In among the faces, Ali. He wore the hard expression of a stranger. His mouth was a line, and his eyes nocked a black arrow at me. You don't belong here, they shot across.

In response, I raised my voice: "My home is peace!" and others took up my cry. Mohsin's men tried shouting louder to drown us out, but we were too many. And we were organized.

After that, swords unsheathed, we clashed at every event either group sponsored. What Mohsin's association lacked in strategy, they made up for in numbers and brute force. And, we soon learned, in police connections as well.

In the days after the Kargil War with India broke out, we organized our biggest rally yet. We reached far and wide among our networks to increase turnout—family members, alumni, even friends from colleges in Rawal Pindi and Lahore. On the afternoon before, we held a sign-painting gathering at Zaheer Books and had to move into the street to accommodate everyone who showed up.

The peace march began at the edge of Sadar and ended at Chowk Yadgar. Shopkeepers gawked, and children jeered as we streamed through the ancient alleys. Some called us traitors and worse as we passed by them.

An older woman stood at her balcony overlooking the street and yelled at us through crisscrossing clotheslines. "You think you are brave, but you are cowards," she called out.

Startled when a clothespin skittered near my foot, I glanced up.

"My boy is the hero. He's risking his life at the border. You are just cowards, cowards." She sprayed spittle into the air and gesticulated with gnarled hands. Gray hair half-stained with orange henna peeked from her chaadar.

I swallowed the point in my throat and raised my voice to join the others. We left her behind. We spilled into Chowk Yadgar, and today, the person with the loudspeaker under the central dome was a woman. A poet and activist many of us admired, she'd been in front of the feminist protest lines back in the eighties. She flew in all the way from Karachi for our rally.

Marjan and I scurried between tasks as we checked the square's perimeter. We expected some counterprotests from Mohsin's crew, but the only interlopers so far were street kids with eyes peeled for an easy wallet. I found Saeed at his assigned station near the Chowk's north end.

He frowned. "It's too quiet."

"What do you mean?" We were struggling to hear each other over cheering crowds and loudspeaker call and response.

"Look at the stores." At the Chowk's western end, a fabric seller pulled his shutter closed with a long hook. Another vendor frantically packed up his hairbands and train sets. At the next shop, a man snapped a padlock onto his shut gate.

"Maybe they're just going for prayers," I ventured.

Saeed shook his head. "Something's wrong. They've been tipped off."

"All right. I'll go investigate. Stay here." I picked my way through the students crouched atop the square's periphery steps.

"Where are you going?" I asked an elderly vendor as he covered the fruit on his cart.

"Na, na, don't trouble me. I have enough worries without you lot." He shook my questions off and wheeled his cart away.

I tried others, but they all refused to speak to me and averted their eyes. Panic mounting, I scurried farther into the market and searched for an explanation when a child tugged at my chaadar. "Baji."

"What is it?" I handed him a few rupees.

He grinned and pushed matted hair from his eyes as he pocketed the money. "Police, baji. Run, run, run!" he shrieked behind him as he skipped down another alley.

"What? But we got permission." I was speaking to no one. The empty street was eerily silent; only the buzz of the loudspeaker from the Chowk crackled in the distance. No wailing, no sirens either, no warning.

An ambush. The realization descended too late. I sprinted back toward the Chowk, but already, at its opposite end, police vans pulled up one after another. Policemen armed with batons swarmed into the crowd. I could get no closer. Bodies stampeded out the Chowk any which way to escape the lathi charge. I couldn't fight the tide. Shouldering across, I crouched in the shelter of a shuttered store-front and waited for a break in the current of people.

When I managed to stumble back to the Chowk, the last of the police vans were retreating full of cuffed protesters. A few dazed peo-ple crouched near the periphery and nursed their injuries. One lay prone and unmoving. Saeed. A gash at his temple bled freely. His torn shirt revealed long bruises blooming across his torso. He was breathing but labored.

I found another member to accompany him when the ambulance arrived and went in search of a phone. We needed lawyers and bail money. Luckily, we already had a plan for both.

Saeed was in the hospital for a while with a concussion and bro-ken collar bone. But he recovered. We got everyone out of jail within a day. The police were only paid enough to bully us and didn't want to bother with paperwork.

Mohsin must have hoped the injuries and arrests would scare us into submission. But everyone knew his family had paid the police off. Our people were incensed. We gained more energy and wider membership. With each action, we gathered more supporters for an even greater turnout at the next demonstration. Mohsin's plans had backfired. He grew desperate.

* * *

I crept into the kitchen—mindful of the late hour and thin walls—and slapped handfuls of cold water on my face at the sink. It had some of the desired effect. The window was propped open, and a chill breeze drifted in to cool my brow. And, too, in came the smoky resi-due of evening. Tandoors snuffed out for the night, coals in a brazier where someone warmed his hands. All silent except for the call of a chowkidar and the occasional car on the main road.

The first year of the new millennium had begun in a blur of protests, classes, and papers. While I was occupied with Pyaar and keeping up with my studies, more than three years had sped past at the university. Enough at our college for a combined bach-elor's and master's. More importantly, it was enough to equip me for my dreams of getting a job and saving some money so I could travel. I'd train to become a grassroots organizer maybe or study activist movements in other countries. I kept in touch with Meghan Jennings over email, and she'd promised she could arrange some fellowship funding in America for me. But first, I had to get this thesis out of the way.

I turned off the stove before the kettle could whistle and poured hot water on the evening's dregs still left in the teapot.

"Enough there for another cup?"

I jumped, spilling water before setting the kettle down with care. "You scared me!" I scolded my father as he shuffled in. "Why are you up?"

"Couldn't sleep." He shrugged.

My father's insomnia was a frequent malady grown familiar over the years. I poured him a cup of secondhand tea and took two nan khatai biscuits from the tin hidden behind the spices. We returned to the dining table, where my books and crumpled notes were spread out, haphazard.

"I don't want to interrupt," he began as I moved some books from a chair for him.

"Well, where else can you go?"

He nodded. The living room had become Ali's de facto sleeping quarters since he'd distanced himself from our shared bedroom. We could hear his snores beyond the curtains drawn across its doorway.

"Anyway," I continued as my father slipped into the chair. "I could use a break. It'll help keep me awake."

"How much more to go?" He eyed the small pile of typewritten pages with skepticism.

"I've got more done by hand," I protested. "I'm going to type up the rest on Marjan's computer. I still have to do the literature review. And then this last bit and then back to—" I sighed and mentally counted out the sections that remained. "It's still a lot," I admitted. "But I'll get it done."

"Will you? You spend so much time on—other things."

The subtle rebuke was the closest my father could come to speaking about my activism. I'd been involved with Pyaar for almost two years, and in the past year especially, we'd grown by leaps. My parents, however, still struggled with acceptance.

"'Other things?' If you mean my work with Pyaar, then come out and say so." I flipped open a textbook. If they'd just try to understand.

After a long pause, my father sighed. "You kids. Both of you reck-less. We were never like you." He gazed at the dark window reflecting back our irritated faces. "I don't know, maybe your mother. Books were enough for me. True, Ali has never been that kind of boy. But you . . . I thought you—"

I shut my book carefully. "We're different, Baba, you and me. But not so much. I love books too."

He glanced back from the window. "Have you looked into that doctorate we talked about?"

"What does that have to do with anything?" I ran a hand over my face and pinched the bridge of my nose where my tortoiseshell glasses rested heavy. Much like his. "I did, I did look. Now isn't the right time, Baba. I'm too busy, and Pyaar is really taking off. Besides, I've already applied for a junior lecturer position in the department for next term."

This last tumbled out to get it over with. It was the first time I'd mentioned my future plans to my parents.

"Hajra." One word. So much disappointment. "A doctorate would allow a different life for you. Respect. A dignified life. Not all this." He waved a hand to encompass the cramped room, his chipped teacup, and frayed kurta. "If I'd been able to study more. But your grandpar-ents—you know we lost everything to come to this country. I had to support the others. But you don't have such responsibilities. You can do more."

There was a pleading in his voice that cut right through me. "Why, why do you put all this on me? What about your son? Ask him to be your surrogate."

"You kids," he repeated and shook his head. "I never spoke to my parents like this. Where have you both learned it? Ali says, 'Ibaadat is more important than thermodynamics.' Imagine. Who is the father?"

I reached over and unhooked the dirty glasses from his face, blew on the lenses, and wiped them clean on the hem of my kameez.

"Here." I handed them back. "Is Ali failing again?"

He waited a beat as he listened for the snores from the living room. Afraid of his son, I suppose. "Yes. Just think. Five years now, and he still hasn't finished engineering. Mr. Malik's son started the year after him, and he just got a job in—Muscat or something. This was all we ever wanted for you both. An education. No one can take that from you, beta. It's the only possession you get to keep in this world. Everything else . . ." He shrugged. "Do you understand?"

"Of course I understand. You've been telling me all my life. What do you think I'm doing here?" I gestured to the piles of notes and scraps that accounted for a year's work. "Don't give me this lecture again. Tell *him*, the one who'll give the shirt off his back to his no-good friends before he'll do anything for his own interests. If they were real friends, if they cared about him, they'd tell him to study. Get a future."

"A future," my father whispered as if haunted by the word. "He says he doesn't need us to pay for his college anymore. When I said we didn't have any more money for it. He's getting a job with the party, he says. With Mohsin's uncle. Secretary or something. He says they'll take care of him. What kind of job is that, I ask you?"

I'd dropped my gaze while he spoke and wore the edge of a piece of paper under my fingernail. I glanced up at his question. "Don't ask me, Baba. You know how it is between me and Ali." I shook my head. "Do you remember, years ago? When I'd just started college. We talked once like this, you and me. About how Ali didn't go to the snooker club anymore. We were so happy. Snooker." I snorted at the concerns of my past self. "You said—we thought—he'd found himself."

My father rubbed his face with both hands and smudged up his glasses again. He brooded for a minute before he seemed to come to a decision. "No, beta, this is wrong. You cannot give up on your only brother like this. What do you have in this country but each other? Look at Chhotu. You wouldn't believe the things he's pulled. How many times I've had to . . . Anyway. He's my brother. He's foolish— that just means he needs me more. You see?"

"Oh, I do see." I stared at my father's calloused hands and the deep lines across his brow. "I have to be the sensible one. Isn't that what you've always said? No. Ali's responsible for his own actions. And here's the thing, Baba." I leaned forward and made sure he looked at me before I continued. "This is bigger than our family. What he's doing—he and Mohsin and the others. You have to know this isn't going anywhere good. We'll all be burned to cinders if they have their way. Future, education, everything you dreamed of to come to Pakistan. There won't be anything left for any of us. We can't let them just—" I searched for the word and failed. "What I mean is, we have to fight back."

My father studied my face as if for the first time. "But why does it have to be you? This is your brother. This war you're both fighting—our home is too small for it. Let someone else take it on, I beg you."

I looked away, embarrassed for him. He'd been taught to keep his head down, and maybe no one would notice he didn't belong. I didn't want to inherit his timidity. I'd fight for a foothold in this land and make it mine somehow.

"I heard you, Baba. I'll think about it. Go back to bed now; you look like a ghost. Get some rest."

After a frantic few weeks, I slapped together a thesis and completed my graduation requirements. That autumn, I started work as a junior lecturer. The pay was meager, but I was determined to save what I could. Besides, the work kept me on campus and engaged with Pyaar—what I really cared about.

After many slammed doors and arguments with my parents, Ali had finally dropped out of his failed engineering degree and taken on some vague duties with the party run by Mohsin's family. Luckily, I wasn't asked to weigh in on any of this. Not much remained between Ali and me to damage. We'd clashed at protests in public for years, but we maintained a frosty silence at home. It was easy enough to avoid him; he wasn't around much.

That evening in December was a rare instance when we both were home. Ali had stopped by for an early dinner before Isha prayers at the mosque. My mother flipped his two chapattis at the stove, her temple dusted with flour when she brushed wisps of hair back from her face. Just beyond the kitchen, I sat at the small dining table, where I folded the newly designed Pyaar pamphlets. Ali came to sit at the table, too, and tapped his foot as he waited for his meal.

I glanced up and studied him for a moment. His face was wan, thinner than I remembered. There were shadows under his eyes, and his beard was ragged. He did not look like a man at ease with himself. I might even bring myself to feel sorry for him. Then, he shifted his gaze to my papers and glared at them with an expression bordering on disgust. My sympathy disappeared. I'd stayed silent to maintain the peace at home. No more.

"What are you looking at?" I could hear the edge to my own voice.

"Why do you do this? All this." He waved an arm across the piles of pamphlets. It was the first time in years he'd openly referred to my work. I was thrown off by his pleading tone. We'd avoided each other so long that his cadence, too, was unfamiliar.

"What do you mean 'why?' This is what I believe in. And why shouldn't I do this?"

He sighed and rubbed both hands over his cheeks and pinched the bridge of his nose under his glasses. A nervous habit he shared with my father. With me. "Hajra, you're more intelligent than that. You should know why not. Be reasonable."

"Who are you to tell me about reasonable? Just come out and say what you want to say." My heart thudded against my rib cage. We'd circled so long around this unexploded anger. I balled my hands into fists and dug fingernails into my palms. Out of the corner of one eye, I could see my mother at the doorway, chapattis forgotten.

"I've told you before." He began slow, as if speaking to a bucking horse to be tamed. "We're only looking out for your own good. It isn't right for a woman from a good family to be shouting on the streets among men. Once you leave the four walls of your home, you become an outside woman. Once you bare your face to other men. It's not right to excite their temptations like that."

The words did not sound like his. "An 'outside woman?' What is that? You're crazy. I wear a chaadar; it covers my sinful hair, even my loud mouth, mostly. Don't pretend this is about religion. You're just scared of us—admit it. You know we're stronger, and you know we're right."

I surprised myself with this last. Ali and Mohsin had every institution behind them, an army on their side. Why should they be afraid of a few peaceniks? But once I'd said it aloud, I understood something of their fear. The ground was shifting—our movement signaled that—and they were afraid history would slide over to our side.

Ali sighed again. His exaggerated air combined the weapons of the adult with those of the teenage brother who knew exactly how to incense me. "I can't talk to you when you're behaving like this, Hajra. It's childish. Ammi, is that chapatti ready? I don't want to be late."

"Oh no. You can't just stop now." I stood up and pressed my palms hard against the table for support. The strength of my new realization coursed through me. "We're not done just because you decided we are."

Ali shook his head sadly. "Don't you know when you allow anger into your heart, you let Shaitaan in?"

"Don't tell me about gods and devils. I don't want to hear any more of that religious bullshit. Say what you really mean. You think I'm an outside woman? A fallen woman, is it? Say what you think of me in front of our mother."

"All right. I don't approve of what you're doing. I'm worried about you. I know you say you believe in this cause, and maybe you do. But it is a temptation from the devil that you must resist. Belief is for Allah alone! You must follow the role Allah has written for you as a woman; that's what the Prophet has said."

"Oh and you know what the Prophet wanted? Or are you just parroting Mohsin Khan as usual? He and his family are playing you, don't you see? Who is he to tell us what to do anyway—does he have a direct line to God?"

"Astaghfirullah, Hajra! Don't speak that way. If he has a clearer understanding, what's wrong with learning from him? You know what—I'll borrow that teaching tonight from Mohsin. 'Women should not parade outside.' It's been written. You can't argue with what's written."

I picked up my stack of pamphlets and hurled them across the table at him. I threw them hard. I meant them to hurt. I wanted him to bleed.

The pages rustled and slipped from the table. Holding out his hands reflexively over his face, Ali stared up at me, incredulous. Then, he rose to his feet. I took a step back. My mother took a step forward.

"Ali," she said, her voice pitched high.

He didn't look at her. His eyes were locked on me across the table from him. A pounce away. "I won't have this insolence." His voice was a low growl. "I've tolerated too much from you already. You are an embarrassment to me and our family, and this madness must stop. I am your elder. You must do as I say."

Even as I tried to stop myself, the words tumbled out: "And how will you make me?"

He stepped around one end of the table. My birdlike mother was all that stood between his rage and mine.

"Ali," she said again, firmer this time. "Go from here. Please."

Slowly, he turned to her. His face bore the surprise of a boy betrayed, not of the man who hulked over her. "But Ammi—"

"Please, Ali. Talk can come later. Now is not the time. Go, go. I'm begging you."

He didn't look at me as he left, but I caught something of his eyes. They reflected what I felt too. We'd found ourselves in a place we could not recognize. Both of us outsiders in our home.

NINE

Sita awoke tumbling across slick floor. There was no time to gather her wits. She was pinned against the side of the deck by a massive crate crushing her ribs. Another lurch of the ship, and the crate creaked backward an inch—enough for her to scramble out. Not a moment too soon. The floor keened again, and women fell against each other, shrieking. The crate smashed into splinters.

One woman wailed, "It is rakshasas come for us! Risen from the black water!"

The ship lurched, and her sentence slid into cries. Above the confusion, Tulsi's authoritative voice rang out, a little higher-pitched than usual. "Calm yourselves, silly girls," she commanded. "It is a storm, nothing more."

Sita wanted to believe her, even as she clung on to a bolt with clammy fingers. Black water beasts were only a tale. But even now, after days on the ship, she still shrank away from the sight of that endless sea. Because maybe there were no devis to save the world and no rakshasas to condemn it. Maybe no nightmare monsters pursued her in waking life. But wild nature still laughed at the foolish joys and plans of people. Nature leapt forth over the waves as everything she'd built drowned.

Eventually, the waters calmed, and the women rearranged their bedding as best they could to return to sleep. But Sita could not rest easy. Her stomach remained clenched in the morning. She was unable to touch a morsel of breakfast. Still, their daily tasks awaited them. She followed Tulsi up the ladder. They were part of the group cooking today.

They squatted on the deck under the beating sun and cleaned grain and lentils. Something of this was familiar. Like rice thrown high to land back onto rattan. Her village, her people laid to waste the water rising the baby wailing the water as high as her hip Ayamma a bony bundle with sickness the sun relentless the earth cracked.

Sita reached for the cumbu. Sturdy grains sifted through her fingers. Again and again, she ran her fingers though clean water, freshly washed hair. Once, she'd longed for such abundance. But this poor man's millet was not rice. And her family was gone.

A nudge from Tulsi. "He's watching." She indicated Raju nearby and tilted her chin back to her own hands picking and discarding dirt.

Sita bent to her task. The mass of cumbu under the bright sun was a blur. Sita squinted to focus her eyes on individual grains. The first wriggle seemed to accord to the ship's rhythmic motion. She scooped the lilting grain along with a few others and brought her hand closer to her face. Another squirm as if to escape and jump overboard. Then more of them were alive in her cupped hands. Wet and tender.

Sita cast the maggots from her body, but they would not let her go. They clung to her wrists and sprang onto her foot. She swatted them and ran to escape them, unseeing until she stopped against the railings, and her eyes were open wide. Far below, the ocean was not the color of the sky or the river. The mighty color stretched and filled the horizon up until the bottom curve of the sky.

Sita's knees gave. She leaned over the railings and retched hard. Then, she relaxed and let them drag her away, shedding grains of millet.

The surgeon smiled. His teeth were yellow and crooked. He shook his head when he spoke and raised an index finger in admonition. This, then, was the same in every language. Stop causing trouble, little girl. The trumpet rested longer and lower on her chest this time.

He sent her below decks with Raju, who said she'd been instructed to sleep off "fever by reason of sunstroke."

"You're lucky the surgeon likes you." He smirked. "But don't expect your antics to get you out of work next time."

She settled back in her corner of the lower deck and shivered. Her section was almost empty. Most women were still topside, except one who was heavy with child and was perhaps also instructed to rest. She heaved herself up off her blanket and waddled over.

"Why aren't you up there with the rest of them, girl?" she asked. "Are you sick?"

Sita only nodded, unsure of her memory. It was entirely possible she'd seen maggots in the cumbu, but her terror had been sourced in something far darker. Decay at the foundation. The ground beneath her feet was no longer certain but instead had become a writhing morass that could swallow her whole.

"Yes," the woman was continuing. "Many people have this nausea on the ships. It will pass. Only remember this when you're expecting a child one day! You will look back on this sickness and laugh."

Sita tried for a smile but failed. No fairy-tale return to her own village could be possible. She'd already accepted that much listening to Tulsi's bitter recollections. No marriage day from her courtyard, as she'd grown up playing with her friends. The past had rotted away and so, too, the image of the person she thought she'd become.

But maybe in this new land—in Natal—she might have a child. Perhaps not in the way of custom. But she might still be able to bear that daughter from her dream who would rescue her from the trials of this samsara. There was hope yet.

The woman, Pushpa, stayed and talked for the rest of the afternoon. She said she would join her husband in Natal. He'd set sail six months ago and then sent for her. It was a land of great riches, she assured Sita. Fortunes abounded for those who were willing to apply themselves. The savages did not work hard; that was why the white people needed to bring others in, Pushpa explained. The five years, the plantations. Her husband told her everything in a letter dictated to a friend and read by the village Brahmin. He'd told her to hide her pregnancy from the agent. They hadn't found out until she saw the doctor at the harbor, and by then, they'd spent too much to leave her behind. Besides, her baby was still at least three months away. Her son would take his first breath in that new land across the ocean.

"I was afraid of crossing the water. But my husband said what we've heard is not true. Those beliefs about black water are just superstition. The whites travel all the time, and they still have their souls intact." Pushpa hesitated here. "Anyway, look at us," she continued.

"Here we are, floating in this ship. A miracle of the white people. It protects us from the evil of the open ocean."

This time, the surgeon laid a hand on Sita. Instead of the trumpet, he pressed a palm to her chest. When Sita inhaled and broke through her fluttering breath, he grinned wide. She watched his hand on her breastbone fall with her exhale. And then again.

Finally, he withdrew his hand. But as she turned to leave, he grabbed her forearm. His fingers dug into her flesh, and his other hand grasped her hair. He ran his fingers down the length of her plait and lingered over the woven grooves. Frantic, Sita reached for the table where the surgeon kept his gleaming instruments. But he caught her and pinned her arms together with one arm and clapped his other hand to her mouth. His wet lips dropped to her neck.

Sita raised her knee, swung back, and kicked his shin as hard as she could. Jolted, his teeth sank into her neck. He sprang back to wipe her blood from his mouth, and Sita struggled loose. She wrenched open the cabin door and ran past the women waiting outside, down the ladder below deck.

"Don't say anything," Tulsi insisted. "They'll believe him. And then he will come after you for his revenge."

"But I have the wound. The wound will prove it."

Pushpa shook her head. "He'll say you made it up. Or else that you're mad. He'll remind them of that day you were fevered on the deck."

"But I can't go back there!"

Tulsi squeezed Sita's hand. "Don't worry. We won't let you go back alone." Pushpa made soothing sounds. Another woman nodded, and another. You won't be alone, they said.

In wonder, Sita glanced at the circle beginning to form around her. Their faces were varied. Scars carved stories across the cheek of one; another's complexion was almost night—a color from which she had once recoiled. Sita had raised herself above them in her mind. But by making this journey, they were no longer different. So Tulsi once told her when she'd pressed food in her palm. So this circle now reminded her. In making this sea crossing, they were strangers no longer.

After the crewmen extinguished their lamps in the evenings, the women's murmured gossip faded into slumber. Sita listened to this drift with her eyes wide open. The hours pooled slow as syrup around her wakefulness. The first few times this happened, she cursed her fate as she tossed in a sweaty tangle. But soon, she came to welcome the nights free from that same repeated dream of pursuit.

One night, restless, she sat up and let her eyes adjust until she could make out the peaks and valleys of the landscape. She stood and placed her foot into a crevice left between a folded knee and another's splayed arm. And then, her other foot eased into another empty slot. Tiptoe by tiptoe, she made excruciating progress.

She didn't get far before she was startled by someone shifting onto her heel. But after that, every night, she got a little further along in this adventure. In darkness, the shapes could be a tiger ready to pounce or a cobra slinking into brush. Creatures forming behind her eyelids, she reached out her palm to find her way forth as real danger blended with fantastic.

A hand closed tight around her ankle. "Sita!" An urgent whisper from below. "Be careful!"

It was Pushpa. By degrees, Sita lowered onto her haunches. Reaching out, she found Pushpa's round belly, where the woman's own palm rested.

"What are you doing?" she demanded in a low whisper. "You almost hurt him."

"I'm sorry, akka! I was just . . . I couldn't sleep."

"Aren't you tired? You cooked lunch today, and that white man made you exercise too."

"Yes. But I lie awake anyway."

"Why?"

Sighing, Sita ran a shaky palm across her face. She hadn't slept in days. Memories of her home flickered. But when she reached for them, they extinguished quick as a candle flame. Her family felt like a made-up story in contrast with the ship's reality. "I think about my village. And where we will go. And what will happen. And—so much." She shook her head.

Pushpa clicked her tongue. "Silly girl," she muttered. "You're just a girl."

"You aren't much older," Sita retorted. She'd grown weary of Pushpa's maternal superiority. Just like Anjali and the other women from the village who looked down their ample bosoms at her. Unmarried, unmother. She wasn't a real woman to them.

"Still," Pushpa continued in her knowing tone. "Maturity comes after marriage. You'll see one day."

Sita laughed without mirth. "Marriage. Not for me, not anymore. The black water ate it up too."

This time, Pushpa's cluck of impatience was sharper. "Come now! All this black water nonsense. Hasn't Tulsi akka journeyed before? Just stories trying to stop us from being brave."

True, Tulsi had returned from the journey. But not unscathed. To the other women, she shrugged and made wry comments about the dangers. "What black water? Ayyo, it isn't black you need to worry about. Worry about white. Watch your back for white skin's black heart." Tulsi made the others giggle at her stories of greedy overseers and harbor pickpockets.

But without an audience, Tulsi's practiced manner fled. Her face was lined by bitterness. Once, as they sweated together over a vat of lentils in the cramped galley, Tulsi muttered, "What use this food? Fattening us like cattle for the kill." Then, as if startled she'd spoken aloud, she pursed her lips and refused to explain herself further.

Sita returned her attention to Pushpa's dim outline. How did she come by such certainty? Only by desperation. She was the guardian of new life, after all. She needed to be sure she was doing right by that duty.

Overcome by this realization, Sita reached out her hand, found Pushpa's, and squeezed hard. Startled, the other woman paused her chastising. "You are right, akka," Sita whispered. "Sleep now."

Pushpa's pains came on while she was cooking with a group of them on the deck one afternoon. She'd insisted on joining them. Tulsi held her hand; another tested the warmth of her brow. Raju came to see about the commotion, and one woman said, "Help us carry her down the ladder. She'll be more comfortable there."

But he turned on his heel and returned with the surgeon. Heaving her up together, the men carried Pushpa away. She called out behind her in pain or fear. Sita and the others trailed after the surgeon, whispering among themselves, "This is not the way. How can men birth a child?" He waved them away.

They sat up late that night, awaiting news. Exhausted, some of the women began to fall asleep. After another yawned and curled up, Tulsi got to her feet.

"I can't wait anymore. I'm going to see what's happening."

Those who were awake looked away. They were forbidden from climbing above deck except for scheduled work, exercise, or washing. And they certainly weren't allowed unescorted inside the officers' cabins where the surgeon sat. So far, none of the women had been severely punished. But they'd all been made to witness the men whipped unconscious on the deck—the ones who'd resisted work and another who complained about the food.

As Tulsi turned to leave alone, Sita made up her mind and jumped up. She would not let her fear of the surgeon paralyze her. She would share in this trial as the others had shared in hers. A cold gust greeted the two women as they emerged from the ladder. They ran across the open deck and hid behind a dinghy. Light spilled out of the galley on the other end, punctuated by the crewmen's voices. This end was cast in darkness. They edged toward the officers' cabins.

Sita shivered as the wind lashed against her bare arms. The ocean was hungry tonight, hurling and beating against the ship like a petulant child. Sita's stomach roiled as she was thrown against one side of the railing. But she followed her friend as they tiptoed inside the narrow corridor lit by gas lamps. All was quiet, and the surgeon's cabin was empty.

Back outside, Tulsi began to climb the ladder up to the highest level. They would be exposed to the rest of the deck if the moon should emerge from behind clouds, and Sita tried her best to crouch as small as possible against the ladder. Tulsi stopped just before the top rung. She sprang back a step and landed on Sita's fingers.

"He's there," she whispered. "Around the corner. He has something in his hands." Her voice wavered. "Something small."

"It must be the baby. I want to see." Sita edged farther up the ladder. Tulsi seemed reluctant to step aside but was strangely limp too. Peering up over the top, Sita saw the surgeon a few feet away. His looming shape was outlined by the flickering lamp Raju held. Their voices were too low for Sita to make out. The surgeon held a bundle wrapped in cloth. Too small to be a person, surely. The bundle was still.

Sita's breath caught in her throat. Where was Pushpa? Why were they standing so near the railing? She wanted to look away. But her eyes were fixed on the surgeon's arms outstretched. Farther, his arms over the edge. An easy tumble. The bundle gulped and disappeared without a sound. No peace, no journey for the child. Only suffering and trial forever tangled in the ocean.

"I saw them take him," Pushpa whispered.

Raju had carried her below deck the next day and deposited her on a blanket. Her face was drawn into shadow, her eyes far away. Sita dropped water between her lips with a spoon. Tulsi massaged her back with a little oil stolen from the galley as Pushpa whispered, over and over, "They think I don't remember. He was a boy."

TEN

Approaching Durban, the plane crosses a sea both foreign and familiar. I once bid farewell to another corner of the Indian Ocean when I
left Pakistan. But even that shore didn't belong to me. I'm a child of
the mountains, not the sea.

Through the plane window, the Drakensberg range's misty slopes
greet me. Imagining the hillsides I have known, I spy dirty blue rivers
snaking between them. Haphazard towns of mud and brick side by
side. Alleys twist darkly, rusty steel gates set all the way along and
houses teetering above. Children balanced on rooftops fly kites into
sunset skies. Grandmothers chew betel nut and shoot red spittle
into steel bowls. Vespas skirt around cricket matches. Wives perch
behind drivers, legs pressed prim to one side. They roar through the
streets and out into the clear-breathing country, where plants in little
clay pots are set in rows along whitewashed garden walls. A baker
slides the long handle of his pan into a fiery tandoor set deep in the
earth. Because the ground is cool at the surface but aflame within. I
imagine I am coming home to you, Peshawar.

Two bumps of tire against tarmac, and we've landed in Durban,
which is about as foreign to me as Peshawar has now become.
Wheeling a creaky cart toward baggage claim, I am briskly aware of
my skin and the skin around me. I am camouflaged against a gra-
dation of my color. Pale beige with freckles and green eyes, warmer
hue on others with tawny curls, dark-brown foreheads, and waist-
length black hair on a pair of sisters. And the brown-black skin of the
woman at Immigration: "Welcome to South Africa," she says with her
stamp on my passport.

Outside is a warm afternoon. Peeling off layers of clothing, I find a taxi, and soon, we're speeding away from the airport. Sleeplessness rakes its fingers through my senses. Everything is in pieces; everything is new. Zululand. I landed in Durban, but that is a white man's name. Sir Durban, no less. Up and down the hills. The city is laid at my feet. Thorny bush, concrete downtown, peeling plaster near the harbor. Midwinter, and I expected yellow grasses. Instead, green adorns every corner. Palm trees persist. Colonial homes withstand the belching highway. Coral, powder blue. Coppery mosque dome and minarets wink at the sky. At a red light, a man raps at my window with a bouquet of feather dusters under one arm. And against a slope rising above is a sight as familiar to my memories of Pakistan as the mountains: a cardboard and tin shanty town.

Off the highway, we turn onto a broad beachfront avenue. Vendors line the walkway with handicrafts arranged on their allocated ground. Across from them, condos rise up high. Restaurants are shuttered, and neon shellfish are unlit.

But something here belies the quiet weekday. This place portends discovery for me. I can taste the thrill of it in each breath of salt air.

We arrive at my reserved accommodation in a block of furnished holiday apartments. An air of decrepitude lurks in the alley between dingy pastel buildings, only a street or two from the beach. A middle-aged Indian man meets me at the front, polyester tracksuit zipped over his belly. His name is Mahesh, but he says to just call him Manny. He pants as he hauls my suitcase up two flights of stairs, and his grin bares several gold teeth. I'm grateful for his hospitality until he calls me "baby," and I become more suspicious of his manner. At my flat, Manny fishes the key out of his jacket and dangles it in my face.

"You'll be here all alone?" He shakes his head. "I just don't know. A bit funny for an Indian girl to be all alone."

I take the key from his hand. "I live alone in New York City. I'll be fine."

"Still, still. Things are different in Durban. If you need help, you just call, and Manny will come to the rescue."

I manage a nod and bolt the door behind me. Inside, drapes are drawn across the far end of the room. I drag them open to a cloud of dust, and afternoon sun floods in from a sliding glass door. In the distance, barely visible from the tiny balcony, is a small patch of sea. It's enough to lift my weariness and the vague disquiet Manny left behind. I run a comb through my hair, lock the flat, and set out for the beach.

The sand is strewn with the strange leavings of the ocean: seaweed like molted snakeskins, shells in pearlescent shards, splintered driftwood. I sling my sandals over a hooked forefinger and roll my jeans up to my calves.

The tide is colder than I expected. Far away, this same giant lowers its muzzle and laps up against Pakistan's southern edges. My zigzag path to this shore feels more unlikely than ever. The stray laughter of a long-dead woman was like a message in a bottle I retrieved on yet another continent. But I've also begun to wonder if her call was never a floating, fragile thing. Maybe my connection to her story is rooted in the earth. And my pilgrimage to Durban was written before I was born. The ocean encourages such improbable ideas.

The waves lap forward. I let my feet sink into sand and sway in time with the tide. A strip of seaweed wraps around my legs like an embrace, then lets go. Did she come here, the laughing woman? She, too, might have gripped the shifting sands with her toes. Maybe she, too, was repulsed and enraptured in equal measures by the slimy touch of seaweed. I wonder if this land was a friend to her sometimes or if it represented only hardship.

When I return to the flat, I'm overcome by fatigue. Fridge empty, I resort to stale crackers and miniature packets of nuts left over from the flight. As I eat, children shriek in the hallway and a television drones through the wall. I'm startled to find my cheeks wet with tears. I didn't think I was sad about my lonely meal. But sobs quickly follow suit as if boiling to the surface. It's so unexpected that I hardly know what to do with myself. When the sobs pass as sudden as they came, my shoulders and chest are looser than they've been in months. I fall into bed and dreamless sleep.

The next day, I explore the network of streets around my building. An alley leads to a modest strip mall featuring a convenience store, a boarded-up chemist, and a takeaway that sells fish and chips, samosas, roti, biryani, as well as a few mysterious items listed on the board: bunny chow, mutton pies, Bombay crush, patra.

At the convenience store, I strike up a conversation with Reshika, the owner. Her plump face is smooth, and her hair is black. But her patient eyes lend her the air of a mother, so I'm not surprised to learn that the teenage boys hanging around are her sons.

Like Manny, she's shocked that I'm staying alone and offers to find me a more suitable situation renting from a "nice Muslim family." Inwardly recoiling at the thought of an aunty nosing about my papers or disapproving of my nocturnal habits, I make polite excuses. I stock up on the limited provisions available: beans, eggs, milk, toilet paper. Reshika eyes my finds doubtfully.

"How you getting around?"

I tell her about the rental car I've reserved, but when she learns that I plan to take a taxi to pick it up, she won't hear of it.

"Young girl staying alone, and now she must take a taxi? Durban is not so cold, even in July."

I manage to keep a straight face and accept her offer to drive me.

Later that afternoon, one of her sons at the cash register, Reshika and I climb into her ancient Toyota and set off. I jump at the opportunity to learn more about her. She tells me she grew up a few miles up the coast in Verulam, a town familiar from my research into the plantations. She's from a large family, most of them still in KwaZulu-Natal. Reshika met her husband at the local Indian high school, she says, and I realize she must have grown up during Apartheid.

She asks about my work, and I share the basics. "I was doing research about Indians in South Africa and the indentured laborers who first came here. I found out about the work they did with Gandhi—protests and marches. Women as well, especially with Kasturba, his wife. I want to learn about those women. I was curious because it wasn't common at the time for women to do anything outside the home."

Reshika snorts. "Nothing much has changed, eh."

I like her more and more. "True."

"Kasturba bai lived here in Durban, neh? I think somewhere in Phoenix. That what you came for? To visit her house?"

"Well . . ." I hesitate. "I saw a picture of three Indian women. They were protesting here in Durban a long time ago. I haven't been able to stop thinking about them. They're even in my dreams! And—" I pause to gather the shadowy details that have eluded my grasp. "It's hard to remember, but I've had this dream before. Or it was different. But they're familiar, I think. Maybe that's crazy."

Reshika is quiet as she pulls into the car rental parking lot. She pulls up the hand brake and sits for a moment staring ahead. "I never read much books and all. But no one taught about dreams in school anyway. They left out everything important, neh? Dreams are important. My grandma, mummy, my aunties, all the elders say so because they know. Schools don't know. You mustn't say it's crazy. We must listen when the world talks. You came here because you listened, and that's good."

We slip out of our seat belts and proceed into the rental office, saying nothing more about it. But I'm buoyed by her response. Her affirmation is the only one I've received for my journey.

I unpack. These first two days felt dredged in jet lag. But now, my rental car is parked in the building garage, and I have spoken my reason for traveling here to another person. My presence here feels firmer.

I hang up my good pants brought for meetings and tuck away sweaters in the bottom-most dresser drawer. I fold them just so, taking more time than usual, because I know the suitcase behind me is not empty. Inside the top flap is the latest unopened white envelope from my drawer. I slipped it into my luggage at the last minute before leaving New York.

Why did I bring it with me? I could shrug and suggest it was a whim, just as I've pretended this whole trip was random circumstance. But I didn't resort to easy explanations with Reshika. She said we must listen. And what is a letter but something—somewhere—calling to me. If I would listen.

Sighing, I retrieve the envelope and slit it open with my car key. The letter inside is thick and folded several times. The lawyer's cursive script glides across the pages.

Dear Miss Hajra,

As-salaam-o-alaikum! I hope this letter will find you in best health. It has been a year or more since my previous letter to you. To be frank, I was upset and decided I will not write letters to you anymore. What is the use? After all, for five years almost you have never seen fit to reply to me. Why do I carry on anyway, you must be thinking. Maybe you are laughing at the foolish barrister who is a stubborn woman.

But I don't think so that you laugh. I remember that you have left your homeland for "pardes," as we say it. You have said farewell to your mother and father and most likely, you have not seen them again in so many years. Maybe you have not found confidantes in that cold America of yours and have nobody to speak your mother tongue.

Today, I am writing in English because that is the language I am used to for my cases. But I do not like this language and I will be happy when I can stop this letter and go outside and hear my own language. So I think, Miss Hajra must be suffering in this "ajnabi" place. Certainly, she must be very afraid so she carries on living there even though she has to do everything in English. When I think like that, I don't feel angry any more and I want to try one more letter to you.

Maybe you are already knowing that Mohsin Khan has gone away. He departed quietly so I did not know at first. But then I received reliable news that he is gone abroad. For some time, we were disheartened that now this man can never be held to justice.

We have tried to find his accomplices instead. And yes, we still try for that. But Mohsin Khan—this is not his first crime and it will not be his last. We must stop him!

So I am requesting you once again, Miss Hajra. Now, we are facing one more chance. Because of some international media attention on women's issues, the government and police are embarrassed. Some similar cases have been expedited, old cases are being reviewed, and rich men have even been brought from America and Europe to face charges. It is a small chance we have been given to try again before the public forgets. I have prepared all the documents and we have received a court date of 30 August with a sympathetic judge in Karachi.

But, Miss Hajra, we will be weak without your testimony. My client is one woman and we must have two. Her word is not enough. As you know, in our country, women must stand together. Nobody believes one woman. But two? Then we can be strong. This is the law of our land. And also, it is true all over the world.

*Please, Miss Hajra, do not disappoint us again. We understand
the danger of coming back. And I think there are some family
difficulties as well. So, I understand why you stay away! I know
about such difficulties myself, believe me. But you must have
"himmat," Miss Hajra. Without "himmat," what are we?*

*I will be waiting for your reply and praying that you find the
"himmat."*

Respectfully yours,
Miss Saadia Hussain, LLM

Carefully, I fold the letter back into its creases. For a moment,
I consider dropping it back into my suitcase and zipping it shut.
Instead, by a great force of will, I place it on top of the dresser, where
I will have to see it daily. Being here in Durban seems to have made
that much possible.

Was I called here? The idea feels too tied up with religious belief
I've scoffed at—no more than an opiate that men in power use to
bend people to their will. But I don't have to let those men take every
belief from me.

Or maybe, it's simpler than that. Maybe I'm here because I admire
those women, and I'm in search of their strength—their himmat—
to steal it for myself. But even if such strength could be taken from
another, how could I imagine it still lingered in the plantations, the
streets, the shore, waiting for me? Only through an act of faith.

ELEVEN

"What did you see?"

The guns and batons wanted to know. The white coats and stethoscopes wanted to know. My own mother was afraid to ask.

What did you see? My dreams and waking reveries were haunted by the question. I knew what I saw. But each question introduced another way of seeing and remembering.

I saw the chaiwallah exchange tea between two pots back and forth. He poured from up high to cool the liquid and top it with froth as bubbles trapped across the surface. A child spun her wooden top into the shallow gutter lining the street. Her dress was once rose-patterned but mostly soot now. Her face was streaked with grime, her hair almost yellow, eyes almost blue.

It was cold. I breathed the fumes of morning, the belches of auto-rickshaws, a dozen nee-nee-nee-nee buses adorned with fists and flowers and screaming messages like *dekh magar pyaar se*. A motorcyclist mummified in woolen scarves sped by. Men squatted and slurped chai atop the median just ahead. Shawls wrapped around their ears trailed into the street's washed-up flotsam trash. I stamped my feet to get the blood pumping. My exhale condensed into cloud.

She wasn't one of the bus stop regulars. Perhaps she was on her way to an interview or to visit a friend. Her eyes were very dark against her pale skin and her black lashes very long. A tiny diamond glittered against her left nostril.

She glanced at me, and I registered that her face was uncovered, as was mine. A tendril of hair that escaped her white chaadar was black, as was mine. The similarity ended. My skin was young and unlined, too, but no jewels adorned the straightforward angles of my face. Her eyes were kohl-lined; mine were rimmed with tortoiseshell glasses. Under my chaadar, my hair was in a hasty bun. Hers was likely teased into fashionable waves.

We were nothing to each other. Two women journeying across an ancient city. But in that single glance, we exchanged something, back and forth. The cold morning that chapped our lips and unfiltered air for our lungs. Our cheeks pink by the effort to gather warmth.

Ordinary sameness. Yet extraordinary because no other woman at this bus stop bared her face as we did. This was an unspoken promise we'd both made: *let us make our way through this world as women seen whole.*

The moment passed. She stepped beyond the curb to peer around the corner for our bus. I bowed my head against the wind and stepped backward against the low wall. That's all that separated me from her. The border between us was defined only by a gentle bending away of my body, a slight reaching forward of hers. It was enough to separate the rest of our lives.

First, the sound. Splatter of liquid on pavement, screech of tires. A voice, just a word. Chalo. Let's go.

Second, she fell like a curtain. A graceful collapse, as if someone would catch her. I tried but failed.

Her chaadar brushed my outstretched fingers as she hit the ground. The car that screeched away was a beat-up blue Suzuki. One that had pulled up to our street a hundred times. My brother had slipped into its back seat for years. I knew the pattern of its dents and scratches.

The driver was lost to shadow, but I knew the front passenger. His aquiline nose, lips thin as a crevice. Morning sun lit up the russet of his beard and caught its hidden gold. Elbow casual over open window of his own car because he had nothing to fear in this city. Mohsin Khan, scion of politicians, didn't need to hide.

Third, the chemical stench. Death without its mercy. She was flat on the ground, and everyone sprang away. They ran from her as if they might catch her misfortune.

A drop of the acid splashed through my own shalwar, through my sock, all the way to flesh. It sizzled my ankle and called me to flee.

On her left side, the acid erased her sleeve. "We need water, water." I remembered one thing from overheard stories of this scourge.

Water. I thought I screamed the words, but maybe they were lodged in my throat. Raw red bubbled up her side. The cold air steaming her flesh as if cooking inside and no water, no one to help. But she was twitching, maybe she was shivering, so I took off my chaadar and covered her with it.

Fourth, chill air settled on the nape of my neck for the first time in years. My chaadar was spread out over the peaks and valleys of her body. One of the embroidered flowers bloomed acid-wet for an instant before withering into nothing.

Fifth, poison against my tongue. My flowers, my chaadar. She was closer to the curb. And because of that, I may never know. The acid could have been meant for me. A woman in a white chaadar at the bus stop. Maybe that's all I was to my own brother now. But she was closer to them. And I will never know.

I managed the needful. Ambulance, police. Later, I stumbled across the threshold of my home, and capability left me. On the porch, my knees gave. My mother tried and failed to lift and help me upstairs. Shook me, yelled for the neighbors. I was frightening her—my bare head and wild hair.

I was in bed. Someone must have helped me, but I couldn't remember. I stared at the ceiling pocked with leaks and spiderwebs. A projection screen for that repeated image. My eyes were wide open to its loop.

His voice. Familiar timbre. My brother's voice was the soundtrack of my childhood. I'd known it always; I'd know it anywhere. Once it spun a safe ward around me, but no longer.

I sprang from bed and rushed to the small kitchen, where Ali stood near the stove with my mother. Abruptly, they turned and fell silent, as if they'd been conspiring.

"Are you rested? Hungry?" My mother felt my forehead as if I'd been sleeping off the flu. "I've made some soup."

"I heard what happened," Ali said. "May Allah have mercy on that poor woman."

"You *heard* what happened?" His face crumpled as he opened his mouth to speak, but I barreled on before he could. "Don't bring Allah into this. What she needs is mercy from you and your men. We all do."

In the long pause that followed, I couldn't decide which I wanted more: an admission of guilt or proof of his innocence. Neither could satisfy my rage.

"What are you talking about?" he asked slowly.

"Are you going to keep on pretending? There's no police here. Why not gloat?"

"Hajra—" My mother's tone carried a familiar warning. Be a good girl. Stay indoors. Lower your voice.

"No!" I bellowed my loudest. "You will not deny this. You cannot excuse him."

"What's going on?" My father stood in the doorway, his brow knotted. "What is it? No, no—" He raised a hand to stop Ali and my mother. "Let Hajra speak."

I glanced around at the strange diorama of my family. Our precisely arranged poses and my place at its center.

"It was Ali." My voice rasped in accusation. "He and Mohsin Khan and the others. They were in the car today. They threw acid on that girl. They were aiming for me."

In the brief silence that followed, I dared hope. But then my father's eyes widened in pity; my mother let out the cry of a wounded animal. And I knew how it would be. They could not cast out their only son. They did not dare believe me. I bowed my head to shut out their questions and exclamations.

Until finally, Ali spoke, "You think you saw me?"

His face was hard, his expression close to hatred. I had no trouble matching it. "I saw Mohsin; it was his car. And the two of you are never far apart. Two days ago, you threatened me right here at the table, if I continued making trouble for him. If I continued being an 'outside woman.' Isn't that what you called me?"

I expected him to shout back his own accusations. Spell out the wrath of a vengeful god. But he only pushed past me—hard against my shoulder—and walked out. He did not return that night.

"What did you see, miss?" The policeman was bored but patient. As he waited for my answer, he picked at his earwax with the pink eraser end of a pencil. He cleared his throat but not in a rushed way. In a gathering-up-a-spitball way. He was content to lean back in our good chair and sweat onto my mother's hand-embroidered sofa-back covers. He drank our cardamom chai and nibbled our Prince chocolate biscuits saved for special guests. Of course he was patient.

Next to me, my mother fidgeted. She couldn't wait to be rid of the policeman and his dirty shoes. And she was anxious. About what I would or wouldn't say, what he would or wouldn't believe.

More than anything, she was afraid of appearing anxious. Usually, her anxiety was infectious. But over the past two days, everything had slowed down and shrunk to a pinpoint. I stared at the policeman's left shoe. I studied the wear patterns and scuff marks left by an uneven gait. I ran my fingertips along the plush grooves of the sofa cushion I'd known since I was a child.

Today, I perched on the seat's edge. I couldn't sink into familiar depths. Because I'd become a stranger in my own home now, less comfortable than the policeman who settled back with unearned confidence.

"Hajra! Beta, answer the man. He's busy, can't you see?" My mother tried to hide the pleading in her voice. But her hands clasped and unclasped.

"It's OK, madam. In these cases, sometimes it is difficult to recall for the fortunate young ladies of good families who do not see such things normally. It is like a shock to their girlish sensitivity, you see." He helped himself to another biscuit and took three-quarters of it in one bite, chewing with his mouth open. Crumbs littered his shirtfront and collected in the crease around his crotch.

Fortunate. Sensitive. My mother shot me a glance of surprise. Maybe this bumbling man knew less than we expected. He asked nothing about my involvement with Pyaar or our battles with Mohsin's crew. Watching my mother's expression turn to cautious relief, I knew she would always defend my brother. She cared only for his protection.

Hastily, she tapped my elbow to rouse me from my thoughts and end the meeting before the policeman suspected more. "You are very kind, Inspector sahib, but even so. Come on, beta, just a quick few words."

I began my story—but not the memory. Instead, a colorless account designed to elicit nothing from my senses or anyone else's. Drained of fight in the days since, this was the story I'd relented and agreed to tell.

He asked the expected follow-up questions. "You are sure, miss, that you didn't see the driver or passengers? But you are sure of the color and make of car? There are many cars, after all."

My mother leaped in. "Of course, the inspector is right. He is a wise man. And he should know, after all, just how many cars there are in Peshawar. Isn't that right?"

"Well, that is to say, naturally I don't know the precise number, but—"

"Of course, of course, but you could find out, couldn't you? And it would be a large number, as you say quite correctly. It's a pity really, for that poor girl's sake, that no one took the number plate. But there you are." She shrugged gamely with a laughter-is-the-best-medicine-life's-like-that smile.

On one side, the hospital corridor was a series of cutouts in concrete. Hexagons collected city grime and birds' nests and filtered the shaft of gray light from an adjacent alleyway. I leaned against a pillar and closed my eyes to the symphony of vendors and rickshaws from the street below. Closer, the trundle of wheels down floors worn smooth.

I'd come and stood against the same pillar twice already without advancing farther. No one remarked on such behavior at a hospital. So many loitered in orange plastic chairs or curled into blankets on the stained linoleum. They waited for information withheld, appointments delayed, or operations in progress. Perhaps a few waited for courage, as I did.

"Please, I'm here to see my sister, Rubina Imtiaz. Which ward have you moved her to?"

I jerked upright at the name. The woman who spoke balanced a whimpering toddler on her hip. She danced a jig to soothe him as she waited. I'd been trying to work up the nerve to ask the same question for an hour.

"Yes," the nurse said as she flipped through her clipboard. "She's out of the ICU today, poor thing. What a tragedy."

The visitor's expression seemed to harden, but she said nothing. She busied herself instead with wiping drool from the child's chin with the edge of her chaadar. The nurse continued her chatter. She found the ward number and offered to escort her personally. I hadn't seen any such treatment for other bereft family members in the waiting room. Perhaps the nurse was eager to involve herself in a sensational case.

Keeping a discreet distance, I followed the women through hallways, up two flights of stairs, and around corners before they pushed open a door. I edged closer as they disappeared inside. The door had a small glass window through which I peered. At the far edge of a row of beds, I spotted the woman visitor lowering her child into the nurse's arms. A privacy screen pulled across the last bed obscured it from my view. Slowly, the woman approached the bed. Her outstretched fingers were tentative. Then she, too, disappeared behind the screen, where indistinct shadows moved.

I waited for a moment. My hand hovered over the door handle. I wanted to speak to the family and confess my role in this woman's disaster. In a burst of courage I'd lacked until now, I'd tell them about Mohsin and even my suspicions of Ali. It was wrong to keep the truth from them.

An orderly sweeping the hallway stared at me. With uninterested flicks, he pushed the same line of dirt back and forth. Maybe he'd been put here by Mohsin to keep an eye on me. Or he could be just another man who stared at women. A new hesitation crept into my throat. I swallowed hard, but the hesitation stayed. I should protect my words and utter them with care now. I should keep my voice low. I stepped backward and away from the door. Another step, out of sight of the orderly, and another until I could turn and escape unseen. Outside the hospital, I gave the gift of fruit I'd brought to a man begging for alms in exchange for prayers.

The street beyond him was lined with shadows. The usual donkey carts and trucks surged through this part of town. But in between their weaving and honking, a presence lurked. Danger bubbled up through every crack in the pavement. A man turned and spit his paan against the wall next to him. A shaft of sunlight from behind the next building cast his beard russet. His nose was hooked like Mohsin's.

I clambered into the back of a rickshaw to get away, but the driver looked at me askance in his rearview. His eyes were narrowed with suspicion. "Where?" he asked, a dozen threats encoded into the word.

I hopped out without an answer, sped up my pace, and stayed close to the curb. I pulled my chaadar like a hood over my face. I could be anonymous this way. No one could know that I was a loud woman, once. But I was alone. The other women shopping along this street traveled in pairs or groups or else tugged small children by the hand. Sometimes they were accompanied by men who trailed them, important and bored.

I used to stroll these downtown streets without care. True, I was always alert to stares and whistles. I knew how to carry myself; I'd been taught well by the women in my family. Careful not to make unnecessary eye contact. Keep the bounce out of your poised footfalls. In this way, ease your body through the streets like a whisper. If a man oversteps his bounds, create a ruckus. Use the rules that govern this world to support your outrage. But most of the time, tolerate them. Men. Tolerate their occasional incursions into your borders.

Once outside your home, the space you occupy is rented. It belongs to them.

Breeze chilled up the edges of my clothes and cooled my armpits and back. My kameez was soaked through with sweat. Over it, my chaadar bunched up and stuck to my body. Perhaps it revealed outlines and curves that must be kept secret. My shallow breath could not keep up with my feet running walking stumbling running again. I tried to inhale deeper and fill my aching lungs, but air eluded me.

I slipped into a stall where women fingered the artificial silk on display. I pretended I was one of their group haggling with the vendor and hung back like a shy cousin. The women glanced, curious, at me for an instant, but the negotiation demanded more of their focus. They forgot me soon enough. I used the respite to breathe. Enough for the rest of my journey home.

Four days after the attack, Marjan came to visit. She was the first friend who came to see me. I learned from her that my mother had warned away everyone else who tried. She told them I was too unwell for visitors. A few days ago, my mother's interference would've provoked a shouting match between us. Now, as I listened to Marjan, I could not muster the energy for anger.

After an initial burst of chatter, Marjan was quiet. Her eyes skimmed over my disheveled appearance. I avoided her gaze. Instead, I traced the tiny mirrors adorning a cushion. My fingertips followed their crisscross path to the four corners outlined in green.

"What happened exactly?" she asked.

She'd pieced together a mishmash of neighborhood gossip and inference, but she knew better than to trust such sources. I paused, unsure how to begin. Marjan and I had stood side by side for years with nothing but our solidarity to shield us. No matter the consequences, I couldn't fashion my tale into something artificial to fit inside her hands as I did for the police. So I excavated the truth, the words dry and loose as gravel.

"You're sure it was Mohsin?" she asked after I was done and we'd both lapsed into silence.

I nodded. "I didn't tell the police though. You know his connections." The rest of my explanation remained lodged in my throat. My silence served my parents. They'd raised me to close ranks and protect our little unit in this hostile country at all costs. But maybe this silence was what I wanted too.

Marjan grabbed my hand. "We won't let him get away with this." Her nails carved little moons into my palm.

I extricated my hand from her grip. Her emotion embarrassed me. Perhaps this silence wasn't my parents' imposition on me but a lesson from my elders who'd survived so much. "We tried what we could. They've beaten us. It's over."

"What do you mean?" Marjan spluttered. "What's over? This isn't a game we're playing with the boys. That poor woman, what about her? Have you thought about her?"

I bowed my head. Rising and falling shapes of bodies in the hospital ward. Smell of ammonia from cracked floors. A woman with fingers outstretched, afraid to touch her sister.

Marjan tried again. "Hajra, this is . . . Look, I understand they've scared you. But I'm with you . . . and other people too. We'll be careful."

When I was twelve, a man sitting behind me on the bus slipped his hand between the seats and massaged my right breast. I realized then for the first time that I had grown breasts. It was the first of such daily incursions that would become commonplace as I matured. That first time, I didn't tell my mother next to me. Instead, I shifted forward and out of reach from the seatback. The hand disappeared. After that, I began to perch on the edge to protect myself.

I glanced up at my friend, who still lived in a world I had outgrown. "Have you seen a body erased?"

Marjan's mouth opened and closed like a fish.

"We forgot ourselves," I continued. "For a while. Now we have to remember what we are allowed to be. Before it's too late for us too."

She pulled her knees up against her chin and rested on her side against the bolster on our creaky divan. Somewhere, a tap dripped an uneven rhythm against metal, and the fridge resumed its shuddering hum. She started and stopped sentences. None of them found their way.

Eventually, she pushed herself to her feet. She wrapped her scarf around her head and tucked stray wisps beneath its folds. She fastened up her abaya.

At the last button, she paused, hand on heart. "Just like that," she said. It was neither an observation nor a question but somewhere in between.

I stole my gaze from hers as I huddled into my corner of the divan. When I looked up again, she was gone.

TWELVE

Sita had been dreaming of Natal for days. The prospect of this new land dominated her imagination. She dreamed of sighting it from a distance. Instead, she learned of their arrival from Raju's smirking instruction to cook a meal fit for a prince because "the land of their fortunes" was in sight. That night, she stayed up distracted, unable to rest amid the unseen commotion on the deck above. She imagined them fighting to bring the ship to rest.

In the morning, Sita waited with a group of women to climb down to the boats pulled alongside the ship's hull. Of land, she could only see the harbor. The country beyond was hidden behind crates and ship riggings. Gulls swooped down to perch on the railings and cock their heads in curiosity at the newcomers.

With her balled-up belongings slung over one shoulder, Sita climbed down the rope ladder with the others. The siding of the ship was a steep drop painted with the slime of the ocean. So easy to place a foot wrong. And another's foot near her head marked by broken calluses and a toe ring. She could slip and tumble them both. Knees weak with relief, Sita reached the boat packed cheek to jowl. She filled her lungs deep, and her chest lifted. Breath by breath, she was inhaling a new land.

The boat knocked into the dock, and she climbed and jostled onto shore. Sita was accustomed to the bustle of a port from the weeks she'd spent at Madras. She remembered well the salty tang on her lip, the smell of rotting wood mingled with jute and seaweed, and the air so humid it was almost gelatinous. Men strapped crates onto their backs and strained forward, a trail of sweat dripping behind them.

White men were in charge, just like in Madras. But, as Tulsi had promised, men of an entirely different race were among those unloading the ships. The Zulus. They were not much darker than the men from her village, and their hair was not nearly so different as Tulsi had given her to believe. Most were dressed like the white men but shabbier. They expressed no curiosity as their eyes flicked over the new arrivals. Their gaze seemed to cast a net over the lot and gather them into a single glance of disgust.

The women shuffled into a long line leading up to two white men at a table. Sita's head ached under the unfiltered sun; it was the middle of the day, and salt air dried her lips. She ached, too, with new realization. She was an unwelcome stranger in a land that belonged to others. The white people who traveled here were just as foreign. But already Sita noticed the deference Zulu men paid to their white supervisors. This, too, was no different from Madras.

And what of their language? She heard two of the Zulu men speaking. Each part of their speech seemed to stretch as long as a shadow in the afternoon. Words lingered and then snapped back into precise place. Sita longed to learn these words or make her own understood. She wanted to explain why she'd come. It was true that she'd chosen to mark a piece of paper and climb aboard the ship. But the tides washed her here because she had nothing left to hold on to.

An hour, three, before her turn with the white man. He wore a wide-brimmed hat that hid his face as he bent over his pen and ledger. He barked a question in what took her a minute to realize was her own language.

"Your paper?"

Sita dug out the precious girmit from her bundle. The man clicked his tongue in annoyance as he unwrapped and smoothed out the certificate. He wrote in the large ledger open before him. Without looking up, he beckoned the next in line. A doctor inspected her eyes and mouth. Raju brought food, and they stood in another line for a tin plate with a puddle of gruel. Sita squatted with Tulsi in a far corner to swallow a few morsels. They were removed from the immediate chaos of the dock here. Surrounded by strewn haystacks and broken planks of wood, she could see farther into the country. Distant mountains rose and disappeared into cloud. A closer hill jutted its fat thigh into the ocean—a mass of green, twisted jungle against sky. Its arc surrounded the harbor.

Further up the slope, brush had been cleared for a clump of shacks surrounded by a wall. The lush hillside appeared pocked with their tin roofs. Tulsi pointed to them with a forefinger. "That is where they will put us—until the agent comes and sends us to the land."

Two weeks or more passed before they saw any more white men. They saw only Raju and other ship crewmen or aloof Zulu helpers from the docks. Their temporary barracks were even worse than the Madras depot. No outhouses and no place to cook except a communal fire under a rigged lean-to. The only comfort of this place was the company of her friends from the ship—she, Tulsi, and some others banded together.

Though their lodgings were simpler, they also enjoyed more freedom without surveillance. At Madras, they'd been closely supervised to prevent escape. Here, they were camped in wilderness on a foreign continent. A wall surrounded their camp, and they were forbidden from climbing it. But their overseers were lax here, knowing they had nowhere to go, and largely left them to their own devices.

So Tulsi and Sita began to take exploratory walks through the surrounding countryside whenever they could get away. At first, they edged deeper into the bush so they'd have some quiet away from camp. And almost immediately, only ten minutes in, a sense of peace descended under the lush canopy. Soon, though, they realized the solitude came with hazards. So many snakes slithered, unafraid, across their path. The darting grass snakes were a pleasant enough sight, and Sita grabbed one by the tail to admire its twisted markings, surprised when the unflappable Tulsi shrieked. But even Sita knew not to approach the fat charcoal-gray snake, more than three feet long as it uncoiled. They watched their step more carefully after. Worse than the snakes, though, were the thorn bushes that left deep welts along their arms and ripped their saris.

They tried another direction on their next walk—a laborious clamber up along the sand dunes. But eventually they were rewarded by views of the coastline on one side and hilly countryside on the other. Beyond the harbor, the shore undulated into dramatic crags. Gulls and cormorants swooped in the foaming shallows near rocky outcrops. A flock of large gray and white birds came up to the dunes to caw at the women curiously. They snapped their giant orange bills at them and wagged their old-man heads.

On their other side, the hillside dipped, and a compound of mud huts was visible in the distance below. One day, they ventured farther into this valley. The rounded huts had whitewashed walls, and their roofs were thatched with dry brush. They approached close enough to spot the outlines of a Zulu woman sweeping the outer boundary of their clearing. Sita wanted to go nearer and greet the woman, try to communicate. But Tulsi insisted that they'd be unwelcome, so they kept their distance. They perched on a rock among the trees to rest awhile before their climb over the dunes back to camp.

What if Tulsi were wrong? Sita could come back here on her own and approach the Zulu woman. Maybe she could offer her labor here instead. She'd be discovered missing eventually at the harbor, but they might not think to look for her among the huts.

The Zulu woman straightened up from her task and turned around. A baby was strapped to her back, snug in the blanket wrapped around her torso. The sight of the child was a jolt. Sita's imaginings had no ground in reality. She would not find a home in that clearing. If she were very lucky, she'd find a temporary refuge. But she had no blood connection to that woman and her child. Sita's ancestors had not lived and died by this soil. She'd never be able to claim it as her own.

On a cooler day when they were still watching for a moment to slip away for a walk, the white man arrived on horseback. The distant thump of hooves rose easily above everyday humdrum. He alighted gracefully, his shoulders squared and back straight as a rod. He was dressed in khaki and wore a bulky hat that shaded his face. Raju and the others scurried like ants around a queen. They called him Mr. Dickinson.

"Strange," Tulsi muttered. "He doesn't look like an agent."

Other speculations fluttered through the crowd until Raju yelled at them all to be quiet and stand in line for inspection. "This is an important man, a landowner," he announced. "Show respect. He could be your master."

"A landowner? He must be powerful to be able to come and take first pick," Tulsi muttered as they jostled with the others to line up.

Comprehension began to dawn on Sita. She might finally escape these barracks, count out her contract, and earn a new life. Conscious of her disheveled appearance, she smoothed back her hair and tugged to rearrange the pleats of her sari.

Mr. Dickinson strolled through the encampment with his hands clasped behind him. He assessed each blade of grass and tin roof with the air of a homeowner returned after a long absence. He came to a stop in front of a man and glared at him, up and down. A shiver ran through the man, and his visible ribs rippled like dark water. Mr. Dickinson sniffed loudly, chin high, and strode purposefully on.

Tense silence hung heavy. Mr. Dickinson continued his assessment body by body, sometimes inching closer to inspect a limb, a cheekbone, a set of the lips. Some of the men recoiled; others stared back with stony contempt. He stared at the women in much the same way. Most lowered their eyes, bent their heads, or hid their mouths behind a hastily tugged mundhanai. Sita watched this dance with mounting impatience. The women were being absurdly coy, as if he were a groom on their wedding night.

So when he came to stop in front of Sita, she squared her broad shoulders and glared back at Mr. Dickinson, just as some of the men had. He was not much taller, so she was face-to-face with him. She'd never stared at a man like this, let alone an important white man. But he'd want bold, strong workers for his farm, she reasoned. And maybe, in the course of everything she had to battle to get here, it was no pretense. Maybe she really had become this bold.

Mr. Dickinson raised his chin higher and appraised Sita down the bridge of his nose. A muscle beside his lip twitched—with amusement or irritation, Sita couldn't tell. He sniffed, then bowed his head and fixed his gaze at a point near his left foot. He beckoned over the man with the ledger and barked an order. The man hopped to attention and flipped through pages with eager fingers. He came to a stop and read out loud with an index finger pressed against paper, the book balanced in his arms like an infant. Sita might have made out the words if she tried. But it took every ounce of her effort to keep her lips from quivering and not relent to the weakness shooting up and down her legs.

Another order. This time, the words were addressed to her. The man holding the ledger translated: "The good sir is asking if you know about children."

Sita was sure she had misunderstood. "Children?"

"Yes, he is asking if you have cared for children. If you know how to."

"My brother's children and my cousins, back in my village, but—"

The man raised a hand and turned back to Mr. Dickinson. Nervousness forgotten in her bewilderment, Sita listened more carefully this time and was able to understand a few words. *Brother, village, ayah.* This last was a word belonging neither to the white man's language nor to hers. But it was one they both knew.

Sita struggled to make sense of it. Tulsi had told her about sugar fields, her calloused hands evidence. Sita came here expecting earth under her fingernails, the sun to paint dark lines across her bent back. She wanted a mind too exhausted for anything but rest. She could not again serve as nursemaid to other women's children—once more a shadow to the full lives around her.

But the white man's order was not a request. She must do what he demanded and leave her friend behind. Because, now, this man owned her. She couldn't be sure when or how that happened. Maybe when she returned the paper to the arkati and agreed to hide inside his cart. Or earlier. On her first day as the only girl in school, sure of a grand destiny. A single thread through the eye of one of those needle-thin happenstances pulled her halfway across the world to stand before this man who, with a sweep of his arm and scribble on a contract, purchased five years of her life.

Sita climbed into an ox-drawn covered wagon. She was to ride with nine others that Dickinson chose from the barracks: two married couples, four children and an infant between them, and two single men who stared ceaselessly at Sita from their cramped corner of the wagon.

She bid Tulsi a brief, tearless farewell. After all, Tulsi herself had already warned that their chances of being employed by the same estate were slim. They'd expected the separation and promised each other that they would reunite soon—a wish without hope. But it felt necessary to make plans out loud. Unspoken was the vow that they would command their own destinies again someday.

The surrounding countryside opened its doors wide as Sita and the others journeyed. Rain fell over distant mountains, and clouds reached spiky fingernails to the ground. Flecks of soil kicked up by cartwheels collected in her outstretched palm as if raindrops.

When they stopped for a midday break, the others huddled close together. The women fussed over their children, and the men passed a precious beedi back and forth. The white driver of their wagon stood apart and cut himself pieces of a leathery snack with his pocket knife. He watched his wards silently, chewing with his mouth open.

Under his gaze, Sita took tentative steps away from the group. Beyond the oxen and the wagon canopy, the road ahead hugged the curve of the hillside. She followed its line and raised her eyes. The sun sighed out from between thinning clouds and lit up hidden peaks. Below them, the hill tumbled green into the distance, unbroken by red earth or habitation. A vast future lay out of her hands, outside imagination.

THIRTEEN

After the attack, I cocooned away from the world in my bedroom. I pushed around the food they brought me and left tea to turn ice-cold on the nightstand.

My mother urged me to open a window, join her for a walk. Sometimes she shook my shoulders and succeeded in wresting me from the nest of my bedsheets. Outside, my pulse quickened. I studied each passing stranger for signs of menace. Back in the safety of my room with the door bolted, I tried to relax my muscles one at a time. But I couldn't be entirely at ease inside either. My parents might have silenced my report to the police out of survival wisdom. Or, more simply, they'd chosen the child who mattered to them. Looking back, that was the moment I lost them. When they chose his safety over mine.

A corner of my wardrobe still contained Ali's good shirts, but he hadn't slept in our shared room in two years. Now he barely lived at home. He only stopped by to collect fresh clothes or scarf down a meal. At these times, I listened to his movements from inside my room. I waited at my window until the gate downstairs clanged shut before I released my breath.

Several weeks passed before I had to go to campus to deal with some paperwork. I'd dropped out of my teaching responsibilities after the attack in December, and a substitute had to finish out the year. But now it was January, and a new term would begin soon. I had to formally resign in person to collect the wages I was due.

Catching the bus from the same stop did not feel possible yet. In any case, my parents wouldn't let me. Eventually, I was allowed to take an expensive auto-rickshaw if accompanied by Saeed. We were mostly silent on the ride. Saeed had always been a reserved man, sniffing often and speaking little. Now perhaps the awkwardness of the situation further muffled him.

At college, he escorted me to the administrative block, where I submitted and signed resignation forms and emergency declarations and receipts. Afterward, I found Saeed waiting in the hallway. "Shall we go home?" I asked, longing for the seclusion of my room.

He cleared his throat. "One more stop. Please."

I nodded and followed him without curiosity.

We caught another auto-rickshaw at the gates and alighted at Zaheer Books. The ginger cat washing her paws at the doorstep next to an empty saucer. The musty scent of old books and cheap ink. Dust motes in a shaft of light falling across a stack of magazines tied together with string. The owner, Zaheer sahib, stroked his salt-and-pepper beard, immersed in a copy of Chomsky's *Manufacturing Consent* behind the counter.

It was too familiar. My old life. A ball swelled in my throat. I thought I might fall to my knees right there in the biography/letters/memoirs aisle and never get up again.

In the back, my friends sat on folding chairs and sipped chai. Not so different from my first Pyaar meeting here two and a half years ago. Even the faces were mostly the same. Marjan, of course. Saeed, quiet at my elbow. The woman I'd once known only as a sociology student, Gulnaz, biting her fingernails and fidgety as always. Salma, her kameez splattered with paint. Serious Bashir, one of those who joined after the riots and became a mainstay.

They glanced up at me half-guiltily. I felt sure they'd been talking about me before I arrived. Bashir found me a chair, and Salma poured the chai. Some awkward niceties were necessary to move past. All the while, I swallowed my questions. It hardly mattered why they'd gathered. I didn't belong among them.

The superficial conversation ebbed soon, and an uncomfortable pause followed. Eventually, Marjan began, "Hajra, look, this is difficult. It's all been difficult. We never thought, none of us did, that what we were doing was so dangerous. I mean, maybe we did, but—"

"We knew it was dangerous," Salma broke in. "We all knew that. After that time with the police in Chowk Yadgar, poor Saeed was in the hospital, remember? But we didn't know how far they could go."

Everyone was quiet as Salma's words hung in the air. Marjan turned her empty tea glass in her hands. Then she placed it firmly on the carton of books that was a makeshift table between us.

"Look, we can't watch you live like this," she said. "It's been more than a month, and your house—what it must be like with Ali still there. You need a break, Hajra. And—" She paused before continuing quietly. "We're worried about your safety."

My throat was dry. "What do you want me to do?"

"Well . . . we reached out to Meghan Jennings. The American woman."

"What? When?"

"Last week." Marjan exchanged a glance with Saeed. They seemed to argue in a silent language before he sighed and took over.

"Look, you've always talked about doing that fellowship with them someday. We thought, maybe, now is the time to take a break from Peshawar."

"You mean . . . you're talking about me going to America?" I let out a shrill laugh.

"Why not? It's an idea," Salma said, characteristically indignant.

I glanced around at their eager faces, and gratitude tightened my chest. Almost more than I could handle. This family I collected piece by piece. Dreamers, every one of them. But I didn't share their idealism anymore.

"Yes, it's an idea," I said slowly. "And you're all . . . so kind. But I can't just leave. How could I afford it? I just started saving last year."

Marjan leaned forward, a gleam in her eye. It was clear she'd been plotting for days. "We've thought of all that. We talked to Meghan Jennings twice. Her organization hosts a six-month fellowship at a university in New York, and there's funding for it. And Meghan said you can live with the church people. See?"

I sat back, heavy, in my chair. Surely this wasn't possible. They'd missed something. "What about visa fees? My savings wouldn't cover it. And a ticket? For—New York?" I tasted the gritty syllables.

"We've pooled money together for the ticket and visa. It's enough to get you there. No, wait, Hajra. Let me finish." She raised a hand to stop my protests. "I know this is hard to accept. But you can pay us back. And we're in this together, aren't we? It could've been me they came after. Let us do this for you."

I opened and closed my mouth. Salt tears bathed my lips. "I don't know what to say," I whispered.

Salma scraped her chair closer to mine and knocked her head against my shoulder playfully. "Hajra in New York! Imagine that."

* * *

The lawyer was waiting in Marjan's living room. I had no idea that evening when I slipped off my shoes at the front door. I didn't wonder at the lights in the living room or the low voices from behind the curtained doorway. I supposed that a neighbor or relative was visiting them. I'd exchange a quick greeting before escaping to Marjan's room to look through the stack of American visa paperwork delivered to her place by post.

The stranger replied to my terse salaam with an appraising look. Marjan turned and frowned. "Someone to see you, Hajra," she said before shuffling from the room.

I took tentative steps toward the woman, who rose and took my hand in that limp, uncomfortable manner that passes for a handshake among convent schoolgirls. I tried to place her features. With a streak of gray at her brow, too old for a school classmate.

"You are wondering who I am," she said. "I will explain. The matter is a delicate one. Sit, sit, please." She waved at the chair behind me as if I'd just entered her office. "My name is Saadia Hussain. I am a barrister."

A lawyer could have arranged to see me for many reasons. But as soon as she identified herself, I knew why she'd come.

I could imagine her little office reached by flights of paan-stained stairs down one of those narrow Sadar alleys. Plaque next to a door: S. Hussain, LLM. A woman—ruined face concealed from prying eyes—might pause there to gather courage before she pressed the buzzer. She would arrive alone because no one from her family would want her involved with lawyers and courts. Just as my parents did not want me "mixed up" in police business. But then, my parents had other reasons to want my silence too.

"You know why I am here, I think." Saadia's gaze was piercing.

I sank into the proffered chair and tucked my hands under my thighs to stop their trembling.

She sat back down, too, and narrowed her eyes. "You know my client Rubina Imtiaz's name, I believe." She reached into the battered leather satchel at her feet and pulled out a file bound with string. "It wasn't easy to arrange this meeting," she continued. "I had your name and address from the police file, but your family—well, let's say their reaction was not unexpected."

"I'm sorry." I could well imagine my mother's panic at the lawyer's appearance. My father's habitual retreat into avoidance. Neither had said anything to me about Saadia Hussain.

She shrugged. "I'm used to it. All the clients I work with have—delicate cases. No one wants to speak to me." She seemed unperturbed as she flipped through her papers and readied a pad and pen. I couldn't interpret her expression.

"So. Let's begin."

It wasn't the interview I expected. Mostly, she provided information about Rubina's slow, painful recovery, her determination for justice. How Saadia found Marjan through the newspaper article about our rally at Chowk Yadgar. From time to time, she handed me pieces from her file—photos of the bus stop, a schematic of the scene she'd hand-drawn. Casually, as if nothing, a stack of close-up photos of Rubina. Topography of the jagged, rippled valleys that now made one side of her face and body. Fused cartilage, scooped craters in flesh. Overripe burst fruit bubbling purple and rotten.

Afterward, we were both silent. Not casual then; her chatter and factual tone were practiced too. An ambush for a purpose. She studied me as I clutched my stomach.

"We need you, Miss Hajra. Simple. I know very well how this must be for you. You have nightmares. You want to move on with your life, but you can't. Your family is worried. Your friends are scared for your safety. And they are right."

I glanced up, surprised.

"Yes, it's true," she continued. "I still don't know why these men attacked Rubina. It could be random. But you were standing next to her. You, who have protested against war, whose photo has been in the newspaper. We cannot rule out that you were their target. And so you are not safe."

Our eyes met for a long, tense moment. How much did she know? Did she suspect Ali?

"What do you want from me?" My words emerged as more of a whine than I intended.

She leaned forward as if preparing to take me into confidence. "In your official police statement, you said you saw nothing other than the color of the car. Blue. But at the scene, you said more."

The scene. Absurdly curled mustache of a policeman. A boy in a ragged gray shalwar kameez in my peripheral vision. My throat hoarse screaming for water that never came. I could not remember what I'd said that day nor to whom. When the police inspector came to our home days later, he mentioned nothing of a statement made at the scene. He treated his visit like an obligatory social call that was unimportant to the case.

"How could you give him our address!" my mother had hissed later as we cleared the teacups. Silent, I'd scooped biscuit crumbs from a side table into my cupped hand and released them into a saucer. I had no memory of giving my address to anyone. So what else had I said and forgotten?

"You know more than I do," I told Saadia finally. "I don't remember much."

"I see," she said. "That's a pity because the police notes from the scene are not very detailed. But there is a name. One I have come across before. The police tried to bury it, but they were careless, so I found it anyway. That name interested me, and to be frank, it's the reason I took Rubina's case. You are the first person to speak this name officially to the police. It's the first time we have a witness."

She'd spoken in Urdu for the rest of our conversation, but now she used the English word—*witness.* Somehow it was fitting that she borrowed the language of others for it. What did the word mean in our tongue? Gawah. A simple translation. To watch, listen, and testify. But in Urdu, the word is braided forever in my mind with the laws that took our testimony from us. Four men. Two women the worth of one man. A word stolen.

"What is the name?" I whispered.

She enunciated clearly as she watched my reaction, "Mohsin Khan."

The courier with my passport and stamped American visa showed up at our doorstep. My parents didn't know anything about it, so I muttered something about research materials as I whisked the envelope away. I opened it when I was alone. My picture on the visa was the only addition to a crisp, new passport.

Reality descended absolute as cold water. I'd already agreed to help Saadia with the case. Though after that, I still traveled to Islamabad for my scheduled interview at the embassy. I left ajar that one hope to happenstance.

My parents would be relieved. They'd urged me to go and stay with relatives out of town. Get out of the house, make a change. America was farther than they'd bargained for, but I was sure they'd welcome the chance to be rid of me.

Which was why I couldn't tell them. I couldn't go. I couldn't abandon Rubina. I still hadn't even met her in person. She was in Karachi for long-term rehabilitation with a specialist. But her first hearing date had just been granted. Saadia didn't need me present for that, but eventually, my day in court would come too. I was already listed as a witness in the filed briefs.

I took another expensive auto-rickshaw to Marjan's place—a ding in my savings, but I didn't need them. I wasn't going to America. Once, I used to walk to Marjan's neighborhood—a long but pleasant stroll if one avoided the main road with its smog-belching buses and mountains of trash. I used to take the side streets lined with rusted gates and pass by dusty lots and tandoors and eucalyptus trees and tailor shops and corner stalls selling tuberoses to the celebrating and the mourning.

Now, the streets streamed past. Wind whipped through my thin chaadar in the back of the auto-rickshaw. The outside world had become a blur the past four months. I only spied it from inside.

I handed Marjan the courier's envelope without a word of greeting. The passport fell into her pale hands, and she flipped through it. "You're leaving, Hajra. Really leaving." Her voice broke a little.

"I can't go now." I bowed my head and found a chair in their living room. "I've got to turn it down," I whispered.

"What is this, Hajra? After everything? You have to go!"

"But the trial. They'll need me. It's the least—it's the *only* thing I can do for her."

"They don't need you right away. You haven't even been summoned yet. It's a long road, Hajra, this justice. Take a break. You'll only be gone a few months."

I nodded, uneasy. I couldn't tell her how much it beckoned—the shimmering idea of a place so far away that no one could follow me. Not Mohsin, not Ali. Not my friends who only saw the best in me. Not my parents, either. The tight net woven by their aspirations and fears had always contained me. I'd only just begun to cast off that net before this happened. And for a shining moment, I'd played the woman out front with opinions writ large on my body and loud on my lips. But it turned out my boldness was only an act. I was never any louder or any larger than the frightened girl clinging to the water tank while my brother, the hero, leapt forth.

This visa permitted that girl to have her way and forget her pretense at bravery. Lodged, safe, in America, I'd have to fight every day to make sure she returned here.

* * *

I dreamt I was wandering through cobbled alleys in the old city. A shoemaker hammered on his last. Gutters perfumed the air. From atop a rusty gate, a child with matted hair peered out at me. Then night fell like a curtain, and the city was hidden.

Silky leaves rustled against my cheek. I was nervous here, away from buildings and people. And it was so dark. But I took a few tentative steps forward. I smelled the earth and mushrooms and decay underfoot and something else too. Damp fur. A bird called in the distance.

Like a fist, fear clutched at my chest. I had to get away. I began to run, faster and faster. My breath caught, and I wanted to pause, but hooves thundered behind me. That musk of danger filled my nostrils. I'd become a fawn or rodent sprinting for my life.

The darkness began to lift and up ahead, a house. It was my home in Peshawar, its porch and parked Vespa so familiar. For an instant, the front door opened, and a girl stretched out her arms to grasp my hand. She had broad shoulders, and her long hair was oiled into a plait. I reached for her. So close to safety.

I sat up in the dark, heart thudding. The whistle of the patrolling chowkidar startled me from my dream. I lay back and tried to drift back to sleep. My packed and bound suitcase waited by the door. I would need rest for my flight to New York the next day. But none came as I tossed among the stifling bedclothes. Finally, I cast the sheets aside and slipped downstairs.

The gate creaked, loud enough to wake the neighbors, and I paused there, listening. I'd never done this; I'd never seen my neighborhood in the dark, not alone. A dog howled in the distance. *It isn't safe outside at night*, a hundred women scolded me in my mind. My days aren't safe either, I protested. At least at night, no one knows who I am.

The paanwallah's stall at the corner was shuttered. Across the street, I could make out the figures of men crowded around a small can of flames in an empty lot. Their voices drifted across with the sickly smell of hashish. A cat slunk past and squeezed into the gap between a gate and a pillar. I jumped at the skitter of another animal in the darkness.

I'd never been out late at night without my family to protect me. But now I needed to learn to take the unknown in my stride and fend for myself. Perhaps forever. I wondered if, with time, I'd grow world-weary in that faraway New York and wouldn't startle so easily in the dark anymore.

I crouched at the step in front of a padlocked tailor's shop. My mind tumbled through the haphazard timeline that led to my flight the next day. A day like any other, waiting for the bus. My brother, who'd been a child once. My parents, who could have stayed in India once. If only I could go back to any one of those moments and twist circumstance to prevent my exile.

Then I noticed the silence. No more murmur of voices from the empty lot beyond. I glanced up, and all four of the men were staring at me. The can of fire beside them cast their faces in a flickering light from below. Their dark, ill-fitting clothes were patched, their cheeks hollow. One of them lifted his hand to his mouth and took a slow drag from his beedi. His eyes stayed on me through his exhale.

How long had I been frozen in place? I got to my feet and stumbled back down the street toward home, walking faster, then faster still. I heard a whooping laugh from one of those men, or maybe it was the bark of a dog. I didn't wait to find out which. I picked up my steps into a jog, then a sprint. I had to protect myself, but I had no armor or weapons. I had no choice but to run.

FOURTEEN

The hatchback rental putters up Durban's hills along a road hazy with red earth whipping off the slopes. I've set out for my first day with some trepidation; I've never been a confident driver, and now I have to deal with South African road rules and the dizzying dips and climbs of Durban's streets.

My first stop is the university I contacted for archival research. Its buildings are a boxy 1950s hulk presiding over the surrounding suburbs. The bastion of learning shining atop a hill. The road curves around buildings outlined against gray skies in red brick and concrete. Students rush across a broad courtyard or sprawl against giant aloe planters.

Many years ago, I was a bookish schoolgirl longing for spirited debate and endless libraries. Later, though, by the time I arrived at the New York campus with its cramped offices and classrooms, the years had transformed me. Universities had become political machinations, burning tires, and effigies. New York students with their sit-ins and petitions seemed foolish—as naive as I once was.

After finding parking, I head to the indentured labor archives: a room banished to a building's basement. Here, floor-to-ceiling murals in garish colors depict scenes of migration and servitude. The receptionist finds my appointment in her book and leads me through a pair of glass doors.

"Dr. Naidoo? Miss Ahmed is here to see you."

On the front edge of the desk before me, a marble slab announces "Vikesh Naidoo, MPhil, DPhil." The man seated behind it wears rimless glasses, and the part of his hair is as straight as a ruler.

"Now, let me see." He smooths a printout of my email to him. "You have come here from New York? For doctorate research."

"Yes, I wanted a preliminary look through your archives today."

"Of course. We are always so flattered when Americans take an interest in us."

Is he mocking me? Surely, he can tell from my accent I'm not American. But he seems too humorless for sarcasm.

"How wonderful," he continues, "that you are interested in Durban's ancestors. You might be interested in my most recent paper, published for an American conference, as it were. But for now, I can show you some books of use when starting out."

He names a few titles, and I'm startled. The illustrated books are designed for laypeople. "That's—kind of you, but I was hoping to look at your primary documents."

Dr. Naidoo smiles. "Eventually, yes. But you must start at the beginning, as we all did." He hands me the pile of books with the air of conferring a great honor.

I'm shuffled out of the office by the assistant even as I protest, and the door slams shut in my face. I climb up the basement stairwell, running through all the retorts I should've thrown at Naidoo when I had the chance.

Eventually, I stop just outside the building entrance and take several deep breaths. I will not let this little man deter me. A shout shakes me from my reverie, and I glance around at all the gelled haircuts and aviator sunglasses. During Apartheid, this was an Indians-only university, and from what I see around me, that's what it still appears to be.

"Excuse us."

I realize I'm blocking the door and hastily step aside. A pair of young women peer at me with curious smiles as they leave the building. Instinctively, I avert my gaze. But—no. I came here to talk to the people of this city, not keep hiding behind my books as I've done for years. I take a deep breath and turn back toward them.

"Hi!" Too loud. "Are you here to look at the indentured labor archives as well?" I can't seem to keep the forced brightness from my voice.

One of them shakes her head politely. "We came to see our aunty. She has an office here."

"Oh. I see." I keep smiling like an idiot, unsure how to break the awkward pause that follows.

The woman who spoke smiles graciously. "Are you from overseas? I'm Ishara." She wears a kameez cut from bright satin, tight pants of striped red and gold, and strappy sandals. Her tunic clings to her curves, but she is still girlish in her way, cheeks bright from the brisk day. Her black hair glitters in the winter sun. In contrast with her friend's pink-and-gray backpack, a little gold purse swings from her shoulder.

When I nod and introduce myself, the other girl in her jeans and anonymous sweatshirt smiles at me shyly. "We have to go to class, but—do you want to walk with us?"

"Sure!" Still that ridiculous brightness.

"Are you studying here or something?" Ishara asks me as we set off.

"Not studying exactly. I'm here doing research. I'm studying about Durban at my university in New York."

"Really?" Ishara's arched brows shoot up and disappear into her fringe. "You're learning about Durban over there in America? And you came here all by yourself?"

There's no mistaking her impressed tone. I'm taken aback by it; I haven't considered what I do as anything special in so long. I manage a nod in response.

"Wow. Only ever saw white girls coming here before. What you studying?"

"History. And you? What do you both study?"

"Accounting," says Rajni.

"I'm doing my B.Comm," Ishara says. "The usual. What type of research you doing?"

"Indentured labor. I came to look at the archives, but I didn't get very far. I'd rather talk to people anyway, people who know something about the migration, but it isn't easy getting interviews. I thought the university would help me, but . . ." I shrug.

Ishara shakes her head. "Ay, this university is falling to pieces. *Definitely* not like when my father went here in the seventies."

"But who did you see down there in the basement?" Rajni furrows her brow. "Not Brenda aunty?"

"No . . . I saw Dr. Naidoo."

Ishara clicks her tongue. "No wonder you didn't get help. Brenda aunty—well, she's not our real aunty. We're cousins, Rajni and me.

Brenda aunty is our grandmother's friend. She knows *every*thing and everyone in Durban."

No women's names came up on the department website, or I would surely have started there. "And she works at the archives?"

"I don't know, eh? She does a little bit of this, a little bit of that. She made them give her an office, I think. Look, today we have class, but if you want, you can come home sometime and meet her. And our grandmother too. She has plenty of stories about the old days, believe me. Don't say there back in America no one helped you out in Durban!"

"Oh, I would never say that!" I flush.

Ishara smiles, benevolent. She pulls out a Hello Kitty notepad and jots down her information before they continue on.

I pick my way down rough-hewn steps toward the parking garage. Cousins, almost sisters. A grandmother. I barely knew my grandparents. They fled privileged lives in India for Pakistan but were little used to the hardscrabble Frontier province and wilted away when I was still an infant. Just one grandfather survived into my childhood, a man with rheumy eyes who told me wistful stories of the Lucknow haveli where his dreams still roamed.

For a moment, I'm seized by envy of these girls and their cozy community. But then I remember that they, too, have roots in refuge. Every generation carries some trace of that separation. We're none of us unscathed.

* * *

Under a relentless winter sun, I take the highway toward Durban's outer suburbs. Developments are going up along the route, but young sugarcane still sways in breezy waves of green. Across the highway, a megamall sprawls, complete with an IMAX theater and condominiums.

It's the day after my futile meeting with Naidoo, but I'm too excited to care. I've called Ishara and secured an invite to her grandmother's home for Sunday lunch. She promises that the mysterious Brenda aunty will stop by as well.

In the meantime, I've decided to visit relevant historic sites. My first stop must be Phoenix, the storied Indian township where Gandhi and Kasturba lived and established a shelter. Remains of their settlement have been made into a museum. The museum's website was vague on directions, but I'm confident I'll find the famous place somehow.

In Phoenix, concrete fencing climbs up the hill like rows of yellowed teeth. Pastel houses cluster, as haphazard as a child's blocks kicked across the floor. Coral stucco, mustard yellow, Kelly green edge out the monotony of red earth. A Hindu temple with white domes topped with gilt. At a red light, I glance over at a thatched fruit and vegetable stall. A woman in a black burqa picks up an avocado and examines it with her gloved hand.

As if cast in permanent sepia tone, Phoenix is chipped wooden stiles along labyrinthine streets. Cylindrical streetlights from a bygone era. Teenagers loiter at bus stops in their gray pants and untucked white shirts. Tin shacks and stray cats and wind whipping through fabric too thin for the season. I've slipped out of time to some place just before the internet and polished chrome—a world more reminiscent of the Peshawar I knew than beachfront Durban.

I'm transported to a dusty stall and glass case lined with grime. Peshawar's old city. The dirt-lined fingernails of an old Afghan man who sold me a pair of red and green earrings. I lost one of the pair a year ago and mourned it as a cherished heirloom. I only packed a single suitcase when I left Peshawar. So little of me has survived from that old life.

For a moment, I fantasize about returning to meet with Saadia. I might wander the alleys, find that jewelry seller, and reclaim what I lost. I might stop at a roadside tandoor and buy a giant naan fresh from its scorched clay oven with a sizzling chapli kebab encased inside. I could eat it there on the pavement and ignore the flies and staring men. I'd burn my fingers tearing morsels of the meat and bread and charred fat. Whole coriander seeds would stick in the crevices of my mouth. I'd tease them out with my tongue later and savor and remember.

I turn into dead ends and circle around, hopelessly lost. The museum's directions were useless. I pull up to the shoulder of a Phoenix side street where three men bend over the open hood of a car. One tinkers while the other two hang around and dispense advice.

"Excuse me," I call from my rolled-down window. "Could you give me directions? I'm looking for the Gandhi settlement."

"Where?" One of them turns to his friends. "You heard of this thing?" The other two draw closer and peer into my car with frank curiosity.

"It's on the Heritage Route. You know, where Gandhi lived, and now it's a museum?"

"Gandhi?" One scratches at the stubble on his chin. "I'm not sure, ay?"

"It'll be near Bambayi!" I remember a detail from my research. The Black township in Phoenix that was settled after the Inanda riots and named in a mispronunciation of "Bombay."

"Bambayi? You can't go there, miss. It's not safe!" They all shake their heads. "Not a chance." "Terrible, terrible."

I smile politely at their admonitions to "bring your brother next time. Not safe alone" and continue on my way. I wonder if Bambayi is any more unsafe than other parts of Phoenix. Than Peshawar, for that matter, where I've seen assault rifles sold at street markets. But Bambayi has more Black people. Everyone knows about this country's scars. Still, Truth and Reconciliation did happen here as an organized event. Perhaps that's all reconciliation means—draw a line, move on, relinquish hope for more.

I try a few more times, even get some hazy directions, but find nothing. Hours tick past. As sunset rakes pink fingers across the sky, I decide it's time to give up and try another day.

Perhaps I invented this place. And maybe Gandhi was never here, either. He never settled in Phoenix, never rallied laborers. Just as I've never helped anyone who asked for my voice to support her own. Alone in my car, no one to interrupt my thoughts, I could believe oppressive silence has never been broken. Not in this country, about which I'd nursed a foolish optimism, or any other. A blink and I might be inside my circle of lamplight in New York, the world dark outside. I cannot be sure I've traveled any farther.

On Sunday, clouds hang low, and only a few tourists brave the beachfront. But my own spirits are finally lifting. Today, I'm on my way to meet Ishara's family.

The address in Overport is a convenience store with bars across windows and door. Ishara and Rajni's grandmother lives in the flat upstairs. The smell of fish permeates the dingy stairwell and grows

stronger with each step. Ishara answers the door with clinking bangles and leads me into a small living room, where at least ten people are crammed. I smile through introductions to uncles, cousins,
nieces; speech seems to have left me.

In the kitchen, three women crowd each other as they stir, chop,
fry. An older woman supervises the operation. Ishara's grandmother.
She takes a corner of her sari to her damp forehead and waddles over
to me. The hand she places in mine is disarmingly soft.

"Come, these girls don't need me nosing in the kitchen." In the
living room, she shoos the men off a sofa so we can sit together.

"So what you looking for in Durban? All the way from America?"
She peers at me through thick bifocals, and others in the room eaves-
drop in between their own conversations.

"I'm doing research on indentured labor. Women laborers."

"Yes, yes, Ish told me that." She pulls Ishara toward her. "But what
you want to know? I know little bit, little bit. Sugarcane . . ." She strokes
Ishara's shiny head and drifts into thought. "It was finish already when
I was born. You know. I'm not so old! But my grandma, grandpa, they
came from India. Tamils, we are. From India. They came in the ship
for the sugarcane. Girmit-karan, they called themselves."

It's been years since I conducted interviews with people in
Pakistan's northern areas for my thesis. Now those instincts return
like a muscle memory. Her words allow me to clear a path, and I feel
my way to the right question for the next piece of her story.

"Yes, I remember my grandma. Grandpa died when I was still
small. He was big. And smelled of smoke always. Grandma was
small but fat, like me." She chuckles. "And dark-dark, more than
all of us. Must be from the sun of the fields. And her hands—eesh."
She holds her own hands out and, with one forefinger, draws lines
across the other palm, up, down, side to side. "All over her hands,
you could see scars from the work. Sugar gets hot, and they should
work all day pulling and chopping, and then the harvest time was
very tough. She told me this. Even pregnant women must do the
same work. Ay. First Grandma came alone; she got married to
Grandpa there on the estate. They needed protection, you see, the
women who were alone."

I grasp at this bit: "I'm really interested in the women who came
alone. Did your grandma talk about how she came?"

"Let's see. She never talk too much about those times. Such a young thing she was, you know, when she came first time. Very scare, she told me, she was of the ocean. Even my mother was scare of the beachfront. And Grandma was scare of both Zulu people and white people. Must be hard, ay, to leave your family behind."

"So why did she leave India? Was she . . . forced by someone? Taken?"

"Force? Why? She was happy to come here away from all that disease and filth and whatnot. India." She speaks the last word with distaste. "She was lucky to get away; she told me so. Nothing left in India for them. Nowhere to go, nobody to be. She and her friends ran away to Africa, and you know, my girl, they could have gone back. After five years, after ten years. No. They wanted to stay in Africa. So."

This is what she's been told. Maybe what her grandmother wanted to believe too. No one wants to tell her children she was taken by force.

It's time for lunch. The meal is a raucous affair, and the food is homey—curried fillings for vegetarian pies and samosas, steaming rice and dholl, a big vat of greens and potatoes. Familiar, though different. The others are more used to me now and free with their inside jokes. The younger cousins whisper over their plates.

When last was I included in a meal like this one? My ex-boyfriend's family dinners in their Connecticut suburb could not have been more different. Quiet enough that my fork echoed when it screeched my foreignness at the table.

Once, this was my life. I was the girl giggling in a corner with her cousins, not a woman desperate to join the chatter of a strange room. But other memories rear up to challenge that narrative too. I also remember resentment and restlessness. Evenings spent serving tea and making inane conversation with visiting relatives about fashion or curtains. And as I fidgeted on the sofa, Ali would wave and slip out the door without anyone to stop him.

Thousands of miles away, my own family is sitting down to a meal at this very moment. My mother will make ghee-layered parathas for a late brunch. My father will throw together his Sunday scrambled eggs with radioactive quantities of cayenne and green chilies. Ali might have brought home a bit of sooji halwa from the shop down the street, newsprint soaked through with grease. Others may have joined them this Sunday—Chhotu Chacha or a neighbor's child. Or maybe my place at the table is still empty.

After lunch, Ishara's grandmother stays at the cleared table to peel oranges and hand around slices. Most of the others have left for home. When the doorbell rings, Ishara's grandmother nods. "Good, good, she came. Go, my dear, bring her here."

Ishara returns with a woman almost as old as her grandmother but different in every other way. Her silver hair is cropped, and she is stylish in a black skirt, tights, and low pumps. The grandmother rises and kisses the new woman on both cheeks. "This is one of my oldest friends, Brenda Pillay."

I introduce myself, a little nervous of this woman's easy confidence. Over black tea and oranges, it emerges that Brenda is something of a local celebrity. She spent a couple of stints in jail as an anti-Apartheid activist and published a book about Durban Indians as well as a memoir about her forced exile to Botswana when she married outside her race. She's been given an honorary position and office space at the indentured labor archives, probably to capitalize on her fame.

Brenda waves away my diplomatic account of the university. "That Naidoo, too full of himself, he is. A few letters to put after their names, these men, they think they added a couple inches to their thing."

Ishara's grandmother laughs and laughs as she clutches bits of orange peel. "Oh Brenda," she gasps. "Just too much. Too much."

"Anyway," Brenda continues with a wry smile. "You don't need him. What you want to know, ask Brenda aunty. We'll help you out."

"I've been researching Gandhi-ji and Kasturba bai. I tried to find the Phoenix settlement, but I got lost. I wanted to find stories about the women laborers Kasturba bai was fighting for. And in New York, I saw this photograph, and I want to know about them." I pull out the copy from its folder and pass it to Brenda. She takes out her glasses to study it, and Ishara and her grandmother also lean in.

A long silence follows. I'm waiting for her shrug as she returns the photograph without explanation. I'm so certain of failure that Brenda's slow nod shakes me as nothing else could.

"Yes, yes," she says, almost to herself. "I recognize this picture. It's beautiful, isn't it? I can see why you were drawn to it." Brenda nods again and takes off her glasses. "I've seen it before. But, my dear, you are mistaken. This has nothing to do with Kasturba bai. Your book took you on a wild goose chase!"

I frown, taken aback. "So, then, who are they?"

"These, my dear, are just a few Durban women. You wouldn't find anything about them in your American books."

"What were they protesting?"

"I don't know, eh? But—let's think." She pauses and drums her finger against the table. Then she glances up with a bright smile. "I know exactly the person you must talk to." She extracts a black leather-bound agenda from her handbag and copies out a few lines into my notebook. "Here, this man can help you." She hands the notebook back to me with a gentle pat on my shoulder as if to set me on my way.

FIFTEEN

It was late afternoon when the oxcart stopped near a house presiding over vast fields. A fine rain was falling, and most of the house was obscured by mist. Sita clambered out and stretched her stiff limbs. She blinked the drizzle from her eyelashes and took in her surroundings. Acres of green tumbled across slopes before them in an undulating symmetry of young cane shoots. It was more land than Sita had imagined could belong to one man.

The house towered through the rain, its outlines barely visible. Wind gusted through the trees in a grove behind them, and a few chickens clucked from the shelter of their coop to one side. Otherwise, all was still in this packed-earth yard. Another gust parted the mist a little and revealed more of the house. Narrow windows were set along the top story, their curtains drawn. Charcoal-gray roof tiles above sloped into a peak topped with a metal structure. A rooster? Spindly, it creaked to and fro, the only being in this place that seemed to move.

A Zulu boy arrived and helped the wagon driver unhitch the oxen. With him came a middle-aged man who greeted the newcomers and bade them to call him sirdar. This man was Tamil but dressed in a cotton coat and trousers—a rough facsimile of what the white people wore.

They followed him through the grove of fruit trees to emerge into a deserted clearing where small huts were set around an enclosure.

"This is where the girmit-karan live," he explained. Though she'd never heard the term before, Sita understood that she, too, was now a person known only by her contract. The sirdar pointed out sections—men, married families, single women. He instructed them to relieve themselves here before meeting him back in the center. He would escort them to the white overseer, who would issue further instruction.

Soon, they returned the way they'd come, crossing the orchard to the yard where the house loomed. The rain had stopped, and a few errant rays of sun peeked through clouds. But the yard was still cold in the long shadows of the house.

Then the sirdar seemed to remember something and raised a hand. "Which of you women is the one called Sita?"

Startled, she stepped forward.

The sirdar gave Sita an appraising look. "You must stay here. One of the housemaids will come for you. The rest—follow me." He continued toward a set of outbuildings. The others stared at her for only another instant before they followed him down the path without a backward glance.

Sita wrapped her arms around herself, cloth bundle at her feet. A tabby cat sauntered up as if to interrogate her and began washing its paws. The small Zulu boy she'd seen with the oxen earlier rounded the corner, and she started. Perhaps he would relay a message. But he ignored her, kicking a stick against the ground as he skipped past.

She wondered if she should approach the house but balked when she glanced up. Its haughty demeanor forbade her. A breeze picked up as the light faded, and the mood of the evening dipped with the temperature. Sita settled herself on the bare earth and hugged her knees for warmth.

A shape emerged from darkness. Slight as a night creature and soundless too. It was a woman dressed in a sari, as far as she could make out.

"My name is Vasanthi," she said and beckoned Sita to follow her to the house.

They entered a cavernous chamber. A kitchen, stone underfoot. A fire blazed in the hearth. Two women—one old, one just a girl—were dressed in long skirts and little caps like cotton flowers. They rushed around a long table in the center. These women were both white and, except for a quick glance, ignored Sita. Heat radiated from their activity, the fireplace, and large pots steaming over a stove. The center of the room seemed to glow with heat, but its sooty corners were lost in the dark.

Vasanthi disappeared, returned with a tin plate, and motioned for Sita to follow her to a corner. In the light from the hearth, Sita studied her: she had a catlike sashay to her step, and her waist curved above the knotted folds of her sari. Her skin was a deep brown, shiny as burnt sugar. The plait of black hair down her back was thick and strong as a rope. When she turned around, Sita was startled by her delicate, moon-shaped face. She smiled at Sita, thrust the plate at her, and disappeared again behind a door at the kitchen's far end.

Sita crouched, as small as possible, her plate piled with rice and a bit of spiced pumpkin. She savored the sweet depth of the vegetable poriyal and stretched it to her last morsel. It had been so long since she'd tasted anything but gruel made from dried grains and seeds.

She tried unsuccessfully to stay out of the way of the bustle. One of the white women carrying a large bowl of frothy liquid in her hands almost tripped over her and exclaimed loudly. Sita shrank as far into her corner as she could. Eventually, the commotion calmed. Vasanthi and a stout Zulu woman took elaborate platters out the kitchen doors into some other part of the house. The white women sat down at the long table and ate their own meal. Vasanthi and the Zulu woman reappeared with dirty plates while the white women prepared new platters. In four rounds, they took soiled dishes through a doorway at the far end. Sita crept around the edge of the kitchen to peer through this door. Beyond it, two dark-skinned men—also girmit-karan, she supposed—squatted on an earthen floor and scrubbed pots while another bent over a large soapy tub.

Eventually, Vasanthi emerged from this washing-up room and dried her hands on her mundhanai before tucking it into her side. She let out a weary little breath. Perhaps this was a break in her tasks for the evening. She beckoned and led Sita up a narrow staircase by the aid of a candle. Sita had hoped they'd talk about the house and how things were done here, but Vasanthi was quiet and seemed exhausted. Sita did not like to bother her.

At the top of the stairs, a passageway stretched into the gloom. Drawn curtains on one side billowed briefly; shut doors were set along the other side. In the dim candlelight, Sita could just make out the shapes of paintings lining the walls in between doorways and curtains.

Vasanthi paused in front of a door at the end of the hallway. She raised the candle to her face and placed a finger to her lips. Gently, she opened the door and nudged Sita into a room where a shaft of moonlight fell through windows at the far end. In the room's center was a high bed. A mosquito net slung over four railings shrouded the sleeper. On tiptoe, Vasanthi approached the bed and lifted a corner of the netting to reveal a child.

Sita bent closer to study the boy. Five or six years old, he lay on his stomach with his face turned to one side. Their candle seemed to glow brighter against the bloom of his cheeks and butter-yellow hair. His brows were knotted together as if his dreams required precise engineering. He clutched his pillowcase in a fierce, tiny fist.

Vasanthi replaced the mosquito net and led Sita to the room's far end. Bedding was rolled up beneath a window. Together, they shook out the blankets, and clouds of mildew and dust rose up. Vasanthi smoothed the blanket and tucked it just so at one end. She straightened and touched Sita's elbow with a smile. "Sleep now," she whispered. "We'll speak tomorrow. I must return to work." And before Sita could thank her, she slipped from the room, taking the candle with her.

Sita stood where Vasanthi left her. Nothing of note had begun, but so much was ended. The sleeping child's murmurs, the door firmly shut—each was a kind of signal. This small territory under the window would be hers when she finished work and her bedding could claim it. She knew nothing about what would be required of her. But she understood the word *ayah*, which Dickinson had used. She understood that her waking life would orbit around this child. She sank to the floor and leaned against the wall, sure that no sleep could come for her that night.

Sita didn't wake until the sun rose high enough to fill the room. Unsure of her surroundings, she tried to stretch her stiff limbs and opened her eyes a little. She gasped and sat straight up, startled out of her yawn.

The child sat cross-legged and somber a foot or two away. He was wearing a long shirt spun from white cotton of a quality far superior to any garment Sita had ever owned. Both elbows rested on his lap, palms supporting chin. He was studying the strange woman in his room with unnerving stillness. Sita was surprised to find that the eyes boring into her were soft brown and flecked with gold, not the blue-green-gray she'd seen among white people. The warmth of this color was unexpectedly soothing. Copying him, she sat cross-legged, too, and participated in his silent communication as the sunlight between them intensified. Heat seeped into stone floor and the folds of their cottons.

The door creaked open, and the spell broke. The Zulu woman Sita remembered from the kitchen last night came in with a tray she placed on a small table. She pulled back a child-sized wood chair and spoke to the boy in a mix of Zulu and English. He got to his feet and sat down to breakfast with eyes still fixed on Sita, staring through each eggy mouthful. The woman brought Sita a steaming bowl of cornmeal, bobbing her head to her thanks.

She was a stout woman of gentle expression. Her dress was long and black, like the white women from the kitchen. But, unlike them, she also wore a square headscarf knotted at the nape of her neck. She pointed to herself and said, "Mary."

As Sita ate, Mary opened a dark wood wardrobe and extracted clothing. Short woolen pants, shirt, waistcoat, socks. Her hands were sure and expert. She was not old. No lines gathered around her eyes when she smiled. Still, motherhood seemed to govern each move-ment she dedicated to the white boy's care. Perhaps she'd developed this ease through the repetition of working for others. Sita wanted to ask if she had children of her own or a family that still lived together nearby.

So far, Mary and the boy in the yard were the only Zulu people she'd seen here. This land belonged to their people, and yet the estate seemed peopled almost exclusively by whites and girmit-karan ser-vants brought here like her. Maybe Mary resented Sita like the men at the port had seemed to. She wanted to ask so many questions, but language was a weight in her mouth.

When the boy was done eating and had used his chamber pot, Mary helped him wash at the basin. He cried out at the first cold splash but then laughed and flicked water at Mary too. They chattered in Zulu as she dried him off and dressed him in the clothes she'd set out. She pulled tight the strings in a pair of shiny leather boots and parted his thick yellow hair down the middle with a wet comb.

When she was done, Mary stood back as if to admire her handiwork, and the boy obligingly stuck his tongue out at her. Mary shook her head with a smile at Sita, then led them both from the room and around a far corner Sita had not noticed the night before. She pushed open a heavy door, and the sickly light of the hallway was overcome by sunshine.

Sita blinked and shaded her eyes as she followed. As she adjusted to the light, the space beyond the door emerged in degrees. Flagstones at her feet were lit up in a dizzying pattern of color. A multicolored pane was set in the window—light poured in from this pane and made blue and yellow shapes on her arms and along the whitewashed walls. Motes swam lazily in these colors of light too.

Ahead of her, a wide staircase swept down and away, its curves lined by dark wood. The broad steps were black stone, rough and cold underfoot.

"Woza," Mary whispered, already halfway down the stairs.

Scurrying to the bottom, she slowed her pace to match Mary's and passed through a wide doorway with her. In this new room, thick rugs lined the stone floors; armchairs were upholstered in silks and velvets, cushions tucked against corners, polished wood tables inlaid with shells and pearls. Small bejeweled objects and glass figures gathered around every flat surface. Intricately woven fabrics hung from walls. A pair of elephant tusks curved over the fireplace at the other end of the room. Sooty tools stood inside the hollowed leg of perhaps the same unfortunate elephant.

Only when the child broke free of Mary's grip and ran across the room did Sita realize that a woman sat on one of the armchairs. Her dress and demeanor so closely matched the room that she almost disappeared into her backdrop. She sat straight against the back of a chair, elbow on each upholstered arm. Her blouse—the same ivory color as the tusks—was stiff against her throat where her starched collar stood to attention. Her navy skirt stretched to cover her ankles.

While her outfit conformed more or less to what Sita had seen on other white women, its effect on this woman was new. Perhaps she had simply never seen the attire in this atmosphere for which it was meant. Amid the room's finery and the plantations stretching all around, Sita was awed by the rustle of the woman's armor.

The woman spoke but had to repeat herself before Sita could understand. She was speaking Tamil or some version of it. "I am mistress of this house," she said.

Sita nodded and hoped it was an adequate response.

"You will call me Madam or Memsahib. And this," she said, indicating the boy who fidgeted to one side, "is my son, Desmond. You are his ayah. You will call him Master Desmond."

The boy was made to stand still next to his mother's chair. Sita nodded again, bewildered by the distance between woman and child. She had no memories of her own mother or her touch. Sometimes, lying awake at night, she tried to imagine the softness of being held by the woman who birthed her. Glancing at the boy, she pitied his poverty.

"You will bathe and dress him," continued the mistress. "And fetch his water and bring his meals from the kitchen. Every day he has lessons. You will take him. Morning and evening, you will bring him to see me. In this time, you have your meals. You will sleep in his room and look after if he wakes. Understand?"

Sita nodded for the third time. Then, beginning to feel she was required to offer more in the way of proper deference, she added, "Yes, Memsahib."

"Now it is time for Desmond's lessons." She switched to halting Zulu and addressed Mary, who responded with a polite bob of her head as she retreated. Sita wondered if she was also expected to perform this action. But before she could attempt it, Mary took her by the elbow and led her away.

SIXTEEN

On September 12, 2001, I crossed the street without looking. I didn't hear the screeching brakes or horns, not until after I'd reached the opposite curb. I traced my everyday steps to the subway. No scraps of charred paper blown into Queens and no gray chalk for my lungs. Greasy-haired men loitered by their cars and ogled as always, but their gaze lingered that morning. Grandmothers appraised from stoops; children paused in play.

I'd lived in their neighborhood for three months since I had arrived from Pakistan. All this time, I'd only been another commuter to Manhattan. Today was different. Now, I was someone to be watched.

The empty platform was quiet but for the drip-drop of the tunnels and a scrabbling rat on the tracks. Perhaps I would be alone on the train. Surely, no one else would be so foolish or so callous as to go into work this morning. That's proof enough that she means harm, someone could reason.

Footsteps. A bleached blonde wearing a leopard-print blouse click-clacked down the stairs. She stepped forward and edged closer to the tracks. Handbag tight under her arm, she started when she saw me. She strode over with purpose to where I stood against the tiled wall. A flag pin was fixed to her blouse lapel.

"Please, train still goes today? Manhattan?"

I raised my eyes from her pin to her face. I nodded, then shook my head. "Not today. You'll have to transfer at Queensboro."

She thanked me before turning to stare down the tunnel.

On the train, I sank into an empty seat. Perched at the edge, I studied the dermatologist's ad and avoided everyone's eyes. Up and down and around me, people turned in or away as the train sped or screeched as lights flickered or dimmed and bodies swayed or stumbled. I closed my eyes and wished someone would scream or point a finger at me. I'd prefer it to the silence.

At the university in midtown, classes were canceled, but a few professors came in. They lingered in twos and threes in hallways and spoke in hushed voices. When I passed them, their eyes rested on me no more than a moment. They knew I had no one here to lose.

I unlocked the office I shared with other visiting scholars. Sarah, my office mate from Taiwan, typed frantically at a desktop.

"Hajra! I didn't know you were coming today." She jumped up with her usual nervous energy. "How are you?" she asked, searching my eyes as if for signs of disease.

"All right. And you?"

"I'm fine, I'm fine. I was worried about you. The news, people . . ." Her words trailed off. "You should take care. People, they should know the difference," she said, shaking her head as she returned to her chair.

I sat at another of the ancient computers: castoffs from the rest of the department. The internet was up, though the phones were still down. My parents might be worrying and waiting for word from me. Or maybe I'd already become a distant, troublesome relative they rarely thought about.

"I can't concentrate." Sarah chewed distractedly on a piece of her hair.

My own computer screen was overrun by slow-motion magenta and lime geometry. "Neither can I."

"Do you want to order lunch?"

"Will anything be open today?"

"Of course—this is New York!"

We fished out our collection of delivery menus from a drawer. New York. A city that belonged to me for now, even if my six-month fellowship was edging closer to its end. Even if I lived in a vermin-infested basement room far inside Queens. No matter. I belonged to this city I once knew only from pirated seasons of *Friends* and British Council library books. A surreal metropolis where people came to surpass their past selves. But even after JFK and MetroCards, my feet never quite touched these streets. I'd levitated through a dream of New York all summer.

Today, I stood on real concrete for the first time since leaving Pakistan. The crushing silence of this day belonged to the same world I'd left—those last months cloistered in my room, afraid to step outside and raise my voice. Today, even in anonymous New York, I'd had to look over my shoulder on the subway. I'd kept my gaze low.

People should know the difference, Sarah said. I suppose she meant the difference between me and those who would wish this city harm. No one would know the difference. I was another brown-skinned threat with a Muslim name here, as I'd been another chaadar-clad woman at the Peshawar bus stop.

"The pizza shop is open." Sarah cradled the phone against her shoulder. "Vegetarian special?"

We tried to work through the afternoon. Around four, Sarah stood and cracked her knuckles. "Let's go . . . let's get out. I can't sit here. I need a drink. I'm sorry, I know you don't—"

"No, it's all right. I'll come with you."

We walked to a nearby Mexican restaurant and sat at the last table available on the street-side patio. Sarah gulped back a margarita and ordered a second. I sipped a virgin strawberry daiquiri, the cheapest item on the drinks menu. We made our way through a basket of free tortilla chips, saying little. The talk at tables around us filtered through in pieces.

"Everything below Canal . . ."

"To give blood, but they didn't need . . ."

"Doctors were scrubbed up, but no one came . . ."

"Thirty-sixth floor . . ."

"Paper raining on the BQE . . ."

"How many miles did you walk . . ."

"Bomb Afghanistan, Pakistan, any -stan, I don't give a fuck, nuke 'em all."

Sarah met my eyes as we both froze over our drinks. Words rushed from me to fill the pause. "Did you get through, I mean, did you talk to your family they must've been worried."

"Yes, thank you," Sarah said, a bit awkward. "And you?"

My throat tightened. "I emailed my father today. I didn't try calling—" I hesitated. Then, grateful when I remembered, I added, "Well, the phones were down, you know."

"Oh!" Sarah's expression changed. "My roommate's landline works. You can phone from our place. It's not far. We can go now!"

"It's OK," I said, flustered. "The office phone will be working by tomorrow, and there's the time difference. But thank you."

She nodded with a polite smile, and our conversation petered out. I slurped the last of my drink. She motioned for the bill. We settled up in silence. I'd pushed her away.

When I arrived in June, I attended every department-sponsored happy hour and free event in the parks. The relief of walking down the street unafraid had been dizzying. I had no history here. I could start over, make friendships, even return to the unencumbered girl I used to be.

On this day, such notions felt absurdly foolish. I was destined to drag this silence behind me everywhere now. The overheard ugliness from the next table confirmed as much; I was an unwanted outsider here as much as I'd ever been in Peshawar. I needed to be careful with what I said, and to whom, to keep safe. It was the policy my refugee parents kept, one I was beginning to understand.

At the corner where we separated for our solitary journeys home, Sarah opened her mouth to speak. But then, she seemed to change her mind and hugged me instead.

I wanted to say something to ease the weight of this day. But silence grabbed hold of me, and I hid inside its familiar shelter. In that moment, against the dying light of day, I made a decision. I resolved to do anything I could to stay here rather than return to Peshawar and make a sound. New York only required this silent Muslim woman of me. I could perform accordingly, to survive.

Sarah let go of me with one hand on my shoulder. "Take care, Hajra," she said before crossing the street.

SEVENTEEN

It's a glorious day to drive the treacherous streets of Reservoir Hills, a historically Indian Durban suburb, where my search takes me next. Far below these heights, sunlight skims the ocean, and the high-rises of an idle downtown point at clear sky.

I imagine Rakesh Govender to be a middle-aged amateur historian. When Brenda scribbled and handed over his name to me, she didn't say anything else about him or how he could help in my search for the woman in the photograph. On the phone, he was terse and spoke only long enough to set up a meeting at his home. I'm prepared for someone just as patronizing as Dr. Naidoo from the university.

At his address, steps lead to a terrace patio, where I ring the doorbell and enjoy the view of tumbling slopes: a mosaic of green shrub and red roof. The metal gate scrapes open, and a man emerges barefoot. He is dark-skinned; his eyebrows and mustache are lustrous but neatly groomed. By way of contrast, his hair sticks up in mad-scientist curls, as if he has been pulling them in agitation. He has a buzzing vitality about him and is much younger than middle age. His manner, too, is softer than I expected. In person, he speaks in the sort of tone one reserves for small creatures. He invites me into a sparsely furnished living room and introduces me to his aunt—a wiry, shy woman who fusses over tea and snacks before she retreats to leave us alone.

Rakesh and I exchange no small talk. He doesn't seem to know how to say nothing. Even of the weather, he observes, "We get used to it, ay, these beautiful days. Sometimes, you need a visitor from far away. Then you see all this, right in front of you." He sweeps an arm to indicate the Reservoir Hills view—that majestic falling of green into light into blue. "Today in the morning, I was drinking my tea, and I thought—this is a good day for a newcomer. So then for a few minutes, I became a newcomer as well."

A slow smile plays across his features, and I'm lulled into the cadence of this conversation. And why not speak with meaning, even to a stranger, rather than sketching out drab niceties to begin every encounter? I dip below the surface with my response too. "What's strange is—I don't feel like a newcomer at all. Sometimes I think I've been to this city before. Especially the mountains. This landscape is so familiar to me."

His smile broadens and sharpens into a dimple on one cheek. "Good, good. Because sometimes people, they come here, and they say Durban isn't friendly. The doors are all closed." Rakesh's face clouds. "And I say, ay, but you must understand as well why you find our doors closed. Do you understand?"

"There is a sadness here." As soon as the words are out, I'm embarrassed by them. My trade is in file folders and books, not sadness.

Rakesh nods, unsurprised. Perhaps he took the measure of me right on the terrace and does not speak this way to everyone. "Think now, what's there to trust for us? This country, you know what about us? Only hatred. And so much sorrow we brought to come here. No one leaves their home from choice. You understand. Or else why would you come here, digging up the dead."

Heat flickers to my ears and chest. Brenda told him about my quest, and he is mocking me. Or else, he is offended. "I'm—I didn't mean to. Maybe I am looking for something from the dead. But only because—" I search for words. A quick breath, and they take shape. "Only because it's the truth. And people need to hear it. So I'm not digging up anyone away from their rest. I want to put them to rest. And . . . I've brought something of my own to bury. Or I'll keep wandering forever."

I'm whispering by the end of my confession. But, despite the noise of traffic and hum of a plane far above, I'm still too loud for the man not three feet away, whose every sense is tuned to the present. He holds the moment like a fledgling in his hands, quiet until its frantic heart returns to an even rhythm.

Eventually, he says, "What if you find something, but it isn't what you want? Then you'll think, 'I came so far just for this?'"

I don't hesitate. "Whatever I find will be what I need to know." With the words comes a flash of memory: wild geese in formation overhead in New York. Guided by a homing instinct they weren't taught. No ancestor pulled me to Durban, but I knew to fly here as if the path were encoded in my blood. I've been confident of so little in these years of fleeing and hiding. But I am sure of this one thing.

Rakesh nods, rises, and leaves the room. I float back to unsteady ground out of the alternate world our conversation seemed to inhabit. I've become so used to easy lies; I'm a novice at teetering over the edge of true.

He is gone long enough that I begin to wonder if he means me to leave or has forgotten my presence. But then he returns with a suitcase. It's the sort of old-fashioned valise a young woman might carry at a black-and-white train platform, steam rising up around her face.

Rakesh places the suitcase on the coffee table and sits next to me on the sofa. I'm intensely aware of the shape of his knees through linen, dark hair lining his arms, his woodsy scent. But I'm not uncomfortable. His physical closeness feels like a natural extension of our conversation.

He snaps open the case and lifts the lid to reveal sections of carefully organized files, pamphlets, and two smaller cardboard boxes. He flips through the labeled folders to extract the one he wants. In between our laps, resting on my knee and his, the file falls open to a plastic sleeve. Inside this sleeve is a well-preserved photograph yellowed by the years. Three women captured. As always, my eyes fall on the one in the middle who laughs.

"Where did you get this?"

"All this," Rakesh indicates the full contents of the suitcase, "was left to me by my great-grandmother. Her name was Maithili."

We establish soon that none of the three women in the yellowed protest photograph is Maithili. Rakesh has family photographs of his great-grandmother when she was younger. She was an unusual beauty with delicate, feline features and cannot be confused with anyone else, no matter how faded or blurry the picture. Still, her treasure trove of papers is the closest I've come to finding the laughing woman I seek.

I return to Rakesh's home every day in the week that follows. I arrive in the mornings when he is at work teaching biology at the local high school. His aunt lets me in and shows me to the table where the archival material is ready for me. I try to engage her in conversation and ask questions about family lore, but she stutters and gets flustered before rushing away. Judging by some of her faraway pieces of speech, I come to understand that she isn't entirely well and Rakesh cares for her because she's unable to live alone.

In the valise, I find newspaper clippings organized into folders with typed labels. I imagine Rakesh processing his inheritance with a steady hand and typewriter and wonder how he feels about it. I am hesitant with questions since our first, surreal meeting, as if the archive has raised a formality between us.

Occasionally, when he returns from work, we talk over my progress. Most days, though, while he's washing up or changing in the other room, I slip away and drive back to my dingy flat. There, I read over my notes, type them up, and fall asleep over my books. The days slip past into August, but I studiously avoid thoughts of courts and letters and Peshawar.

I'm careful not to intrude on Rakesh's routine because I don't want to overstay my welcome and lose access to the materials. Excavating them feels urgent, a matter of survival. Typing my notes one day, an irresistible notion seizes me: that I've been waiting for this discovery ever since leaving Peshawar. My life has not merely been a haphazard escape route, and Durban is more than another hiding place.

I stare often at the yellowed photograph. So far, the only additional piece of information I've gleaned is that the women are protesting in front of a whitewashed structure, maybe one of the old colonial buildings downtown. I've learned nothing new about the women's identities. But I surmise that Maithili knew these three women. I wonder why she wasn't at the protest herself. Maybe she was able to live a full life and pass on papers to her descendants because she did not participate that day—and her friends were not so lucky.

I search for other clues about a younger Maithili but struggle to find any information about her indenture. All Rakesh knows is that she arrived as a laborer. Among newspaper clippings about Gandhi and his wife, there's a group photograph in which Maithili stands proud in a back row next to the man Rakesh points out as her husband, his great-grandfather. He tells me that after her contract was over, she got married and went on to work for the rights of Indian coal miners in South Africa. We guess that the picture of the three women was taken during this period. But which of the mining protests took place in Durban? I know of the march Gandhi led from Natal to Transvaal. And protests in response to the infamous Asiatic Registration Law, including the bonfires they made of registration certificates. But none of those fits right with the timeline or context of this photograph.

Rakesh and I sit on his terrace and sip instant coffee, bitter from the bottom of the tin but sweetened with lots of sugar. He has convinced me to take a break, and Aunty has placed little meat pies on a table between us.

It's that magic hour after school and before homework, but no children play on this hillside street. It wouldn't be safe, Rakesh explains, or that's what their parents believe. He gestures at a sprawling bungalow at the street's upward curve and tells me they had a break-in last year. The whole family was held at gunpoint for hours while burglars emptied the place and took everything they could fit in a van. Even light bulbs.

He points out other houses up and down the block and lists his neighbors' grisly misfortunes. Knives, guns, murder. I'm reminded of the university researchers in Johannesburg who interviewed South Africans about violent crime and compared their accounts to the far milder police statistics. Of course, a ledger could not tally up their stories in black and white. Our lives take stranger shapes than paper permits.

Durban returns me to the precipice I thought I'd left behind in Peshawar. Life balanced on a knife's edge, calculating how many bars on the window could keep me safe. The same edge keeps the swing set in the yard next door creaky and empty of children. And the lawyer, Saadia, has asked me to return to Pakistan, where danger slithers inside my own home. No locks could keep it out.

As Rakesh begins another tale of violence, I burst in: "Why did it all turn out like this? This beautiful country?"

He snorts out a laugh with a cynical grate. "Why? We had a bloodless revolution, as the world loves to say."

It's the first time I've heard this note in his voice. Not despair but scorn—more caustic than disappointment. Embarrassed, I bite my lip. With my foolish question, I've adopted the guise of another naive, post-Apartheid Westerner with stars in my eyes. I should know better. I already understand simmering resentment in my bones. My life was shaped by its demands before I was born.

In silence, we watch the day sink into darkness. Though sunset must have lent a brief interlude between the intensities of night and day, we do not register it. We only remember that afternoon light, blink to adjust to the dark. We cannot reconcile the two.

His chair scrapes to break the quiet, and our empty mugs and plates clink as he piles them together. "Sorry," he says but doesn't explain.

I can find nothing to say. How long they have waited. He must yearn for the reconciliation that never arrived. We all yearn for it. The dream my grandparents fled their homes in India for, that my parents built with their hands in a new country. How well I recognize disappointment so caustic it could burn through cotton.

"I thought—I hoped it would be better here than my country," I venture at the front door. "And it is. But not the way I expected." I hesitate, unsure how much to reveal.

He relaxes against the doorframe and studies my face as I continue. "I mean, I know it's foolish to think everything would have changed here so quickly. But seeing all this suspicion and separation, still. It gives me no strength to take with me. I didn't even know I was searching for that. But I was."

He nods and opens his mouth as if to respond but then seems to think better of it. He looks away. And the moment is gone.

I gather my papers to leave for the night, refusing Aunty's invitation to dinner. Rakesh walks me down the front steps to my car. He holds open my door for a minute and gazes into darkness.

"People are afraid when they don't know," he says. "We still don't know each other here. But now, we can try at least. Before, we had no chance to meet. So in some ways—there are some things that are better."

With that, he smiles as I slide behind the wheel. He shuts the door.

My headlights trace a winding route up and down suburban hills as I head back toward the beachfront. People are afraid when they don't know, Rakesh said. I couldn't fully know the path Ali had to hack through Peshawar to survive. He was a child of refugees in a city that did not tolerate soft men.

But Ali could have chosen another path. He didn't have to align himself with Mohsin's violence. Unlike so many others in Peshawar, Ali did not want for an education. Our life was simple growing up and our parents' resources limited. But our home was filled with books of all kinds, from Agatha Christie to Kahlil Gibran to the Ramayana to Keats. The wide world of ideas lay open before him too.

In the blistering summers, we were often sent a couple of hours farther north, where Chhotu Chacha was posted for a while. His whitewashed house was surrounded by fruit orchards, butterflies of many colors, chipmunks bold enough to beg for food. And also bazaars where one could purchase smuggled machine guns. My childhood memories consist of the butterflies. The ripe mulberries we crushed and rubbed as rouge for our cheeks. Apricot perfect in my small fist, pit cracked open to marvel at its edible innards.

Perhaps for Ali, such moments of beauty pale beside the suffering that marked our family's circumstances. We were born into an impoverished city that hosted us with reluctance. I felt the loneliness of our refuge too.

But he could have let beauty shape him. He could have been a better man. Instead, he chose the rotted sediment underfoot. And I cannot forgive his choice.

EIGHTEEN

Between the kitchen, bedrooms, drawing room, and passages lined with paintings, Sita often lost her way. On her first day, Mary took her by the elbow and taught her the purpose of each corner of the house using a mixture of language and gesture. Later, Sita tried to remember Mary's directions and the rules that governed her movements. The front staircase, the dining room, to be used by her at only these times. The parlor had two doors, but she was only permitted this one.

Heart racing, she creaked open door after door, searching for Desmond's chamber. What if she burst in on the master in his library or the mistress taking her tea? No gentle correction could be expected from them. She'd understood this much when Mary slipped, fell, and broke a teacup one morning while preparing Desmond's breakfast tray for Sita to take upstairs. Without pausing to attend to her twisted foot, Mary glanced around the empty kitchen and swiftly gathered up the shards. Sita followed as she carried them out behind the chicken coop and buried them there, digging with her bare hands. After, she shook the earth from her fingers, the steadiness in her posture gone, and shot a hunted look at Sita. Understanding, Sita reached out and rubbed her arm to assure her of their secret. Neither spoke.

Sita's mornings began early. The sky was still cast with a rosy hue when she crossed the backyard to fetch water and take it to the worker quarters to wash and relieve herself. At that hour, the quarters were empty. The kitchen servants had to prepare breakfast and scrub the house before the master and mistress rose. And the field-workers had already left well before dawn to toil over cane. Sita could call these few minutes her own; not surrounded by unfriendly faces, not waiting on Desmond.

But she didn't have long before Desmond would begin to stir, so she had to run to take up his water and breakfast. Most days, she made it back in time, and he woke to the clink of spoon against plate as she set up his little table. Sometimes, he stuck out his face, frozen in a ghoulish expression, between the mosquito net curtains so that his head appeared disembodied. She jumped back in mock horror and yelped until he could hold the expression no longer and broke into peals of laughter. She mimed annoyance, then grabbed him by the middle and dragged him to his meal.

While he ate, she made his bed and set out his clothes and shoes. The first couple of mornings, she was flummoxed by the many folded and hanging garments in his wardrobe. She'd only seen white men's clothes from a distance and never paid close attention. But Desmond came over, pointed at the items he needed, and led her solemnly through the buttoning and strapping process.

Washed, dressed, combed, Desmond couldn't wait much longer while she tidied up his breakfast dishes. In the couple of minutes she spent bent over the table, he might win a sword fight with the rocking chair or attempt a somersault, mussing his hair and covering his fresh clothes with dust. Once, she had to change his clothes and bring him downstairs five minutes late. Mrs. Dickinson reprimanded her in a mixture of English and broken Tamil. Though Sita understood only a few of her words, their tone was humiliating.

The only contact she had with her employers was these brief exchanges when she dropped off and picked up Desmond for his visits. Most evenings, Mr. Dickinson paged through some paperwork and made no acknowledgment of Sita or the boy. As she left, she saw the mistress push Desmond across the room and urge him to greet his father in what Sita supposed was the correct manner. She never stayed long enough to learn the outcome of this greeting or whether Mr. Dickinson put aside his papers to regard his son. Whether these people embraced their children.

In the mornings, she might stay longer as Mrs. Dickinson questioned her about Desmond's care. Had he cleared his plate at mealtimes? Slept well? Nervous, Sita stumbled over her answers. She was tasked with caring for this woman's only child. The responsibility intimidated her into greater eagerness than she might otherwise have mustered for an employer she'd never chosen. But the mistress showed no emotion in response to these brief reports. If anything, she matched Sita's enthusiasm with equal sourness.

Afterward, Sita took the boy to his schoolmaster—a pinched man with a permanent scowl—and rushed to clean his room in his absence. All of her tasks concerned Desmond's care: washing, ironing, and mending his clothes; emptying his chamber pot; cleaning his bedroom and playroom; bathing and dressing him; fetching his water, breakfast, morning snack, afternoon tea, supper; putting him to bed at night.

Twice each day, when Desmond was with his parents, she looked forward to the moment when Vasanthi handed over her meal and they exchanged a greeting before each hurried back to work. Sita longed to sit down with Vasanthi or even meet others from the quarters. But she was separate from all of them. The other house servants ate breakfast before dawn and an early meal before preparing the master's supper. Sita could never join them because she ate around Desmond's schedule. The relative ease of her work and the hours she was permitted to rest while Desmond slept meant that she enjoyed a better position in this household. As ayah, she was not a common servant. And yet, in this role, she felt as though she'd been cast beneath the rest.

Mary was the only person she spoke to regularly. That moment over the broken teacup seemed to forge an early bond between them, and Sita began to look for her when Desmond was with his parents. Often, Mary could be found in the kitchen or the adjoining room, where she tackled freshly washed clothes with a coal-filled iron. They could only exchange limited English at first. But with gestures and Sita's growing Zulu vocabulary, they managed to communicate.

In this fit-start way, Sita learned that Mary did have a child: a baby girl who lived in the village with other family members. Mary herself had a room in the quarters she shared with two other Zulus employed by the estate. After work, by the light of an oil lantern, she crocheted little dresses and caps for her daughter in preparation for her next visit to the village at Easter. When the baby was older, she would go to school, Mary explained. She had come to work for the white man in service of that dream.

A few weeks after Sita's arrival at the estate, the mistress told her she would take Desmond with her into Durban very early the following morning. There would be no need for her to come along. She assigned plenty of chores to keep Sita occupied for the day—she must air out Desmond's bedding and beat the rugs from his playroom. But for the first time, Sita would be able to join the other house servants for meals. Perhaps she could even work alongside them.

The next morning, she had Desmond dressed and ready to go before dawn. As soon as he left, she dashed to the kitchen for breakfast. But it was empty, the fire almost out. She realized she'd never seen other girmit-karan eat here at the house. Only the white cook and occasionally Mary.

In the yard, the air was chill, and fog further obscured the eerie half-light. No chickens clucked; no maids swept the veranda. Near the worker quarters, she inhaled the distinct aroma of woodsmoke mingled with fried mustard seeds. Of course. Vasanthi brought in Sita's meals from the quarters because they would never be permitted to release the smells of their foods in the white people's kitchen.

Sita crept toward the wafting smoke. She was unsure how she'd be received by the field-workers she never saw. Around the corner, a woman of indeterminate age sat beside a wood stove. With a large ladle, the woman pounded the contents of a pot over the grate while a naked infant kicked the dust by her side. Sita couldn't see anyone else in the semidarkness, but she was aware of a flurry of activity all around. The distant rumble of hurried conversation, bare feet on packed earth, clink of bangles, the lilt of a small child's question. The woodsmoke was gentle as a feather as it brushed past. Warm as the crook of her grandmother's arm.

By degrees, she lost her sense of presence—she was neither in that other place nor this one. Disoriented, she stumbled back and stepped hard on a bit of rotting food against her heel. Only it wasn't food; it was a dead lizard. Head now yellow crush, dotted black eyes. She shrieked before she could stop herself. The woman at the stove started and looked up to see her. She rose from her stool, tucked one corner of her sari around into her waistband with purpose, and walked up to peer into her face. Sita was reminded of Anjali—less by her features and more by her expression of disdain.

"Who are you?"

"Sita," she said, then added, "the ayah."

The woman nodded, no longer interested, and returned to her stove.

Sita glanced around. A few children watched her saucer-eyed, but otherwise, no one seemed to pay her mind. She emerged uncertain from the shadows and gazed at the stove. This familiar ritual of a pot over embers.

"Come and sit here with us." Vasanthi was doing up her plait a few feet away. She smiled as she flicked her hair over one shoulder.

Sita wandered over to the cluster of younger women seated on the ground near Vasanthi. They balanced tin plates on knees or palms and stared at Sita in between morsels of balled rice dredged through steaming rasam.

Vasanthi handed Sita a plate. "Don't mind her." She stuck out her chin to indicate the woman still bent over her pot. "The married ones say we will taint their food with our bad luck. We make our own." She snorted and didn't bother to lower her voice. "They're just afraid of letting us near their husbands. As if we would want them." The older woman remained focused on her task but began to pound the pot with greater force.

Sita ate with relish and listened to the chatter about work, a coming day off. Dawn's haze began to lift into light, and the shapes of the girls' sun-dark faces turned clearer, as did the calluses and burn scars on their hands. They were shy around Sita. Surely, her dubious stature as ayah was not the only reason for the distance. Judging by their speech, they—like the women on the ship—came from lower origins. Maybe they'd noticed Sita's own smooth hands and light skin.

Only Vasanthi appeared equally at ease with everyone as she snatched pickle from one girl's plate with a laugh or slapped Sita's arm to emphasize the punch line to a joke. With a pang, Sita remembered Tulsi, who'd similarly been the natural leader of any group and unconcerned with old-world hierarchies. She'd guided her to this new land and was so easily lost by the harbor. She could be anywhere, and her fate might well have proved harsher than Sita's own.

Soon, the others left for the fields. Vasanthi and Sita headed back to the house. For the first time since she'd arrived, Sita worked alongside others. She rushed through the chores in Desmond's room and brought downstairs any tasks she could. She followed Vasanthi and

Mary around the house as she mended Desmond's clothes and polished his shoes. Sometimes, she paused her own work and helped
them instead. At lunch, one of the girls came up from the fields to
collect the overseer's meal and smiled shyly at Sita. They knew each
other now.

Vasanthi and Sita squatted in a corner of the back veranda for
their own midday meal. With the white cook nearby, they could not
be nearly as free with their talk. Still, Sita was overwhelmed by the
luxury—to speak and listen, to be together. She had learned to live
without connection. And yet, this slip into friendship was so easy,
like waking from a brief slumber.

As they cleared the remains of their meal, they heard a flurry of
activity behind them. Mrs. Dickinson, still in her traveling cloak, had
swept into the kitchen. She issued orders to the cook for dinner and
supervised the man who carried in her brown paper purchases from
town. Vasanthi had been telling the story of a wedding she'd attended
as a young girl, when she danced suggestively in the village square
and caused a minor scandal. But now she stopped midsentence, and
her mouth hardened into a sullen line. The tap of boots on stone
broke through their silence as Mrs. Dickinson stepped out onto the
veranda.

"Sita, go inside at once!" Her clipped Tamil was always ugly but
harsher today than usual. Sita glanced at Vasanthi in surprise, but her
friend's gaze was cast to one side, and her jaw was clenched.

As Sita reached the kitchen door, a river of stowed vitriol seemed
to break loose from Mrs. Dickinson. Most of it was rapid English that
she couldn't catch. But she gathered that Vasanthi was lazy like the
rest of her kind, she was influencing the ayah with her bad habits yet
again, and had either of them considered how their behavior might
affect the young master?

Vasanthi said nothing. Her glare spoke for her. Stony, she stared
unblinkingly at the white woman. After a moment, a contemptuous
sneer began to curl her lip, and she sniggered her disdain audibly. But
this was too much for the mistress. Taking a sudden step forward, she
swung her palm across Vasanthi's catlike face.

The slap reverberated through Sita's own pulse. Everything was
still for that single beat. She stood frozen, one hand at the kitchen
door. Slowly, Mrs. Dickinson turned around. She narrowed her eyes

at Sita, and they exchanged a glance heavy with implication. Then, unexpectedly, instead of her unleashing more abuse, Mrs. Dickinson's face slackened. She pushed Sita aside roughly and stormed back inside.

The kitchen resumed behind her. Even the pecking chickens and breeze in the yard seemed to return to a steady rhythm. Vasanthi rubbed her reddening cheek and began gathering their plates. Sita raised an eyebrow at her, but she only shrugged.

"You should go to the boy," she said in a dull undertone.

Sita crept up the back stairs. The boy she was to raise in his mother's stead had returned home and was waiting for her. But just for a moment, she stopped on the flagstones because her breath was too quick. Perhaps it was the shock of Mrs. Dickinson's violence. Or the years of servitude that stretched ahead now, steep as these stairs.

She opened Desmond's bedroom door gently in case the child had tired and fallen asleep. But she was knocked almost to the ground by the ball of blond hair that barreled into her.

"Ayah!"

He was tall for his age, so his head hit the base of her sternum. Gentle knock from his brow to her heart. Neither of them spoke, but this stranger's child had missed her. She knew, now, that he loved her. The realization was not a surprise but a sadness. Could she ever return his love? He was only a child, not responsible for his parents, his people—and yet.

Stroking his yellow head, she remembered Pushpa, whose tiny bundle was cast overboard by the surgeon without ceremony. Perhaps the same waters had claimed a phantom baby of Sita's too. Her imagined life with her groom-to-be, the children she should have already borne. Though in this new world, there was still time. So Tulsi had assured her. Sita was neither old nor tainted by disaster, as she'd been in her village. Here, she could still dream of making a home.

And yet. Because of Desmond, many years must pass before she could have a child of her own. Unlike the field laborers, she could not be house servant and mother. She could not be ayah and wife. Her hand came to rest against the boy's neck. She kissed the top of his sweet-smelling head.

When Sita had the dream again, it was different. The road was red. She could see it stretching into the distance like a string pulled taut. And at its far end, a plume of dust darkened the sky. It approached fast along with the sound of hooves or thunder. She waited and watched. Her heartbeat pounded all the way to her temple.

Out of the dust cloud, the shape of a girl emerged. Behind her, an elephant wild in musth.

Sita stretched out her arms. Her fist closed around the girl's reaching fingers. She pulled, laughing in triumph. But then, she looked past the girl's black curls. Behind her was an older woman still left in the street. She would not survive the beast. It was too late for her.

* * *

Tulsi came to visit one day at the end of the harvest season. She'd memorized the name *Dickinson* when the women parted and had promised to find her friend one day. Sita herself had held out little hope. Tulsi was a face from that other shore. Everything else from her past had been ripped away, so why should this one good thing survive?

Fortunately, Tulsi did not abide by such fatalism. She asked every stable boy and peddler and friendly merchant until one agreed to take a message next time he stopped by the Dickinson plantation. So Sita learned that her friend was situated at another estate some thirty miles up the coast and that she planned to visit when she could.

Just after the harvest and threshing were past, when cold began to edge around the first and last light of day, she came. Tulsi's master was a lenient man who always allowed his servants their Sundays off. Now, he had even given them three full days for rest and feast after the busy season. Some arranged a caravan to the city for the day, and Tulsi had them drop her off in the morning and promise to collect her that night on their return.

So she turned up at the kitchen door and asked for her. When Mary came up to tell Sita she had a visitor, she knew it was Tulsi. She dashed out and embraced this only figure familiar to her in all the land.

"You'll squeeze the life out of me, girl," Tulsi said with a wry smile, same as ever.

She stepped back off the veranda and gazed up at the house, shading her eyes. "What a strange place. Is that a chicken up there?" She let a theatrical shiver run through her. "Cold, it feels like. And so big!

So many windows to clean. Our master has five children and nothing like this. Well, they must be very rich."

Luckily, it was one of the days Mrs. Dickinson took Desmond into town. So Tulsi could follow Sita around for her chores. But her usual laughter gave way to brooding the more time she spent in the house. The weight of its silent opulence seemed to affect even her. When they entered Desmond's room, she shivered again, but it was no act this time. Subdued, she wandered around and ran a hand over the smooth lines of the dresser. She opened a drawer to exclaim over the boy's fine linens.

"They make you sleep in the house?" She stood over Sita's neat roll of bedding in its corner. "All alone? I've never heard of such a thing." She frowned and ran a quick glance over Sita's body, up and down.

Sita shrugged and wiped down the breakfast table. She'd assumed all ayahs had to sleep in the nursery, having never met another. And that all white people inhabited houses as vast and unnerving as this one.

Tulsi lent a hand for the rest of the chores, so they went double-quick. After, the two friends slipped away to the worker quarters for the luxury of some quiet conversation before the field laborers came in and Tulsi's people returned to fetch her.

Though the day had a chill edge, they found a grassy patch at the women's end and huddled in a nook there, safe from winds and prying eyes. Sated with the small treats Tulsi brought from their harvest feast, they told stories of good meals from their past. Sita brushed quickly past her memories lest their luster fade under scrutiny.

But Tulsi's sharp eye did not allow easy nostalgia. "Why?" she shot back in her pointed manner. "Why would you remember the village so fondly? What did they ever do for you? Me, I'm glad to be here among the Zulus. I'm just another girmit-kari to them. They don't care about my marriage or name. I can be anyone I choose among them. Better than our own people, always gossiping and fighting. I'm better off here—you are too."

Sita leaned back against the wall and watched a beetle near her foot climb a blade of grass. Anjali's face rose before her, resentment carved in early lines around her mouth. Also, though, the faces of the Zulu men at the docks. The boy who took care of the Dickinsons' oxen and never returned her nodded greeting.

"But they don't want us here," she said in a low tone. "Do you not see that?"

"Some, yes," Tulsi reflected after a pause. "But not all. And anyway, can you blame them? We came here to do the work they resisted. They are stronger than we were, look—we just lay back like a common whore and let the whites have their way with our land. Isn't it?"

Tulsi laughed, and Sita tried to join her but could only manage a weak smile. The other woman's easy language made her uncomfortable. Under her grandmother's tight watch, coarse talk had never been tolerated in their household. But Tulsi's words were also a reminder that Sita was no longer that girl constrained by her family's requirements. No one here cared about her manners. Such freedom also brought a dizzying sense of falling. Without the rules to govern her as tether, she could drift away through night sky.

"Maybe that's true," she allowed. "But what future do we have here? I used to know who I needed to be back there." She hesitated. "There's a dream I've had since I was a child." In a tumble, she told Tulsi its contours, adding, "You probably think it's foolish to set store by dreams. But I was told—that's my daughter. This girl who will reach out to save me. And now? How can I make an ordinary woman's life here?"

Tulsi cocked her head to one side. "I don't think dreams are foolish. But are you so sure you understand its meaning?"

"Ayamma said it was my daughter."

"And maybe she was right at the time. Things have changed. Even the dream changed, no? Who knows. Maybe the other girl is your daughter. But is she your own? Is she your blood child?"

Sita started, confused. "What other kind of child can there be?"

Tulsi yawned and stretched her arms wide. "What do I know, ma? I'm only saying to ask questions. Don't be so sure about what you remember. Did you ever belong in that village, a girl like you?"

A memory of the river. Under water, the world had been silent. She'd blown bubbles under the surface, and women's voices engaged in women's work had been far away. Colorless fish darted past her belly.

"I don't know," she said finally. "But . . . it was still our place. The soil was known to our ancestors, and they taught us to plant it. Here, I don't even know the name of this fruit with its prickly skin and the pale flesh inside. I wouldn't know how to peel it—couldn't know food from poison even—if the other girls didn't tell me."

"So. There you are." Tulsi jabbed at the air, her finger sticky with litchi juice. "We make the land ours. One girl helps another, and she tells the next one." She burped and scratched at a bit of peel caught between her teeth. "Listen, ma, this is all talk. But—land. Land is real. It's why I returned here." She gathered a fist full of red earth, uprooting bits of grass, and let the damp grains sift through her fingers. Ants scurried to and fro over the little hill she made. "You don't remember my seeds? What did they tell you about your payment? Some of these arkatis don't know much themselves. When you finish, you can take a ship back. Or you can take land. They will give you a small piece if you choose."

"For yourself? That you can own?" Sita was incredulous. An unmarried girl owning land?

Tulsi snorted. "You're a funny one. Make big eyes at everything, like a child."

Sita blinked. "I haven't been a child in many years," she shot back. "Not since the day my father died."

"Yes." Tulsi sighed after a pause. "I see that. And you got here too. This journey made old women out of all of us. But still, you have something of the child. You have dreams, and you remember them."

Sita shifted from her crouched position and stretched out her legs. The close examination was making her uncomfortable. "Forget all that. Tell me about the land. Is it really true?"

"I heard about it. I didn't meet anyone who took it, but everyone says it is so. Me, last time, I took the passage home. Where would I find money to build a house on this land? You have to buy seeds and animals for a farm. I went home. I won't be so stupid this time. Home!" She spat out the peel she'd finally teased from its crevice in her teeth. "What is home for one such as me? Imagine how they greeted me. Those people who decided what we are. They're not our people, Sita ma. This is our land now."

As time went on, Sita began to see the other women as often as she could. Most often, she snuck out after Desmond was asleep and slipped down to the quarters. On those nights, she pushed her evening meal back to Vasanthi and whispered, "I'll eat later, with you."

Vasanthi ate only after the Dickinsons' supper was done, the kitchen scrubbed, and each fork put away. She and Mary and the men in the scullery were permitted to gulp down a few bites separately when the white maid and cook sat down to their meal. But Vasanthi preferred, she said, to go back to the quarters and eat later without rush. She would rather stay hungry for the sake of this little pride.

Though the women from the fields had already eaten by the time she came, some stayed up and kept her company for her lantern-lit dinner. Whenever possible, Sita engineered her way into these late-night sessions where Vasanthi reigned supreme.

After Desmond's room was dark, she crept to a corner near the door and waited for the house to settle. She could make an excuse if Mrs. Dickinson saw her on the back stairs—a cup of warm milk for Desmond—but she would rather avoid the woman's temper. Besides, Vasanthi would still be at work in the kitchen this early.

Soon, she heard the clack of heels on the stairs. Mrs. Dickinson was turning in. The master would work in his library until much later; running into him on her return from the quarters was always possible. But the risk was nothing compared to the reward: a couple of hours to sit with ease and hear her own language and laugh all the way from her stomach.

Taking her chance, she slipped out and ran down the back stairs, through the narrow passageway to the kitchen, and into night. Only then did she let out the breath she'd held. A rush of sweet air filled her lungs to replace it. Packed earth cool under her feet, she half skipped through the yard, past the chickens clucking in roost. A shortcut through the litchi grove took her to the clearing around which huts were arranged. Some distance away were the old worker barracks, now abandoned, where men sometimes went to drink and smoke dagga.

Sita made a wide circle around the perimeter to avoid the areas for married couples and single men. At the former, she was not welcome, and at the latter, she was a little *too* welcome. Finally, she reached the women gathered around a fire, her friends, who said, "Sita, you have come tonight; we are so glad." Two of them moved aside to make room, and she sank down cross-legged.

Vasanthi had not yet arrived with their food, but she hadn't been in the kitchen either. Where could she be? The other women offered some of their paltry leftovers. But Sita refused with thanks; she savored the sharing of a meal with another and would wait.

One woman was speaking of a laborer who always contrived to work near her in the fields and whispered lascivious remarks. "I want no quarrel with his wife," she said. Some of the others gave her advice or told their own stories. "And if he doesn't leave you alone," one of them said, "just tell Vasanthi. She'll put him right."

They all laughed. As if on cue, Vasanthi came rushing up out of breath, her hair loose. Someone took the bundle of food she carried and offered a portion of cumbu and steamed eggplant to Sita. Vasanthi grabbed her own and ate ferociously, hardly pausing to swallow or speak. But then, once fed, she stopped and stared at Sita.

"What are you doing here?" she barked. "Why did you come here alone? You should have waited for me."

Sita's face burned in the firelight. Vasanthi never spoke to her like that. Yes, the first few times Sita visited the quarters at night, she'd waited for Vasanthi in the kitchen, and they'd walked down together. One night, though, she waited for hours before she gave up and returned upstairs, disappointed and hungry. The next day, Vasanthi apologized and muttered something about having forgotten. But something in her demeanor told Sita otherwise. Maybe Vasanthi resented her like a clinging little sister. She resolved to find her own way, and since then, she came here by herself most of the time.

"Why do you care?" Sita retorted now.

Vasanthi started as if the answer were obvious. "Because it's not safe alone, foolish girl."

For a moment, Sita was too confused to remain indignant. "Not safe? What do you mean? You came here by yourself. You go back and forth alone every day."

Vasanthi was quiet as she ran her tongue around her mouth. She rose, deliberate, to her feet and seemed about to leave. But then she turned and tugged the tucked end of her sari loose from her waist. She rolled down the folds there at the small of her back until they could all see the swell of her buttocks and the beginnings of the crease.

Ordinarily, Sita would avert her gaze; she'd always been embarrassed about glimpsing the hidden places of other women. But now, like the others in the circle, she was transfixed. Not by Vasanthi's uncovered skin but by what was pressed against her side, held there by the fabric. A flat, worn piece of wood attached to a leather sheath.

"I go back and forth alone," Vasanthi said as she slid it from her waist and removed the sheath, "because I always carry a knife."

In the moonlight, the short blade shone cruel. It was sharpened and ready. Vasanthi replaced the sheath, hid the knife again, and pulled up her sari. When she bent and turned, Sita tried to catch a glimpse of the weapon's outline beneath cotton. But it was hidden too well.

The other women were subdued by this revelation and the ominous tone in which it was made. Their chatter faltered to a murmur. When Vasanthi left to relieve herself, they began to gather their things, though it was still early. As Sita helped tidy up, she overheard a whisper: "Does he not see it, then, when she undresses for him?" And the response: "Maybe he likes it."

She stood up straight to see who had spoken, but all of them fell silent. Not one would meet her gaze. Before she could ask questions, Vasanthi returned.

"Come," she said. "I'll walk you back."

Sita was still annoyed about her earlier scolding, but Vasanthi's tone now was kind. She couldn't bring herself to refuse. They walked together in silence and came to a halt near the chicken coop, where Sita muttered her thanks before continuing to the house. At the door to the kitchen, she glanced back. The moon was at least half-full and the night clear. Vasanthi stood still where they'd parted. Her arms were wrapped about her own body. She made a frail statue. Durga without the strength of outstretched limbs. Moonlight found the dips of her clavicles and lingered over the valleys of her cheeks. Then, as if startled awake, she came to life and disappeared into shadow.

When they met in the kitchens or over meals in the next few days, Sita observed Vasanthi more closely. But she was mischievous and light of step, same as always. For a while, Sita avoided the quarters, not only because of Vasanthi's warning but also because of the strange things she'd overheard. She turned the words over and over through her chores. Perhaps it had been a joke. But the insidiousness in that voice and the cynic's response told Sita otherwise. And this thought, too, made her wary of returning to the campfire: If the women saw Vasanthi as their protector—a dog they could set on men who did not behave—then who would protect Vasanthi?

Eventually, she began to visit the quarters again, though she was more guarded around the other women now. They must have noticed because they were solicitous and tried to include her. They asked about her daily routine, what it was like to care for Desmond. They were curious about this child who was rarely seen near the sugar fields.

"Is he like his mother or his father?" a woman asked.

Sita had to think. "Certainly his temper is very different from the mistress. I hardly see the master. What is his temperament?"

"Oh, the baas rarely visits the fields. The overseer and sirdar are our masters. The baas does walk through to observe the crop every now and then. On those days, we must look sharp and work twice as fast, or the overseer will bring out the whip."

Sita winced and ducked her head. The women often spoke casually of the overseer's whip. Though this shrugged resignation was perhaps natural, she could never become accustomed to it. House servants did not face the whip except for very serious transgressions. Sita had never seen its use in her months of work thus far, only the rumor or threat of it. To avoid the subject, she picked the earlier thread back up. "He is still very young, the child. It is difficult to compare him to the parents. But I think, one day, he will be like his father. That is the way."

It was a line she repeated to herself often—a reminder to harden her heart against this child only temporarily under her care. The women nodded knowingly.

One added, "But the ayah, too, has influence. An elder in my village returned after working as ayah to a British family in Madras for many years. She raised all the white children. Never married herself. And the youngest called her Amma, so she told us."

Sita believed the story. She mothered Desmond in every sense of the word. But as he grew older, Sita would become another dark-skinned woman who served him. This, too, was the way. At best, she would remain a pleasant memory from his childhood. The thought recalled a question she'd been meaning to ask. "Who was the ayah before me?"

The women fell silent. A few exchanged glances. The one who spoke before leaned in: "No one has told you about her? About what happened to her?"

Sita shook her head. Because of Desmond's age, she assumed the previous ayah left when her five-year contract ended. She hadn't imagined any special reason for her departure.

The woman leaned in further with the air of revealing something sordid. "She was thrown out. The mistress cast her out one fine morning. Raised the young master since he was an infant, and she was not even allowed to say goodbye to him."

Another nodded. "They say the young master cried himself feverish for weeks after she left. And no wonder."

"But why?" Sita was bewildered. No misdeed of the ayah's could supersede Desmond's own well-being.

The woman gave her a sly look. "She was a young, pretty thing. The mistress was . . . suspicious."

"What? Of her husband? Surely not—white men would only lie with their own."

One of the women snickered. "Come now, Sita," she said. "You know better."

She considered. Yes, the surgeon on the ship had grabbed her and other women as well. But that was on board a ship where no white women were available to satisfy their desires. Here on the estate, a couple of the white farmhands did smirk or whistle when she passed them, but that was the way of men everywhere. She shook her head. "The mistress must have been mistaken."

She left the quarters early that night to return to the house. Vasanthi had not yet arrived, so Sita hadn't eaten. But she didn't want to stay and listen to more gossip. Her head spun with questions over the familiar route back to the house. *You know better*, they said. But she was no longer sure of what she knew and what she hid, even from herself. A cricket landed near her foot, and she bent to scoop it into her cupped hands. It chirped once and leaped into her face. She had to stifle a laugh as she batted the cheeky creature away.

Tulsi had mocked her a few weeks earlier for being a wide-eyed child. *You have dreams.* Her implication: that Sita was naive to hold on to childhood preoccupations. And here, more proof. Only children played in the dirt with birds and insects. Grown women never paid much heed to what scrabbled at their feet. It was time Sita entered that adult world and abandoned this other foolish one made up of dreams and wild creatures. She'd nurtured its flame through so many storms, but now, the time had come to snuff it out.

As she emerged from her brooding, the litchi grove seemed newly sinister. The pathways between trees crisscrossed with shadow and silver on this clear, moonlit night. Shapes alive with malice leapt in her way as the wind shook branches and leaves whispered in her ear. She quickened her pace and longed for the peace of Desmond's room, devoid of intrigue.

Ahead, she could smell the chicken coop and the way out. She crept forward as quiet as she could. The open yard just beyond— visible from the kitchen—was the easiest place to get caught. Her footsteps were noiseless, but theirs were not. She heard them before she saw them.

At the far edge of the grove, his white skin gleamed in darkness. They are so vulnerable to sight, to sun, Sita mused. Their skin is their traitor. By comparison, Vasanthi melted into night. She was a shape-shifter, a water creature. Sita recognized her only by the white skin she blocked from the light. Her head was a curved bite of the man's shoulder, her arm a snake that twisted around his waist and split him half. And then her laugh, unmistakable. Her arm slipped from the man. She pushed at him playfully, and he pretended to fall back. She laughed again. He reached for her, but she was too quick. She slipped away and ran toward the quarters. They had been in the midst of goodbye.

The man did not watch Vasanthi disappear into the grove. He did not sigh to himself a little or look up at the stars. He indulged in none of the things Sita imagined for a lover when his beloved leaves him. Instead, he turned smartly on his heel and took long strides back toward the house. He did not try to soften his footfalls to conceal them. He did not dash through the open, risky yard.

So even if Sita had not seen his face caught by the moonlight, she would have known that Vasanthi's lover was the master.

NINETEEN

When I pull up to Rakesh's driveway on a Saturday morning, he is crouched into a ball in his little garden. I spot his yellow shirt in among the green bush and venture closer.

"Didn't want to miss the light filtered through the clouds," he says, still unmoving. His back is all I can see.

A click and I finally understand he has a camera in hand. Slowly, he rises and turns around, a dazed look across his features. Without speaking, he gestures to the unremarkable grassy patch beside him. When I shake my head in confusion, he beckons me nearer, and we both bend down. He points to a tiny pale mushroom sprouting next to the desiccated remains of a millipede. A few pink petals have fallen here too.

"You were photographing this?" I turn to him. His curls are made lush by the humid morning, and a film of sweat lends his neck a bronze sheen.

"It's just a hobby." He rises quickly, and I realize that he might have thought I was mocking him.

"But it's beautiful. I would never have noticed, even." I stand up, and blood rushes to my head. Unsteady, I reach out for balance and find his elbow. The skin there is like soft leather.

He glances from his arm to my face and smiles. "Let's see. I'll show the print to you when—"

But the rest of his sentence is lost to an immense thunderclap. Together, we turn our gazes skyward, and in that same instant, rain crashes down in sheets without a single drop of warning.

For a beat, we are frozen in place. Far away, a girl screams. Cold streams down my back, and I let out a shriek that is also a half-laugh.

Rakesh grabs my hand, the camera cradled under his other arm, and we leap over the drive and up the front steps. The rain is pummeling my scalp hard. I cry out when I miss a step and slip, but Rakesh has my hand, and he pulls me onto the covered terrace in time.

Panting, he lets go, flicks the rain from his eyes, and shakes off his camera. In between catching my breath, a laugh wheezes from me. He matches it, and in a moment, we are both overcome. I laugh until my sides hurt. I have to grab the railing to steady myself because I'm dizzy with it all: the soaking downpour, pungent mushrooms in the garden, and the drumming of rain against red earth.

I begin to look forward to the end of each workday when Rakesh returns home and we have a few minutes for conversation before I return to the flat. He's not my only social connection here. I've struck up other tentative friendships in Durban too. Reshika has had me over for dinner, and twice I've met Ishara and Rajni for coffee along fashionable Florida Road.

But Rakesh is different from them. His thoughts meander a path of his own. His close attention to the ordinary makes it brighter and stranger at the same time. He's different, really, from anyone I've met. This thought startles me, but then I remember—he's a research contact. No wonder his musings fascinate me. I've struggled to understand my connection to this place and its people, the precise nature of the excavation that drew me here. Rakesh is fluent in dreamlike liminal spaces, and he can help me in my quest. That's all.

So I begin to relax into our conversations on the terrace. He tells me that the outlandish birds perched in his trees are purple-crested touracos. They are so bizarre in appearance, they must belong to a distant planet. The towering tree next door turns out to be a jamun, familiar to me from Pakistan. Rakesh calls it naaval maram and tells me its fruit stains the driveway every summer. Like the noisy mynah birds, this tree, too, is a species introduced to Durban by Indians.

I'd assumed the monkeys that dash across the road and through his kitchen were brought from India as well. But they're native to this region, he says. Vervet monkeys. Humans encroached on their world, and that's why they're here in the city like bandits who steal food and stuff their mouths with orange cheese curls. So many layers of invasion in this city of sediment. The monkeys dangle from the eaves and taunt us with their acrobatics even as we clap our hands and shout to chase them away.

It's my mother's birthday, so I buy a phone card and call Peshawar from Rakesh's landline in the middle of a workday. Though we're still a continent apart, the time difference between my mother and me has narrowed to a couple of hours. I forgot that, so I'm confused at first by her greeting:

"You're awake so early?"

I've mentioned nothing of this trip to my parents. When I last called two months ago or more, I filled the twenty minutes with questions instead: family gossip, the price of tomatoes. I said nothing about my own life beyond perfunctory reports about health and studies.

I clutch the receiver and gaze out the window. A young woman with beads threaded through braided hair is climbing up the street beyond Rakesh's yard. What shall I tell my mother about who or where I am? I couldn't hope to scale the chasm between us. I must begin where I stand.

"I'm in South Africa. Durban, on the east coast. For research."

She pauses, perhaps considering the nature of our silences. "Africa?" she says finally. "I didn't know you were studying it."

"I didn't know either."

She laughs. "That sounds like you. Go to China if you must, to gain knowledge. The Prophet said that. You went farther!"

I smile. I didn't know it was "like me" to abandon everything and travel so far on impulse. But she would know. My mother. Eager to hasten the thaw, I volunteer further details. Our creaky speech warms into a conversation as I reveal bits and pieces of my research.

"And when will you go back to America?"

I hesitate. My return flight date is fast approaching. And so is August 30, the court date from Saadia's letter. Carefully, I consider what to say. "I'm thinking about changing my ticket and visiting Pakistan on my way back. I have a stopover in Dubai anyway, so—" I come to an abrupt halt, unsure how much to reveal.

"You'll come here? To Peshawar?"

"Maybe. I don't know. What do you think?"

"What do I think? But this is your home. Of course we want you to come. We have been waiting for you to return—all of us." This last phrase tremulous with implication.

In an instant, my mouth is awash with bitterness. *All of us.* My mother and I never speak of Ali. Long ago, I insisted on that condition for my phone calls home to continue. That *all of us* is the closest we've come in years. Now, I wonder if my brother still lives in the room we shared as children and sleeps under my sun-and-moon bedspread. No consequence for his actions. Or maybe he left and found a new home camping near the Afghan border, dressed in khaki with a gun strapped across his chest. These and worse imaginings wake me from sleep before I banish them.

Once my mother learns about the court date, her message will change. She won't welcome me home when my testimony poses a threat to her golden boy. Swallowing a hard point in my throat, I lie and say the phone card is almost over. I'll call again once I decide about my travel, I assure her.

Afterward, the neighborhood around Rakesh's home is quiet. A fine rain mists the valley below. I gather my scarf closer to my throat and tuck my chin inside.

That afternoon, I'm unable to concentrate. After staring out the window for much of the day, I pack up my notes. Rakesh pulls into the driveway as I'm edging out the front door.

"Leaving so early?" he asks when he gets up to the terrace.

I shrug. I'm in no mood to explain. "You're early too."

He gazes at me for an uncomfortable moment. I expect him to ask more questions, but instead, he says, "I'm here to get my camera. I'm going to the nature reserve nearby. The light's good—finally." Another beat and then, casually, "Want to come?"

Without waiting for my answer, he disappears into the house. I don't feel like company. But if I say no today, maybe there won't be another invitation.

"I'll just come for a little while," I tell Rakesh when he emerges with a camera bag slung over one shoulder. "I have a lot of work."

"As you like," he says.

I follow Rakesh's old station wagon along his neighborhood's streets as they broaden into wide avenues and a shopping center.

Down one more curve, we pull into a small parking lot tucked beside a trailhead. Beyond a board with a graffiti-covered map of the nature reserve, a path disappears into brush. As Rakesh and I head down the trail, I'm already fighting the urge to leave. I want to burrow underground today. Still, I continue trudging behind Rakesh because it's easier than making the effort to turn around.

With each step, the bush reminds me that it is alive. The undergrowth rustles, and birds flutter in the treetops. The path narrows, winds around, then stops. Rakesh steps aside so I can see beyond him. We're at a small pond. Bright pink lilies bloom across its surface. A tiny frog near my foot leaps in, and green water ripples behind him.

Rakesh crouches down, and I step back to allow him light and space. We make no sound save the clicks of his camera. But his concentration is a kind of language. It draws my attention to the worlds I would miss while lost in sadness. Droplets caught by the forked petals of a lily. A clutch of white eggs on a dying leaf. Lichen like fingers stretching a sinister pattern across a branch.

Eventually, he straightens up; we return down the little path and choose another. Red earth muddied by the earlier rain kicks up at our feet. Around the corner, a vast gorge opens up and stretches far above us. The bush here is winter yellow, and a lazy stream trickles below. Generations layer through in earthen hues along the gorge walls. We clamber down to the base. Here, a few teenagers silently pass a joint back and forth. One raises a hand in greeting, and we return it before continuing along the bank. Rakesh discovers a patch of mosses growing in a gap among the rocks and stays to investigate. I continue wandering along the stream's edge and collect pebbles in my pockets.

Eventually, I perch on a large rock and gaze out at the gorge's expanse. For a while, I'd forgotten my cares, but the world is still gray. Rakesh finds me, sits nearby, and joins my contemplation.

He has not asked me a single question. But, unexpected, I decide to speak anyway. "I called my mother today."

"Oh?" He pauses. "Was it difficult?"

Most people would respond with a trite phrase. Not Rakesh. I glance at him with a smile, surprised by the tears that well up in the same moment. I turn to hide my face and blink them away. "Sometimes I feel so alone."

He's silent awhile. "I know how that can be. When I feel that way, I come here."

I look back at him, up and down. "You feel lonely? But—this is your home."

He laughs gently. "Yes. And wasn't it like that for you there, in Pakistan?"

In between our words is something I want to understand, but it's like the sun in eclipse. I can't look at it directly.

He continues: "I never really fit in around here. That's how it is for some of us, isn't it?"

I nod slowly. "You're right. I never really fit in either. In Pakistan. I'm not sure; maybe it was because my parents weren't from there—or something else. I was always saying the wrong thing. Or saying too much." I pause. "I suppose, I thought, it was different for you. You have this community. Your students. But—" I tighten my arms around myself. I haven't thought through any of my assumptions with care.

"It's not so simple, and I think you know that. This land is and is not mine."

"You don't think of South Africa as yours?"

"South Africa." He shrugs with a wry smile. "Words rich men made up to suit them. Words can't change the land. The ashes of my ancestors didn't nourish this ecosystem into being. So, that's how it is. Yes, this land has sheltered me like its own. But there is something sad between us too. You can call it loneliness."

My breath catches. I want to extend a hand. Instead, we watch the horizon begin to tinge with pink. When we cannot stay any longer, we rise and dust ourselves off and retrace our steps to the parking lot.

On an evening when I'm cataloging the last of Maithili's materials, Rakesh insists I stay for dinner. "Aunty has cooked something special. She wants you to stay."

I've been there all afternoon, reading and taking notes, but Aunty hasn't breathed a word of invitation herself. She's been in the kitchen most of the time and communicated only with shy smiles when she did scurry through. Maybe Rakesh is using her as an excuse. But he doesn't seem the sort to need excuses.

The table is crowded with dishes. Save the basmati rice, the rest are unfamiliar to me. A pungent smell of fish presides as Rakesh and

I take our places and Aunty fusses back and forth from the kitchen. She seems content to watch us eat from the doorway, but we refuse to begin until she sits down.

I slop large spoonfuls of rice onto my CorningWare dish. I'm looking forward to the meal. My experiences with home-cooked Durban food so far at Ishara's and Reshika's have mostly consisted of comforting but unexciting casseroles and potato salads. Perhaps Rakesh's family hails from a different region, or maybe his aunt cooks closer to her Tamil roots, but everything on the table is foreign to me. I ladle a soupy concoction onto my bed of rice, and watery gravy floods my plate. Gray dumplings plop out, and I catch a strong whiff; the fishy aroma definitely came from this. Aunty smiles at me encouragingly from across the table. Rakesh busily composes his own plate. I spear a dumpling with my fork, but instead of slicing in two, it tears open like a water balloon and spills a mound of tiny white specks.

"Fish eggs," Rakesh observes. "You've tried this kind before?"

"No." I try not to sound appalled. "And these are . . .?" I wave my fork over the dumplings.

"The egg sacs, cooked fresh in curry. A childhood favorite of mine. But you don't have to eat it."

Rakesh tucks away his own meal unperturbed, but I catch his aunt's face eager for approval, and I don't have the heart to turn away. I try a forkful—heavy on rice, light on egg sac—and give Aunty a thumbs-up. I'm afraid I'll gag if I try to speak.

I make my way through the meal with a kind of heroism. My efforts are stymied for a moment by a particularly vile preparation of beetroot—never a favorite—which tastes as if it were dredged in sand and fried in blubber. But I get through most of the helping Aunty has thrown onto my plate and hide the last few morsels under empty mussels shells. Afterward, the three of us linger around the table, and I gulp down mouthfuls of coffee. Three cups will likely ensure a restless night but help cover up the fishy aftertaste on my tongue.

For most of the meal, we've been silent or spoken of everyday things: Rakesh's day at school, a small café I've discovered near the Botanic Gardens. But now, Rakesh turns to the research: "So how's the reading? You found some good stories from my great-grandma?"

I'm relieved that he's raised the topic, though nervous as well. I've wanted to talk through my findings, but I've felt unsure about how

Rakesh connects with his migrant ancestor whose life was burdened with suffering. Clearly, he feels some kinship with history, having preserved her materials with care. But then, the past is not a photo frame on his mantel. It has been locked away in a suitcase.

"They've been tremendously helpful, the archives," I say carefully. "She must have been a methodical woman to save everything so neatly."

"Ah yes, that is said about her. Focused, always thinking of the future. They all were but especially Gandhi's crew."

Encouraged, I plunge ahead. "I found one photograph of a whole group of female volunteers with Kasturba bai. And Maithili was right there in the back row! Remarkable. You must be so proud."

Rakesh is quiet for a while. "Yes, it's true," he agrees. "She was a lady ahead of her time. But hard, eh? Even now, but in those days, even more. To do important work and then come home to your husband and cook and care for your babies and all that. Not easy to do everything. My grandmother, she had a hard time. She had to look after her brothers and sisters because her mother was always gone away. Maybe tonight, she'll spend the night in jail; who knows."

It is my turn to be quiet. I'm embarrassed of my fanciful ideas about Maithili's activism and my envy of her perseverance. Our actions always come with a trade-off. "I suppose, brought here against her will, Maithili's activism was a way to exert her will," I muse, almost to myself. "Defend others who were brought after her."

Rakesh frowns. "Against her will? Who told you that?"

My cheeks grow warm. I should have known to expect this response, especially after my conversation with Ishara's grandmother. I've taken for granted the academic knowledge that most single women laborers who arrived when Maithili did were kidnapped or tricked by the notorious agents. "Well, anything's possible, but that's what the research suggests about many of the women. I just thought—"

"Not forced, Granny was." It's Rakesh's aunt who speaks. We snap our attention to her end of the table; we'd almost forgotten her quiet presence. Until now, she has only spoken small words to me: *hello, thank you, bye, eat.* It's the first time I've heard her utter anything like a sentence.

Rakesh seems surprised as well. "You heard her talk about it, Aunty? About coming from India?"

She bends her gray head and fiddles with a corner of her place mat. Aunty is the only person alive, as far as I know, who actually knew Maithili. Maybe she even remembers her stories.

"She did talk, she did sometimes." Aunty clasps her hands together. "One time, I remember. She was old, neh? I was the baby. When I came, she was already old. But she should sing to me. A little song from India. I can't remember the song, ay. Lots of things I can't remember now."

She glances up, nervous, at me, then Rakesh. He smiles at her with soft reassurance. Aunty continues: "I remember one day, she was singing, see, like that. And she said her granny should sing for her, in their village back there. I aksed where was her granny. And her amma and daddy. She came sad, like. Cry little bit. First time, that day, I seen that. She say they sleeping, back there in India. I want to aks her how come they sleep and sleep, but I was afraid when she cry. So then I just keep quiet, and she keep talking and talking, like she forgotten me. She say bad-bad things come to her village, many hot days and everybody getting sick. So she must run away to town. Over there, this man say, 'Come on my ship. I'll take you to a new place, far away. You'll be a laani there, not poor place like India.' So she came."

Aunty looks up from her hands. A girlish joy has played about her face as she tells the story. Another migrant seeking better. I've been wrong so many times. And who am I to take the measure of that long-ago woman's victimhood anyway? Her choices died on the vine.

"Thank you, Aunty," I say. "How amazing that she came all this way alone! And had to work in the fields and earn her way out and . . ."

I stop short as Aunty's face clouds over. She still wears the determined air of one who has cast off her cares, but her smile has faded. Now she stares darkly into a corner. "Not fields. She worked inside a house. Oh yes, oh yes, I know about the house." She narrows her eyes as if the house is a wayward child standing before her, awaiting punishment.

Rakesh and I have both questioned the conspicuous lack of information about Maithili's indenture. The suitcase is filled instead with her life after indenture: her activism, education, her family. The local archives store the indenture certificate of each laborer who arrived.

But my attempts thus far to obtain a copy of Maithili's certificate—
which would include the name of her "employer"—have turned up
nothing.

Rakesh prompts for more. "What did she say about the house,
Aunty?"

She glances at him. "A bad house, she say. She always say be careful, you know, of the white people. Because what they did in that
house." Her eyes flash as if she is telling her own story of trauma
remembered. Though, in a way, she is. Her blood remembers.

"What did they do?" Rakesh asks.

Aunty waves him away. "Don't aks me. I don't know. She never
tell me. Saying I was too small. But it was a bad thing, what happen,
because she say those white people must go to a court. You know, in
front a judge. All that."

A courthouse. Though I am loath to interrupt the moment, I can't
help it. I scrape back my chair, grab the photograph, and half run
back to the table. I crouch next to Aunty's chair. "Look, look at this
picture, Aunty. Do you know who these women are? Did she ever say
who they are?"

She turns to me and smiles. The earlier focus in her gaze is gone.
She strokes my head. "You're a good girl. Nice to remember Granny."

Afterward, Rakesh tends to Aunty, who seems more withdrawn than
usual. Not wanting to intrude, I slip out onto the dark terrace. The
neighborhood is tucked away for the night. A few windows down
the curve of the hill are lit with the flickering glow of televisions. My
heart beats, loud, against the oppressive evening. I push my hands
into my jeans pockets.

Court. A trial. I resist the urge to look over my shoulder. Saadia's
words from that folded letter crowd around and find form not only
in my present but in this land's past too. They assail me in Saadia's
voice and also in the laughter of the woman who stands full-throated,
broad shoulders back.

"Himmat," Saadia said. Gather it up around yourself, draw it to
your bosom like a cloak, and wear it until it becomes you. Himmat.
A word on the tip of my tongue on this terrace, days before, when I
spoke to Rakesh about his country. I told him I am searching Durban
for strength, but it was only a poor translation of the word. Strength is

a force one owns. Himmat is the choice to embrace courage in the face of danger. To be daring. It's a quality no one ever asked of me before.

I was raised to be polite. Intelligent, thoughtful, but not too much. Don't talk back. Speak only when someone asks for your opinion. Don't splay your limbs in a vulgar manner. Instead, crouch inside whatever crevice you are permitted.

For a time, I shouted my convictions out loud. But it was a performance. Other women wear their himmat proud. I only read about them.

Rakesh finds me later in the kitchen with my hands in soapy dishwater. He takes a dirty plate from me and insists he'll clean up later. The excitement of the evening tired Aunty, he says.

"I'm sorry, I pushed her too much." I wipe my hands on a towel.

"No, no, don't feel bad. This is how she is. Since I remember." He rinses off the dish and squirts green liquid onto a sponge. "My mother took care of her when I was young. I took over after she died. Aunty always needed help. She's getting worse, though. Some days she talks again like that. Sometimes gets quiet."

I lean against the counter, my hands awkward without purpose. "I just thought the photo might help."

"And it might have. You were right to try. But you know, we have something now that we didn't before."

"We do?" Caught in the tumble of my own emotions, I hadn't thought to look through her words for information.

Rakesh tosses the sponge from one hand to the other in a messy juggle. "For all your professor-ing and researching, you need me to point it out?" The intimacy of his light tease brings a swoop to my chest.

"Fine, fine, you're cleverer than me." I laugh and duck my head. "Just tell me already!"

"We now know there was a court case," he says with the gleeful air of a conjurer pulling back his curtain. "And where there are trials, there are court records."

His eyes shine, and warmth sparks through my limbs in response.

TWENTY

Before Sita discovered Vasanthi and the master in the orchard, the house had always seemed a vast stranger. Though she came to know its rooms and passages over time, she could not feel at ease inside its walls. Now the house assumed a newly sinister identity, taunting her with creaks and groans, doors that slammed accusations. At dawn, she raced to and from the quarters as one pursued.

Vasanthi had given her body to a man who belonged to someone else. He was powerful enough to harm Vasanthi and those who befriended her. It was unwise for Sita to risk her own safety by keeping company with such a reckless woman. And yet Sita could not abandon Vasanthi. She was indebted to the friend who cared for her and felt connected to her. It wasn't only because of their work together in this house. An emotional bond had emerged between them, stronger than any Sita had felt in years. Beyond even that: so what if Vasanthi lay with the master? What did she have but her beauty to survive this land. Like Sita, she arrived with nothing but her body and her name.

Still, she couldn't help but see Vasanthi differently now. She could not meet her eyes. The first few times she greeted Vasanthi awkwardly when taking her meals or passing her in the kitchens, Vasanthi was busy and appeared not to notice. But when Sita tried to brush past silently for the third day in a row, the other woman stopped her and gestured a question with her twisted hand. Cheeks burning, Sita shook her head and rushed away.

The next time they saw each other, the silence was mutual. Vasanthi carried herself with frost, made all the deadlier by hurt simmering beneath the ice. Without her friend's chatter, Sita's days echoed ahead, empty of her own language. Afraid of running into Vasanthi and the master again, Sita hadn't returned to the worker quarters since that night. Besides, she felt uneasy about the other women and what they'd guessed. Vasanthi's affair with the master was an open secret, it seemed. So it could not remain secret from anyone for long.

Each moment, she watched for one of the many disasters she dreaded. Perhaps Mrs. Dickinson was withdrawn or irritable today. The master hummed a soft tune when he passed by Desmond's room last night. Cracks began to splinter through her lonely routines.

When she fetched Desmond from his evening time with his parents, she often ran into Vasanthi, who cleared the dishes from afternoon tea at the same time. No longer did the two women share a silent camaraderie in their tasks. Instead, Vasanthi was a study in nonchalant efficiency. Nervous as she gathered up Desmond's books and toys, Sita inevitably dropped something and elicited a sharp reprimand from the mistress.

Meanwhile, Mr. Dickinson remained lost behind his papers as his foot tapped to a melody of his own. But his facade broke on occasion. When Vasanthi reached out for his cup, his foot ceased tapping. He cleared his throat and folded his newspaper. He made a show of handing the cup to her and managed to caress her hand with two fingers. Perhaps he wanted to make Vasanthi uncomfortable. If he succeeded, she showed no sign of it.

Crouched a few feet away, Sita was overcome by fear. She ducked her head and stole a glance toward Mrs. Dickinson. The mistress observed the exchange with a glacial calm. Her gray eyes followed Vasanthi, whose posture remained deliberate. The arc of her spine was as precise as a trained sapling. When Vasanthi bent over a table, her plait slipped over one shoulder in an uncoiling surrender to gravity so pleasing to the eye, the action appeared almost rehearsed. Sita wondered if all of Vasanthi's actions were carefully choreographed.

Mrs. Dickinson now angled her neck in her husband's direction. He, too, had watched Vasanthi's every movement. After she left, he slowly unfolded his newspaper and disappeared behind it again. Mrs. Dickinson returned to the embroidery in her lap. Her steady hands traced the outline of a petal without pause.

"You are sad," Desmond observed one evening.

Sita was preparing him for bed. It was still light out, but she drew the heavy curtains, so the room was cast in darkness, and wavering candlelight illuminated his hazel eyes.

She retrieved his discarded shirt from the floor and folded it with care. She placed it on the bed beside him. Then she sat, too, the shirt between them. She'd never before sat on his soft, white bed. She only made it every morning and pulled back the covers to tuck him in every night.

She nodded. "Yes, I am sad," she replied.

Desmond searched the shadows around her eyes and the hollows of her cheeks. "Why?" he asked.

But no language could give voice to the worries and sorrows invading her mind each night as she tried to sleep. And even if she could find the words, she couldn't burden a child with such ugliness. Even this child, whose parents were responsible for her misery. Desmond was not responsible. Not yet.

So instead, she tried to smile and shrugged to imply that she didn't understand. Desmond appeared unconvinced. He gazed at her face with a troubled expression too old for his years. He found her hand on her lap and held on to it with both of his.

"Please," he said. That seemed to be all he could think to say. *Don't leave*, she heard, underneath.

Sita had vowed this would not happen. She'd worked against this feeling. But now, submerged in loneliness and fear, she could no longer protect her heart from this boy. Even though he would only hurt her in the end. She would receive nothing from these people in return for her love.

Maybe it happened this way for Vasanthi too.

Sita squeezed Desmond's tiny hands hard. Then she rose, picked up his shirt, and put it away.

That evening, she sat awake while Desmond drifted to sleep. She tried to busy herself with mending, but her work sat untouched in her lap. Instead, she gazed out of the sliver of window she'd left uncovered. Beyond the manicured lawn stretched row after row of young sugarcane like strung jewels. Sunset sky gripped each plant in a tight gold bezel. But only for an instant before the land was drenched in night.

She had no clock to measure the hours, but her instincts were honed by the rhythms of the house. When it was time, she crossed the room and opened the door. She made no sound. Her muscles responded to the memory of stealth, though many weeks had passed since she last left Desmond's room at night. Down the back stairs, she was alert to every rustle and creak. She paused and listened at the kitchen door. Some distance away, clinks and splashes from the men in the scullery. Closer, scrape of rag against stone floor. Sita slipped into the dim light cast by the hearth.

On her knees, Vasanthi wrung out the rag in a bucket. She was so small for one so fierce. Startled, Vasanthi glanced up at Sita. She studied her face as she might the map of a foreign land. Then she knotted her brows and returned to scrubbing the floor as if she had seen nothing there worth visiting.

"Vasanthi." Sita heard the shake in her voice. "I want to speak with you."

In response, Vasanthi only pushed harder against stone, the muscles of her neck taut in sharp relief. Clearly, she would rather scrub her hands raw than speak. Sita took a few tentative steps forward.

"Please," she said. Reminded irresistibly of Desmond, she crouched and reached for the other woman's cold hands. At her touch, Vasanthi paused but did not look up. "I have been unfair to you. I know. But please, let me explain."

Another long silence. Sita had come down here sure of her purpose. But she hadn't accounted for Vasanthi's obstinacy. She knew her friend was a warrior, but now Sita faced her defenses from the other side for the first time. As an enemy.

She let out a breath. "All right. You're angry. I have kept my distance and said nothing to explain. But I want to talk to you now." No change in the other woman's gritted countenance. The immovability loosened a confession Sita had not intended: "You and Mary are my only friends here, so—I didn't want this wall between us. You have many friends; you wouldn't understand how it is for me."

Finally, as if losing a battle with herself, Vasanthi raised her gaze. "Then why?" Her voice grated raw with hurt.

Sita faltered. The chastening morality speech she'd carefully rehearsed now seemed so unkind. Besides, Vasanthi was world-wise and did not need advice from a girl who'd never even known a lover's embrace.

"I am sorry," Sita said, at last. "I don't know why I was angry. Can you forgive me?"

Vasanthi stared, one dramatic brow arched high. "You think I don't know what's bothering you? It's easy to see. From the way you look at me. At him. At *her*." The last word a bitter morsel spat out. "You act like a frightened animal around them. Like a pet they brought home for the boy." She tossed her head back in undisguised contempt. "No one put you in a cage, you know. No one except yourself." Her mouth twisted in a mirthless dagger of a smile as she crossed her arms, prepared for the next round.

Sita sat back heavily on the cold floor. No longer sure of her intentions or mission, she glanced around the kitchen. "I don't know what you mean," she whispered.

Without warning, Vasanthi reached out and grabbed Sita by both shoulders, shaking her hard. The shock was too much. The days of guarded anxiety broke into sobs, each one rocky as it tore from Sita's chest. Vasanthi clapped a hand over her friend's mouth and hissed at her to be silent. One of the dishwashers peeped in from the scullery at the noise, but she waved him away with her other hand. After a smirk, he complied. Even the men were afraid of Vasanthi.

Sita pushed her hand away from her mouth. She pulled up her knees and pushed her face hard between them and bit the fabric. Her sobs quieted only when her teeth had torn through and pierced the skin over her kneecap. The brief pain recalled her to this kitchen and the sleeping masters above her.

She raised her head to peer at Vasanthi over her knees and was gratified to see concern dart across the other woman's face. "Why?" Sita whispered. "Why are you doing this?"

Vasanthi shrugged. "Doing what? Shaking you? I thought you'd come to your senses. Say what you mean, for once. Stop being so afraid all the time. I must be an idiot to think it could do any good."

"You know what I mean. You know what I'm asking."

Vasanthi glanced at her up and down, perhaps to consider her worthiness as a confidante. "Why do you care?" She narrowed her eyes as she spoke. "You've been here long enough now to see how it is for us. Mind your business, do your work, and leave when they let you go. Everyone knows this. So what does it matter to you what I do or don't do?"

Sita wiped her face on the ripped edge of her sari. Slowly, she crossed her legs and straightened her back, hoping this position would lend her a dignified demeanor she did not feel. "It matters for many reasons. It affects me too, for one thing," She raised a hand to stop Vasanthi from interrupting. "No, you must see that. We are friends; the mistress knows this. I know what happened to other ayah. What if she suspects me too? Where will I go? I have no one left, not here, not there." She indicated *there* with a quick thrust of her chin. The place that once was home but no more.

"None of us have anywhere to go," Vasanthi muttered, but she did not contradict Sita either. This much, then, she implicitly conceded: that she'd brought danger on both of them.

Sita was emboldened by Vasanthi's unspoken acquiescence. And yet what she had to say next was far more difficult. She took a breath before dashing forth: "It's not just that. Also, I care for you. I don't want them to hurt you. They are . . . cruel people. Sometimes I think you've forgotten. You only remember how strong you are. You forget that they are stronger."

Vasanthi started, her eyes wide with anger. "What do you know about strength?"

"I know enough." Sita felt more centered now that she'd said the worst of her piece.

"You don't know! You don't know anything about what it takes to survive here. You're a slip of a girl, just arrived from the village. Look at your hands! You've never had to rip burning sugarcane. The way you stare big-eyes at the world. It's never beaten you down. I protected you; I felt sorry for you. And you—*you*—say I'm not strong enough? You don't know what it means."

"I know enough," Sita repeated, even though (or perhaps because) she knew how much it would anger Vasanthi.

Vasanthi grabbed at her own hair as if to tear it out, her whole body shuddering the scream she could not let out. She took a deep breath before continuing: "All right, then. You know enough. Do you know *enough* to survive? Do you know what it takes to survive in a place that doesn't want you? It's not *enough* to be a good girl and listen to your masters and work hard. You can toil until your bones shatter and the sun burns your skin to ashes. It won't be enough."

"But enough for what?"

"Aren't you listening? What do you think you'll do after five years? You'll go back? And what's there? You think you'll have enough money to live there? You think anyone will accept you, marry you? Or you want to stay here—maybe you think you'll charm one of these coolie idiots into marrying you and keeping you on the rocky, worthless land they'll give you. Some toothless old fuck who gets drunk and beats you every night, beats you till you die giving birth to your tenth starving baby. If you're lucky, that's the kind of husband a woman like you will find. A woman who stepped outside her family and traveled on a ship by herself. An unmarried girl who has lived in a white man's house."

Somewhere over the course of this speech, Sita's shoulders slumped, elbows on knees, head bowed. The same thoughts crowded Sita's own sleepless nights. Stories she sketched and smudged and pushed away to her mind's edge. To hear them recited by someone else was newly harsh. Still, she would not let Vasanthi cow her. Not when she was only circling around her own reality.

"So," Sita whispered. "You keep saying this isn't enough to survive, that isn't enough to survive. That I don't know the things you know. So what do you know? What have you discovered that the rest of us haven't? You think *he* will help you survive?" Sita spoke this last line in sarcasm—surely Vasanthi couldn't be foolish enough to believe the master would help one of them. But she saw immediately from Vasanthi's expression that she'd been wrong.

"So what if I do? It's worth a chance." Vasanthi shrugged the words with a careless air, but it was clear she did care a great deal.

"Oh, Vasanthi! We don't matter to him. You must see that!"

"You don't know what he's like with me. It's different when we're together. But I know what you'll say, so don't bother. I'm not dreaming that the master will leave his wife to marry me or anything like that. I know I'm not the first. I'm just another pretty servant girl for his bed." Her lip curled with bitterness; it took something for her to say that aloud.

"Then . . . ?"

Vasanthi lowered her voice and drew closer. "He noticed me. He *chose* me. That might help. I don't know yet how. But it's better than before. It's better than just . . . waiting to die. I mean, what is life for us after this, Sita? It's no better than wasting away." She shrugged again. "So I please him. I let him please me. It means I *do* something, try something."

Sita shook her head. "I don't understand. You aren't doing something. He's taking advantage of you."

"Look, I know why you can't understand. This is who you are. You catch your sari when it shifts and make sure the folds cover your shape. Your hunched shoulders, your folded arms. You think making yourself smaller will hide your body from men. But it won't. Your scurrying and hiding—it only makes them think they can own you. As for me, my body is my weapon. I'm not ashamed of it. Let them stare. I'll use it to own them. The sooner you understand this, the sooner you'll have a chance at survival."

Sita couldn't find an argument against this logic, though, instinctively, she didn't like it. But, too, a current beneath Vasanthi's words rang false. She was determined to expose it. "So that's all it is for you, then, laying with him? Survival?"

"What else? I know better than to expect more."

"You don't . . . love him?"

Vasanthi's eyes flashed. "Don't be ridiculous! Who could . . . why would I? I already told you I know better."

"But I saw something. I saw you with him one night in the litchi grove. I saw the way you caressed him, the way a wife does. You can honestly say you share his bed, embrace him, watch for his approach, kiss him farewell, and you have felt no love toward him?"

Vasanthi sprang to her feet. "No! I would never feel love for that beast. For any of these people. I would never allow it." She wrapped her arms about herself as if to protect her heart.

For a moment, they were both quiet. Sita thought about Desmond lost in his innocent dreams upstairs. She thought of the scent of his hair and his serious expression. His face when she entered the room to take him from his parents. There was no repressing a child's joy: his rush to join her and help gather his things so they could leave together.

Already, he loved her as he would a mother. As he did not love his own mother. As perhaps no child of Sita's own would ever love her. She knew the truth of Vasanthi's words. No worthy man would want her now. She may never know motherhood beyond this proxy forced on her.

But for now, she had a child's love. And sometimes, she couldn't help but return it. She drew from this memory as she spoke, "I understand. But it may not matter what you allow. Your heart knows its own will."

Vasanthi gazed down at Sita still crouched on the floor. She clasped her arms tighter and shivered though the night was warm. "You're wrong," she said. "I am master of my will. Of that much, at least."

After that night, the two women resumed a wary friendship. The kind forged over a shared secret. Their bond was stronger than before but also more watchful. Each had so much to lose by the other's misstep. As they passed each other during their workdays, Sita tried by glances and quick brushes to convey her desire to regain her friend's trust.

But this was not easy when she did not trust Vasanthi herself. She wondered if Vasanthi knew that and also approached the space between them with reticence. In the weeks that followed, neither brought up their conversation of that night again. Nor did they acknowledge the relationship that she assumed Vasanthi was continuing to keep with the master. They spoke to each other in soft tones, as if each was aware that she had broken something precious to the other.

But perhaps the break allowed a subtle rearrangement of shards and something new at the joins too. Vasanthi's words lingered through Sita's days. She paused for a moment now before entering the Dickinsons' sitting room. She imagined the doorway as a cage meant to restrain her. Picking up the boy's things, she was aware of her body's crouched shape—an inconsequential animal scrabbling in the undergrowth whose predators lounged on thrones far above.

Sometimes she was startled by such dark thoughts. But they were her frequent companions now. She remembered Tulsi's words from just a few weeks earlier. The older woman had called Sita a child, a dreamer. Now she longed for a time when she knew less, when she still yearned to satisfy her employers or do enough to escape their notice. Vasanthi was to blame for introducing this resentful rebellion in her.

But in some ways, Vasanthi was more optimistic—maybe even more naive—than Sita herself had once been if she thought she could earn any favor from the master. Or that her choices could have any consequence but disaster.

Sita no longer took up any extra chores while Desmond was busy with his lessons each day. Instead, she rushed through a shoddy version of her basic tasks and wandered the house the rest of the time. She still took care to stay out of Mrs. Dickinson's way, but that woman's strict schedule made it easy to avoid her. At this precise time, she took up her embroidery hoop. At this other time, she changed shoes for her promenade across the lawn to supervise the gardeners. At midday, she sat down to lunch at the long table, where she ate alone.

During those hours, Sita explored rooms draped in cottons to protect their furnishings. Her fingertips traced whitewash whorls along cold walls. She pressed her palm against a covered seat, and a dust cloud rose to greet her. In another room, she came across a locked trunk and its stout key hidden under a corner of the rug. She lifted the trunk's heavy lid and found humble treasures. A rag doll with orange yarn for hair. A bolt of pale green cloth. Several rolls of paper, which turned out to be watercolors of a house overtaken by creepers.

She was crouched, one hand scrolling open a painting, when Mrs. Dickinson walked into the room. It took Sita a moment to recognize her, as if she'd returned from a journey to that cottage. The white woman's eyes widened. She rushed over, seized the papers, and tossed them back into the trunk.

"You thief," she growled, arched over Sita.

Heat crept up from the stiff collar of the mistress's blouse and bloomed across the tender skin of her throat. A bubble of spit burst at her lip. Sita remained crouched. Here it was, the moment she'd feared. She almost welcomed its long-awaited arrival.

Her calm must have been apparent. Mrs. Dickinson's eyes hardened, and the flush of her cheeks receded. She stood up straight, and for an instant, Sita wondered if the white woman's rage would come to nothing. Idly, she imagined the mistress as an ordinary girl who might show her treasures off to Sita and chatter. Even laugh.

The kick caught her unaware. The woman's boot was pointed and Sita's hip mostly skin and bone. Pain flared through her side as she toppled onto her knees and gasped.

Another kick, with the base of the woman's wood heel this time, and then she swung her leg back with force for another blow, but Sita scrambled to her feet first. As she rose, she noticed for the first time that she was an inch or two taller than the mistress. And they were alone.

The white woman raised her eyes to meet Sita's gaze, as if startled by this realization too. Sita took a single step forward, her fists tight.

"Ayah?" Desmond's voice rang from the silent hallway. Neither woman turned toward the sound, but the moment's stillness broke.

"Get out," the mistress said, her voice low. Then louder, a bark: "Get out!"

But Sita paused. She narrowed her eyes to muster the stony contempt she'd seen on Vasanthi's face on the veranda.

"Yes, Madam."

She made sure to lean over the slighter woman as she curled her lip around the word. And though her hip protested against its bruises, she was careful to stalk out of the room without a limp.

Because she'd come to understand that it didn't matter if she hid and cowered. She may as well keep her head high since, in this house, danger would claim her anyway. Sooner or later, Vasanthi's flesh would not be enough to satisfy their gluttonous appetites. Sooner or later, they would come for Sita.

TWENTY-ONE

I'm eager to pore over court archives right away after that dinner with Rakesh and Aunty. I want to tear through the records to find the women from the photograph and the story behind their protest. But Rakesh asks to come with me, and I can't refuse his request. Maithili's story—and that of the women whose image she preserved—is his birthright.

Besides, I want his reassuring presence when we scour detailed reams about laborers brought before judges. I know they were dealt public lashes and worse for minor infractions. Their names and brown faces have grown familiar to my imagination.

I've been a scholar for years. Once, I could turn off names, faces, and voices at will and reduce people to data points. A talent or professional hazard, I'm not sure which. But something has changed now. I can't turn from empathy to anonymity so easily anymore. It began when I wandered into that room at the conference center and saw the projected images of women who resisted.

Since then, my attempts to categorize people and file them away fail. The names and faces of people I've met in Durban flit to and fro as I try to sleep, cheap blinds on the balcony door fluttered by sea breeze. The bags under Reshika's eyes. The children she and her mother and mother's mother raised. Rakesh's faraway glance and his murmured asides to ship passages. The spark in Aunty's brief connection to her memory, the struggle behind Brenda Pillay's wry smile, the pinpricks of light inside Ishara's tossed hair. They knit together my connection to the city where I learned to listen again—to the world and also to myself, because I am part of the world.

Now, I can't seem to return to my scholarly cocoon. Disarmed this way, I need Rakesh. He is a teacher of biology. He understands how land lingers and evolves inside cell walls when we breathe its dust and eat its fruit. Generation after generation, different lands meet and twist and become new inside us. So, to find what I'm seeking, I need to reach beyond my familiar papers and ink—and even outside our common speech. I need someone who knows our bodies.

I wait until Rakesh is able to get time off the following week to join me. In the meantime, I keep busy with preparations. I meet again with Brenda Pillay and Dr. Naidoo for advice. Naidoo cowers in Brenda's presence; he is all sulky cooperation around her. We draw up a list of next steps. Archives at various libraries, the names of legal historians. A path that soothes my scholar side.

On our first day, Rakesh wants to start at the old courthouse. Neither Brenda's nor Naidoo's suggestions involved the place. They assured me it's a tourist trap. But Rakesh insists, so we set off together toward town with him at the wheel. He takes us down the backstreets where Durban's residents have lost their battle with verdant bush. Green intrudes through cracks in the sidewalk, lingers over missing roof tiles, and blooms across vacant lots. This city was meant to thrive without us.

In town, combis line up at the depot, commuters already deposited, and wait for the lunchtime round. Mynah buses trundle down West Street past the department stores and rickety pie stalls and vendors hawking beaded lizards and painted masks. As we fly over a highway ramp, Victoria Street market teems far below us. The dome and minarets of its famed mosque cast shadows over the tangle of buyers and sellers. Weak midday sun glints off Gandhi's pate in front of the old train station; his bronze likeness seems to perspire in the tropical winter.

Near the harbor, salmon and mint stucco buildings are scattered around old Durban. We circle a few times before we find a parking spot and pick our way through grimy port-side streets. The old courthouse is the oldest surviving building in Durban and is now a colonial relic and museum. Surely, Rakesh has seen this place countless times supervising school field trips.

For a time, I bite my tongue. But once the building looms, I can't hold back. "Why are we here?"

"Because the place matters. Not just the paper." He turns to me with a smile. "I can see you think we are silly to come here. Humor me, please."

His tranquil nature evokes the opposite in me. Sighing, I follow him with downcast eyes and don't notice he's standing still until I walk into him. "What is it? Is something wrong?"

He stares up at the old courthouse steps away. "You don't recognize it?"

"Do you mean the building? Sure—" I halt as his meaning strikes me. "This is the place?"

"I think so, yes." He flips open his satchel, removes a folder, and holds it open at eye level. The plastic-covered photograph inside is secure under his thumb. Three women stand in the foreground. One of them shades her eyes from the sun. The building behind them is out of focus, but here, in the right context, it's unmistakable.

I try to examine the scene like a scientist. "They would have stood here, their backs to the courthouse, and what would they have seen?"

He strokes his chin as if peering through the years. "I believe this would be the road for horses and carriages. Where people would come to the courthouse."

"So the subject of their protest was these carriages and their passengers." My mind races. "Maybe the judge, maybe the white people in a case. Maybe an estate owner?"

"I thought they were raising awareness for worker rights," he murmurs. "Like a rally."

"I did too. But I'm not so sure." As I glance again from photo to daylight, the screeches of traffic melt away. We might as well stand face-to-face with the women we seek. I shake my head to dispel the ghostly outlines that rise before me. "It's almost as if I can hear them," I whisper.

"Maybe you can," Rakesh says after a pause. "Have you heard of Charles Babbage? The air as library? No?" He frowns as he remembers. "A nineteenth-century philosopher, I think. Or mathematician. He believed everything humans ever said was recorded in the atmosphere, like witness testimony. And with the right device, we could rewind and listen."

"An interesting theory." I manage to make my voice casual, though the humid air prickles at my skin.

Inside the courthouse building, we find nothing of value. Only waxworks of early sugarcane plantations and photo exhibits of Apartheid in sports. We avoid the gift store on our way out.

We make our way to the legal archives on our list. When I came here before meeting Rakesh, my stumbling conversations with the librarian ended in frustration. She had little patience for a foreigner without clear direction.

Today, not only do I have a specific question, but I am also accompanied by a handsome Durbanite. The librarian is eager to assist our search for Maithili and her connections to a court case that the three women might have protested. But the name brings up nothing. She doesn't exist in the indentured labor records—not with her married name, which is all we have.

For two days at different libraries, we search without success. It's only when an archivist suggests searching the record of deaths that we find Maithili's name in an ancient ledger.

Maithili Iyer, the looped handwriting states. Died aged sixty-eight. No date of birth available. And the name of the man who came to report her passing: Krishnaswamy Iyer. Husband.

Rakesh nods. "My great-grandfather."

In my mind's eye, I lean over the shoulder of a stooped man in a pressed suit. Grief like winter's dawn casts a shadow across his face. He bends low at the registrar's desk and fills out a death certificate for a woman with no other records in this country. And I'm grateful because his entry is all we have of her on paper.

Maithili's name has turned up almost nothing, but the search for Krishnaswamy Iyer is more fruitful. We return, one by one, to all the archives and find that the footprint of a privileged-caste man—rather than an indentured woman—warrants record.

At the end of a particularly busy morning, we gather up our notes and add them to the growing pile on the back seat. Today's destination has brought us closer to Overport, just past the glinting dome of the Soofi mosque and the street where Ishara's grandmother lives. Rakesh looks through our list for the next destination, but my stomach growls out a singsong protest.

"Time for lunch, then?" He grins. "I know a place."

I button my sweater up against the wind before I get behind the wheel. I hope he's taking us somewhere warm. We wind onto the neighborhood's main drag. Schoolchildren with loosened ties sprint across the street, and men knock at my window offering bags of tangerines. In the mess of stop-and-go traffic, I double-park while Rakesh gets out and dashes through a narrow alley. Soon, he reappears and slips back into the passenger seat carrying a white plastic bag. The heady aroma of turmeric and garlic is almost more than I can stand.

Through a side street, Rakesh directs me to a parking lot near the large polytechnic. We stay inside, where it's warm. On the car stereo, Radio Lotus plays synth-y eighties numbers—this one is from the *Janbaaz* soundtrack, I remember with a start of recognition. Carefully, Rakesh opens up a square Styrofoam container and hands it to me with a stack of paper towels. Inside, flaky roti is curled around a generous mound of spinach in a pool of oil. I scoop up a large mouthful and lean back in bliss.

We are quiet as we devour the roti. Once my hunger recedes, my thoughts return to the pile of papers in the back. My hands are too greasy to reach for them, so I rifle through my memory of the material. So many newspaper clippings by Krishnaswamy Iyer about Indian remedies applied to African illnesses. And the irresistible image of herb bundles and paper twists of powder conjured up by that word—*apothecary*.

"Did you know he was a plant specialist? Your great-grandfather?"

Rakesh nods, his mouth full. He smiles as he swallows. "Everyone was always telling me. I find an injured bird or bring home a snakeskin, and 'Oh, you are just like Thatha. It's your great-grandfather's spirit in you.' Irritated, I use to get sometimes. But can I tell you something?" He takes a gulp from his bottled water and turns in his seat to face me. "I loved it. I imagined we were the same person. I told my friends they must respect me as their elder."

I snicker. "How did that work out for you?"

He shrugs with playful nonchalance. "I decided to start keeping the truth to myself. They weren't ready."

We laugh and tell childhood stories as the radio twangs its nostalgic playlist. But my thoughts keep circling around that idea too: of a bright flash reappearing at random across Rakesh's family tree like bits of gold in a pan of gritty water.

I watch the bob of his Adam's apple as he recounts another memory. Our friendship. Surely, our connection will fade once I return to my solitary box of a room across the ocean. And, too, my link to the woman I seek will wither. Soon, everything alive between us will get bound between dissertation covers and relegated to a campus basement.

Brooding, I turn to gaze out the window. Classes must have let out at the polytechnic, and a group of young women clamber into a combi at the corner. Just beyond their shouts, raindrops drip from the branches of an overhanging tree. Its trunk is pocked by the hearts and arrows of students with pocket knives. Still undaunted, the tree towers over the sidewalk and dirt lot to one side. Its leaves flourish into a verdant sphere. I'm almost certain it's the same species of tree that dips its tresses over Rakesh's yard—the naaval maram. I've eaten its astringent fruit flavored with salt in Pakistan. But back then, I never looked up the tree or knew how to recognize the shape of its leaves from another. Not until I found it again here with Rakesh, so far from its origins.

"Where did you go?" he asks after a pause.

We are so close. The car feels too small. He's still waiting, so I shake my head. "That marriage certificate we found with Maithili's name today. I was thinking about that. We found her only when her name was joined to Krishnaswamy's. Otherwise, nothing. Like she was never here." I pause and struggle to pull together the tangle of my thoughts. "What does it mean?"

"She was a woman," he says simply.

I nod. No one has ever recorded women without men to accompany them. Her erasure from history is an ordinary circumstance. I wipe the grease from my hands. "Let's go. It's getting late."

Our next stop is a small archive in a town north of Durban. We've retraced our steps here because we only searched for Maithili's name in court records earlier, and now we want to try looking for her husband. I'm not optimistic. Krishnaswamy seems obsessed only with plants. I'm sure he would consider any kind of legal proceeding insufficiently relevant to the natural world.

When our search returns a result almost immediately, I jump to my feet in surprise. Unsupported, my chair spins away a few feet as we all peer at the loading document on the screen. It's the record of a trial at which Krishnaswamy Iyer was the primary witness.

The newspaper microfilm is poor quality, so the photograph is blurrier than the copy in Rakesh's file. But the caption is clear: "Miss Meera Iyer and Coolie Women Protest against Dickinson Plantation."

We read it out loud together. After a brief pause, the text seems to click into place for Rakesh: "Meera Athai! So young here, I never recognized her."

"Meera Athai?"

"That's what my family called her. She passed long before I was born. I've only seen pictures." He points at the stern woman holding the left edge of the banner. "My mother's great-aunt. Krishnaswamy's older sister. They all called her Athai."

"What do you know about her?"

"Not much, eh? She traveled a lot. Lived somewhere else, maybe London, I think. In old age, she came to Durban to stay with the family. I only have photos of her from that time, when she was old. My mother told me about the strict old aunty who never had kids."

"But who are the other women in the picture, then? Others from your family?"

He shakes his head. "I don't think so, eh? But hard to be sure. So blurry. And people change so much. I didn't recognize young Athai all this time."

We return our attention to the figure next to Meera Athai—one of the two the newspaper has called a "coolie woman" and nothing more. Her laughter is the thread that pulled me across the world. I've memorized her square shoulders and posture. I could count each pleat in her sari if I closed my eyes. But I am still no closer to naming her.

TWENTY-TWO

Sita rarely visited the quarters after dark now. But tonight, she made an exception for a special occasion. A child was born to a woman who was kind to the unmarried girls and included them in her ritual celebration. They crossed over to the married quarters to wish the new babe and mother well. Others clucked their disapproval at the break from tradition. It was wrong to allow fallow women to look upon a new child with their longings and regrets. To ward off evil eyes, the baby was marked with a black spot on one cheek.

Afterward, they returned to their end of the quarter with their blessed sweets. Vasanthi seemed withdrawn and did not participate in the huddled gossip around the fire. Soon, she rose to wash and turn in, and Sita decided to return to the house.

"I'll walk you back," Vasanthi offered. Sita refused. She preferred a solitary walk to the other woman's sullen mood. Also, she supposed Vasanthi wanted an excuse to return to the house and meet the master. Though she couldn't alter her friend's chosen path, she did not want to aid her in it either. But Vasanthi resisted all protests with her characteristic mulishness and set off by her side.

They walked for a time in silence before Vasanthi broke in with an abrupt question: "Do you wish for a child? Of your own?"

"Of course. As all girls do."

"All girls do not wish for a baby. I don't."

Sita glanced at her in surprise. It was a cloudy night, and as they passed through the shadowy orchard, Vasanthi's expression was hidden. But her tone had been straightforward. "I didn't know that. Why not?"

Their footfalls were soft, so it was a moment before Sita realized Vasanthi had stopped short and was no longer at her side. She turned to peer through the darkness and found the shape of her friend a few feet behind her.

"Look at our lives!" Vasanthi raised her voice high above the whisper they maintained during their nighttime walks and startled a creature in the brush nearby.

Sita glanced around as she hissed, "Be quiet!"

Vasanthi let out a humorless laugh. "Be quiet, sit down, get up, fetch, clean, scrub, clap your hands, stamp your feet." She recited the words in a singsong and danced a jig at the end.

"Have you gone mad? Lower your voice!"

"Is this madness? Speaking like a normal person? All right, I'll do as you say, Sita ma, but only for you. Not for them would I lower my voice." She skidded to a stage whisper by the end of her sentence.

Sita took a guarded breath. "Is something the matter? What happened?"

"You asked me why I don't want a baby. I'm trying to tell you. If you would listen."

"I don't understand."

A breeze picked at the seams of the humid evening and cooled the sweat on their brows. Leaves fluttered, and litchis—leaden globules whose floral scent overwhelmed the stillness—swung to and fro around the women.

"What will come of our lives here?" Vasanthi's voice dropped so low, Sita had to step closer to catch her words. "We don't belong here. Why bring a new child to life here, his skin as unwelcome as ours?"

The breeze seemed to pause with bated breath as crickets resumed their dominance of night. "But I thought," Sita tried. "I thought you had some plan for your future. That you were hoping the master . . ."

But this turned out to be quite the wrong thing to say. "The master!" The syllables in her cry were carved raw with bitterness. "Weren't you the one who said we don't matter to him?"

"Yes, but I thought you felt different. That perhaps you knew different. Has something changed?"

"Nothing has changed. So everything has changed."

"Tell me what happened. What pains you so?"

"Is stupidity the same as pain? When you cut your own hand, is that foolishness or pain?" Vasanthi sighed. "I asked him for something. A small thing to him. But it would help me make a life after my girmit ends next year. I hoped—but no."

"What did you ask of him?"

"Does it matter? Forget it."

"But what will you do, then? Next year?"

"Don't worry. You won't be rid of me that easily. I'll be here another five years if he has his way."

"You'll stay here?"

"He's not done with me. Why would he help me leave? So I have to stay, and that's easier for him than pursuing a new conquest. Easier than you, surely." She laughed again.

A wave of dizziness struck Sita. Words and sensations clashed. Caress of dark against light. The warmth of an embrace to dull the sameness of each day. Fog carried across sugarcane, obscuring trysts among green shoots. Which of those images were real, and which had emerged from her imagination? She knew so little, after all, about skin. She'd been taught only to guard against incursions into her body's territory by men, a lesson repeated since her childhood. She'd never heard whisper of a woman choosing pleasure—what that might look or feel like. For a moment, she allowed her gaze to travel the length of Vasanthi's bare arms gleaming in moonlight. How the dip of her collarbone might feel under the press of Sita's own calloused finger.

She shut her eyes, and imaginings, tight. "You said he pleased you," Sita whispered. "I thought you wanted him. I thought you chose to be with him."

"'Chose to be with him'? Yes, he pleased me. I did say that. But 'chose'? What does that mean for us, Sita? Did you choose to come here?"

"Yes, I did. I marked that girmit with my own hand."

"All right. Believe that if you like, dear friend."

"What do you know about me? I tell you, this was my own cursed choice." She spoke with as much force as she could muster, but her own memories rushed in to challenge her. Anjali's words: *Your father is dead; we have to live.* Sita shook her head. "You don't know my story."

"Your story? You don't have one anymore. No one will tell about you. No one will remember you. You're just ayah in their story. You think you chose this place? They bought and brought you here, same as cattle, same as the rest of us."

"It's not true. You don't know. I came here; I wanted to leave there. I wanted a new start. Because there was nothing there, only the eyes of the dead and the echoes of your belly. And those who should have fed you ready to feed on you. And those who should have loved you as a sister ready to leave you to die in the forest. Why would I stay in such a place? I chose to leave it. It was my choice. Mine alone."

The tears ran faster than Sita could catch them. She thought Vasanthi would reach out to brush them away, but she only stood still and stubborn to the end.

"So what kind of choice was that?"

Sita inched open the door to Mrs. Dickinson's bedroom. She'd never dared enter this room before. Since the mistress had caught and attacked her, she'd been more careful to limit her explorations. But on the morning after that conversation in the orchard, a new recklessness seized her. She was not as timid as Vasanthi supposed. After all, she'd been the girl who fought to attend school with the boys, who stole away from her village in a strange man's cart under the cover of night. This boldness was part of her too.

Inside the mistress's bedroom, she was startled to find disarray. Mary must have cleaned it during breakfast as always. But the mistress had come back since to change before leaving for town. The armoire doors were flung wide open. A lone powder-blue glove lay on the floor. She'd left her skirt where it fell from her waist in a crumpled pile. Beyond the mosquito net, other items of clothing were strewn across the bed. Their quantity suggested that she'd considered several outfits before making her decision.

Sita reached out and scratched an ivory bead at the throat of one discarded dress. The bead lay within an intricate lattice of ribbon and lace threaded together so tight, you could never find the stitches sewn to keep it in place. The network extended across the bodice and met creamy fabric scalloped along the sleeves. She gently picked up the dress by its shoulders, not expecting its heft. Before it could fall, she grabbed it round the waist like a lover would. As if to satisfy this image, the dress relaxed on her arm and arched gracefully onto the bed, sleeves trailing. Sita jumped back as if scalded by this image. She withdrew from the bed and stumbled on uneven ground behind her—the edge of a fireplace where a few embers still glowed.

It was a warm day, as most were in this country. In the year and a half since Sita's arrival, she'd only shivered through a couple of wintry weeks. On other cool days, her work was sufficient to keep her warm. But a fire blazed in the sitting room every evening throughout the year and in Mrs. Dickinson's bedroom too. Some said the mistress arrived in Africa as a bride from England. They said this was the way of the English. They lit fires everywhere. Perhaps they were a superstitious lot, and the fires were meant to ward off demons from their homes. Or maybe they were a race particularly fearful of the cold.

A sudden movement across the room caught Sita's eye, and she started. But it was only a play of light. Clouds had released the sun, and it curled silky fingers along the dressing table, burnishing cut-glass bottles and their amber liquids. Sita approached the table and pushed the bristles of a silver hairbrush hard with two fingers. She coaxed the stopper from a little bottle, and the cloying scent was so insistent that she clamped it shut. It was worse than a siren blaring her trespass.

Behind the bottles, jars, and combs was a larger box—teak inlaid with mother-of-pearl designs. Sita gasped. She'd inherited a box much like this one from her mother, who brought it as part of her trousseau. Ayamma said it was originally crafted in Delhi or Burma or a place like that. Sita had never seen anything like it in their own village.

She ran her fingers now over the dips and curlicues of the carving. She remembered the high ledge where she hid it and the baubles she stowed within. Curiously shaped pebbles from the river. A poem traced on bark tucked inside her schoolbooks by a secret admirer. The cheap twist of a ring given by her best friend. A tiny elephant Maalan whittled from sandalwood for her when he was still unmarried and cherished his sister.

Sita lifted the decorative lid, almost convinced that she'd find her treasures. But it was filled instead with useless jewels that sparkled at her disappointment.

Nothing remained of Sita's past. Her box was lost in the flood. It had likely splintered against boulders on its way to join the river when the waters receded. Mrs. Dickinson's box was safe from disaster. The riches it contained protected her from false choices. She would never need to trade her body for a man's worthless promise.

The mistress never ornamented herself; she only hoarded such wealth. So she wouldn't miss a sliver of it. A single piece might purchase a new life for Sita far from this house. She already understood—better than Vasanthi, it seemed—that the world would make no shelter for her except what she took and created by her own hands.

Besides, it was only a small tax, a paltry exchange for her labor. Without pausing to weigh or choose a piece, because all of them were equally repulsive, she uncoiled a jeweled length of green from the box and tucked it into the folds of her sari. As she'd seen Vasanthi hide her dagger.

Sita shut the bedroom door behind her, alert to every sound. She should run and hide before someone discovered her. But hadn't she done enough of that already? Not just in this house, either, but from Anjali's curses, from the withering of her village. Every turn of destiny's wheel that had pursued her, none of them subject to her power. But standing here in danger's current and pushing fear aside—this was intoxicating.

She did not run and instead drifted down the hallway as if afloat. The blue and pink petals on the curtains ahead seemed to throb with the half-light that filtered through. She was painfully aware of the tender nape of her neck and longed to check if anyone lurked behind her. But she would not turn around. She was no longer a timid girl.

Her steps light, she descended the front staircase. One step, a beat, another step. She had not forgotten the masters of this house nor their cruelty. But she took another step anyway. The polished wood grain of the railing was smooth under her fingertips. She stopped to marvel at its red hue and the many stripes and whorls this once-tree had sacrificed.

Out the forbidden front door. Who dared stop her from stepping over this threshold? *Let them come*, she thought, as if thirsting for a fight. She imagined kicking and biting the Dickinsons into submission. The vision was exhilarating.

A graceful drive wound away from the entrance. So much land and all of it deserted at this hour. Sita wandered across the manicured lawn without direction, thrilled at her own daring. Anyone watching from the front windows might reprimand her: go back to the little square where you are permitted. She threw their censure from her shoulders like cloth.

As she approached a stone birdbath carved with playing children and fruit, a mynah bird alighted at its edge. She froze, only a foot away. The mynah cocked its head to one side and considered her, then seemed to decide she was no threat. It hopped into the shallow bowl and fluttered in the rainwater collected there.

Sita had seen this inquisitive bird every day in her village. She recognized the yellow stripe across its eyes and its unremarkable brown plumage. But it had become remarkable here. She'd never before seen a mynah in this land. Unable to contain her curiosity, she started forward. The mynah screeched and took wing into the lawn's stillness. Hand outreached as if she could convince it to stay, Sita watched the shock of the bird's white underbelly recede into sky. When she looked away, the shape was imprinted on her vision everywhere. It lit up a bit of fruit afloat in the shallow bathwater— maybe the mynah had dropped it. She scooped up the purple flesh and rubbed it into her palm with one thumb. A half-rotted naaval pazham.

Unmistakable, the mynah trilled from a distance, and she glanced up at the call familiar from so long ago. She could try to find it. Mynahs could be tamed and taught words. Maybe this one would speak to Sita and become a companion.

She ran in the direction of the bird's song, forgetting the house and its rules. Forgetting, even, the reckless persona she was trying on. Around the side of the house was a low stone wall and an overgrown outbuilding with a padlock on its gate. Beyond that, the grass turned wilder. The gardener had not bothered to continue his work here past the sightline of the front entrance. Grass gave way to brush as tall as her shoulder, but she parted the bushes and scrambled beyond them. Thorns scratched her arms, and gnats buzzed at her neck. Still, she snapped and swatted her way in.

The bush seemed to hiss at her approach, but she could also hear the mynah above the din. Though, not a mynah either. She paused and listened. Voices. Or just one voice. A woman's voice in a language she did not know. She tasted the texture of the words—*lll b k all ma ll b k.* Like a melody. Probably, it was just the mynah—a pet taught a song by its master.

She continued on, following her senses. She needed no pretense here. The forest seemed to let her in. She stepped out into a small clearing beneath a tree taller than the rest. Splashes of darkness carpeted the ground. Naaval maram. The mynah lived here, of course, in the shelter of a tree it remembered from the land of its ancestors.

The fallen fruit would stain her feet and clothes, but she didn't care. She clambered over and among the tree's roots and eased herself into a nook, where she fit. If only she could hide here and eat naaval pazham all day. The space under the tree was dark and the surrounding bush thick. Here, she didn't need to summon the foolhardy courage she'd seen others wear. Flurries of activity up inside the branches and creatures that crunched along the forest floor, so she'd never be alone.

She shifted her weight after a sharp prick at her side. Jewels. Trespassers to her body. She slipped them from the tuck at her waist and held them up. The crushed fruit from the birdbath had stained her hand purple. Against the darkened lines of her palm, the jewels were iridescent green.

She did not want them. Here among the tree's roots, where she felt steady comfort, the rash decision to steal them made her uneasy. This recklessness did not belong to her. She wanted to climb trees and read books, not hoard riches. The jewels would trap her all the tighter into this house's web, one way or another. She should sneak back upstairs to return them while she still could.

But then Vasanthi's face rose before her. Her careful plans to make a new life. Maybe she was right to plot and scheme to survive the white man's house, and Sita's impulse at honesty was naive. She would need whatever safety the jewels could purchase. Crouching to one side, she dug a hole in between the roots and dropped them inside. She covered them with scoops of earth made dark by the gifts of the naaval tree.

* * *

In the days that followed, Sita often thought about that hiding place among the naaval maram roots, though she did not return there. She felt uneasy at the memory of her actions, but she swiftly pushed the emotion aside. Instead, she thought about the seeds she might purchase and plant in her own land one day. She'd let trees grow tall and wild in her orchard and climb them herself to collect fruit for market.

Adrift in thought, Sita was in the kitchen preparing Desmond's midmorning snack to take up to his schoolroom. She'd just finished his tray when Mrs. Dickinson swept in.

"Where is she? The coolie woman."

The mistress crackled with electric rage. Strands of hair were loose from her bun and seemed to flame darker when freed this way. Her face was flushed, her skin blotched with red patches as if diseased.

Mary hunched her shoulders over the table to make herself smaller. The younger white maid continued scrubbing carrots without pause but shot the mistress a sideways glance. The old cook was less cautious. She stopped rolling dough to wipe her calloused hands on an apron and stare.

Sita's mind skipped to the dark earth that hid the jewels. She pulled her mundhanai around and tucked it secure before she stepped forward. "Yes, Memsahib?"

But Mrs. Dickinson only spared an impatient look for her. "Not you. The other one."

The white cook barely suppressed her glee. She hated Vasanthi's confidence and superior air. Eagerly, she pointed outside and followed Mrs. Dickinson's stomping to the screen door. She and the white maid positioned themselves there to watch. Mary found another place near the window, and Sita squeezed in beside her.

In the yard, Vasanthi pinned up laundered bedsheets on the line with her back to the kitchen. She turned when she seemed to hear Mrs. Dickinson's brisk approach. From the window, they could see Vasanthi's face clear enough. She was composed as she wiped damp hands on her sari. Mrs. Dickinson spoke with her voice raised, though she was too far for the precise words to carry. Her back ramrod straight, she gestured her agitation. Vasanthi's lips were set, grim, as she glared through the mistress's rage. Then, pouting, she turned her back pointedly. She picked up a mound of white linen from the basket and expertly tossed it over the line.

Their movements became an exaggerated pantomime—one of the traveling puppet shows Sita had seen in her village. From a distance, they were shadowed figures against white linen. Mrs. Dickinson's hand was a claw that grabbed Vasanthi's plait and pulled hard. Her grip was as bone tight as a storied beast's. Even from a distance, Sita felt the wrench of hair and instinctively reached for her own plait. Vasanthi started and lost her balance. As she fell, the wet sheet in her hand slipped from the line like a shroud for her body.

Tangled in the sheet, Vasanthi struggled to stand. She grabbed at the fabric to haul herself up. But Mrs. Dickinson had not released her. She dragged her by the plait with both hands as Vasanthi fought to free herself from the sheet and the snagged line. Her arms and legs were tentacles from their bundle. Chickens squawked in feathery chaos, and farmhands emerged from the sheds beyond to watch the women's fuss.

The white woman dragged Vasanthi across the dirt yard to the veranda, closer to the windows where Sita still stood, stricken. She could make out the terror on Vasanthi's face. The sheet was bloodied where rocks scraped her fighting limbs and the clothing line chafed her skin. Abruptly, the line snapped as if the cord to a dramatic curtain. A row of damp linens came tumbling through the mud. Some resisted and tore before they would endure the struggle; others were pulled along anyhow.

The snap of the line broke the spell on Sita too. She extricated herself from the kitchen, pushed aside the cook and maid crowded at the screen door, and ran out to the veranda. The door slammed behind her, and Mrs. Dickinson glanced up at the noise. The pause was enough for Vasanthi to wriggle free from her grip and kick off the sheet as she gasped for breath. She crawled to the curb of the veranda and heaved herself off the ground. Rushing forward, Sita pulled Vasanthi up to sit on the step. She wrapped an arm around her friend's shoulder and crouched down beside her.

Vasanthi shook like a brittle branch in a thunderstorm. The wet laundry had left her skin and clothes damp. Scraped skin bloomed blood along her legs, back, cheeks because her pinned arms were unable to protect her. A trickle of blood ran down the side of her face—she'd hit her temple. Eyes shut tight, she cowered as distant from her pugilist self as Sita had ever seen her.

A bark from the mistress. Mrs. Dickinson's face was still a deep red, but she was no longer a madwoman in her rage. She seemed to have returned to her dry manner. Another word. She pointed a finger at Sita. *Get back.* Sita shook her head and held her arms tighter around the trembling Vasanthi. A sharp splinter of thought: Could her own theft be the reason for this punishment? Maybe Mrs. Dickinson suspected Vasanthi. She could hardly breathe for the guilt. She could not let them hurt Vasanthi. She wouldn't let go.

The mistress called to the two farmhands loitering near the shed. They straightened up, clearly perturbed at being noticed. One of them chucked away his smoke as they jogged over, caps in hand. Mrs. Dickinson spoke to them in brisk English. The angle of her chin indicated her superiority, though they were easily a head taller than her. They nodded and avoided looking at Sita and Vasanthi. After the mistress's instructions, the older man ran back toward the shed and disappeared around the far corner. The only other buildings in that direction were the stables.

Perhaps she wanted Vasanthi sent away immediately and had ordered the horse and cart. Then Sita would leave, too, and come back for the jewels at night. Together, they'd make their future by selling them. They had nothing else of value to their names. No farewells to make.

Unbidden, Desmond's face appeared before her mind's eye: the silky hair pliant to comb, his chubby hand linked through hers. She pushed the image away. His was only a temporary love. And she did not have the luxury to mourn it.

The young farmhand was speaking. He was gesturing at her. *Away, away,* he seemed to say. Sita shook her head again. She'd wait for the cart with Vasanthi. If she were left behind, she might never know where they took her. Mrs. Dickinson flushed deeper and shouted at the young farmhand, who sprang to action. Roughly, he grabbed Sita's shoulder and tried to pull her from Vasanthi. He waved at the kitchen door with his other hand—*Go back inside,* his urgent gestures pleaded. *Do what she says.* Sita might have expected him to gloat over their suffering, but his expression was grim. His face was dark from the sun, plump and unlined. He was no older than she. Sita wrenched her shoulder from his grip and flashed him an angry stare. She tried to channel the kind of piercing intimidation that Vasanthi would have worn with ease.

But the farmhand was stronger than Sita. He seized hold of her armpit and pulled hard. She locked her grip around Vasanthi, but he loosened her intertwined fingers one at a time. She tucked her head onto Vasanthi's shoulder and curled like a babe to her side. Perhaps there was no reason for this obstinacy. She might feel foolish later when it turned out they were only trying to help Vasanthi—if the older farmhand returned with bandages.

But she'd made up her mind. Some intuition filled her with dread even before the mistress dragged Vasanthi across the yard like the corpse of a slaughtered animal. The sudden fall of that damp sheet over her friend's body struck Sita with foreboding.

She struggled against the boy's attempts until approaching foot-falls caused them both to glance up. The older farmhand ran up to them. Sita straightened in surprise, and her grip on Vasanthi loosened in the confusion. She'd become convinced he would bring a horse and cart from the stables. The boy saw his chance and pulled harder at Sita. At the same moment, the other farmhand drew close enough that she understood what he brought his mistress. He carried a rope. And a horse's whip.

"No!" She thought she'd shouted the word, but it only emerged as a whisper that could not count as protest.

The boy managed to extricate her grip enough to pin her arms and drag her aside. She screamed at the top of her lungs, as hard as she could. The boy tried to clamp one hand over her mouth, but she bit down, and he pulled away with a yelp. Even then, his grip was too strong. He still had her pinned.

Mrs. Dickinson pointed to the kitchen door and yelled at the boy. He tried to comply. But Sita fought, kicked, and scrambled, and for every few steps he managed toward the kitchen door, she dragged them a foot back across the veranda. Closer to where Vasanthi still crouched against a pillar. The other farmhand handed that worn leather snake to his mistress. He stepped back immediately, perhaps hoping to slip out of notice. But there was nowhere in the open yard to hide.

Sita's throat was hoarse. No one was coming to help them. Surely, the master would want to protect his lover. He would not want the flesh he feasted on to be harmed. But then, as Mrs. Dickinson took the measure of the whip, a cold realization hit Sita: all that was finished now. The intensity of this cold hatred could not be summoned for the theft of mere jewels.

Mrs. Dickinson caressed the leather with her fingertips as if to test its power. She glanced from the coiled weapon in her hands to the woman before her, and her eyes welled. But if the mistress was reconsidering her decision, the momentary emotion seemed only to confirm it. Setting her jaw square, she held the whip's handle in her fist. Her knuckles were pale as bone against dark hide. She called out to the older farmhand. He rushed forward and pulled Vasanthi up to stand like a broken doll against the pillar. She was no weight for him. She half-stumbled, her eyes open but glazed. The wound at her temple bled freely now down one side of her face. Her hair was matted with blood.

Mrs. Dickinson issued another command. The farmhand pinned Vasanthi's arms around the pillar and slipped back to tie the woman's wrists in a quick knot with the rope. It was enough to keep Vasanthi upright, though her head lolled to one side, and her knees shook. It took every ounce of Sita's will to keep her eyes open. Looking away would be a betrayal of every kindness Vasanthi had shown her. And it would betray what separated them—only a few feet of earth and circumstance.

The whip uncoiled scale by scale at Mrs. Dickinson's side. Her hard gaze swept up and down Vasanthi's body. She drew the whip back with force. She seemed to rise up with the leather as each breath quieted in anticipation of its return. The slap of cured hide against skin was muffled by a shriek. Through blurring tears, Sita saw Vasanthi's back arch. Tightened tendons in her neck. Again, a quick slash through air. Two dark maroon welts plotting parallel paths from waist across belly.

Another flash and another. Would the woman not tire; would nothing interfere. But no one appealed for mercy except Sita, who whimpered and kicked in the stony boy's grip. Mrs. Dickinson's strength only seemed to expand with the appearance of welts, as if they were soldiers she must fight. Her face was flushed with effort.

Pricks of blood crisscrossed Vasanthi's torso. They bloomed through her faded sari where she was still covered. Perhaps once, many washings and wearings ago, small flowers the colors of spring adorned this cotton. Now those blooms were red once more.

Vasanthi's knees gave. Like a sail keening in the breeze, she collapsed and folded forward into ground. Her wrists slipped down the pillar, though they were still bound behind her. As if disappointed,

Mrs. Dickinson cast the whip aside. She lifted her skirts from the dust and stormed into the kitchen.

The farmhand released Sita, and she rushed to Vasanthi's side. Trembling, she undid the knotted rope. Vasanthi flopped forward like a marionette. The young farmhand caught her before she could fall. He lay her gently on her back, arms at her side.

Sita winced at the darkening welts. "Help," she said to the boy.

He stared at Vasanthi's motionless body.

"Help her!"

He shook his head. "No one can help," he said in Tamil. She had no time to register surprise.

"Do something. You watched. You did nothing."

He glanced back at Sita with defeated eyes. A shadow fell over them. Mary.

"John, isangoma samandiya," she whispered to the farmhand. When he continued to stare, Mary flapped her hands at him: "Hamba!"

This last word seemed to snap him from his daze. He lifted Vasanthi with both arms. It was impossible to avoid the bloody slashes mapped across her body. But even though the farmhand's touch must have shot pain through her, Vasanthi did not rouse.

It felt like an age since Mrs. Dickinson first came into the kitchen, but it was only midday. Still, darkness was closing around them as Mary and Sita followed the farmhand. Thunderclouds had gathered while Vasanthi suffered Mrs. Dickinson's wrath, and now the sky was coated in soot.

The cook and other servants stayed indoors after Mrs. Dickinson left. Some peeped out through windows, but none dared to emerge and close the chicken coop or clear the yard of the muddy laundry in preparation for the storm. Perhaps they thought if they stayed in their dry kitchen, they would be safe.

As cold drops splattered across her arm, Sita hurried after Mary and the farmhand toward the stables and followed them into the earthy interior. She had never been here before and was surprised to find that the grassy odor of the horses was a comfort. She reached out to a dark-brown mare, who lowered her muzzle to her palm. She seemed to expect a treat, though, and not receiving one, shook her head and backed away.

Farther in, the farmhand and Mary settled Vasanthi into the back of an unhitched cart. The cart was packed with hay bales, and he took care to place Vasanthi on a layer of sacking. He hooked the back of the cart shut and wheeled it to the stable entrance. Mary slipped her hand into Sita's while the farmhand chose the same brown mare for this journey. He hitched the cart to the horse so quickly and easily that it was clear this was his primary job.

Hoisting himself onto the seat, he patted the mare and took up her reins. As he shifted and readied himself, he said, in Tamil, "I'll be back by nightfall. I'll try to find you to let you know."

"What?" Sita had watched him prepare the cart in a daze. But now urgency seized her. She caught hold of his pant leg and tugged. He gazed down with a mixture of pity and exasperation.

Mary clicked her tongue. "No time, Sita. Ngozi!"

"No, Mary, vumela." She brushed away the woman's hands. To the farmhand: "I won't let you take her. I don't trust you!"

The boy's mouth set in a firm line. But she didn't have patience for his feelings or time to consider why Mary wanted her to stay. She was going with him. Irritated, he gestured to the back of the cart with his chin. Mary sighed in resignation and helped boost her up. Clambering into the back of the cart, Sita scraped her thigh hard against the back bolt. Somehow, the scratch was a relief. She did not deserve to be whole while her friend lay bleeding.

The farmhand threw them loose blankets from his seat. "Cover yourselves up. The fewer questions, the better."

Sita saw nothing of their journey in the rain. Sometimes their progress was too slow; other times the mare clopped along with such speed that they tossed in the back under wet blankets. At these times, Vasanthi woke only to moan or mutter before slipping away again. She never seemed fully conscious, only toying with the idea.

After more than an hour, the cart came to a halt. She heard the farmhand slip off his seat and his feet thud to ground. She dared not move and feared the worst as she heard the farmhand speak English. The authorities might have stopped him. A set of footsteps came closer.

The blanket was roughly thrust aside by a man. He was brown-skinned but not dressed like a girmit-kare. His garb was more like the master's. He placed round spectacles on the bridge of his nose to peer more closely at the women.

Sita sat up. The rain had stopped, and they were in a narrow alley set with small doors, no windows. The ocean and its putrescence filled the air.

"Take her inside," the man said in clipped Tamil. And then to Sita: "Come, come, there's no time to waste."

The farmhand lifted Vasanthi from the cart, and Sita followed both men over cobblestones lined with decades of slime and filth. The man pushed open a door and held it as the farmhand entered sideways, careful not to hit Vasanthi on the doorjamb.

Inside, she followed down a dim hallway. A slim shaft of light shone out ahead, and Sita felt—though she could not have explained why—that they had reached a safe place where everything would be all right. But she reminded herself sharply that this was not true. She and Vasanthi had left the property without permission. This man could not protect them from the Dickinsons, no matter his fancy clothes.

The hallway opened out into a bright room like a clearing in a forest. Green leaves and vines were abundant in every corner. For a moment, Sita wondered if they'd come to a courtyard garden. But above her stretched wood beams and spiderwebs. Here and there, brick and peeling paint emerged between the green. An ordinary room. But life filled every crevice. Plants grew from pots, saucepans, old jam jars, and glass bowls. Shutters close to the roof were propped open and let in the only sunlight. It seemed, miraculously, to suffice.

The men laid Vasanthi out on a hastily smoothed sheet on a cot in one corner of the room. The farmhand retreated, cap in hand, and wiped sweat from his brow.

"I will have to examine her wounds. I am an apothecary, you see," the bespectacled man explained to Sita as he moved some of his plants aside.

"An apothecary? She needs more than a few herbs!"

"I understand," said the man simply.

He rapidly cut open the knots in Vasanthi's sari, her sleeves, even the front of her blouse. He held a ragged sheet over Vasanthi's body for decency as he examined her welts in uncovered sections.

"Help me turn her over," he commanded. Something in his demeanor reassured Sita that he had knowledge and would not hurt Vasanthi with ignorant remedies.

Together, they gingerly lifted her slight frame. Vasanthi's back was less wounded because she'd been roped to the pillar. But, then, most of her wounds were across the front of her torso, where they would cause the most suffering. This thought seemed on the apothecary's mind, too, and he shook his head. A woman staggered into the room with the weight of a full bucket and cotton rags under her other arm. She was dressed like Sita, but her cotton sari was pleated and ironed to perfection. Her blouse was trimmed with lace, like white women's dresses.

She set her bucket of steaming hot water near the cot and exchanged a few words with the apothecary in city-clipped Tamil. Nimble at work with tinctures from his shelves, he measured drops from one bottle and a few from another into a silver bowl. He poured the mixture into the bucket and instructed both women to soak rags in the hot water and clean Vasanthi's wounds. As they began work, he prepared another tincture in the bowl. This, he said, they were to dab directly at the wounds after they washed her. And with that, the apothecary and the farmhand disappeared down the hall.

Sita worked silently, too focused to wonder about the woman beside her. Together, they removed the last scraps of muddy clothing and thoroughly washed Vasanthi, then applied the medicine and a rough bandage to her forehead. After, they wrapped a clean sheet around her to preserve Vasanthi's modesty. Only then, as they straightened up and stretched, Sita noticed the clink of the older woman's gold jewelry and her clean fingernails. Her skin was smooth, not tanned to stiff leather like a laborer or farmer. She seemed too old to be the apothecary's wife. The woman, too, appraised Sita up and down. In silence, they collected bloodstained rags and Vasanthi's ruined clothes in the bucket.

Vasanthi stirred. A moan began low in her throat and gathered force. Sita touched her friend's hand. The moan continued its trajectory among the books and plants as if seeking respite. Then the front door creaked open and shut. And Vasanthi was silent once more.

The apothecary hurried in with another Tamil and a Zulu man. Both strangers were dressed like white men in their waistcoats and collars and leather shoes. Their foreheads shone as they shifted in their heavy clothes. The Zulu man carried a leather case in one hand. He squatted near the cot and peered at Vasanthi with grim fascination. As he reached into his case, he spoke to the other men in English.

"He's asking what they used to hit her," the apothecary said. It was a moment before Sita realized he'd addressed her with the doctor's translated question. "Did she use anything other than a whip? Did she push or throw her?"

Sita must stand forward and tell what she had seen. Everyone should know what the mistress had done. But what of her own part in the story? She'd sauntered in and stolen the mistress's property, as if it were nothing. Such actions brought consequences. Vasanthi was blamed, either for this theft or for her own transgressions with the master, she couldn't guess which. Either way, Sita should have trusted her own fear when it had urged her to flee the house weeks ago.

A hand on her elbow interrupted her reverie. "Come now," the older woman said, firm as a schoolteacher. "Better tell what happened."

Sita nodded, grateful for the gruff kindness. And in that instant, the certainty in herself she'd found crouched among the roots of the naaval tree returned to her. A moment when she'd known her true self. Not the reckless bravado, not even the fear that kept her contained. She found she could still hold on to that certainty, even now, and drew on it as she spoke. She avoided mention of jewels or Vasanthi's affair with the master but did hint at Mrs. Dickinson's jealousy and added the rumors she'd heard about the previous ayah. When she was finished, the apothecary whispered with the other men and turned back to her soon.

"Time will tell," he said to Sita's unspoken question. "When she fully regains consciousness, we will know better. The doctor thinks the wounds from the whip are not worrying. But she appears concussed, and we don't know how badly her head was hurt. The white hospital... Let us see what we can do. But the doctor will give her medicine for the pain and will stitch her temple to stop the bleeding."

Numbness overtook Sita as she observed the doctor tend to Vasanthi. Her friend's body was laid out like an object of study, separate from the laughter and beauty of its creature movement. The men stood around and discussed her in clinical tones—all except the apothecary. When the other man moved the sheet to examine Vasanthi's body, he turned his gaze and waited until the examination was complete. When the doctor pulled her skin together with needle and thread like seams on a rag doll, the apothecary did not flinch. But his expression betrayed a common sympathy. Sita concluded that he was a man who cared. Perhaps even about women.

Hours passed. The men smoked their pipes and discussed other subjects. The older woman left and returned. The apothecary brought Sita a meal and shrugged whenever she asked about Vasanthi. "We must wait."

Eventually, the men got up to leave, and she was told to stay and watch over Vasanthi. The apothecary explained that he would be in the other room and she must alert him if Vasanthi regained consciousness. "Just call out to me or my sister, Meera. My name is Krishnaswamy Iyer."

Iyers. Living in such a humble place. And they had given Sita water from their own cup. Without pause, they touched Vasanthi, whose skin color hinted at her birth. This was a distant land indeed.

Darkness descended. Meera brought Sita an oil lamp and another meal and sat with her while she picked at it. For the first time, she spoke about herself. She was Mr. Iyer's elder sister. Sita wondered at the lack of vermillion at her brow. She did not wear a widow's garb either. Perhaps she was a spinster. For the first time, seeing this woman's grace and eloquence, Sita allowed that the fate of a spinster might not be so terrible.

She learned that the siblings came to this country some years ago from a university in London, where both had traveled from Madras. A woman who traveled abroad for study! As Sita listened to her speak, she understood that Meera Iyer could do anything. She need marry no man.

"Why did you and your brother leave—Lon-don?" she ventured to ask.

"Gandhi-ji wrote to us. He told us about the injustice here. We thought that Tamils should be here, too, to help our comrades in the plantations."

"Who is Gandhi-ji?"

Meera laughed, not unkindly. "He is a lawyer. But much more now. I do not always . . . like him. There is much we disagree on. But he has ambition. I thought so when we met him in London too. So we're all here in Natal, for now. We shall see."

In the lantern's dim light, Sita's eyes began to droop. Eventually, Mr. Iyer came and sat down near them. "She's still not conscious," he said. "And we have to consider what's best. You understand?"

Sita shook her head wearily. The apothecary's subtleties were too much to interpret when the day continued to pound her head.

Meera took the situation in hand. "What he's trying to say, my dear, is that you have to go back. For your own good. We will take care of your friend. Don't worry."

"Go back? What do you mean?"

"To the estate," Mr. Iyer said. "You both left without a pass. There is heavy punishment. Even now, they may have reported you. But I think not. After what has happened, they will be nervous."

"I can't go back there! What will they do to me now that I've left? What if they do this to me too?"

Brother and sister exchanged glances. Meera spoke again, "Yes, of course, we are worried about you too. That is what the other Tamil man was here about. We want to defend Vasanthi and keep you both safe. We are making plans."

"What kind of plans?"

Mr. Iyer began slowly, as if to a child. "Surely, you understand, this is a crime. Even against one they would call 'coolie.'" His voice gathered passion, and he punctuated it with sharp gestures. He seemed to speak to a much larger room filled with people. "These acts have become too commonplace, and the Protector still sits on his hands. This is exactly the kind of injustice we must fight against. Enough is enough. What use the reforms, the Protector, the Commission? No, they will be sorry. We will make sure of it."

Sita stared at both of them. "But what has that to do with me? What about my safety?"

Mr. Iyer raised his arms. "We know, but staying here is impossible. The risk you face is too high."

Sita jumped to her feet, hands balled into fists. "Don't you mean *you* face risks? You show us this place, this safe place, and then you just throw us out, back to the dogs. What kind of people are you? Even if you are Iyers, I thought you felt some common humanity for us."

Sita paused and realized she was shouting. In the corner, Vasanthi stirred and gasped. All three of them turned toward the cot and waited for more. Sita crept over and felt her wrist. The pulse there was feeble. Vasanthi's expression contorted. She seemed in the grip of a terrible vision. With a jolt through her body, her eyelids sprang open. She stared straight up at the ceiling, still caught in her nightmare.

Sita whispered her name. With the air of disbelief, Vasanthi turned toward the sound. She gazed at Sita for a blank moment. Then she closed her eyes again and would not rouse no matter how many times Sita called her.

TWENTY-THREE

The evening is eerily still. Twilit clouds hang close as a damp cloth to the mouth. Rakesh and I trudge to the car. The squat buildings of this suburb are shabby against pale pink sky and streaks of indigo where night has burst through.

We have dug out everything we could from the archives about the Dickinson trial. Photocopying and organizing every page, we've worked so long that it's dusk by the time we begin our journey back to Durban. The streets are quiet here, and we pass only a few cars. On the highway, too, we are almost alone; all the cars speed past on the other side of the median to escape the city for the night.

Inside the car, Rakesh and I are lost in our own reveries. Everything we've learned is summarized in stacks of paper piled on the back seat. This story has been locked behind obscurity for so long. Freed, its demands are suffocating. I want to turn around, fill my arms with papers, and cast them out into the forgetfulness of night.

But it's too late to turn away. I cannot forget the precise number of lashes sketched across her body. I cannot forget her name. Vasanthi.

Rakesh slows to a complete halt, and the sloping highway ahead of us is dotted with red brake lights.

"Traffic jam?" I roll down my window and crane my neck to see.

Brow creased, he opens his door and steps out. People around us are doing the same. I join Rakesh in front of the car and tiptoe to see farther down the highway.

Acrid odor. A murmur in the far distance. Sounds rise and fall, and I begin to recognize a drumming rhythm in them. The faraway shouts of a riot.

"Toyi toyi," Rakesh says. I shuffle through my mind for this phrase and what little I've read of South African protest rallies.

"What could it be for?"

"I don't know." He hesitates and then seems to come to a decision. "We should leave. This isn't a show."

"Oh? Do you want to take the side streets back to Durban?"

"Probably not a good idea." He rubs the stubble on his cheek with one palm. "No," he adds. He seems to come to a decision. "We can't get back any other way easily. And I think they've blocked this highway, maybe with burning tires. It might be a while. Let's go."

I swallow back my questions and follow his lead. We buckle in, and he nods at me once before he begins to reverse. A few more cars have slowed behind us but not many. There's still enough space between them to maneuver a path. We're a few yards from an exit, and Rakesh makes his way there in reverse.

"Where are we going?" I ask as he takes the ramp.

"You remember Brenda aunty? She lives nearby, outside Verulam. I thought we might visit while we wait for this to pass. We can call and let her know."

"She won't mind?"

He shrugs. "She's a family friend, known me since I was small. She is lonely out here sometimes. And she likes you. Believe me, she'll be very happy to see us." He turns to me with a wry smile, as if to imply something more.

I raise a questioning eyebrow before I remember my last meeting with Brenda. The sly questions and references to Rakesh, *such* a nice young man. I laugh a little as I begin to understand. Brenda has held the strings from the start.

"You are such bad children," Brenda scolds as she emerges from her front door. "It took a riot to bring you here! After how long?"

"Sorry, Aunty," Rakesh says with a grin.

Shooing away his apology, she bustles us into her small bungalow. "Sit, sit," she bosses us. "Now tell me what you want to eat. You both look worn out."

After some halfhearted politeness, all three of us end up in her kitchen, where Rakesh and I chop vegetables and boil rice for a simple meal. Brenda sips wine at the kitchen table; we insisted she relax, and she agreed readily, laughing: "I'm a terrible cook."

In between sizzling onions and cumin seeds, we tell her about the discoveries we've made today.

"Ah." Brenda nods. "The Dickinson trial. Yes, I've read about that."

"Where were all the witnesses?" Rakesh wonders aloud. "Krishnaswamy spoke at the trial, but he wasn't even there when the woman attacked Vasanthi. What about the other Indians on the estate?"

My shoulders tighten as I stir the onions and scrape the bits that stick to the pan. "They couldn't have helped much anyway," I venture. "It would have meant risking their contract, or a beating, or worse. I'm sure they wanted to help."

Brenda nods. "It wasn't easy to speak up. I know very well." She nods again and seems to trail into memory.

"Come on, Aunty, you're not so old! How would you know about the witnesses in this case?" Rakesh teases as he spoons out and tests a few grains of rice between finger and thumb.

"Ag, silly boy. I don't mean this case. But you know I was in jail—how many times? I don't remember. Apartheid time. Sometimes, my friends were in jail, and I was hiding. You think I should go to court to say, 'Yes, I was there too. Arrest me'? No, baba. What sense in going to a court full of white people. No justice in there. Better outside." She takes a big gulp of her wine and pats her lips. "Look at this protest tonight, the reason you came here. The radio said it was mill workers. I know very well which one. The conditions are terrible. You don't think they tried talking before they burned tires on the highway? It's still the same."

"Yes, well. South Africa." Rakesh sighs. "What about Pakistan, Hajra? It's different there, isn't it?"

I start as if caught out. "Is what different?"

"Courts, justice. When the judges and lawyers and police are your own people."

I turn to the stove and lower the heat to simmer. Silence hangs heavier as it lengthens. "They're not my people," I mutter and busy myself with wiping the counter clean. I'm still trying for more words when I notice Rakesh's unsettling stare from the corner of my eye. "What is it?"

"Sorry." He adds gently, "You were involved in something like this? Am I right?"

Brenda's gaze sharpens on me, but she doesn't say a word. My nerves spark with the urge to flee. In that moment, I'm certain that he's always known. "What are you talking about?" I try and fail to sound casual.

"Why did you leave Pakistan?"

I shrug. "Why does anyone leave a third-world country? Fame. Fortune. The American dream."

"Maybe." He hesitates. "I don't believe everyone really *chooses* to leave home. Look at what we found out this week."

"Indenture, yes. No one chose this. I mean, even those who wanted it didn't really want it. People were escaping famine and all the rest. But that's different—" I stop, confused by my own logic.

"What's the difference?"

"It's very different! I filled out my visa application and stood in a line at the consulate. I gave them my passport through a window. I didn't press my thumb to a certificate that I couldn't even read."

"So you're better than them?"

"I didn't say better! You're twisting my words. You don't know—you've lived in this one city your whole life. How could you understand?"

"I wouldn't understand? And why do you think I've gone with you from library to library all week? This is my family; this is who I am. And I have shared it all with you, without condition. You've shared nothing."

"Enough, Rakesh baba." Brenda's authoritative tone cuts through. Rakesh turns away. I take the chair next to Brenda and stare at a point on the floor. I'm trembling. I can't help the tears, but I do my best to brush them aside before anyone notices.

There's no hiding from Brenda. I hope she'll change the subject, but I also hope she won't. When she speaks, each word is deliberate. "I don't know, eh? Why you've come all the way here. You will tell us when you are ready. But the little bit I have seen, what I've come to know about you—I trust you." She shoots a chastening glance over at Rakesh. "Sometimes we make one decision. And then we think there are no choices left. But no, my girl. There is a choice."

I am pressed into my mind. A rodent in its corner. "I want to believe that. But I ran away from danger. And each day, I am still afraid." Tears run fast and hot on my lip as I lick them away. "There was a woman. They hurt her. I saw. I was supposed to help. But I was scared. Without me, it all fell apart. I never went back." I spit the words out as if I could expel this poisoned version of myself.

"Why didn't you go back?" Rakesh asks, surprising me. His tone is harsh or just matter of fact; I can't tell.

"Because—maybe it was my fault."

"Your fault? Did you hurt her?"

"No! Of course not." But how do I explain? Because what would he and Brenda say. *Oh, we've heard about these Muslims. Honor killings in the newspapers.* I would be another of those voiceless women to him. And Rubina would become another victim too. Nothing more. "It's complicated," I manage to add.

The silence stretches out, and Brenda sighs. "Come now, we need energy for all this hectic talk. Let's eat."

Rakesh and I settle down with stiff politeness to the food we've cooked. Thanks to Brenda, the meal is not as awkward as it could have been. Without avoiding the substance of the conversation we've begun, she tells us her own stories of complex allegiances in the struggle, easing the pressure off me. I'm grateful for the break.

She's recalling a sit-in organized by a sugar worker union when she pauses and puts down her fork. Rakesh clears his throat, and we continue to stare at our own plates.

"You know," Brenda muses. "That reminds me of something." She scrapes back her chair and wipes her hands on a napkin. "You children clean up. I have to find a map."

She scurries from the kitchen. We get to our feet and begin stacking dishes without a word. I'm spooning leftovers into a plastic container when Rakesh finally speaks.

"We're wrong," he says, as if continuing a train of thought. "About the witnesses. Someone did help Vasanthi. They were there at the courthouse holding a banner. Just not inside it. Outside, like Brenda said."

"That's true." I press the container's lid into place with a satisfying click.

"My Meera Athai was there and the other women in the photograph." He dries a dish with a towel. "They stood up for Vasanthi. They risked everything."

I lean against the counter next to him, glad we're talking again. "They did. And that woman in the middle just laughed! As if it was nothing. It's like an animal sound, not language or words. Laughter. She was just being herself."

Rakesh reaches out and touches my shoulder. Each fingertip is so welcome. I close my eyes and sink into warmth. I want him to say, You did everything you could. You are still as good as you were. I want him to brush away my failings and embrace me as he would a woman still worthy of love.

"They were very brave," he says instead. "And Brenda too. We cannot all be so brave all the time."

I open my eyes, stung. I want to argue, but Brenda saves me again.

"Here! I found it." She walks in waving a ring binder and opens it up on the table. "See? This is an old map of the sugarcane plantations." She points at a photocopied page. "The Dickinson farm is marked, see? That's not far from here."

Rakesh peers at the faded markings on the copy. "Yes, here is where they've built that big mall."

"Of course, of course, all that land was sold and parceled, no? But there is still sugarcane here and here—even now." She taps her finger before glancing up at me. "You should go there, my dear."

"Visit the plantation?" I'm startled. But as soon as she says it, I'm seized by the idea. As if I'd meant to go all along.

"Yes, dear, write to them with your American university email, and they'll show you around. It will all become cement and high-rise buildings soon. Go and listen to the land while you still can."

I have gone from room to room, book to book, searching for a woman. But what of the land where she stood as witness. I have not sought that land.

The radio tells us the highway has been cleared. We bid Brenda farewell and get back in the car. The suburban streets are quiet. In the distance, endless fronds of sugarcane are black needles in silhouette against the streetlights. Through my weeks here in Durban, the crop has inched gently above ground.

"I want to go to those sugarcane fields from the map," I tell Rakesh without preamble. "Now. Will you take me?"

"Now-now?"

"Yes. I've waited too long already."

He considers. The sensible option would be to contact the owners or even simply return in the daytime. But my heart is laden with Brenda's words and the memories this evening's argument sparked. I cannot wait for permission any longer, not anywhere.

"All right," he says. "But we will just look from outside."

We proceed, quiet, along the sleepy streets. More than once, he pulls over and compares the map Brenda gave us with a current one in the glove compartment. Eventually, road becomes gravel becomes dirt path. We are skirting around the boundary of a large plantation. Sometimes the road fades into bush, and we have to reverse and try another path. Eventually, Rakesh finds a spot to park quite close to the fencing. He turns off the headlights, and we stare out as darkness presses against the windshield.

"Now what?" he asks.

"Let's walk around a bit."

"Wait—" he starts, but I've already opened my door. Though I don't know my way, I feel an irresistible urge to escape my timid self. I take a step and then another.

"Here, slow down." Rakesh switches on a flashlight and picks his way around to me. "We have snakes here, real ones. Watch where you go."

He takes my arm, and we edge forward through the brush. Our arms are braced against snagging twigs. Small animals scuttle at our approach. A loose flap of wire fencing. I slip under before he can stop me, and after an impatient noise, Rakesh follows me. Lights twinkle at the farm's distant outbuildings. Our footfalls feel like a giveaway, and I listen for a shout or the bark of a dog. But, alone in the fields, we are indistinguishable from swaying cane.

The cane is taller than it appeared, high as my waist. I run my fingers over a new tendril. In Pakistan, I have drunk salty sugarcane juice cranked out of diesel-fueled machines on the street corner. I have sucked on cold slices of ripe cane twisted tight in plastic bags and sold by small boys running along railway platforms. I've spat the spent bark from each piece out the speeding train's window into the countryside beyond. But I have never known cane while its limbs are still alive and rooted. Here, the crop belongs, whole-hearted, to earth.

"Many years since I saw sugarcane like this." Rakesh is a row away; a line of green stretches between us.

"It could have been here," I say. "Vasanthi's attack. Just there, near those lights."

I point toward the outbuildings and take a few steps through the rustling stalks. The beam of light at my back flickers and then dies. Rakesh says something about batteries and fumbles in his pockets, so I pause. But my eyes adjust. There's enough moonlight to see my path forward, and I can't wait any longer.

Without the flashlight, my hearing sharpens too. Crickets play their evening symphony in composed waves. A chorus of toads issues a full-throat complement. A birdcall—two chirrups and then a long trill, almost too high to make out. The song tugs hard at a memory. It's an almost-memory of sound just out of reach. I was standing in the fields at dawn, and the same birdsong surrounded me. But I have never stood in a field before.

I rush forward to follow the call. I pause only when the rows of cane give way to a dense thicket. I clap and stamp and hope it's enough to send any snakes slithering away. The birdcall repeats louder now, almost as loud as my thumping heart. I have always lived in a city, and every sense is sounding an alarm. Still, shielding my face from thorns, I elbow forward through bush. I've already crossed oceans to be here. I can't stop listening to the world now.

The night air changes. The texture in my breath and the scent of tilled earth. They all drift into the background, and it feels as though every creature is listening with me as I stand still. I can hear a voice but discern no words. A person speaking. I'm not as afraid of snakes and spiders as I probably should be, but I am afraid of people. Living ones, men especially, but not only them—everyone who has reduced me to a figure crouched low. I press forward, on guard now. The voice continues its lilt. The bush clears, and my foot catches. I stumble to my knees. My hands grasp a knobby tree root and feel forward by cautious fingertips. Roots ascend into cracked bark. I crawl forward and extend my arms around the trunk, expecting my hands to meet on the other side. But my forearms only flatten out.

Only by closing my eyes can I take the measure of a tree that extends far beyond my understanding. I listen to the branches that push leaf by leaf into the canopy and the rotten fruit that started as flowers and the ants that climb through tunnels in the bark and roots that reach out into the fields and link with sugarcane underground. And the voice, too, that is stored here—perhaps pinned like a letter inside one of the thickened tree rings and muffled by the years.

". . . roar through the fir trees." Only once is a sliver of the voice clear enough to make out. I repeat the words and taste them. Cupping my hands against my mouth, I whisper them again and again. They become only echoes of sound.

I, too, want to record a secret here. I cast about for something hidden I've wished to speak. But the words that come forth startle me. They interrupt the quiet before I can stop them.

"Labbayk Allahumma labbayk." A prayer I was taught in another life that's never felt right on my tongue before. But I have submitted to this call, in my own way, by being here. And I've called out, too, searching, in my own way. Here I am. I am here.

I retread my steps back out of the clearing and walk into a beam of light. Shielding my night eyes, I stumble again, but Rakesh catches my elbow this time. He pulls me to him roughly. I've worried him with my disappearance. I expect to be reprimanded; it's an old expectation. But he says nothing, only rests a hand on my cheek. I reach for his face too. His lips are as soft as bruised fruit on mine.

I pull back from his scent and warm skin. *You've shared nothing*, he said at Brenda's table. So I told him about Rubina. But even then, I couldn't manage to tell him why I fled. Now that I've declared my being here out loud, I must be present wholly. And I cannot protect Ali any longer. That's what I've been doing all these years. Letting him hide behind my shame.

"The woman I told you about this evening. Who got hurt. I didn't hurt her. But my brother may have been part of it. I can't be sure. But she was dressed like me. And he hates me because I spoke out."

Rakesh is quiet a moment before he asks, "You think your brother wanted to harm you?"

I manage a nod.

He shakes his head. "Only your own family can hurt you so much." Sighing, he's quiet awhile. "I have no brothers or sisters, you know. I always wanted one. Many days, taking care of Aunty, I wish I had someone to share things with. But then I remember. I have my family."

He bends and rises, his hands cupped toward me. Inside, a tiny cricket chirps and startles me into a tearful hiccup of a laugh. And with the strange sound from the back of my throat, a lightness spreads through my body. I'm lifted from my mind's secretive misery.

Rakesh releases the creature and twists a finger around a frond of cane. "Maybe this will sound silly, but—when I remember that I am just a small part of this world, the loneliness of being an only child fades away. The land saves me, over and over again."

* * *

"Granny, she should have diffren' name when she was young," Aunty says as Rakesh helps me file our research at the dining table the next day. Perhaps one of the many photographs or court transcripts spread out across the table triggered her memory.

"What was her name before, Aunty?" Rakesh asks, carefully casual.

"I dunno, eh? But I remember she say, when she get marry and start new life with Grandpa, she took a new name."

Rakesh promises he will try to learn more about this name change. But I grow tired of my own scholarly persistence. I begin to lose the thread of my research. English print cannot help us read the pain snaking across our family trees.

A woman's laughter was strong enough to pull me across the ocean. So what if I haven't found her name misspelled in a ledger by a British clerk. I've come to the land that joins us. The bit of earth just outside another woman that holds the echoes of both our stories. It's the closest I can come to her.

* * *

The waitress eases in between tables to fill our water glasses. "And how is everything?"

I swallow my mouthful of seafood pasta hurriedly to answer, but the child at the next table flings his fork to the floor with a clatter, and she rushes away to rescue it. Rakesh gives me a wry smile, but I'm not certain because our candle anchored in a tiny bucket of sand has flickered out. We can barely see each other.

It was my idea—this awkward, mostly silent dinner date. I wanted to thank him and thought an evening away from paper cuts and microfilm was overdue. Maybe I'd entertained other vague ideas too. It's been days since our brief embrace in the sugarcane field, and we haven't spoken about it once.

We haven't had much time together. He's back at work, and I've been filling in the gaps in my research with Dr. Naidoo's help, careful to distract myself from thoughts of the plane ticket I've bought to Karachi. It's not as if I have time for romance. Romance! An idea meant for blond girls and Archie comics. Sri Devi in a red sari at the beach.

I give up on the rubbery bits of squid left on my plate. Rakesh is valiantly attacking his greasy fish and soggy chips.

"You don't have to finish that," I tell him with a sigh.

"Yes, but I enjoy a challenge," he says.

We burst out laughing, and I think my relief is reflected in Rakesh's expression too. I've found a friend in him, and I'll always be glad for that much. Warmth suffuses my chest. Friendship is enough for someone with my preoccupations.

"I think you've earned your medal already. Shall we go?"

Outside, the breeze is a mildewy breath from the nearby port. This close to downtown, the buildings are all peeling-paint storefronts with padlocked grills and alarm systems.

"Let's walk awhile." I'm reluctant to return to the car; it feels too soon for the evening to be over.

"Hmm. This area at night . . . but the main road will be fine. Over there."

A couple of turns and the streets are brighter. I vaguely recognize some of the shuttered department stores, but the atmosphere here is transformed at night. So many people are out to enjoy the mild evening. Men in shalwar kameez linger in doorways, smoking cigarettes. Two women brisk-walk past us on the sidewalk in burqas and sneakers. I catch a few words of their conversation—Urdu.

"Is this a Pakistani neighborhood?" I'm amazed that I never knew.

"Yes, and Nigerian and Bangladeshi and Zimbabwean and everything else. Like New York, yes?" Rakesh smiles at me. Unexpectedly, he takes my hand and threads his fingers through mine. I'm frozen in surprise, but I manage to give his palm a weak squeeze in response.

A middle-aged man emerges from a convenience store and hands out small, wrapped packets through the open window of a parked car.

"Paan!" I'd recognize the triangles of newsprint anywhere.

"What is that?" Rakesh squints to figure out where I'm pointing.

"You've never had paan?"

I drag him by the hand over to the stall with its many Urdu signs and ice cream freezer at the doorway. I bound up the steps and give my order with a surge of joyful authority: "Do meethe paan!"

The skinny teenager behind the counter hands them to me with a shuddering yawn. On the pavement, we peel open the wrapping, and I demonstrate how to stuff the whole green-leaf triangle in one corner of my mouth. There is no elegance to paan, I realize too late. It's not exactly date food. Rakesh chews with careful suspicion, his cheeks puffed. The betel nut crunch is so loud. He frowns as he works his jaw through all the bursts of texture. What a ridiculous notion this was. He's probably cracked a filling.

He swallows the last of the paan and smiles. "Very . . . interesting. So many flavors." He laughs. "Who came up with this?"

I exhale the breath I've held and laugh with him. "I like the bitter ones better, but I thought we'd start you with sweet."

"A naughty plan." He reaches out and tucks a strand of my curls behind my ear. His touch lingers there at the edge of my neck.

A loud squawk and we jump apart. At the corner, a few feet away, an older man in shalwar kameez spreads a stained bedsheet on the sidewalk. On the ground next to him is a large cage and, inside it, a green parakeet. The man squats and fans out scraps of pastel-colored paper across the sheet.

Two midnight-skinned men in long robes and caps approach from across the street and watch him set up as they smoke. Mesmerized, we saunter closer, too, and join the crowd beginning to form around the man and his bird. He opens the cage, and the parakeet hops onto a stick that he swirls around him. He brings the stick up to his shoulder, and the bird hops off to nibble at his hair.

"Are we dreaming?" Rakesh leans closer and whispers in my ear. His scent is pine needles crushed underfoot. I turn to answer his question, but I've forgotten what I was going to say. His lips are inches from mine.

"Mitthu see Mitthu see everybody amaze everybody amaze," the man calls out, singsong.

I laugh at Rakesh's bewildered expression. "He's a fortune teller," I explain. "I've seen this in Pakistan."

"Oh? Well, then, what are we waiting for? I have some questions about destiny. Thank God he's here."

Rakesh strides forward, squats before the man, and counts out some change. The bird seems to recognize this cue. It hops from the man's shoulder back onto his stick and then to the ground. There, it paces back and forth among the pastel notes as if considering before bending and grabbing one with its beak. The man tugs at the note adorned with blue flowers, but the parakeet doesn't want to let go. It flutters from the bit of paper and swings side to side as if dancing. We all laugh and clap at the performance, and, satisfied, the bird releases Rakesh's fortune.

The fortune teller smooths out the paper with appropriate solemnity and shows Rakesh the creased image of a tall tree heavy with fruit. "Much money your life. You must to make investment." He glances up at me and back to Rakesh. "And much love coming for the rich gentleman also."

He twirls the paper around Rakesh as if to bless him, then folds and replaces it in the fan on the ground. Rakesh gets to his feet, and two girls wearing floral hijabs push past him, impatient for their turn.

"It's a good thing you're destined for riches." I smirk. "You just lost your money for nothing, I think."

Rakesh puts his arm around my shoulder, and we wander away from the crowd.

"Not for nothing. The bird knew a bit, I think. Or no—was he wrong?"

"Who am I to argue with fate? Especially when predicted by a parrot."

I pause and reach to cup his face in my hand. This time, when we kiss, I'm not anywhere else but right here among the streetlights and ocean breeze.

TWENTY-FOUR

It was the middle of the night when Sita slipped into the house. Mr. Iyer and John, the farmhand, planned it this way. The men discussed it all in English and gambled with Sita's life without seeking her opinion. Luckily, things turned out as they'd planned. Everyone was asleep—or appeared to be—by the time John drew up to the stables. Woodsmoke curled up from the direction of the worker quarters. A dog barked, and the chickens rustled fretfully in their coop. But otherwise, no one seemed awake for her reentry.

Sita ran across the yard, shutting out the memories it provoked. The kitchen door was unlocked as usual. Moonlit shadows fell across the stone floors. The back stairs were pitch dark. Desmond's resting breaths were visible as small currents under the covers. Her own bedding was rolled up as she'd left it that morning. Nothing in this little life had changed.

She sank onto the cold floor and wrapped herself around the rolled mat for comfort. Her fitful sleep was interrupted by dreams of green vines grown vicious. Vasanthi's unseeing eyes wide open.

In the morning, Sita picked up objects and replaced them, undressed the child, and dressed him. She was a doll with strings to guide her. Her departure and absence must have been noticed, but no one said a word. Not the white cook or maid in the kitchen, their expressions superior. Mary's hand brushed hers in sympathy when she handed over Desmond's breakfast tray. But even she did not ask after Vasanthi, perhaps having learned what she needed from John. The girmit-karan in the scullery refused to meet Sita's eyes when she brought Desmond's dishes to them.

This house was the reality she'd known. But now another reality resided in that room filled with plants, where her friend struggled to wake. She could not reconcile the two. Soon, she had to take Desmond for his morning time with his mother. She last saw Mrs. Dickinson cast the whip aside and disappear into her house. Maybe now she would reprimand Sita for leaving without permission. Laborers had been banished across the ocean for less.

Inside her sitting room, Mrs. Dickinson sat, composed as always, in her armchair. A small book lay in her lap. Though the book was open, she was gazing out the window at the lawn beyond. Desmond rushed forward with a drawing he'd brought and placed it over the book's unseen pages. His mother returned from her reverie as if surprised she had a son at all. She studied Desmond's face and his gesticulating hands with the baffled expression of a young girl.

But only for a moment. Collecting herself, she glanced up at Sita with hard eyes and waved her away. "Come back later," she said. Nothing in her tone was different from every day.

The dismissal could not have come sooner. At the doorway, rage surged inside Sita as a tidal wave. She wanted to rush back inside and lunge at the white woman's tidy throat. With her ragged fingernails, she'd shred the starched lace collar and trace a network of scars identical to those she'd washed on Vasanthi's body. But it was not enough to hurt her in this room surrounded by her beautiful possessions. Her own people must see her thrown on the ground and humiliated in the middle of town.

Sita sprinted up the back stairs into Desmond's quiet room. She could not scream here, not anywhere. Her sleeping mat was insubstantial as a weapon but the only thing in this room that was hers. She lifted it high and smashed it against the wall, again and again. Dull thuds and clouds of dust were the only result.

Revenge on the mistress meant nothing—not here but not even in public. She could stand up and come back to her husband and son. She could not be humiliated because nothing she loved could be taken from her.

Mr. Iyer had promised he would get word to Sita. But twilight fell, and she heard nothing. She sat by Desmond's window and listened to the rhythm of his slumber. Rest was impossible when the mistress could slip into this room at any moment to attack her. The master, his desires left unsatisfied, could come in search of Sita's flesh. It was hard to believe she'd ever slept easily here, especially in the days since she'd stolen the jewels. Only her own willful ignorance had permitted that rest. But she could have no peace in their house now. She could no longer avoid the gravity of her situation.

Without caring to quiet her footsteps, she ran down the stairs. In the kitchen, the cook was still tidying after dinner and stared down her presence. But Sita did not stop to make excuses. She slipped out and raced to the stables. She searched for John, the farmhand, who was now her sole connection to the safety of the Iyers.

The horses were already scrubbed down for the night and the stables were empty of humans. She crept across to spy on the outbuildings where the white workers lived and where she was never allowed. But she saw no one. Returning to the stables, she crouched just inside the half-open doors. Perhaps the farmhand would come back here. She could not bear to return to the house before speaking to him.

She roused to the rooster's crow and a smudge of dawn against sky. Her limbs protested as she uncurled from her position and sprinted to the quarters to wash and return to the house before she was missed. Some of the women there cast curious glances at her when she arrived covered with bits of hay. No matter. Not one of them asked after Vasanthi, their erstwhile entertainer and defender. Sita didn't care what they thought.

All day, she seethed at the Iyers' betrayal. They were callous to leave her in this place. She could have been whipped or worse for her absence without leave. Rich people like them could not hope to understand. Sita resolved to get Vasanthi out of their clutches as soon as she could. She would go in search of the farmhand again that evening. But before she could do so, he found her.

Early in the evening, she brought Desmond's dirty dishes to the kitchen after putting him to bed. Making something of a clatter while taking the tray from her, Mary whispered, "Outside. John s'there. S'wait you." She angled her chin toward the stables.

Mary took the tray into the adjoining scullery. After a beat, Sita followed her. The dishwashers squatted there and gulped down their meals before the pots and pans from dinner piled up. Her own portion sat near them too—a tin plate covered by a towel in the corner. Sita swept past the men toward the door and the gathering dusk behind them.

Before she could leave, Mary pressed a tiny packet into her palm. "For Vas'thi," she whispered.

Clasping the gift in her fist, Sita ran across the yard. A soft voice stopped her at the corner: "Sitt-ah."

John emerged from the sheds with a black and white dog panting at his heel. He beckoned her to follow as he took a circuitous route around the outbuildings toward a part of the estate she did not know. The dog trotted alongside him but also stopped occasionally to check on Sita as if she were a sheep that required herding.

As the evening grew darker, the shrubbery around her came to nocturnal life as bats swooped and crickets sang. The dog was the first in their party to come to a halt. Earth scent and green leaves bloomed; night seeming to press against them from all sides. Neither distant light nor murmur hinted at the surrounding estate. Sita could make out the dog's ears pointed, alert, and nose sniffing eagerly at the air.

Soon, a man emerged from the brush, and the dog's excitement could not be contained. He sprang forward, and the stranger bent to embrace the animal. When he straightened, a shaft of moonlight illuminated his face. It was Mr. Iyer.

"You!" Sita cried out without disguising her contempt. When she first met him, she was intimidated by his highborn speech and the white man's clothes on his back. No longer. "Where have you been? What have you done with my friend?"

He made her a ridiculous bow by way of greeting. "Your friend is healing. I have come with the happy news that we believe she will make a full recovery. I apologize that I could not come sooner to inform you, but it has not been easy to arrange this meeting."

"And it has not been easy to return to this house! Everyone behaving like nothing happened. That woman's blood runs cold as a serpent. For all you knew, she might have killed me already." She stopped just before she could add: for all you knew, she might have found me out as a thief.

John cleared his throat and turned to play with the dog as if embarrassed. Mr. Iyer began a careful response, "Our friend John here has kept an eye on you, though he could only do so from a distance. Of course, you took a great risk returning here. I commend your bravery. But the risks would have been greater had you not returned. The punishment for deserting the contract has, at times, been grave. And Dickinson is influential. We have to be very cautious, you see."

He spoke as if to a child on the cusp of a tantrum. Sita was tempted to fulfill his expectations and stamp her feet. "And where will your care take us? How will it help me serve out my time in this house?"

Mr. Iyer nodded solemnly, but he did not answer her. Sita muffled the frustrated noise that rose to her throat. He couldn't understand the crush of her emotions. There was too much she'd kept from him about her own culpability as thief and Vasanthi's relations with the master.

John moved closer to Mr. Iyer, and an urgent discussion ensued between the two men. Intense fatigue overtook Sita, and she crouched down. She opened her eyes to a wet sensation. The dog swiped her ear and cheek with a slobbering lick. He smelled of damp linen and sweat. The memory of still-wet laundry dragged across earth and body. The dog nuzzled her chin, and his cold nose pulled her back to now. Sita rested her brow against his matted fur for comfort. He sniffed at every fold of her sari and found a small knot that interested him. It was the little packet Mary had given her. Undoing the layers of cloth and paper within, she found a thimble-sized nugget—some kind of ointment.

Mr. Iyer came over and crouched beside her. "You should return to the house. The hour is late, and you must not be caught. I came only to inform you about your friend's health."

Sita sat up. "But what happens next? Will she return here?"

"Don't concern yourself with that. We will take care of her."

"You? Who are you to take care of her? What is she to you?"

He looked away, awkward. "I do not mean myself alone. My sister as well. And others want to help her—a lawyer especially. There are many of us working hard on your friend's case."

"She is not a case! We don't need you and your friends. As soon as Vasanthi recovers, we will leave this wretched place forever."

"Oh? Where will you go? With what funds?"

His dismissal was so casual, confident in his worldly knowledge. And yes, she knew nothing about how to trade jewels for a new life.

Maybe the impetuous risk she'd taken would come to nothing. But, too, this rich man did not know what she knew—how to survive in a foreign land with nothing to her name. So, voice low as a threat, she replied, "We found our way here; we will find our way out."

He frowned. After a frosty silence, he said, "All right. As you wish. But please listen. In the days to come, keep to your work and out of the way of white servants. Do not make any trouble with anyone. Do not gossip about what happened. If other girls ask you about Vasanthi, say you don't know where she is. Do not speak of that day or of her. You will do this? You will listen to me?"

As he spoke, Sita folded her arms about her chest. Warmth rose to her cheeks. Who was he to issue instructions? Forbid "gossip"? He knew nothing of her loneliness. In response, she shrugged and held out Mary's packet. He took it with a sigh. Bidding her a gruff good-night, he shook hands with John and turned to leave.

But then he paused. He called over his shoulder, "Sita, listen, ma—"

A gentle syllable, a brotherly word. She could hardly recall what it was to be "-ma" to someone. She who was once "little girl" to each person in her home. The very notion of being small and deserving of protection had grown alien.

"Be careful," he added before disappearing into the bush.

Sita slept as little as possible in the days that followed. For most of the night, she remained alert to the sounds of the house. She stole ground pepper in a paper twist from the kitchen and kept it tucked at her waist, ready to throw at an assailant.

She watched for John too. Taking Desmond around the house for his lessons or to see his parents, she searched out of each window. Whenever she and Mary were in the same room and out of earshot of other servants, she asked about him. She stitched together the shape of his routine.

Three days after their clandestine meeting with Mr. Iyer, she was ready. She put Desmond to bed as early as she could, then half-crouched, half-ran past the stables. She hid nearby and waited for John's usual evening trip from the estate. Though proud of her stealth, she had not accounted for John's dog. The animal bounded up to her and began to lick her face as she tried to shoo him away. A whistle and he sprinted off. Sita rose with as much dignity as she could muster. She picked the twigs from her hair and dusted leaves from her sari. She nodded at John; he responded with a tired smile. Placing a finger to his lips, he motioned her to follow.

Inside the stable, a covered wagon was already hitched to the mare. Boxes and packages were piled up inside. He cleared away a gap between them, and she climbed into the hiding place as small as possible. Just in time. A voice boomed at the stable entrance—it was the overseer. He had brought another package for the trip into town. John loaded it alongside the others and strapped everything together with rope.

The wagon trundled onto the muddy road beyond the estate, and Sita let out a deep exhale. At least the ride would provide some respite from the days of vigilance. She considered sleeping for a while, but excitement overcame her exhaustion. From a peephole, she caught sight of the passing countryside. Oxcarts, horse-drawn wagons like their own, servants and laborers on foot. Some carried large baskets; others led cattle at the end of their day. Once they reached Durban's outskirts, her view changed. The road was steadier, and she saw more carts, some drawn by multiple horses. A giant vehicle larger than a train carriage sped down the street, pulled by several horses. People sat inside, silhouettes at windows both upstairs and downstairs.

Sita wanted to see Durban, the metropolis she'd heard about from Tulsi and others. She'd never been to a city. She hadn't even seen Madras, only its port. She wanted to see wide avenues and the dockside quarters where sailors were said to indulge their vices. She'd heard one could climb stairs inside the clock tower and see for miles. But John turned into a side street before they could enter downtown. He wound through narrow roads in between peeling houses where the air smelled of urine and spices. Soon, they arrived at the shabby alley she remembered. Alighting quickly, she pushed the Iyers' door open and paused for John to follow. But he stayed atop the wagon and waved her away.

In the dark hallway, the room at the other end shone bright. Laughter burst forth, and she smelled onions and mustard seeds in hot ghee—rich foods from weddings and festivals. Conscious of her faded sari stained with sweat from the day's work, she crept into the room. The people gathered inside did not see her in the shadows.

Vasanthi reclined on a cot. She was wrapped in a blanket with two pillows against the wall to support her. She was so much herself. Her hair was plaited and coiled around one shoulder. Her complexion was a little gray, but her skin gleamed, and her lips were twisted in that mischievous smirk. Around her, men waited in the manner of attendants at a ruler's court—two Tamil men as well as the Zulu doctor. One of the Tamil men seemed to be translating for the Zulu man, who nodded in great amusement. The other leaned toward Vasanthi, perhaps with some murmured witticism. Mr. Iyer stood a few steps in the background. He appeared smaller among these other men.

"Oh, Sita? We did not expect you. But why are you hiding here?" Meera. Sita ducked her head and shrugged but was rescued from the need to respond. In her commanding manner, Meera pulled her into the room and announced, "Look who is come!"

The men examined Sita with varying degrees of curiosity. The Zulu man's expression was warm; one of the Tamil men seemed apprehensive, the other uninterested. Mr. Iyer's face was all pained disapproval; by stealing away, she had not followed his orders.

Vasanthi pushed herself up to sit and slid her feet onto ground. "Sita!" she cried, her voice hoarse. The men implored her to remain in bed. Vasanthi waved them away like buzzing flies, which only made them more insistent.

"You better go to her." Meera laughed. "Before one of them lays an egg with all that clucking."

Sita crossed the room, aware of all the eyes on her. Vasanthi reached out with both arms and pulled her close. "Come," she murmured. "Sit here. Tell me, are you well? Has anyone harmed you? I ask these people every day, but they refuse to bring you away from that place!"

She flashed an accusing glance around the group and lingered particularly on Mr. Iyer. He pinched off his spectacles and began cleaning them on a handkerchief. "We explained this to you," he said without looking up. "It was only for her good."

Vasanthi sucked her teeth dismissively. She turned from the men and peppered Sita with questions about their time apart. The effect of her withdrawal was dramatic. The men seemed extinguished somehow. They lit their pipes and attempted to kindle the embers of their own conversation. Soon, though, their presence nearby faded from Sita's awareness as she was swept into Vasanthi's infectious spirit.

"You are so well," Sita ventured after they'd shared immediate news. "I hoped, but I did not expect to find you so recovered."

A sardonic twist returned to Vasanthi's smile. "What, you think we are so easily defeated? That pathetic cockroach of a woman could not knock me down for long." Her chin pushed out, she was irresistibly impish. Sita could almost believe her bravado.

Not for long. Vasanthi's sari was arranged precisely across her chest, and long sleeves covered her arms. She'd almost succeeded in concealing her wounds. But as she played with the end of her plait, it shifted to reveal a scar that curled like a snake from her breastbone across her collar and almost to her ear. Sita shut her eyes, and behind her eyelids rose a vision of that other Vasanthi. A broken doll.

Warm fingers threaded through Sita's. The hand was as rough and chapped as her own. She'd know it anywhere—she'd brushed Vasanthi's hand every day taking meals from her. Her pulse quickened at the touch she'd so missed. She opened her eyes. Vasanthi's smile had faded into a tired expression. She leaned against the pillows more heavily. "You tried to stop her, da," she whispered. "It is a great comfort to have a friend in this strange land. No . . ." Her gaze drifted beyond the corners of the apothecary's room. "Not a friend. You are a sister."

Sita bristled at the word, though she knew it was a compliment. She did not want to be Vasanthi's sister. Confused by her own emotion, she only smiled.

They ate dinner on enameled plates lit by oil lanterns. Sita had imagined a grander scene for these people whose skin matched her own but whose cadence, clothing, and habits were so foreign. But the only thing foreign about the meal was that a man helped his sister prepare and serve it. The group's discussion seemed to become more agitated as the evening wore on. Meera held forth and contributed as much as the men, who attended her remarks with respectful silence.

As she helped clear away the dinner things, Sita ventured to ask Meera about the few sentences she'd understood. The older woman rolled her eyes with a pronounced sigh. "That little brother of mine. Sometimes I think I have raised him better than other men. And then sometimes he is like the rest. He didn't tell you anything about our plans?"

When Sita shook her head, Meera explained that one of the Tamil men was a lawyer who worked on behalf of indentured laborers. The other two men were helping him bring a case against Mrs. Dickinson because her assault on Vasanthi might have broken new laws protecting Indian workers in this land. Sita would be called on to help with the case as an eyewitness. All those assembled in the room were part of a group loosely connected to the man, Gandhi.

"They allow women to join?"

Meera threw her head back and laughed. "Let them try to stop us!"

When she moved and spoke, Meera did so with her uncoiled body. She didn't restrain her muscles from their natural expression as most girls were taught. She never attempted to make herself as small as possible. Vasanthi was the only other woman Sita knew who took such room without caring whether it was permitted. But Vasanthi's body was her weapon; she said so herself. Meera's body was a vehicle in which her mind and heart thrived, whose free movement she refused to stifle.

All too soon, John appeared at the door. Meera and Mr. Iyer offered him some food, but he shook his head. At the doorway, Meera pressed something into Sita's hands. "This is a loan," she said. "Finish it and bring it back."

It was a thin, worn book, folded and unfolded many times. An English book. Sita glanced at the older woman in surprise. Meera was smug. "I know you can read it. I saw you listening to our conversation and peering at the newspaper. This will help you get better."

For a moment, the exhilaration of paper between finger and thumb overtook her. It might even be a story that she could escape into, like the books she'd borrowed from the nuns years ago. But then bitterness replaced the excitement. She was going back to that house, where her safety still hung in the balance at each moment. She thrust the booklet back at Meera. "What shall I do with this? Will I use it to kindle the boy's fireplace? Or mop his brow? This is of no use to me."

Meera was quiet for a moment. "Keep it anyway," she said. "Bring it back next time."

It was easier to acquiesce than argue. Sita mounted the wagon and crouched in her place. This time, she did not try to find a peephole and spent the journey in darkness.

Back in Desmond's room, she hid the book behind a loose panel at the back of the boy's wardrobe. She was careful not to read the book's cover before putting it away. Meera and her rich friends were dangerous. Sita must protect herself from the temptation of ideas not meant for her.

She was unable to steal away to the stables again for a few days. Once, she ran into the mistress in the corridor when she tried to leave and had to make an excuse. Another day, a suggestive smile from the master when she picked up Desmond kept her awake all night and too nervous to venture out.

But finally, she managed to slip out. She was racing past the chicken coop when a voice called behind her. The overseer stalked over to her. She'd heard tales of the man's fearsome temper in the fields. His shirt buttons were taut over his gut, and a package was clasped under one burly arm. The skin of his neck was a bright-red wattle. His face, too, was as red as an overripe fruit, but she could not tell if he was angry or if it was his natural complexion.

"You," he said. "Why you run here, coolie?"

The overseer's eyes were blue pinpricks in that meaty face, and her mind was blank. Then the overseer looked over his shoulder at the sound of footfalls. Mary rushed up, breathless.

"Mina bathola! Mina bathola!" She held out Desmond's wooden train—carriages connected by string. He liked to play with it on the veranda, where Sita sometimes set up an obstacle course of rocks and twigs. "Bathola," panted Mary as she held the train out. *Found.*

It took a fraction of a second for Sita to understand the proffered excuse. She dipped her head in thanks, took the train, and held it up to the overseer in mute explanation. He grunted and continued toward the stables. John watched from there, half-hidden in shadow. He might never agree to take her into town again. By helping her, he was risking his own employment and perhaps trouble with the authorities too.

But the next day, he sent her a message through Mary again, and she met him at the stables as instructed.

"It is bad to go town without pass," he said. "But you will." He shrugged as if life was full of such inevitabilities. "Next time, please, wait for my dog. Evening time, he will come at veranda and bark. Then to follow him."

Amazed at this ability of the mangy animal, Sita muttered her thanks and turned to leave.

"Where you going?" John called. He grinned. "You here already. Come." He held up the sacking on the cart for her.

She began to get Desmond to bed earlier and earlier in the evenings by devising games that exhausted him in the afternoons. After he was asleep, she brought his dinner dishes to the kitchen and waited in the scullery or on the veranda. There, she ate her own meal and watched for the black and white dog to trot up. She often chatted with Mary in the mixed-up language they shared. Sometimes, the other woman's companionable silence was enough. In any case, Sita preferred it to any conversation she might have with the estate's girmit-karan. She could not forgive their indifference toward Vasanthi.

At the Iyers' home, preparations to take Vasanthi's case before a judge became busier each visit. Men and even a few women labored over stacks of paper. Pots of rice and lentil were left to turn cold in the kitchen, and people helped themselves as they grew hungry without regard to mealtimes. The lawyer spent an evening interrogating both Sita and Vasanthi with various questions about the attack.

He asked about other things too: the house, other servants, Mrs. Dickinson. Both women skirted around any mention of Vasanthi's relationship with the master, and the man did not ask. He seemed more interested in their work and the parts of the house it took them to. He even asked them to draw up a schematic to indicate where each member of the household lived, ate, and slept. Once, he was joined in these interrogations by his wife, a serious woman with a ramrod posture. Meera introduced Sita to her with pride, as if she were a bright pupil. But that only made Sita feel guilty.

Back at the estate that evening, she retrieved Meera's book for the first time and took it to the dim moonlight by the window. A woman's name on the cover. Annie Besant. *The Political Status of Women.* Sita flipped through it with care and sounded out a few sentences under her breath. "In a free country, a vote means power"; "Women appeal to reason, men to instincts." She struggled with some of the longer words.

But she resolved to try for Meera's sake. She hid the pamphlet inside her sari's folds and studied it whenever she was hidden from view. The project became a welcome distraction from the anxiety that pursued her workdays. Pausing at the door to Mrs. Dickinson's parlor, she repeated one of the sentences she remembered like a chant behind her tongue. *Ex-er-ci-se-of-the-fran-chi-se. Ex-er-ci-se-of-the-fran-chi-se*. And another unbearable moment passed.

One afternoon, Sita looked up and found Desmond paused in play, staring as she mouthed out words from the pamphlet. After an apprehensive beat, he raised a finger to his lips and smiled. He would keep her secret.

On their way downstairs to meet his mother the next morning, Desmond dragged her instead toward his schoolroom. Sita tried to remind him that it was not yet time for his lessons. She was more cautious about punctuality now, nervous about exciting his mother's wrath. But he was so insistent that she acquiesced and followed him even as she listened for the chime of the clock.

She'd only ever seen the schoolroom briefly when dropping off Desmond. This morning, dust motes swam in a shaft of sunlight that fell across two desks, a small chalkboard on its easel, and stacks of books. Books. The walls were lined with low shelves crammed full. But they must be young children's books with shapes and drawings. The boy sometimes paged through these with his mother.

Desmond pulled her to the far end of the shelves, where the book spines grew thicker and leather-bound. These were meant for older children. Many were worn and well-loved. Perhaps they once belonged to his parents or other relations. Thrilled by his own cleverness, Desmond pulled out books and pressed them into Sita's hands. She laughed. It was the first time she'd laughed inside this house from the back of her throat. The sensation broke loose stiff muscles in her shoulders, prompting a relief so powerful that tears sprang to her eyes.

The clock chimed, and they hurried to replace the books. They rushed downstairs full of their secret, giggling all the way, and arrived at the parlor, breathless and shaky. At the door, a pause. Lightness deserted her. Sita rested her hands on the laughing child's shoulders. Desmond's grin slipped into confusion at her somber expression. Sita shook her head hard and placed a finger on her lips in imitation of his own gesture from the day before. The boy nodded in his eager way. Their pact was complete. Sita allowed herself a tight smile as she tidied a stray lock of yellow hair before sending him in to his mother.

After, she returned to the schoolroom when she knew it would be empty. She chose two books that would fit in the hiding place at the back of the wardrobe: *Alice's Adventures in Wonderland* and *Heidi*. They turned out to be easier to read than Meera's booklet. And better respite, too, from watchfulness and the twist of pepper at her side. As often as she could in the days that followed, she let her mind drift to melted cheese and mountain goats.

Once, after reading late into the night to find out if the little girl would be reunited with her grandfather, she overslept. The morning was agony because she did not have time to run to the quarters and relieve herself before dressing Desmond. After dropping him off with the mistress, she had to find a bush in the grove behind which to do her business. She washed her face at the trough meant for animals and raced across the yard to fetch Desmond in time.

Distracted, she tripped and tumbled onto her hands and knees. For a moment, she stared breathlessly at her fingers splayed across the chicken feathers and red dust of the yard. With effort, she pushed the ground away so she could stand. And she also pushed away that image of the Dickinson woman and her jewels and the fearfulness that lingered in her mind. Over this much, she had sole dominion. Deliberately, she replaced the woman's face with a picture of snowy mountains and a ladder to an attic hideaway, the sense of certainty in herself she'd found among the roots of the naaval tree. She shook the dust from her hands and walked with purpose into the house.

The next time she visited the Iyers' place, she slipped Annie Besant's pamphlet back to Meera. "It was difficult," she admitted. "But I tried. Do you have anything easier? Stories?"

Meera sniffed with a distinct air of disapproval. "Stories," she repeated. But then she seemed to change her mind and turned cheerful. "I will look," she said and patted Sita's arm. "I am glad you want to read."

Sita wanted to tell her all about the schoolroom and how much faster she could read now that she was practicing. Perhaps Meera had even visited the Alps and cupped real snow in her hands. But before she could ask her about any of these things, Vasanthi called her over.

She was seated on her cot with a paper folder before her. Her eyes gleamed.

"You won't believe this, da." With an air of ceremony, Vasanthi uncurled the string that bound the folder and revealed a strip of newsprint inside. Tiny words and no picture. Sita bent over the paper and sounded out the words. The largest ones said: "Coolie Takes Dickinson to Court."

"It's about me!" Vasanthi jabbed a finger above the folder and took care not to smudge the newsprint. "In *their* newspapers. The lawyer says we will get more. I'm going to keep them all."

Sita smiled, uncertain how to respond. She'd wanted to tell Vasanthi about Heidi, but the words felt awkward in her mouth. Vasanthi wouldn't care about a world so far away, one only made up for children. Ensconced in the apothecary's safe home, she did not need escape. A gap had opened between the two of them, and now Sita felt it widen.

Mr. Iyer emerged from the kitchen with a steaming pot. As he'd cooked through the evening, the room had gradually filled with the aroma of ghee and good rice. He set the pot on a low table already stacked with enamel plates. "I wish everyone an abundant Pongal festival," he announced in his stiff manner.

Sita started. How strange to live in a country where the season for special foods could come and go with no one to celebrate them. Vasanthi clapped her hands and kneeled over the pot. She inhaled the steam and looked at Mr. Iyer with glee. Her eyes were twin stars in liquid sky. Mr. Iyer smiled back at her sheepishly, as if he had cooked the meal for the reward of her reaction alone.

Glancing from man to woman in their moment that excluded everyone else, Sita felt the ground beneath her feet shift as she began to understand. Her distance from Vasanthi would become a chasm. Everything would be different now. Married to a rich man like Krishnaswamy, Vasanthi would make a new life for herself. A real one, not a made-up wonderland. Her new world busy with husband and children would not include Sita. There would be no patch of land that the two of them could live on and shape with their own hands. Sita's imaginings of their life together were just more naive foolishness on her part. Who would ever let two women do that.

Mr. Iyer spooned out a portion of pongal for Vasanthi. His delicate care for her was so obvious in every movement, Sita had to glance away. She should be happy for her friend. And perhaps joy would come in time. But for now, she could only feel sorrow.

Wrapped up in such thoughts that night, perhaps she did not pick her way from the stables to the house with enough stealth. When she crept into the kitchen, a figure rose from the chair against the half-light of the fire low in its grate. At first, Sita thought the cook had fallen asleep in the kitchen. But then an oil lantern flared fully and illuminated the gaunt cheekbones of the mistress.

"You, too, a whore." Her voice was flat, as if she were merely stating a fact about which she did not care. How did she know this word in Sita's language—*whore*? It was not a word she could read in a book. One learned it by overhearing raised voices or drunken accusations. "Your job, stay with my son. But you run and lie with dirty kaffir in stable."

"No!" All these weeks and it never occurred to her. John's dog. Hiding behind the outbuildings. Disappearing into the stables. Late-night returns. The conclusion everyone must have drawn was suddenly obvious. "No, it's not true. I just . . ." She stopped short. The truth—leaving the property without a pass—was an even worse offense.

The white woman's mouth curved into a crooked smile. She was a cat inches from her prey. "You want to help Vas-Anthi." Her face soured at the name. "Good. Friends. Friends are good." She seemed at a loss here. Sita could not tell if she was struggling with what she wanted to say or the language in which she was trying to put it. "But . . . Vas-Anthi not good friend. Not a good girl. You are a good girl, I know." Bewildered, Sita decided not to point out that she'd been a whore a minute ago. "Mr. Dickinson, me, we help good girls." The mistress touched her chest with her right hand as if swearing an oath. She remained still, hand on heart. Sita nodded, uncertain.

"Good, good," the white woman continued. "Stay with Desmond. Be good girl. Three years more, we help you." Then, quick as it came, the smile slid from her face. "If no good girl, then no help." Her hand dropped to her side. "Then we hurt you."

Sita had resolved not to show weakness to this woman. But she couldn't help it. She drew her breath, sharp, at the naked threat. Mrs. Dickinson was clearly pleased to hear that gasp. "Be good," she said. "Stay in house. No talking at court." For this last, she used an English word, and it changed her. The muscles around her lips relaxed. She was in familiar language now.

In that moment, Sita knew with certainty that nothing would come of the case. The court belonged to these people just as much as the words in her books, as the coat on Mr. Iyer's back, as the ink in the lawyer's laborious hand. Secure in their own court before their own countryman as judge, the Dickinsons would triumph.

Satisfied, the mistress clutched her skirt off the dusty floor with one hand, held up her lamp with the other, and swept out of the kitchen. Sita remained where she stood for a long time and stared into the dying fire. Her eyes adjusted to the semidarkness.

She made her way to the veranda the following evening aware of each glance toward her. She tried to guess which servant reported her absences to the mistress. If she managed to steal away with John that evening, it might be considered an even worse rebellion so soon after Mrs. Dickinson's threat.

The dog did not bound up that evening, nor the next. John must have received warning. Still, Sita waited for his signal each day. She would not be defeated so easily by—what did Vasanthi call her?— that cockroach. But four days elapsed with no sign, and her worry gathered steam without release. She no longer believed in the success of the case, and her spirits gradually slid into despair. Perhaps Vasanthi would be forced to return to the estate, and her life would be in danger again. And what of Sita's own remaining girmit? There could be no safety for her in this house once the Dickinsons were assured of impunity.

Another thought lingered like an aftertaste too: Vasanthi no longer needed her. She'd made a new family at the apothecary's. Krishnaswamy and Vasanthi would get married, and then the rich people would find a way to keep her safe now that she was one of their own. Sita would be alone, unwanted again. Here on the estate, the truth of those stolen jewels would catch up with her in time. And yet, even through her worry and pessimism, she yearned to return to the Iyers' little room crowded with intelligent words and earnest effort. The longing for community tugged through her days. She could hardly believe she once survived without such sustenance.

On the fifth evening, Sita ran to the stables without a care for who saw her and hid inside the doorway. John arrived soon with two packages wrapped in brown paper under his arm. Without his dog to alert him, he started when Sita emerged from the shadows. He recovered and assumed a weary expression.

"No." He shook his head. "Too dangerous. Mistress knows now. Bad for you. Mr. Iyer say no."

"But it's even more important now that I go. I need to help them." She stuck her chin out and tried for that willful expression that Vasanthi deployed with such success.

But John was not convinced. "You go, mistress catch you, new problem for everyone."

Sita huffed in frustration. "How long can I hide here without company or word from the others? And I need to be with people who are . . . like me. You wouldn't understand."

John ducked his head and busied himself with loading the cart. When he turned around, she held her breath. He nodded slightly, and she rushed over before he could change his mind. As she climbed into the cart, he touched her elbow to help. She'd never looked at him closely before. Not before that word—"kaffir"—from the mistress's late-night accusation. This close, his eyes were dark brown and old as earth. His complexion had not been turned ruddy by the southern sun, but it was not pale either. Instead, he was the color of weak coffee. Under his cap, his hair curled tight. "I understand, Sitt-ah," he murmured. "More than you think."

When she arrived at the apothecary's, Mr. Iyer scolded her roundly for taking the risk to come. The others shushed him, but his tongue-lashing stayed with her, and she sulked in the shadows for a while. She was quiet also because her mind tumbled with questions about John and his role in the Iyers' activism. When he reappeared tonight, she'd ask him about his people and how he'd come to understand Tamil so well.

". . . and then she pinned my arms with rope." Vasanthi's words snapped Sita from her reverie. The lawyer was helping her rehearse. Her account was much smoother than the last time they had covered it together.

Sita asked if she'd missed many of the practice sessions. The lawyer did not answer her question and busied himself with his papers. Mr. Iyer also avoided her gaze. "I can catch up," she added as she glanced from one man to the other.

"It's not that," Mr. Iyer said hastily. "Well, we don't want to put you in danger. We all agreed it's best you stay away from the courtroom."

"What do you mean?" A bubble of laughter rose to her throat and burst out in an unexpected peal. The two men started at the noise. "But I'm the only one who saw it. Who else can speak for her? Vasanthi—tell them." She turned to her friend.

But Vasanthi, too, averted her eyes. "I agree with them, da," she said.

"But why? You said yourself, the mistress is a pathetic cockroach. If you're ready to fight her, I can too. Anyway, it's my choice to make, not yours. And definitely not *yours*," she snapped at the men.

The lawyer cleared his throat. "Yes, young lady, but there are other factors we must consider as well from a legal standpoint. What's best for the case, as it were. You want the case to succeed, of course."

"What kind of case is it without an eyewitness? I'm your only one. Except John, I suppose—" She paused.

"Just think about it, Sita," Mr. Iyer said. "How it will appear in court. John's testimony makes our case stronger."

She thought quickly. "How could he make it stronger than I can? He's not one of them, either. He's a Black man." She spoke this last revelation carefully, though she saw at once that it was a secret to no one.

"He is a man." Meera's commanding tone rang through the room. "They don't want you, Sita, because though they are careful not to say the word aloud, they still think of you as just a 'coolie girl.' They are afraid the judge won't believe you. That he'll question and intimidate you, and you'll just drag them down." She shot a scalding look at the lawyer. "Why don't you speak in plain words?"

The betrayal was a stone knotted in the folds of Sita's sari as she sank into sadness. The men's voices faded into muffled sounds as Sita withdrew to a corner. Another voice. This one did not wait for her attention. It said what it came to say, and she had better listen. Meera, who else.

"Don't despair, child. Don't let them defeat you."

"But Meera-akka. A woman beats a woman. In the court, the lawyer is a man; the judge is a man. Who will understand about us?"

Meera shook her head. "They can only decide what happens inside the courtroom." Her expression was fierce. She had not lost this fight easily. "They cannot keep us away. They cannot keep us quiet."

"I don't understand. They said—"

"We will be there," Meera interjected. "And so loud, they won't be able to hear themselves think."

Sita nodded without assent. Meera's bravado seemed like a delusion. Sita was convinced already of the Dickinsons' victory in court. And now she'd have no chance to speak up, either. Vasanthi had snapped even this one remaining thread linking them.

"Listen, Sita. Life is long, ma. The world is big, and you have many battles ahead of you. I can feel it to be true. Your path lies elsewhere. Save your strength because they cannot stand in your way forever."

Across the room, the lawyer and Vasanthi repeated their practiced lines. The words washed over her as familiar as the room's smell of stale clove cigarettes and burnt rice. Then a line new to her.

"I have never cleaned the mistress's room. That is not my work. And I have never seen the necklace you describe."

Sita gasped. "What—what is this necklace?" she asked Meera.

"Hmm. I think they managed to get some information about the defense. The Dickinsons are saying Vasanthi stole jewels. Some ridiculous thing. The witch says she punished her because of it. They claim punishment is permitted for cases of theft. A weak excuse. Why do you ask?"

So it had been her fault, after all. The attack rippled out from that single moment in the mistress's bedroom. If she could return and gently lead her past self away from her pointless rebellion. Was it too late to confess? Perhaps if the lawyer knew the truth, it would change the case and improve their chances against the Dickinsons.

Just then, Vasanthi glanced at Sita. She twisted her mouth into a wan smile—a kind of apology for her part in the betrayal of her testimony. The smile was tinged with persuasion. Sita had seen her use it to manipulate so many men. She could recognize it a mile away. Vasanthi's own reckless decisions were part of this story, too, she remembered. Sita was not the only culprit. Vasanthi had said her body was a weapon. Its use bore consequences too. Now she was wielding that weapon again to carve her new life with Mr. Iyer. And she'd cast Sita aside without a thought.

Sita's heart hardened as she looked away. She shook her head to answer Meera. "No reason."

When John arrived at the end of the evening, he did not linger. Mr. Iyer rushed Sita to get ready and leave with him.

"You cannot wait to be rid of me," Sita muttered.

Mr. Iyer twitched and opened his mouth to protest. But before he could speak, Vasanthi bounded up next to him.

"Da, I wanted to tell you. They want me to change my name after this court case. So those people can't find me for their revenge. And anyway my name will change after—" She glanced at Mr. Iyer with a mischievous smile, and he turned away awkwardly. "Well, I've just decided on my new name. I choose Sita! See? We will be as one."

Her eyes were wide with triumph. Perhaps she thought it was a kindness.

Sita kept her gaze at the door as she spoke through gritted teeth. "You cannot have everything. My name is not yours to take."

"But—I thought you'd be happy."

Sita could hear the pout in her voice. She stared at the door and searched for a response. It didn't matter anyway. Because there could be no confusion between two women with the same name if their lives never intersected. Sita would only be a distant memory of girl-hood friendship for the married woman busy with her everyday.

"There are many names. Find another," she said finally.

"Come, Sita, enough delay." Mr. Iyer shooed her out of the hall, and she followed. For once, she was glad to leave.

Back at the estate, she didn't run across the yard with its sleeping hens tonight. Instead, after Sita left the stables, she picked her way around the side of the house and reached the low stone wall toward the front of the property. The moon was almost full, so she was able to slip from shadow to shadow easily enough. But now she hesitated. The bush grew thicker beyond the wall and would block the light. Once she entered the dark wood, she'd have to make her way by memory alone. For a moment, she turned to glance back at the house. Her sleeping mat lay behind one of those shuttered windows. But that modest possession, too, was not hers to own.

She had no way but forward. Shielding her face with one fore-arm, she pushed aside the bush with her other arm and felt her way. She had to be stealthy here but not too much either—she must make enough noise to warn away snakes from her path. She stopped occasionally to pick palm-sized beetles from her hair because their pincers hurt, but she didn't bother the many smaller insects that alighted on her clothes. Nor did she duck to avoid the bats that swooped overhead. She belonged here with the moths and nightjars. Even the snakes were only trying to survive.

Farther in, she let her eyes drift shut. There was no purpose to keeping them open. No light reached this part of the wood. Her other senses took over. She remembered that the bush had grown thornier here and the leaves underfoot were soft as mulch. Catching the scent of rotten fruit and the spores it attracted, she moved toward her memory.

Her feet knew she'd arrived before any other sense. She opened her eyes. Silver moonlight cascaded through the branches of the tall naaval maram and cast dappled shapes across the small clearing. She clambered over the naaval's roots and ran her fingertips along the bark. Caressing the trunk, she circled over and onto its rooted landscape to find the nook that had fit just right around her. She reacquainted herself with this old-world god.

She knew it as soon as her toes gripped the root. This was the curve where she'd found comfort. She crouched and touched the bark where she'd leaned back against the tree. This moment seemed to call for worship, but all of her grandmother's prayers were lost to the ocean. They did not belong to her anymore. Instead, some bits of English words from *Heidi* rose to her mind's surface. They would have to suffice.

"She heard the wind roar through the fir trees, and she was at home." Sita pressed the bark hard enough to leave an impression on her palm.

She began to dig. First gently. Then, as her tears fell and mingled with the loam, she plunged her fingernails harder into earth and stones and splinters.

Here. Like a miracle or secret, jewels nestled in their hole. They shone in the sliver of moonlight afforded them. The lawyer's rehearsal echoed as she ran her fingers along each facet.

Have you seen an item of this description? A necklace. Six green stones, large ones, set among many small white ones.

No, never.

It is not gold jewelry as you may be accustomed to in India. Think carefully.

No, I have never seen it.

His description did not capture the depths of color. Not the green of spring leaves or young cane. Each stone was the eye of an endless ocean.

When she buried them, she'd imagined using them to escape the estate with Vasanthi. Here under the tree, she'd also realized that stealing the jewels was a mistake, though she hadn't guessed every-thing that might follow. Still, a new steadiness had coursed through her on that day. But not because of her theft or the pretense at brav-ery that led to it. Instead, the mynah and naaval tree had appeared as if to guide her from a silence that had plagued her for years. The same secretive silence that had tempted her to trade her own precious self for jewels.

If she'd listened to herself, she might have known that the adorn-ments of a cruel woman could spark nothing but suffering. And now they were no good anyway. Her friend had found herself another life. Jewels could not purchase the love Sita had lost. They could not be her companion.

Their cold seeped through her skin. It was too late to confess. She imagined unwrapping the jewels from her sari at the Iyers'. Their sparkle would catch every eye in the room. Would the rich people protect her when they found out she was the thief? No. They would gladly throw her to the authorities in exchange for Vasanthi's safety. She did not possess Vasanthi's womanly charms, after all. Her awk-ward angles would make an easy sacrifice.

Vasanthi was wise to care only for herself. She'd clambered out of here by any foothold she could find. Sita's fist closed around the trea-sure. She would protect herself. She would buy her own path.

TWENTY-FIVE

The plane circles lower, and my stomach contracts against my seat-belt buckle. A distant Pepsi-Cola sign; red lights flash out the Urdu letters, though the sun has not set on Karachi yet. Rickshaws and camels crawl along packed streets, and it's as if I can breathe the smog already. Sand between my teeth, sweat down my back.

A bus trundles over the Attock Bridge a thousand kilometers north of here. This bridge chaperones the meeting of two rivers sprung from mountains high atop the world. Far below, the rivers crash and burst foam over smoothed rocks, but their colors will never quite meld. The orchards must be verdant now in the summer. Once, we picked figs off those trees, and syrup ran down our chins. These were the peaks and valleys of the northern homeland from which I was cast out.

Two bumps against tarmac. Our plane touches down in the desert. Karachi, a city far from home. I trudge toward the booths at Immigration and join the line marked "Pakistani Nationals," even as most of the passengers from my flight wander toward "Foreign Nationals." The green passport in my hands still bears a crescent and star. America has never let me forget it. On the conveyor belt, thread-bare suitcases drift ungainly after taped cardboard boxes marked with repeated addresses and a roll of bedding tied with rope. Children run races with luggage carts.

Bags secure, I push my cart through customs to the sliding doors beyond. The glass is tinted, so I can see people outside, but they can't see me. Men jostle against the barriers to offer taxis. Among them, Saadia Hussain waits with a sign in her hands.

Doors slide apart. Heat lashes against my face. A man reaches out for my bag, but a guard's baton cracks down on his knuckles. I search through the chaos of faces and voices and find my name on paper. I meet the eyes of the woman who bears it.

In the years I've been away, Saadia has amassed wealthy supporters. They've arranged a car to transport us safely from the airport. The driver is armed.

Karachi is obsessed with weapons. En route from the airport, we pass a covered pickup with a row of policemen holding machine guns in the back. In front of every hospital, office building, and fashionable boutique sits a man in shalwar kameez clutching a rifle. As we leave the highway for ritzy Clifton's wider avenues, I even spy a sniper perched atop the roof of one of its mansions.

Aside from polite niceties about my flight, Saadia is tightlipped. We spend most of the hour-long ride in silence. The flat she takes me to is small but luxurious. Thick rugs brighten tiled floors. The bedroom has an air conditioner, and there's even a generator in the kitchen for Karachi's frequent power cuts. White sheets obscure most of the furniture. The owners—donors to Saadia's cause—live in Europe, and the flat is their pied-à-terre. Someone has been here to scrub away dust and fill the water cooler. Saadia checks on these essentials before she leaves me to sleep off my jet lag. After she's gone, I wander the empty spaces of a land I should know. Silence and shadow lengthen against white walls.

At the Durban airport parking lot, Rakesh and I stayed and talked in the car until it was almost too late.

"Who am I in that place? I don't like what Pakistan made me. A coward."

"No one changes just because they get inside a plane. It's memories that live in a place. Durban has no memories for you. You could return to yourself here—like all of them who came before."

In Rakesh's absence, loneliness stalks me like an old familiar. I'm tired of it, this wallowing in the past. I want none of the memories that live here. But when I shut my eyes, Pakistan rises from my senses like a monster from the swamp. Vendors calling wares, trucks caterwauling, the building's guards at their post beneath my window. Sweet mist of rotting fruit and budding frangipani against the balcony. Air like warm mud.

It is too much. I switch on the air conditioner, and it shudders out the rumor of home. Inhaling the anonymous laundered sheets, I drift to sleep.

Even while inside the dream, I know I've been here before. It's the alley that leads to my parents' house in Peshawar. Like that last night, I'm running from unnamed dangers that pursue me. The familiar house ahead is so close and, here, the same vision of a girl in the shadow of the screen door. She's propped it open. I expect her to help me inside and reach forward. But instead she steps out and lets the door swing shut behind her. We're face-to-face out in the street.

I sit up in a tangle of sweaty sheets. The power's gone out, and without air conditioning or ceiling fan, the room is a humid tomb. I consider trying to figure out the generator but settle for opening a window instead. A sea breeze drifts through and cools my damp brow. Inhaling the ocean's scent, I ache for Durban. The steadiness I found in myself there. But it's the middle of the night, so even if I had a phone card, I can't call Rakesh. Besides, I've made my decision. I have to sit still with the memories and dreams that live here.

The following day, Saadia brings provisions for breakfast. We remove the shrouds from two dining chairs to sit down to a meal. We speak of ordinary things—heat and wakefulness and sea breeze. But at the close of each banal sentence, I am alert to where our conversation will turn next.

"Have you contacted your family?" she asks. "Do they know you are here?"

I play with the flaked edge of a cold puri on my plate. Grease films like wax on my fingertips as I shake my head. It's a familiar hiding place. Head bowed against the world, the hollow beneath my chin has become a comfort. But it's time to spring forward. I lift my gaze to find Saadia's.

"They will find out," she says, measured. "Your brother is testifying."

"You sent him a summons?"

"No. Not me. He isn't speaking for us. Mohsin Khan's barrister has called him forward. He will be there on Thursday."

Here, without the armor I constructed around my life in America, my tears have nowhere to hide. "He will defend Mohsin? Even after all these years?"

Saadia digs around in her handbag and offers me a handkerchief. It is ironed square. An embroidered peony blooms at one edge. "That, we don't know." She watches me unfold the creases. "They may have compelled him to appear. He is on their list of character witnesses. That is all I know."

I twist the starched square in my hands. Questions jostle against each other.

"I know this must be difficult to hear," she continues. "And it is possible they've called him for this reason."

"Which . . . what reason?"

"To cause distress. Intimidate, pressure. Scare you away from the courtroom."

"No!" My hands are fists. My chair screeches as I push back hard. High-pitched discord echoes through the room. "No. They can't get rid of me. Not anymore. They won't."

Saadia allows herself a brief, grim smile. "Good. Then maybe we can ask one more thing of you." She doesn't explain any further. We wipe crumbs from the dining table before she spreads out her files to begin preparing me for court.

Bird calls ring out over the rustle of papers. We're bewildered before we realize it's the doorbell. At the door are two women. Both wear chaadars over their floral shalwar kameez. One has pulled the scalloped edge across her face, revealing barely a hint of nostril and lip beneath long-lashed eyes. I stumble backward a step, and my hand slips from the doorknob.

Saadia ushers the women inside and guides them to seats at the dining table. I follow with tentative steps and lean over a chair. Rubina glances up at me. Wordless, she drops the chaadar from her face and unravels its folds from her shoulders. It slithers from her and pools around her hips and the seatback.

She is a patchwork creature that others have joined together. Skin grafts like meadows and lakes, suture pathways like roads and rivers. Jagged geology layers purple and terracotta histories. Dotted by the flesh prints of generations. Scars mark each attempt to recreate her image.

When she speaks, her voice is her own and is free from repair. "Welcome home. Please sit."

Rubina's memory has been an anguish. A haunting. She's never been a person. Now I learn that she speaks in urgent passages and frequent pauses. Her thoughts run ahead of her and spill all over the conversation. She has recently picked up the thread of her abandoned education. Because six years ago, she was a college student. The cousin who accompanies her today recalls that, back then, Rubina never paid much heed to her studies. Her family scolded her about her tendency to flit across interests.

But now she wants to be a lawyer. Rubina smiles at Saadia when she talks about her aspirations. Her lips curl one cheek into girlish pleasure; the other half of her face remains frozen in melted grimace. Asymmetry is made beautiful by her. To see her uncovered is to start back from erased flesh. But once I adjust to her reality and we spend the afternoon in careful preparation together, the crevices of her profile settle into familiarity.

Her mouth half-carved is not grotesque; it is magnificent. Her flaws are shaped by the hands of her attacker. But also they reveal her own resilience. They resemble the kindness of strangers. She does not hide her easy laughter behind imperfection. Luster spills and brightens our somber task. It burnishes my shame until I can barely recognize the burden I have carried.

"So you will speak to him, baji?"

"Speak to whom?" I glance, bewildered, around the table.

"I didn't ask her yet," Saadia says to Rubina. "I thought the request was best . . . coming from you." She has the grace to appear abashed.

Rubina turns to me, and we both understand our positions. She wants no more favors extended out of pity. But she is why I've come here. I've been so caught up in my shame and indecision that I'd forgotten, somehow. I traveled far searching for the laughter of a long-ago woman. I wanted to inherit himmat from her, even though we share no blood. And Rubina needs himmat from me.

"You want me to speak with my brother?"

She nods. "Saadia baji thinks—well, we both think he will listen to you."

A yelp of disbelief escapes me. "And just what can I ask of him that he will hear and obey?"

"It's not about obey." She is earnest. "You are his sister. If he sees you are suffering, he will help us. He will speak the truth about Mohsin Khan there in court if you ask. If you will just meet him. Saadia baji says he has agreed to meet you."

My mind spins away to conjure images of a reunion with Ali. But we are lost to each other, even in imagination.

They've set up in Saddar near the ancient nihari joints and cloth bazaars and in among legions of stray cats dodging paan spittle in the shadow of garbage mountains breathing motorcycle fumes. A strange place for a protest art installation.

Saadia told me about the young women from the arts college who've constructed a temporary chai stall in the heart of the old city. Here, women usually scurry past with shopping bags or else are chauffeured in air-conditioned remove along the main road. They do not tarry in the market, where men are able to roam at will.

But for a brief time, women have claimed a square for the most banal purpose: tea and conversation. For anyone who longs for such things out in the open air. Saadia suggested Ali and I meet here in a public place that will also send him a message about who is in charge.

I emerge from a taxi into humid dusk. Maghreb azaan, and a dozen competing loudspeakers echo trained enunciation and croaked syllables, and one muezzin so young, he might be a woman. Their crisscrossed lilt keeps pace with my path through puddles and broken glass.

The students have painted a banner inspired by the lurid palette of truck artists. Beneath it, they've arranged thermos urns and little glasses on a counter. In a cleared space around them is a motley collection of plastic tables and woven mudha stools. Women gather at a couple of these tables and sip chai. One has brought a box of Prince chocolate biscuits and passes them around to her friends. Men gawk. Some stop to inspect the curiosity of women pouring tea in public. Others are content to sing out a lewd Bollywood lyric as they stroll past.

I select a wobbly table and pull up a mudha. Behind me, Saadia and two of her assistants take another table. We behave here as strangers to one another. But every so often, I glance over, and we exchange reassuring smiles. So I'm not alone in this after all.

He's late. I fidget and pick at loose fibers on the seat of my mudha. Saadia made the arrangements and said Ali did not hesitate when contacted. He wanted to meet me. I'm checking my watch yet again when a shadow falls across the table. A man stands before me. Glasses pinch the bump on the bridge of his nose. His hair is a tangle of unkempt curls, much like my own. I point to the bench across from me, and my brother slips into place.

The market streets around us are deafening. Our silence is a cavern amplifying each sound that rushes in to fill it. I've thought carefully about what to say. The request Rubina has asked me to make but also old questions that must be raised.

But he is the first to speak. "I haven't told Ammi that you're here in Pakistan. It would hurt her that you haven't called."

A dozen retorts spring to my lips, but I bite each one back. "I see. Well, there's no need to drag this out."

His expression clouds. His emotions were always writ across his face. And no beard obscures half of it now. The lines around his mouth score deeper than his years. A tired and thin man, he sets his jaw working in childlike irritation but says nothing.

I begin my planned questions. "I hear Mohsin's lawyer has summoned you. Do you know why?"

His foot begins to tap out a nervous rhythm and sets the whole table shaking. "I don't know why. I've tried contacting Mohsin, but we haven't spoken since . . . well, in many years. I spoke to the lawyer's assistant. He told me where to show up. Said I'd be arrested if I didn't come."

"I'm quite sure that's not true."

"Yes, that's what Uncle Mukhtar said—you know, Baba's lawyer friend." He glances at me with a reflexive smirk as the memory of the stolen Jeep flickers between us. In that same instant, he starts, and the smirk slips. Siblings or enemies. Neither of us can remember the precise location of the line between us. "Anyway, Ammi didn't want me to come. But everyone else agreed it was better if I show up and get it over with. I have nothing to hide." This last with an arrogant tilt of his chin.

"Nothing to hide?" Anger sends up a flare in my chest. "You're crazy."

"Why?" He spreads his palms wide as if to prove his innocence. "Why is it so hard for you to believe me? I told you six years ago I had nothing to do with this. I'll say it again in court. It's as simple as that."

His face is earnest. An old man's cares are twisted into young delusion. He has aged too much and frozen in childish place at the same time.

"You want to know why I don't believe you? Let's say I believe you weren't in the car that day. You spent every spare moment with the man who did this—who I saw there with my own eyes. In all the time you spent with him, you never caught a whiff of what he was capable of? That he could come after your own sister?" A catch and I stop before the quiver cuts through my voice.

Ali seems to have forgotten his bravado. He's hunched over and doesn't look at me when he speaks. "I didn't know, Jerru. I swear it. They didn't tell me. I thought we shared everything, but they didn't. They planned it without me. They left me in the dark."

I could almost pity him. My own flesh. As children, we constructed cities from the mud by the riverside, when we were assured of our shared universe. But he kicked away what we made together— generations of our blood and bone. And redemption must be earned.

I lean forward. My hands are calm in my lap. "I hope that's true. Maybe you didn't know he could hurt your own family. But you understood what he is made of, and still you bound yourself to him. This woman he threw acid at—she wasn't the only one he harmed. You took part in everything else he did. Your support gave him strength. It helped him think he could get away with this. So even if you didn't act that day, her face is ruined because of your decisions too. Do you still think none of this is your fault?"

Soft laughter trails through the wake of my words. Teaspoons clink and disperse sugar. Ali is silent and stares at a point on the ground. I cannot guess what the years have made him. He may have opened up to the world since I left. Or perhaps he is scornful of women who gather outside in ordinary chatter and mingle hope with diesel fumes and milk.

Slowly, almost reluctantly, he speaks. "They were doing good; that's what I thought at the time. I wanted to be part of that. Part of something."

I imagine him alone on a wintry Peshawar street without direction. All these years and he has never shed that boy. The refugee.

I thought I came here to beg from him. Instead, I have the power to extend a hand. To a drowning man who stepped on my neck. Does he deserve kinship? No more and no less than I did.

"You can still be part of something. Something good. So think about it. Will you defend the man who betrayed you? Or will you speak up for your sister?"

I rise to my feet. Behind me, I know Saadia and her friends stand up too. They will fall into step with me. We'll make our way together.

TWENTY-SIX

Though a week remained to the court date, Sita did not return to the Iyers' after the night when they dismissed her testimony. They had no further need for her. And besides, they asked her to stay away. But in the evenings, when she sat by her darkening window listening to the rhythm of Desmond's sleeping breaths, she could not be so sure of what she believed.

Images and voices—easily suppressed while she worked—rose insistent when her body was still. Sometimes Vasanthi arched as a brazen temptress who controlled the men around her. But sometimes men stood as if soldiers to attention. They moved in unison, and their words were law. At those times, Vasanthi bent double, a creature in pain.

And yet. Vasanthi did not want her to speak. She did not need Sita now that she would have a real family with Mr. Iyer. Sita may as well hide here on the estate forever. Perhaps she could care for Desmond's children one day. She'd enjoy a long half-life.

When she next took Desmond to see his parents, she paused a moment in the doorway to examine the mistress anew. Hair scraped back from her face. Her only accessories were an ivory pin at her throat and a gold band on one finger. From the simplicity of her adornment, one could never guess this woman owned jewels so valuable that one piece could alter the course of Sita's life.

She always knew some people were richer than others. For most of her childhood, she was the one with and others without. Her mother's dowry had included saris of silk woven so fine, you could slip them whole through circled finger and thumb. As a child, Sita wore silver rings in her ears when her friends' piercings were threaded with neem splinters.

Once, she traveled to a nearby town and saw a white man with a gleaming pocket watch on a gold chain. He rode a carriage pulled by four horses just for him. She understood then that her family occupied a rung rather lower on a ladder that might reach dizzying heights. But at the time, the realization was nothing. She still continued to lord her own possessions over the other girls.

But after she knelt to pick up the discarded shoe of another woman's child. After she took that woman's jewels and was only the poorer for it. Only then did she feel others to be the rich ones and herself beneath them.

On lonely evenings, she brooded over memories from the past few days. John's worried glance when he came to collect her from the Iyers' that last night, guessing she'd learned about the substitution of his testimony for hers. When she'd been frosty with him that night, his disappointment was palpable. For weeks now, she'd noticed how carefully he watched her, how he blinked away when their eyes met. She knew her rebuff would hurt. Good. She'd tug at his emotions because she could. Like Vasanthi would.

When her own land was her home, she'd been assured of a man's sturdy support since childhood. Her husband would light her body's hearth and fill her belly. After crossing the ocean, she'd come to think that kind of family was no longer possible for women such as she. Sometimes she fantasized she'd find a way back to the joy of ordinary things. But did she still want them? Maybe she'd never really wanted a man's shadow darkening her own step. *Did you ever belong there in the village, a girl like you*, Tulsi had asked. It was possible she'd understood more about Sita than she knew herself.

Though Vasanthi, too, had said she wanted no man's child. And then she'd gone on to claim the protection of husband and family for herself, after all. Maybe Sita could return to that expected life, too, with John.

Time became a languid span of silk that undulated but never quite moved. Each time Sita crossed paths with the mistress, a meaningful look passed between them. It might be a warning or an accusation. Perhaps it was fear.

One night at the beginning or end of this time, she had the dream again. This time, she was calmer as she stood at the threshold and waited for what would come. The beast approached slower, one earth-shaking thud at a time. A girl emerged from the dust and reached out to her again. Thud. Sita grabbed hold of her fingers. But this time, the other girl was the one who pulled hard. Thud. Sita stumbled at the doorstep and released the girl's hands as if scalded. What was this? The girl stood still. Her arms dropped to her sides. Thud. Behind her, an older woman appeared. The one they had abandoned to the street. Once, Sita thought she was her mother.

Now Sita saw her clearly for the first time. Silver hair streaked across her temple. Thud. Mud was splattered across her clothing. She opened her mouth wide—to scream, Sita was sure, because the beast was almost upon her. Thud. Instead, she laughed. An animal sound. She was the beast.

She was the beast.

The beastwoman disappeared into the dust cloud. Her heavy footfalls echoed down the street.

Sita woke with a start. It was still pitch dark, but she could not return to sleep. She stumbled down to the kitchen and curled up on the cold veranda. The dream had been with her so long, she could have recited its shape. But now it had changed again.

Ayamma had told them an old story about a girl who cursed her own people and was banished and bound to a naaval tree. What had Ayamma said at the end of the story? The girl became the witch of the forest. She rode the beasts and came after children who did not do as they were told.

The home where Sita had lived was long gone. Even her dreams had transformed since she'd left that world. And the older woman alone in the street—whose fate Sita had once pitied—was not what she'd seemed, either. She was a wild creature who did not need saving.

A baby was tossed to the ocean's maw. Everything new was dashed before first breath in a new land. The babies she thought to have when she was still certain of what kinship meant. Her family's betrayal was an uprooting. But it was also a beginning of what she could be. A becoming.

As if an omen, the sun began to lift the sky from slumber. And Sita remembered—though, of course, she had known already—that it was the day of the trial.

She got to her feet. Upstairs, she took the necklace from the hiding place in the wardrobe and hid it in her sari. She did not glance at the sleeping child as she left. She needed strength. The sorrow of leaving him would sap her reserves.

The estate was beginning to stir. At the worker quarters, the laborers were preparing for the day's toil. Her erstwhile companions from the fireside were even now tying new plaits of their hair or wrapping new pleats in their saris. A knot loosened in her chest as she remembered the contours of each woman's face. They were only afraid of losing their shelter. Those women who could not step forward for another.

She ran the familiar path past the stables toward the outbuildings where John and other Zulus lived. His dog bounded up to greet her.

"Sitt-ah?" He was dressed carefully, a borrowed coat uneasy on his shoulders. "What is it?" he asked.

"I need to go with you to the courthouse," she said. "I must."

He frowned and hesitated but then beckoned. "Hurry."

At a brisk pace, they followed a winding path that took them behind the buildings and in between tall cane fronds. Of course. John's trip to Durban today was not endorsed by the estate. He could not use the buggy for it. Maybe he wouldn't even be able to return to work here after his testimony. Beyond the estate, an old man snoozed atop a donkey cart until John shook him awake. He scowled when he saw Sita and argued. Finally, though, he shrugged and gestured at them to climb on.

It was the first trip during which she didn't have to hide. Not since she arrived at the estate too numb to notice her surroundings. Some of the sights along the way were familiar. The oxcarts, the people carrying large baskets to market, the horse-drawn buses as they got into the city proper. But then they approached the heart of downtown Durban, where she had never been. Several rickshaw pullers waited alongside a roundabout and fountain for their first rides of the morning. Hawkers and newsboys called their wares.

They turned onto a wider avenue with grand multistory buildings. That private smell of the ocean traveled over a breeze whipping curls at the nape of her neck. After another turn, the very end of an avenue. An imposing building loomed ahead. Its walls were white and roof a dark green. Other carriages slowed and approached the building, but the donkey-cart driver came to a halt when they were still some distance away.

John and Sita jumped off to walk the rest of the way. As soon as they were out of earshot of the cart, John touched her arm.

"After today, don't come back."

Her pulse dipped into dread. "Why?"

"They will hurt you. Till today, they were scared. But now—"

"I have nowhere to go," she interrupted, though her mind lingered over the jewels at her side too. "Anyway, I have my girmit. Three more years."

"Worse punishment if you come back after today. Miss Meera will help you go away somewhere. She wants you to study. She said you can read books. Please." His voice was urgent.

John slipped his fingers through hers. It was early, but there were already many around who might see them.

"I thought you, that we—" Sita stopped. She wasn't sure anymore what she wanted from him. She'd tried too often to be a woman she was not. But he said she should go away to study. Not to marry. He already knew what she'd only begun to understand. She was no Vasanthi.

"You will see many places, Sitt-ah, far from here. Miss Meera will help." He squeezed her hand once, then let go. With long, brisk strides, he rushed away. She followed with slower steps. Soon, he was a blur in the distance. And she was almost at the courthouse.

Near the building's grounds, apprehension began to gnaw at her again. Maybe coming here was a mistake. Would she stand in the back of a vast room and watch others speak? But she could not remain at the estate staring at her idle hands while Vasanthi tried to convince a white judge that her blood had value. She might have chosen a different path from Sita's own. But they were joined, too, by a kinship stronger than their choices.

Sita had come here in search of Meera, who possessed resources she had never imagined for a woman of her skin. Meera was adamant that she would be here today. Many horse-drawn carriages assembled along the roadside. Some of the drivers whistled low as

Sita passed them. Others sneered at her in contemptuous silence. As she approached the graceful building, she felt reduced to such a small creature.

She might not be permitted to stand here at all. She stood to one side of the pathway lined with flowers and shrubs planted for white people. One of the uniformed guards at the entrance spotted her and glared. He might force her to leave.

"Sita!" There was no voice she would rather have heard. At the far corner of the green, a rickshaw had pulled up. Meera climbed out and another woman too—the lawyer's wife. Their starched saris were pleated precisely; their buttoned white blouses were adorned with lace. Sita's own hair was wild from sleep, sari patched and faded.

"Sita, there is much danger for you here, ma." Meera and the other woman stood on either side of her, as if to shield her from malevolent eyes.

"I know." She tried for the bravado that Meera seemed to command with ease. "I want to stay with you."

Meera and the lawyer's wife exchanged glances. A silent war of wills seemed to take place. The lawyer's wife seemed to acquiesce, and Meera turned to Sita with a grim smile. "We are here to lodge our protest. Do you understand? We will stand outside the building, and we have written some words in English so their people may understand us. The court and police will be angry. They may hurt us. We are prepared for this. Are you?"

A heartbeat elapsed, then two. The noise around her grew muffled. The horses, voices from the street, even the chirping of the birds. She'd thought Meera and women of her class invulnerable, even from the white man. But she realized now this was untrue.

Morning sun warmed her back. Red clay dusted the spaces between her toes. Her cracked soles were so strong and capable. She loved her darkened patches of skin at elbow and knee. Swallowing was a miraculous collusion between jaw and chest. Could she sacrifice such gifts?

"I am ready," she said, her voice not as steady as she'd hoped. But she was grateful for her tongue's willingness to speak at all. It had cooperated against her body's safety, after all.

Meera and the lawyer's wife led her away from the gathering crowd. They pointed out the grassy patch directly in front of the courthouse where they planned to stand and unravel the canvas on which they had painted some words. They would wait until the precise moment when the Dickinsons and the judge pulled up because they may not get a chance to stand there very long before they were taken away. Vasanthi, Mr. Iyer, John, and the lawyer were already inside.

They waited for an hour, maybe more, as the sun rose higher in the sky. The two older women shaded their eyes and spoke of new books, the strange habits of people who lived in faraway places, women in India and other countries who demanded mastery of their own lives. Sita listened to them. The tightness in her shoulders began to dissipate.

After this day, her future may come to a halt. Or, for the first time, she might shape it using her own hands alongside other women who made their own choices.

It was time. Together, they edged a path in between the crowd gathered on the street. The lawyer's wife stepped over the shrubbery border. Meera took Sita's hand as she began to follow. "Are you sure, child?"

She nodded and managed a tremulous smile. They stepped onto the grass beyond. She stood between the two older women. They unrolled the sign out between them and grasped its edges back from the insistent breeze that picked at her hair and cooled the sweat at her breast. A hush fell on the crowd and then murmurs and a warning shout in the distance. Soon, the Dickinsons would see her too. Because she chose this moment to demand of them, writ in their own words, *Justice for our sister.*

She should have been afraid. But instead she was bursting with life and love, and so, of course, she laughed.

Meera turned to her with a raised eyebrow. "Why do you laugh?"

Sita wanted to say, I am so happy here. She wanted to say, not when my own starved and betrayed me, not when I succumbed to the ocean's hunger, not when I suffered the acrid love of another woman's child. Never have my feet known such steady ground. Because I am standing in the right place.

But she did not yet have the words gathered together, so she simply shrugged and laughed again.

Acknowledgments

You who beat and did not beat the odds, you who knows that any
good thing you have is the result of someone else's sacrifice, work.

—ARACELIS GIRMAY, "YOU ARE WHO I LOVE"

I'm glad I didn't know what this book would cost me when I started it almost fifteen years ago. But I've always known how I got through the hardest of those years—buoyed by the work and sacrifice of both loved ones and strangers.

I thank the past and present stewards of this Turtle Island, in particular the Lenape, whose precious, unceded land has sheltered my mind and body.

Thanks to those who put their time and money into believing in this book (even when it seemed no one else would). I'm so grateful for Julia Masnik, my tireless champion, astute reader, holder of the spit bucket round after round. The selection committee, board, peer reviewers, and editorial and marketing teams at the University Press of Kentucky, thank you for seeing this book's potential. Endless gratitude to the University of Michigan's MFA program; Helen Zell, my cohort; and especially the generous, brilliant, and unflagging Peter Ho Davies and Eileen Pollack. For grants, residencies, and community along the way, my gratitude to the New York Foundation for the Arts, Thomas Lynch's Moveen residency, the Marble House Project, Djerassi Resident Artists Program, Surel's Place, Bread Loaf Writers' Conference, and the Collegeville Institute. Special thanks and love to Hedgebrook, where the seed for this book was first planted.

My incredible readers! So much gratitude to those who told me when my book had spinach in its teeth and did so with kindness: Nawaaz Ahmed, Meghana Nayak, Tricia Khleif, Maha Hussain, Anca Szilagyi, Chris Castellani, Michael McGregor, and Atreyee Phukan. And my thanks to others who showed up with friendship and encouragement for this journey when I needed it most: Patrice Gopo,

Lizzie Elston, Ilana Sichel, Sarah Gambito, V. V. Ganeshananthan, Jeremy Lehrer, Kate Baldus, Emily Ahn Levy, Hasiba Haq, Aamnah Khan, Fabliha Yeaqub, Tamiko Beyer, Sejal Shah, Serkan Görkemli, Kamilah Aisha Moon, and Maggie Ritnour.

Much gratitude to Aracelis Girmay for allowing me to begin this book with her powerful words.

The labor of so many brilliant researchers helped me weave Sita's story. I'm especially grateful for the scholarship of Ashwin Desai and Goolam Vahed, Gauitra Bahadur, Prinisha Badassy, Surendra Bhana, Betty Govinden, and HSL Polak, as well as the resources of the Gandhi-Luthuli Documentation Centre at the University of KwaZulu-Natal and Ike's Books.

The people of Durban—neighbors, classmates, lifelong friends—who gave my family refuge when we had nowhere to go, and whose stories forever took hold of my imagination, I thank you.

I would be nothing and nowhere without the love of my parents, Nasim and Suboohi; my brothers, Imran and Rehan; sisters, Isabell and Kanthi; and my best friend and niece, Aila. Everything I write is in loving memory of my grandparents, Rafi and Rafia Siddiqui, who bequeathed me their delight in words.

Last but most of all, I offer my insufficient thanks to Shiva, my family, my home, unwavering champion, co-conspirator. With you, I belong.